Salomé

Daughter or Demon

William Freeman

SALOMÉ

SALOMÉ

DAUGHTER OR DEMON

WILLIAM FREEMAN

For our National Park Services, State Park Agencies, park volunteers, and their partners.

Many thanks for your service and devotion.

BOOK ONE

Salomé
Daughter or Demon

The name Salomé conjures suspicion, enchantment, and resonates throughout the old world. Two thousand years have elapsed since anyone demanded a head on a silver platter. But I can handle the reactions and the remarks.

If I had attended Catholic school and kids harassed me because of my name, let's say they wouldn't survive the day without a good beating. Fortunately for all involved, I attend a public school where most kids learn to mind their own business.

Unfortunately, some kids refuse to learn their lessons. "All right, I know you're following me." I lower myself into a warrior's stance. A six-inch boot knife points at a five-foot-tall holly bush with an unnatural shadow. "You better show yourself."

A pimpled face boy, with heavy eyeliner, jumps out from behind the bush. Arms wave high above his head. Forearms bang against his red, spiked Mohawk, flopping side-to-side. "It's OK. It's only me!"

"I know darn well who it is, and it's–not–OK." What

did I ever do to deserve a crush from a freshman foreign exchange student? "Alfie, haul your British butt somewhere else before this blade samples your pathetic gothic blood. Which I imagine, must taste horrible."

"The other kids in school said you *liked* company, and you would *appreciate* learning about our popular underground bands in the United Kingdom. I thought after class we could–"

These end of the school year pranks test my patience. "Seniors don't hang with freshmen. You should also know to leave me alone. Do I look like I enjoy people tailing me?" Hate to sound cruel but I got a rep to uphold. "International lesson: Learn to distinguish whom to trust. Now–go!"

Alfie says, "Sorry" and runs off before I can say another word.

What's the scoop on these Goths wearing collars around their necks, anyway? Their parents would have done better to raise pets. With animals waiting for adoption at the shelter, a mature adult could pick a willing dog or cat. The animal gains a home, and the caring couple saves on school supplies, a win-win scenario. I'd rather own pets than children any day. I know I'm staying children-free. You can count on it. I tell you, I'll never figure this world out.

Sometimes, I swear I exist outside of this world. I wander, attend classes and meet up with friends. Several cherished friendships prevent me from drifting and disconnecting from reality. If you share such bonds, you know what I mean. If you don't, I feel sorry for you.

Which brings me to my parents, I'm adopted. My birth mom either fell sick or died fourteen years ago. I forgot the whole story and had buried the issue deep in the past. My foster parents Jim and Tina are copacetic, but my biological father and I amassed a few unresolved issues. They may explain my charming personality. Maybe.

Bio-dad, if I forgot to tell you his name, is Frederick, but he prefers Eric. We distance ourselves because we both enjoy our freedom. I inherit the loner trait from him. He provides money when I need it. Eric inquires, "How much?" His warmth makes me cry. A sarcastic remark if you cannot tell.

In the past, I imagined Eric was a mobster who hit banks for cash. The problem with the theory? The man is too righteous. I settled on him inheriting a bunch of dough. It's as good a scenario as any I can think of.

A counselor once commented I live too much in my head and doing so is unhealthy. She recommended healthy venting to relieve teenage stress. To humor the counselor, I keep a journal.

Tina and I stayed up nights discussing journals. We didn't want an expensive bothersome journal laying under a mattress. We compromised and decided the practical and useful way was best.

For the past five years, I transpose thoughts in black and white notebooks. I consider the quasi-journal a collection of dreams, ideas, and favorite recipes. If you practice Wicca, you could call it a *book of shadows.*

I felt reluctant at first in deciding what to write because I lacked experience in writing a journal. Yes, I felt intimidated but overcame my first doubts. That journal grew into dozens of notebooks now stored in my parents' spare closet. I take pride in calling those dozens of single composition notebooks, "my journal."

Graduation happens next week. Afterward, I move out of Jim and Tina's place and relocate to New Mexico. It took a whole year to snatch the full-time park job.

I'll start off with an entry level position. That should

allow me time to get familiar with the park before committing myself to a park ranger career. I have heard stories that switching college majors at the last minute can be a pain sometimes. So, I have a whole summer to decide what to do.

A career outdoors with nature, it's a life's dream coming true. Plenty of people support my career choice too, even Eric. Bio-dad is overseeing my financial, college and job paperwork. I can figure out some of the forms but Eric excels in managing projects.

"Salomé! That the car?"

I spin around to the source of the outburst. Agnus Stulman points towards a brown Pontiac four-door heading our way. She and her husband belong to the new neighborhood watch group. Her house sits at a busy intersection. She sees more going on than the average person.

"It could be the one, Mrs. Stulman." The car rolls up to the stop sign. Driver and his mates spot us staring in their direction. A passenger's hand pokes out with a particular erect finger to express the owner's distaste for his audience. "Good possibility it's them," I said.

The car cruises the intersection to prove a point. The driver blares the horn. Four teens inside grin wide. One older teen displays a baseball bat and blows a kiss. I dislike both. "Mrs. Stulman, it's them." Must catch their plate number. "Call the police. Gotta run."

Agnus waves in agreement. Before she disappears, Agnus cautions, "You take care of yourself. It's not worth you getting hurt." I race after the car.

The USPS halted mail delivery for several neighbors because a couple of dirt-bags smashed mailboxes with a baseball bat two weeks ago. Parents and I had traveled out of town. When we arrived home, we discovered the family's mailbox and pole in the vacant lot. Neighbors reported the vehicle's description to police. Local citizens watch for the group of deviants if they show up again.

I sprint around the corner focusing on the car's trunk. The car prowls the street. The lower left side of the bumper displays a red and yellow sticker. Cannot make out the writing but the identifier could help to locate them.

"Hey, Shitheads!" The occupants hear my shout. Multiple fingers greet me this time. The smell of burnt rubber saturates the air. The car speeds away. The Pontiac screeches a right toward the highway. Spoke too soon, lost them. "Darn it."

After a feeble try waving my arms in the air, I tramp downtown. Boots scuff along worn concrete sidewalks, my mind reminisces. These hooligans compete for the town's troublemaker award. Our town history shrouds itself in old predicaments, but no place is perfect.

Two years ago, vagrants wandered our streets and harassed townsfolk for donations. The homeless problem lasted a full year until the mayor got serious. He declared, "I promise to purge and eradicate this dilemma. I swear the good folk of this town will once again parade its streets in peace." A notable political statement, right? Citizens voiced their doubts.

Neighborhoods started watch groups to conduct patrols after business hours. Churches held sales and raffles to help the hungry. Local town police increased foot patrols. Within time, the mayor's promise materialized.

"You chasing cars? My dog Charlie did that. Miss the old boy." A white-haired old man stands on his wooden porch. His jibe interrupts my musing. The man wears a thin blue flannel shirt, tucked in beige trousers pulled up above the waist. Both hands buried deep in his front pockets. His polished, heavy silver belt buckle catches the sun, reflecting sunbeams upon the sidewalk. "Those the scalawags?"

"Mister Thompson? Didn't see you standing there." Brad Thompson's family has lived in the same house for generations. He belongs to the neighborhood watch group and speaks his mind.

"Too busy to turn your head and check your surroundings? Stupid if you ask me; a great way to get sideswiped." I drift in his direction. The man descends the porch stairs and lowers himself onto the second bottom step. His black oxford shoes gleam brighter than his buckle. "Girl, you better learn CYA," he said, in a commanding voice.

I remark, "I know how to cover my butt and take care of myself." He reaches into one of his pockets and produces a piece of folded paper.

"What's that?" I ask. He stretches out an arm and hands over a page torn from a yellow legal notepad. A single word covers half the page written with a blue gel pen. "You're kidding me," I said, reading the writing twice.

"Nope. New prescription. Was easy to read." Mister Thompson leans back. Both elbows rest on the top step. "In my day we handled problems ourselves." He gleams over his gold-framed eyeglasses.

Darn, a personalized license plate. I focused too hard on the car's rear and missed the tags.

"Ya know, I'm older than I look," I said making a slow, exaggerated wink.

"I'm retired Army and nobody's fool. I know of you and your friends' shenanigans. You keep your vengeance out of the equation, you hear?" Mister Thompson rises to his feet.

"I believe you'll handle the rascals your way. Time and place for everything. I always enjoyed night maneuvers myself. Plan your assaults before you act rash," he said, taking two steps. When he reaches the top step, he turns. "Keep your protectors close. I imagine they're lurking somewhere."

"Thanks for the plate," I said. Mister Thompson reclines in his outdoor chair. He pours himself a glass of iced tea. I head back to the sidewalk.

Glad he spotted the plate number. I fold the paper and tuck it in my pocket. The investigation can wait, but I'll catch them. Payback, just another task provided and delivered by The US Salomé Service. And speaking of mail, Jim and Tina await theirs. My destination is another ten minutes' walk.

Why did Brad Thompson mention protectors? He may credit his son. Bradley Thompson, the mayor of the town, served in office when the town's trouble started. Back then, strangers stalked me. Thought people lurked and hid in the weirdest places. The shadiness soon disappeared, leaving me sheltered from the town's troubles. I visualized guardian angels protecting me from hidden dangers. Unseen shadowy hands that reach out of the Ethers to end any threat.

Nobody bothers me anymore. I come and go unnoticed. Life developed into a sea of decoupage. Cutouts of ordinary moments and varnished with a dense coat of blah. I swear moments exists where I do not. Wish the whole sky could fall and crush everyone. No, wait. Everyone but me. I want to hear the screams. Darn, teenage life sucks sometimes.

I arrive at my destination and postpone today's daydreaming. *Addison's* convenience store sits on the corner of First Street and May Drive. The Postal Service operates a satellite office in a front corner of the store. Long ago, the store ran a butcher shop, working drugstore, and soda pop counter. The owners remodeled the store several times since then.

A quick scan of the store shows four people standing in the grocery line and nobody at the Postal counter. I pick to collect the mail first.

The mail clerk with curly, collar-length ash-brown hair stares in my direction. He closes a counter drawer and places his eyeglasses in a shirt pocket.

"Greetings, Mister Bell. Any mail today?"

His ritual scowl follows my question. "You know full well we have mail." He points his square jaw to the upper back corner of the store. An olive-colored finger points at an official USPS logo. "The United States Postal Service always has mail," the clerk said with a sneer.

I had repeated the same question for the past two weeks. The running gag lost the appeal with the clerk after two days. But the wisecrack's luster lingers for another few more visits. Mister Bell is destined for a stroke if he stays this deadpan.

"Yes, you do. I meant any mail *for us?*" I said with a crooned tone.

"Sure you did, and no. None today. Help yourself to a store flier. And a free Carefree sampler." A devilish spark shines in his brown eyes. "How's your mailbox? Fixed yet?" The playful smile broadens.

Turnabout's fair game. I ignore the personal stab. I say, "No sir. Not yet, but soon. Have a good day."

Mister Bell haunts the local gym. The man's burly physique blends well with his tan, olive skin. With no wish to challenge the clerk's patience, I move to my next chore on the list. Groceries.

I spin on my heels. Cashier received help from the assistant manager. Line shortens. If I hurry, I can conclude my business before the line grows. I march to the storefront and claim a cart.

Convenience stores stock shelves according to local demand. Quality overrides quantity for product brands. Customers can preorder specialty items, ditto for bulk orders. Cannot beat the personal attention or service one receives in a mom & pop business. All this help makes it easier to complete my list.

Several items prove elusive. The receiving clerk assists and a question or two later, the scavenger hunt ends. One short list completed. If the shop owners could fine-tune the floor plan and move the milk to the front of the store, my shopping experience could guarantee total bliss.

Check out offers no complications. I place the items on the counter. The cashier, Camila, a classmate, furrows her brow. She mumbles, "… cannot believe she… not right… best to respect…, I could…"

I stifle a hardy laugh and reply, "Yep. Found everything I wanted." I hand the cashier a fifty-dollar bill.

Jerry, the assistant manager, glances over and sizes up Mister Bell from afar. "You should leave the man alone. He started the job six months ago, and he doesn't appear to appreciate your humor." Jerry checks the fifty with a marker.

"Eh, whatever," I said, with wide eyes and a finger twirling my hair for added measure.

Jerry assists with bagging to hasten the line. I suspect him and Camila crave their smokes, both exhibit withdrawal anxiety. The sooner I conclude my transaction, the faster they can step outside for their break. I refrain from any comments, collect my bagged groceries, and exit the store to step into the sunshine.

A perfect invigorating June day to walk downtown. Fresh air sure beats slouching on the couch watching television. Let me clarify. I enjoy movies, but no way do I waste life. Clicking a remote through a hundred channels and declaring "nothing on" is wasteful. My free time is valuable.

A familiar silver Mini Cooper drives around the corner. The car sports a black hardtop with the black side stripes. I love the clean lines and the roominess. The car is perfect for driving around town. Gorgeous car, except for its one unique characteristic involving a vivid, lime-green roof decal. No sane person could specially order an eyesore on a classic automobile. The owner of the Mini-coop boasts, "The decal impresses Godzilla puked on the car." What makes matters worse, I know the owner.

The Mini Cooper beeps twice and pulls to the curb. A voice shouts, "What's happening?"

Theodore returns from work. He is one of those friends I mentioned earlier. The kind one can count on and trust. We enjoy our friendship and have plenty of history together. Our exploits are legendary in this town. We agreed that adventures don't end up on paper, including private journal entries. Doubtful the everlasting pact will break.

Theodore maintains thick, collar-length, wavy dark-auburn hair that boys envy and girls adore. Forget any tall, dark and handsome descriptions. Theodore's five-foot-eight-inches tall. And once his metabolism slows, a pudgy belly waits in his future.

"Passing by, I thought you might need a ride back home. Interested?"

I blurt out, "Sure" and climb into the passenger seat. I place the grocery bags on the floor. The ride back home works in my favor. Pacing concrete sidewalks for the past hour caused aching feet. I could use a breather.

We pull away from the curb. Traffic, this time of day, is light. Theodore says, "Want to hear how my day went?"

"Sure. Don't I always?" A *Pfft* comes out both our mouths. We each ignore the other's small talk. The rumblings help vent the day though, so we humor each other. I will add several nods and "ah–huhs" to smooth the ride.

Theodore works part-time on the other side of town, in a woman's clothing store called, *The Real You*. His whole family ventures in the clothing industry, been in his mother's family for years. I laugh every time I picture him unpacking the lace panties. Theodore likes to work and earn his keep. He saves most of his paycheck for after graduation.

Sometimes eccentric describes Theodore. He can talk your ears off on horror movies. I too watch horror films. Who doesn't enjoy a good fright? You relax on a sofa, lights low, with snacks on hand and hope the movie delivers. When it ends, we discuss the film afterward but who chats forever? Theodore rambles on with the back-stories, the director, drawing boards, and history of the actors. It becomes annoying after a time.

Although I rarely complain. Occasional trivia facts can emerge from Theodore. Who knew when Godzilla first made his debut, the original script called for a cow in Godzilla's mouth dripping blood? Theodore once explained the scene required re-shooting because the audience thought it too gruesome. The original version sounded much better.

I appreciate the older horror movies and their early special effects. I prefer to witness the victim's blood squirt everywhere and enjoy the screams echo throughout the night.

People run or visit the gym to relieve stress. Me? I put a

vampire movie in the DVD player and I'm stress-free. If I am lucky, the movie inspires an entry for my journal.

Theodore wants to be a Priest. This idea of *Father Theodore* began back in grade school. I thought it a fad at first, but he refused to abandon the idea. His interest grew through our school years. We participated in debates several times. I tried to tempt Theodore and reaped shocking expressions for my futile attempts. Theodore blushed. True to his future profession, he acted admirably.

I surmise Theodore's professional career choice is more of, I hate this dead quiet town and I want out. But then again, his family is Roman Catholic so that may work for him.

The Church demands a strict criterion from Theodore: high grades, mentoring, paperwork, reports, and altar boy service on Sundays. Which leaves little time for hanging out. I wish him luck though, despite losing Theodore's company.

Theodore rounds a street corner. The sunset gleams over the horizon to my left. I substitute one of my prac-ticed "ah–huhs" with a whispered, "Please slow down for the sights." Theodore casts a glance but makes no reply. He felt tempted to remark. He knows I refer to the hori-zon's light show, so why comment.

Sunsets have held a special meaning since my younger days. Warm colors of yellow and orange mix and dance, blending with the midnight blue sky. The blazing scene delights, but I lack a rationale for the sensation.

In my youth, the family celebrated birthdays. Friends and relatives partied throughout the day. One year I asked Jim and Tina if we could throw an outdoor party. For some unknown reason, celebrations outside always felt more natural. My plea fell flat because of a locust swarm. No biblical plague but according to rumors, "the Rocky

Mountain locusts resurfaced and were to swarm." It didn't happen. The locust faced extinction over a hundred years ago.

A news team discovered a group of fraternity pledges had pulled the prank to prove themselves. The town presented experts on our local TV channel and radio stations explaining everything locust; their eating habits, their transformation, and the last recorded swarm destroying the Midwest farms. Experts proved unsuccessful in convincing everyone, but the story proved enough to force my party indoors. I remember feeling pissed. I figured if the swarm happened, the party could have moved indoors easy enough.

What was the issue? We have no large farms or croplands. This town pursues light industry. The college boys entered their fraternity. The public criticized the so-called experts for their foolishness, assuming they were innocent of the gag, and my parents denied the outdoor party.

I'll tell you what, if I could transform into a powerful eating machine, a few fraternity boys might become headless. Their bodies dropped over a high cliff. Yummy, Bang, and Poof. Do you know what I mean?

I wanted a party under the stars for my sixteenth birthday. My parents said, "We'll think it over," which usually meant, "Yes." Then, for no reason, Eric insisted we celebrate the party indoors. He later proclaimed, "A sweet sixteen party is a special day in a girl's life." Clueless why he fussed. You can ask anyone in town. They can confirm I was never, ever, "sweet."

To make matters worse, Eric missed the party. Dearest father didn't apologize to a living soul. But the party turned out OK. Eric hired an excellent local band and catered food with plenty of leftovers. Guests brought food home for their lunch the next day. Nobody complained, but I bet Eric enjoyed the night somewhere.

Meanwhile, I'm stuck wearing a fluffy, lavender dress. I later tore the darn dress to shreds. Yes, I gained a court-martial for my actions. No, I didn't care. The dress was destined for total and complete annihilation, never to see daylight ever again. I rated the party mediocre because of the dress.

My wardrobe consists of other styles besides black or leather clothing, but I don't wear fluff. The pictures of that monstrosity lay in my parents' bedroom drawer with the rest of my childhood collectibles. Photo extinction awaits when boredom strikes. No hurry. I'll heist the pictures, eventually.

When we arrive at my place, Theodore pulls to the curb. I pick up the groceries and offer goodbyes to my ride. Theodore and his parents travel this weekend for an interview. I daydreamed through the details but attained the basics.

I wish Theodore "good luck and safe trip."

"Later." The retort stays short.

As Theodore drives away, I utter a silent prayer of thanks. Glad this week ended. One long hectic exams week finished. Grades arrive at the end of the week.

Tonight, serious downtime.

CHAPTER 2

Two short beeps from the Mini Cooper tells me Theodore arrived.

I called Theodore before I cleaned up after breakfast. This way he meets me at the curb. He works in the late afternoon, so he has time to drive. Have a wonderful feeling about today. Slept well last night and now feel energetic. Plan to take advantage of it and run afterward before dinner.

I shout, "Later" and dash out the front door.

The car door swings open and I step back a step. "What gives? You sleep on the lawn?" Theodore wears the same clothes he wore yesterday.

He replies with a stupid expression like what a dog makes when caught in the act of guilt. "Stayed up last night watching the late horror shows. Fell asleep on the couch. Sorry."

I roll down the window. Mental note, leave time for Theodore to shower and change. "You could have left a window open," I said, turning the vent fan up two notches. "Let's go and get this visit with Eric over with."

Theodore knows where Eric lives. Thank the gods we'll arrive soon.

We park on the road. Bio-dad mows the front grass. Cutting the lawn keeps him and the grass trim. He wears a faded, orange, plaid, unwashed pair of briefs with an old screen-printed top. From his sweat-slicked hair and reddened skin, he has been outside for a while.

What is it with males and dirt? For an unknown reason, they must either wear soil or roll in it. The shirt's print displays a bright yellow smiley face with a dead expression and a bullet hole in its forehead oozing blood. The smiley face should be smiling.

The loud lawnmower shuts itself off. Theodore and I exchange stares. Both of us shrug before exiting the coop. I add a deep breath for luck.

Theodore exits and strolls around the front bumper.

"Salomé, papers inside the house. Theo, refill the mower and clean the grass clippings. Thanks," Eric said in his economical voice.

Eric knows Theodore for the past dozen years. He refuses to call him by his proper name. Bio-dad calls him Theo. Theodore dislikes the nickname, but he doesn't complain.

Theodore heads straight to the lawnmower and puts on the gloves left on top of the machine. He mouths, "Good luck." I raise an eyebrow and head to the stairs. Glad Theodore's chores occupy him while I am inside. Eric and I can bicker among the best of them. Neither of us wants Theodore sandwiched between us.

I trail after Eric, taking the brick steps two at a time. No screen door blocks our approach entering the lobby. Eric tied the front door with packing twine and knotted it tight to an old, rusted, bent nail hammered into the railing.

Bio-dad prefers his place sparse. The living room stays

barren, including any lighting fixtures. Eric likes to putter around the house. He accomplished a couple of projects. He remodeled the bedroom and bathroom years ago. Eric later removed the closets in both rooms and ripped the bathtub out to install a shower stall. One day I asked why. He answered, "Wanted to open the house and let the place breathe." Breathing houses, who knew?

An oversized armoire covers half a bedroom wall. A steel storage trunk rests next to the armoire. A Californian king-size mattress rests on a makeshift platform stand pushed up against the opposite sidewall. Bathroom sparkles with white ceramic fixtures. Unlike Eric's lucky work clothes, the house stays spotless. The smell of freshly-painted, blue walls permeate the hallway and explains why the open front door airs the house out. The rest of the house retains its painted flat white walls.

Eric leans his butt up against the kitchen counter. He waves a hand towards the kitchenette set. "Take a seat." I prefer to stand, but seize a chair, anyway. "Water?" he asked. I exhale and chew my lower lip. "Fine. Don't answer."

Bio-dad crosses his arms. He says, "Wanted you to know I changed my schedule. I'll be attending your graduation."

Eric watches for my response. I rest an elbow on the table and stare at the ceiling. It looks freshly painted, maybe a week old. "Congratulations. I'm proud of you," he said fishing for my attention.

"Gee thanks. I guess," I said, almost yawning the words.

"Not why you are here."

I rock the metal chair with my toes. "Figured that," I said while halting my rocking. I try to recline, but my derriere slides off the edge of the seat. I reposition myself and sit upright.

My birth father reciprocates with a blank stare and pours himself a glass of tap water. Eric narrows his eyes. He takes sips from the tumbler. "Been talking to Tina and Jim about your move," he said in a rapid tone.

Eric empties the rest of the glass with one long continuous gulp. The empty glass ends up in the sink, Eric in a chair next to me. "You have reached the age where you need to take more responsibility in your life. Time for changes."

Now what? I take a long cleansing breath.

"After the long bus trip to Los Alamos, how do you feel about living in your own place? No roommate. Your mother and I had our apartment at about your age. This move could be the perfect time to start your independence." He leans forward to emphasize. "Up to you but your folks cleared it. So, any thoughts on the subject?"

My mind blanks. Today's plans consist of receiving money and signing consent forms the park wants me to complete. I came unprepared for much else. Eric and I avoid father-daughter chats. However, since he asked, I consider his proposal. To my surprise, he patiently listens to my mind dump.

Bio-dad quietly listens to what I have to say about my move, job, and career path for twenty-minutes. The only comment he makes afterward is, "I understand. I'll see what I can do." He rinses his hands and face in the kitchen sink. Then dries himself using a kitchen towel. Eric pulls money out of his billfold. He says, "Theo's waiting. Take this twenty and treat yourselves."

I grab the bill and leave saying, "later."

When I exit Eric's house, I find Theodore waiting on one of the Cooper's fenders. His wide grin tells me he finished the chores. He leans back with his ankles crossed and arms folded over his chest. Grass stains his trouser legs. I guess Theodore beginning the day with fresh clothes would have been a waste of soap.

Eric exits the house after me and heads straight to the mower. He gloves up, starts the engine after two pulls, and continues cutting the lawn. Eric pays no further attention to us. I shake my head at nothing in particular. Theodore and I jump into the car and drive off. We wasted too much time. Need to get this day moving.

"What happened? Theodore exclaimed.

"You want the boring summary of our conversation or you want something to eat?" I recline the seat and stare upwards. "*My* treat." I check for a reaction. His gleeful expression confirms what I know. Theodore rarely refuses food.

We use a fast food drive-thru. You cannot beat the value menu, besides, its almost lunchtime. We order a few items to curb our stomach pains. Once the food arrives, we both pay more attention to our snacks than to each other. Theodore worries about work. And me? I watch a faded brown Pontiac pull into the parking lot.

Nobody eats or drinks in Theodore's new car. When hunger strikes, we head into the restaurant lobby. I insist on a window seat facing the front of the restaurant. In part, to people watch, but also because of safety reasons. Strange people enter businesses. If you spot them first, you gain an advantage.

I memorize the four twenty-year-olds inside the Pontiac. I tilt my head in their direction. Theodore notices them too. He peers through signage on the window and recognizes the car. "We in recon mode?"

I nod and give him a thumbs up. "Already got their plate number. Want faces to match it." With any luck, the drive-thru line slows down enough for me to commit their faces to memory. The signage on the glass shields our privacy.

"Not surrendering the plate number to the police?" Theodore finishes his burger and crumbles the wrapping into a small wad. He reaches for the fries and offers ketchup packets. "I don't use these. Do you want to smear condiment on the jerks' windshield? Could be fun."

Yea, it could be. Then race around town in the cars later. No. These turkeys pissed me off royally. "Remember how we dismantled the shed back in eighth grade?" I know darn well he recalls the event. It's also a sore subject.

"Bugger off! You want to strip their car?" Theodore leans over the table and whispers. "I got my butt chewed last time. And my father's closest friend is Officer MacGregor in the Masons." Theodore leans back and tries to hide his face behind palms. My old accomplice pleas, "Please not again."

Theodore and I once thought we had found an old, abandoned tool shed. The shed nestled in an overgrown field bordering the woods. Kids in school knew nothing about the old thing. We figured nobody used it anymore. Five of us kids met one weekend morning to take it apart, board by board. As you can guess, someone owned it and was upset to see his family relic leveled to the ground.

Police called our parents to witness the damage we had caused. An officer labeled me as the instigator. No surprise there, but in my defense, I offered to rebuild the shed. Theodore, to this day, hears comments because of the friendship between his father and the responding police, Officer MacGregor.

"Relax. I don't work with metal." Theodore's puzzled expression asks for clarity. "I'm thinking of dismantling them! One finger at a time, what do you suggest, ax?" I slide his fries to the side. Theodore's forehead slams the table. "Jesting." I chuckle to lighten the mood. "We could *Krav Maga* their asses into the ground instead." My smile widens and eyes sparkle at the idea.

"I left my deviant youth behind me. We are almost adults. Drop them in a volcano if it amuses you, in Fantasyland." Theodore stands with a tray in one hand and clears the table with the other. "In the real world, the police handle troublemakers. You know, as they handled us." He marches off and dumps the trash.

The garbage I spy on drives away. Their faces burned into my memory. Theodore made a good point, but he is not me. I play rough. Besides, my mailbox rocketed, not his. This is personal.

We drive off back to my place and reminisce about events that did not involve the police.

Theodore parks in front of the house. Both my parents wait outside by the steps. What the heck? What gives? I unfasten the seatbelt and exit the car. Theodore says, "Thanks for the snack" and beeps the horn as he drives off. Hope he stops for a shower and a change of clothes before work. The grass stains and the new ketchup-mayo spill doesn't help his outfit any.

I face both parents with a puzzled expression. Tina promises, "Everything's fine dear. Eric called right after you left. We wish to discuss a few things with you."

Lucky me, today's talk to Salomé day. Hope our discussion does not last forever. Hoping to add an evening run before bedtime.

Jim holds the front door open. Tina and I enter the house. My mom wraps her arm around my shoulders and offers a hug. After today, I welcome a hug or two. We take our usual seats in the living room, and the chat begins.

"Your mother and I are more than proud of you. You studied hard, and your grades reflect it."

"What he's trying to say is we both love you and wish you the best."

"Yes, we do. And we want you to do what's best for you."

"Jim, please. Let me finish."

"Honey, tell her…"

Parents mean well, but to listen to them is like watching a ping-pong match. I'll summarize the high points.

They say, do not worry about money and enjoy my new park job. Plenty of opportunities to meet new friends. Everything works out for the best. And they both will miss me. If I ever need something, call them. If an emergency arises at my job, they'll drive down to New Mexico to visit.

We rise from our chairs for group hugs. Once we reseat ourselves, Mom recommends I should rest.

Dad says, "Dinner will be ready when you awake. Forget about the chores tonight. I'll take care of them myself."

A high-pitched clatter disrupts our chat. Tina worked in her flower beds earlier today and left the ringer set on high. Jim excuses himself to answer the landline phone. "Yes? She'll be pleased to hear it. Thank you. I'll tell her. Bye."

Jim replaces the headset back to its base, the princess phone back on the table. Dad has this quirk; he favors keeping the whole phone on his lap when he talks.

"That was Eric. He says it's a done deal."

Eric pulled my living quarters off pretty darn quick.

Bio-dad made an apartment ready within one afternoon. Father of mine possesses mad connections. He scares me sometimes.

"Thanks, Dad. If you two don't mind, I'm heading for a nap."

I hop off the couch and retire to my room. Upon reaching the doorway, I pause and assess the distance to the bed. I lunge into the air and land face down. The pillow resists my efforts to tear it into pieces and fights back. Each pillow corner wraps around my head. I fight them off but cannot halt the attack. The down-feather wrestler triumphs and muzzles my scream.

When I awaken from my nap, dinner is ready. "Everything OK at work?" I asked Dad at the dinner table.

Jim paused between bites. "You mean why I came home early?" Tina and Jim exchange stares. "Took half a day. Strictly job-related. No worries."

Pure consequence. Nothing to do with Eric. Right.

After dinner, I praise Tina. "Thanks for the delicious meal, Mom. It hit the spot. A full stomach sure improves a person's mood."

I help with cleanup and fill Theodore in on the news. We chat for a full two hours on the phone. Wanted to talk to him longer but a horror movie was on and Theodore wanted to watch it.

Parents rented a DVD movie. I join them in the living room. Quality time while it lasts. In one week's time, I start my career. The move out of state scares and excites at the same time. Emotions can be fickle that way.

I understand how Theodore falls asleep on the couch. My eyelids droop heavier than twenty-pound dumbbells. I can barely watch the movie. A fuzzy blanket blocks the breeze from the ceiling fan. Pillows support a tired head. Neither protects me from an invading dream.

~

Fell asleep watching the movie last night. Dad draped a comforter over me and Mom tucked me in after removing my house slippers. The way I felt, I'm surprised I didn't sleep for the whole week! I woke up yesterday energetic, but the energy pooped. My evening run went with it.

Today is Sunday. Parents and I grocery shop after breakfast. We might pick up food supplies for my move. The pouring rain kills any outdoor plans. A great phone day with friends unless the rain stops. Lucky for me I plan to prevent wasted days.

Boredom escapes me in this quiet small town. It scurries around sniffing but vacates before infecting my spirit. Small towns offer plenty to discover and explore if you are inquisitive. If a person runs out of ideas, they can read books. Even this tiny nowhere town incorporates a library and two used bookstores. A good read lifts anyone's spirit, especially on rainy days. I guarantee it.

Seniors enjoy half school days for the last week. Plenty of time to reread *Lord of the Rings*, but I prefer horror and fantasy stories with exotic interests. Vampire stories satisfy urges, but with erotica, nothing beats a werewolf in heat, especially when the moon waxes to full. A girl craves romance too, you know.

I checked out a dozen books from the town's library. Three stacks of books written by different authors rest on my trunk where I store off-season clothing. In case I dislike one, I picked extra books, but I favor no particular author. Plan to read one a day. With luck, time passes and rids me of any anxiety.

CHAPTER 3

$\mathcal{A}$nticipation regarding the trip made the week drag as classmates and I said our goodbyes. A week's worth of books helped move the time. I recalled several vivid dreams last week, all about vampires! At least the ones I remembered. Usually, I dream of abstract colors or shadowy shapes; I seldom see people.

Most books that I read were about werewolves in heat or is that werewolves in romanceable moonlight affairs? So, why the vampire dominance in dreams? The stories featured vamps, but no characters important enough to cause any fixation. I'm sure I skimmed most of the vampire parts, anyway. It could be cool though to take part in a romantic vampire affair.

Imagine if dreams lasted forever. Nobody said dreams couldn't be part of one's real life. If you think about it, they are part of your life. They're just temporary. Although, my dreams and books seem more real than this mundane life. If fate handed me the chance to join the night, I would. The chances of meeting a real werewolf or a vampire? Sorry, my reality borders on dull.

I cherish a certain intimacy with dreams since my early teens. My first vivid dream happened the night after my dreaded sweet-sixteen party. That night's particular dream made a stern impression. Sure "stern" is the best word to describe it. Similar to laying down the law, in a possible loving way. Weird, I know. The dream experience felt strong and meaningful.

Once I awoke, I wrote about it in my journal. Every blue moon, stern-type dreams reoccur. Not the same repeating ones but similar. Stranger still, is how these stern dreams appear more often as I age. It couldn't be from the fantasy romance novels, could it?

My last day in this town begins with a long, hot shower. Just what a girl needs to perk herself up in the morning. Moisturize the skin and attack the hair with a heating gun. A low setting prevents any frizzy hair. And, today's makeup requires a special touch.

When I vacate the bathroom, Tina waits outside in the hallway. "I'll return the library books for you. Don't worry," she said with a wink.

My mom is a devoted soap opera fan and reads romance novels. She'll read a book or two before placing them in the bin. I guarantee she'll blush. Tina deserves the simple pleasures in life. She helped me through some tough years. All the power to her.

Tina outstretches an arm dangling a brown paper bag. "Dear, your lunch for the trip. Your necessities packed?"

"Thanks, Mom. Yep," I said, hugging her close. We exit the house together and wave to Jim.

Jim warms up the car after loading my suitcase in the trunk. I prolonged my bathroom time, and Dad's patience wore thin. He wants to say his final, "Be careful." Although, I'm sure I'll hear them again before I board the bus.

No sign of Eric or any mention of his name. Then there rarely is. I swear my Bio-dad lurks more than the characters in the books I read.

I meander out of the house and lower myself in the back seat of the Camry. Bountiful memories in this old house resurface. I'll miss living here. Leaning over the front seat, I stammer a last request. "Dad, can you circle the block once?"

Jim cocks his head. He replies with a prompt, "Can do."

Tina reaches for my hand and offers a gentle squeeze. I return the gesture with a half-smile and reel back into my seat.

When we arrive at the bus depot, I pick up tourist brochures. I'll read them on the bus. The roller bag I check in with the driver. The long bus ride includes several rest stops along the way. Plenty of time to eat and stretch the legs.

We do one last round of silent goodbyes and tight hugs. I say, "Don't worry, everything will be fine. Call you when I settle in the apartment." I board the bus and seize a seat on the side where Jim and Tina tarry. My backpack lays next to me.

My attire serves a particular purpose. I sport a mix of dark flannel and black denim cuffed trousers. My trusty boot knife, I conceal in high-laced combat boots. Extra time in the bathroom earlier allowed me to apply the smeared makeup and heavy mascara. Hair is in chaos.

If anyone pays me any mind, I resemble a vagrant who slept on the streets for months. I made sure this endogenous attire screams, "I don't give a shit." My unique way of manifesting solitude on the bus could use improvements, but a girl can only use what is available to her.

When the bus drives away, I ride solo. I pray it stays

that way. Love it when plans work out. I wave goodbye to Tina and Jim. They wave back. We smile, but our waves radiant with sadness.

The bus reaches the highway in less than thirty minutes and will arrive in New Mexico tomorrow morning. Cannot believe school's over. I left my old life for a new career and a fresh start in life. Man, life takes an entirely new, well—a new everything!

Before my head spins, I redirect my attention and pull out the travel brochures.

They'll provide the much-needed distraction.

CHAPTER 4

The long, uneventful ride makes me antsy. I left the bus at each earlier stop to stretch. Tina and Jim's bag lunch tasted delicious and saved me money and time to seek elsewhere for food.

We drive over the Rio Grande Gorge Bridge. I contemplate the hidden symbolism of beginning anew and leaving the past. Wish there was a chance to disembark and gaze over the bridge railings to observe the canyon. I bet views exceed any panoramic picture in the brochures. However, buses seldom stop in the middle of bridges. This one included.

I sense something exceptional and exciting ahead. My park job awaits, but something is amiss. The red desert ground with the spruce trees spread throughout the landscape looks spectacular. Incredible how these vast mountains glow bright red when the sunset hits them. But they don't explain my anxiety.

Cannot put my finger on it. As hard as I try, the familiar words elude my memory. Fate forces me to wait and discover the nature of my apprehension, despite patience not being my strong suit.

The bus pulls in to the next bus stop. I hurry off the bus for coffee. Few people follow my departure. Most passengers stay in their seats sleeping. Twilight passed hours ago. I slept poorly and felt weird throughout the twilight hours. I make a mental note to write it in my journal later. I also want to clean up before morning, no need to scare my supervisors or any potential new friends.

The bus station accommodates a courtesy nook with the essential ingredients to throw a drinkable cup of coffee together. I say a private prayer and waste no time grabbing what I need. Once back on the bus I can relax and enjoy my fix. I take the traditional first sip. A fresh pot of coffee. Prayers answered! Adding a drop of milk, I place the lid on top and head for the restroom.

Before I left the bus, I scattered belongings and trash on my seat. Upon my arrival, I find the seat unoccupied. Five new people boarded the bus, a married couple, tourists, and a nosy man. The latter wears a taupe short sleeve shirt with matching trousers. A white guy parked himself across and one row up from my seat. He tries to misdirect his stare. I execute a stare-down.

I project thoughts into his skull. "That's right. How do you relish the scrutinizing? Keep your eyeballs in their sockets where they belong." Guy flinches and squirms. He scowls. I can count his forehead wrinkles. Did he hear me? I estimate he approaches his early forties. His baseball cap does little to cover his receding hairline.

Once more, I mentally announce my distaste. "Mind your own business." I sip the coffee in the aisle, making sure this idiot and everyone else on the bus, hear my slurping. I beam my last comment at him. "That *A* on your hat stands for more than the Anaheim Angels!" My eyes meet him one final time. Strike three. Stay away. He pretends his innocence and twists to glance out his window.

Amazing what one can do without saying a word. I settle in my seat and enjoy the rest of my hot coffee. Next stop, Los Alamos, New Mexico.

The bus drives into the station, my final stop, an hour after sunrise. Missed the chance to watch dawn's light. The clouded sky blocked any sunlight, but I don't devote time to sunrise or mornings anyway.

My last coffee fix neglected to replace lost sleep. I meander the aisle. Backpack swings low and bumps into the unfortunate knee or two. Clouded thoughts counteract any apologies passing my lips.

On a chance glance out the bus window, a park ranger waits at the tourist center's front doors. She greets everyone on the platform with a cheerful appreciation. Guess my contact enjoys the wee hours. I sling the backpack around my left shoulder and leave the bus.

The park ranger strolls over and introduces herself as Aby. The bus driver unlocks the lower storage bins to allow passages to pull out their bags. Ranger Aby smiles a broad, white-tooth smile and offers me a large cup of steaming hot coffee. The logo on the paper cup leads me to believe the ranger purchased it from a famous java store. Don't care what brand of coffee I drink. Just make it, hot, fresh and with milk. I reach for the cup with my left hand. The ranger and I shake hands while I balance the backpack to keep it from sliding.

Nobody explained what to do when I arrive. Aby doesn't mention Eric's name, but I'm sure he orchestrated this intro. And supplying my morning coffee fix. Once I pick up my belongings and finish a third of the cup, Aby begins her story.

"Good to meet you in person. I kept abreast with your earlier paperwork for the last year. Pleased you wish to join us here in the park." Pretty beat after the bus trip. Some of my body parts still sleep but I do my best to pay attention.

"You must complete new hire forms from HR and papers need your signature. I expect it should take part of the day. We received your new address, emergency contacts, and your bank account information for your directly deposited check."

Park Ranger Aby continues, "Another park employee will offer the introduction tours and other formalities before the day ends. You may begin Saturday, or on Monday if you wish this weekend to unpack. You'll work on weekends. The summer months are busy."

I worked other summer jobs, and I didn't care what days I worked. I like two consecutive days off though, but HR can decide which ones.

"Monday is fine. I look forward to working here."

"Your room will be ready by the time we're done with the paperwork. More of your belongings arrived late afternoon yesterday. The movers unpacked the largest share of your items. It won't be long before you can settle in and take a relaxing soak in the tub."

Haven't taken a soak since grade school. I take long, hot, showers. My teeth pinch my lower lip, the sharp trivial pain reminds me to respond with courtesy. "Thanks. I appreciate everything you're doing for me."

Aby acts pleased with her accomplishments. I surmise she dealt with Eric in supervising my relocation. Positive Aby can, and has, handled new hires without fanfare.

We chat on the platform and watch passengers board the bus. A glimpse notices my old seat unoccupied. Last night's stranger repeats his performance. I struggle to see the man staring through the bus window's reflections.

I face away from Aby and reciprocate the stare-down.

This past April for National Poetry Month, I memorized Emily Dickinson's *A Day*. I silently mouth, with a creative emphasis on every third word, the first two stanzas. For an extra effect, I add an audacious hand gesture after the stanza's exclamation point. To my surprise, he has the gall to appear dumbstruck. Unsure what the dumbass expects. Nobody I know appreciates strangers gawking.

The bus drives away, and I hunt for a trash receptacle. Two tall cans border each door of the building's entranceway. I toss the now empty cup into the bin labeled "Landfill." I pass on the facilities inside. "Thanks for the coffee. It hit the spot. We riding straight to the park?" I asked Ranger Aby.

"Yes. I promise a quick one-hour ride. I'm sure you will find the scenery calming."

I place both suitcase and backpack in the backseat. We climb into a silver Jeep Wrangler Sahara, a two-door with the hardtop and head southwest toward the Bandelier National Monument.

Driving through the park is surreal. Trees line the road and block any traffic noise. Nature at her finest. We pass people on bicycles along the way. People around here enjoy the outdoors. My teen life prevented camping and hiking. Schoolwork and personal time took precedence. Now a high school graduate, I hope to create new opportunities.

Ranger Aby drives through the entrance gate and parks her Jeep in the parking lot facing the Visitor's Center. I exit the jeep and whip the backpack on. The suitcase rolls behind me. Its small wheels bounce with excitement. Aby and I walk around the Administrative Building's corner.

We enter through a door marked "Private. Employees only."

I follow Ranger Aby through the darkened lobby into her office. No sooner do I reach Aby's desk, her office phone rings. "One moment," she says, taking the phone call. While on the phone, Aby taps the top of a thick pile of papers on her desk. She whispers, "Do the best you can with them. I'll see you shortly."

The office intern hands me the stack of forms, a black pen, and leads me to a table and chair.

He and I pass a small round table loaded with a spread of morning donuts. Sugary delight awaits for eager, grabby fingers. The intern scoffs, "Help yourself. I don't eat junk food myself." The lack of his athletic built and slight belly roll tells a different story. Two honeybuns whisper my name. Easy enough to burn the extra calories. For now, a cup of hazelnut decaf from the single-cup brewer will serve.

"Shout when finished. I'll deliver the forms to HR. My nametag says Christopher, but I prefer Chris," he said while expanding his chest in self-pride.

Sure, scream your name in the workplace. Don't hold your breath.

I mumble, "Thanks." Christopher steps aside and returns to do whatever interns do. The papers I spread on a table and quickly scan them. I flip through them one at a time.

Forty-five minutes later, I take a break and head for the snacks. Forget the honeybuns, too sticky for fingers. I snatch the sole chocolate donut coated with chocolate icing, sprinkled jimmies, and drizzled hot fudge. The lonely, shredded coconut, strawberry iced, vanilla cake donut tempts me too. I commandeer both and stray back to my table to scarf down these babies.

Seven hundred empty calories disguise themselves as handmade, customized, sugary pastries of delight. Depending on what else I eat today, these goodies add thirty minutes to my run time. A price I gladly pay to avoid extra pounds on my hips.

Another fifteen minutes fly by, and I complete the forms. Christopher walks around a room partition. I wave and blurt, "Done."

The intern stands a full foot taller than me. In another year, I bet he'll reach a growth spurt. His eyes focus downwards. He suggests, "We should drop them off to Human Resources." Christopher is destined a kick in the shins. I'm sure nobody will find HR located down my blouse.

I sidestep behind him and wave him onward. I bellow, "Lead the way." Heads peek over the office partitions. I dismiss the intern's perplexed expression. Two strikes for Christopher.

When we arrive at the HR rep, she announces, "You must watch our training films. Christopher can escort you to the training room. One of your supervisors will let you know when we're ready for you."

"OK, thanks." I spin on my heels and face Christopher. Lead the way, Chrissy-boy, I said to myself.

Two large, maple office tables butt up to each other widthwise in the middle of the training room. Five computer monitors rest on a custom, matching maple counter built along the far wall. I assume the computers and accessories lay hidden inside the lower cabinets. Three of the four walls display local scenery artwork of the park. Posters generate aspirational energy for the workspace. Two curtained windows border a projector screen for PowerPoint demonstrations on the fourth wall.

I seat myself facing a monitor. Christopher hands me a list of topics to watch on the park's computer. "You know how to use a computer?" He leans unnecessarily over my shoulder and brushes against my back. Strike three.

My body stiffens. Christopher's demeanor toward women needs improvement. I leap to my feet and leer deep into his eyes. "What do *you* think—Chris?" I said, with a knee to his groin.

Christopher muffles a wild howl. Erratic arm waving exhibits a total and complete surrender. My love-tapped message tumbles to the floor. An easy read for the bent over Chris. No manager desires an employee screaming bloody mercy, but I insist he stays out of my intimate zone. Computer training doesn't require a doofus rubbing against one's back.

"Christopher? Any login or passwords for the computers?" I asked, innocently.

Did you ever watch a baseball smack a man in the groin? The man stands afterward trying to convince people he's not in agony. Yep, not convincing. Poor Christopher squeaks, "They're listed on the bottom of the sheet." He recoils for self-massage, straightens himself up. He asks, "We good?"

"I'll manage. Thanks." Christopher hobbles around the large tables. "Dude, you stick to eating doughnuts and leave me the heck alone. Understand?"

"Will do. I swear it." Christopher lowers his head and exits the room. Time for another short break. Coffee dominated too much today. I race towards the restroom.

Hours of training pass. When I log out, a man enters the room.

The long strides and exposed defined arm muscles suggests he runs long distance. His high cheekbones, long, uncut, raven-black hair, braided and tied with cord hints of Native American ancestry. He looks foreign wearing business casual. Outward first impression says he's in his thirties. My inner intuition tells otherwise. He's much older.

"Salomé? I'm your shift supervisor." He veers around the tables and stands an arm's length from my chair.

I rise to my feet. "Perfect timing. Just finished the videos," I said, and offer him a handshake.

He accepts my offer and greets me with a two-handed shake. "Name's Parker." The firmness of his grip causes a slight tug towards him though it could be my imagination. "Saw you finish on the cameras." He lifts his left hand and points to two concealed cameras on opposite sides of the ceiling. "Maybe be careful of witnesses next time. Better yet, leave me with the discipline?" He releases his handshake, smiles, and waits for a reply.

Oops. Enter one awkward moment. Sorry. Next teen-jerk is yours to reprimand. I reel back and claim, "Been a long day, tired. Sorry." If Parker watched the cameras, I should not need to explain myself. "Hope *Chris* is all right."

Parker studies my reaction. "Close to lunchtime. Doubtful you brought your own lunch. What say we order food? My treat. I'll add your lunch to the office's order, a sandwich from the deli?"

Guess he drops the issue. I answer, "Sure. An Italian cold cut sandwich with oil and vinegar could hit the spot."

"I'll make it happen." Parker sends a text message to the deli. He seats himself in the closest chair and places his phone on the table. He asks, "You up for an impromptu interview, while we wait for the delivery? We can discuss what position works best for you. Once you reach eighteen and are enrolled in college, we can start your park ranger training."

"Sure." I grab a seat opposite Parker.

When the food arrives, Parker leads me to a small break room. "We set the drink machine to *No Charge*. Help yourself." I nod. "By the way, I keep an open office policy. Stop by if the need arises?" Parker again waits for my reply.

A slight reminder to leave the interns in one piece? "Um, sure. Talk to you first. No problem. Good to meet you. Thanks for the sandwich." Parker squints.

During my interview, Parker decided I'm best suited to work in the park's gift shop. I plan to complete my park ranger application and enroll in Basic Law Enforcement classes by next year. One year as a stock person is a cakewalk. I can make do working indoors for a while.

Parker heads out through the doorway. I rip open the bag and attack my sandwich. Stomach growls from lack of real food. This sandwich should appease the discomfort.

Thirty-five minutes after lunch, I meet Dorothy, the HR person. We chat about possible work issues. She rechecks my paperwork while I watch park employees come and go. I grow impatient with paperwork. The stuff bores me.

I start idle chitchat. "Do any of these people work in the gift shop?"

She replies with a sideways nod. "You feeling antsy? We'll finish the paperwork soon." Dorothy picks a green folder from a stack of mixed colored ones and adds a pre-printed label to the folder's tab. She straightens her eyeglasses and inquires, "Do you have any questions?" The final question or statement in an interview.

Today's events covered a broad spectrum of activities and boredom. I shake my head. "No ma'am, no questions yet."

The best part of the day included meeting Ranger Aby. Feeling neutral about the intern, he's inconsequential. Stomach calms after the lunch break. Parker left for the day. He mentioned a pressing engagement and needed to leave.

Aby joins us at Dorothy's desk. Aby checks the forms. She says, "I'll drive you to your apartment. I received a phone call moments ago from the moving crew. They informed me all's well." Aby hands the paperwork back to Dorothy. "Their project manager returned their second set of keys. An hour remains before we leave." Aby passes me a park brochure. "Why not explore for a while? Meet you near my Jeep."

I stand. Legs scream for a run. I grasp the brochure tightly instead. "Goodbye, Dorothy. Been nice meeting you." Using her name will help me remember it. If HR is similar to the principal's office, I'll be back.

Dorothy says, "Good to meet you, Salomé. Stop by when you need us. You know where we are." She opens my file and adds the paperwork. "Enjoy your new apartment. I wish you luck in your career at the park."

With a simple brochure in hand, one I read several times beforehand, I rush out the door to explore.

I visit the Tyuonyi pueblo. It once held four hundred rooms, including storerooms, was two stories high and housed a hundred people. Walls vanished years ago, but you can see the foundation stones and layout right off the main trail.

I climb a ladder of tied branches and enter one of the cavate cliff dwellings. The smoke-blackened, plastered floors, walls, and ceilings keep the volcanic tuff from crumbling.

Oh, I forgot. During my exploring, a park sign read, "Warning, bat colony." One of the caves shelters bats! Want to explore it later at night sometime. Every job includes fringe benefits. Right?

I finish my quick exploration of the main trail and find

Ranger Aby waiting at our prearranged meeting spot. She waves. I plop backpack on the car floor at my feet and climb into the passenger's seat. My shaky legs appreciate the immediate relief. Aby places my suitcase behind us on the floor. I had left the suitcase with Aby but kept the backpack, in case. Don't ask for explanations. Incoherent, mumbling words explain nothing.

The ride to my apartment draws me to sleep. My eyes strain to stay open. Sure, Ranger Aby understands why I give her the quiet treatment. Forget that hot shower I planned. The shower must wait until tomorrow. Bed calls.

I squint at Aby. She says, "Go ahead." I reach under the seat cushion and adjust the seat back. One quick power nap, coming up.

CHAPTER 5

Six o'clock last night I dragged my sorry butt out of the ranger's Jeep with gear and up two flights of stairs. Ranger Aby escorted me to the stairs. I recall her pointing. "Up," a non-vocalized command. Not her fault, mind you, I wanted to do everything myself.

"This is my move," I remember saying.

I could barely stand yesterday evening, much less make it up the stairs but somehow, I miraculously made it to my apartment.

"I insist." I remember saying those words too.

Aby trailed and opened the apartment door. I'm glad she did. Otherwise, I may have slept on those stairs. So much for power naps. Between the dull bus ride, the excitement with moving, and the fresh air trekking through the park, I could use quiet-time. Not complaining, mind you, but I reached my limit.

I fell asleep and slept in my clothes last night. I kicked off shoes before hitting the bed but felt too tired to remove any clothing. Woke up after two hours to visit the restroom, and then crawled back to bed afterward.

Another difficult time sleeping last night. Strange after yesterday's arduous adventures. My body experienced tugging throughout the night. Mysterious hands forced me to stay awake. Music played in my head too. Remember none of the specifics, but then, I don't remember dreams. Cannot analyze it now, too groggy. I predict a mood improvement after a mug of fresh coffee.

A wet bar, of sorts, lays next to the double sink in the new kitchen. It includes a white, four-cup coffee machine and two ceramic, indigo, glazed mugs. Paper filters and a sealed can of Columbian goodness wait on a wall shelf next to a white microwave oven. I open the upper cabinets. Boxes of mixed tea bags stack the shelves. Eric should know better. I do not drink tea often enough to justify this volume. If I find receipts, I will exchange the tea for coffee.

Placing a filter into the basket, I break open the vacuum foil seal. *Psst.* The fresh aroma greets me. The coffee smells heavenly. One substantial scoop should be enough. The bottom cabinet stocks 500ml water bottles. Perfect for the four-cup machine. I pop open the case and pour one into the reservoir, closed the lid, and flip the switch.

I take a mug and pour when the pot level reaches half-way. Fresh newborn drops drip and sizzle, striking the hot plate. As the pot finishes its brewing, I plop milk and swirl it into the aromatic java.

"Mmm." Cannot imagine tasting a beverage better than morning coffee. I scout the kitchen, mug in hand, taking sips.

Eric thought and planned for everything. He loaded the refrigerator with items that Jim and Tina kept on hand. With the cabinets' cache of readymade and canned foods, I could survive for months.

My first apartment. This place rules and differs from

sharing living space with parents. Apartment exceeds my expectations. Quiet too. Heard no morning noise during my tossing and turning.

Hard to live in a quiet apartment. I lived in a busy household with Jim and Tina for fourteen years. Total silence belongs in a graveyard, not in a home. Might play a CD or keep the radio on low to create white noise.

I'm making my first solo breakfast! In the mood for fried eggs, and two slices of toast. I remove an iron skillet from the bottom stove drawer and place the heavy pan on a burner. Wrist strains with the weight. I refill my mug, click the coffee machine off, and prance off to a good, long, hot shower. Breakfast can wait.

After the much-needed shower, I prepare breakfast. The kitchen sink serves as a handy table. A shower and a full belly ranks right up with the first sip of fresh java. A close second, at least. I explore my new apartment with a third fill-up of coffee in hand. Dishes can soak in the sink until I explore outside.

I walk up to the bay window. This building lacks balconies. If I wish to sun, I'll need to lay elsewhere. The main apartment complex I cannot see from here. Foresee an exploratory hike in my immediate future.

Before the bus departed, Tina had said, "We wanted to buy you a going away present. A personal gift, something you can enjoy. Jim ordered it for you. We hope you enjoy your new bike."

"Personal" meant Eric had nothing to do with the gift. No small feat. Eric hides behind the scenes somewhere. Glad parents pulled off their surprise. I appreciated the loving thoughts. The bike could help in my explorations.

Glad I live on the third floor too. Especially when kids jump on beds, while I try to sleep. Eric insisted on a top floor apartment, but it makes sense.

I finish four full coffee mugs within an hour. A caffeine buzz lurks in my near future. But that's OK, plenty of water in my near future too. I test the living room's recliner and review yesterday's events.

I look forward to the thirty-minute bus ride from the apartment to the park. It could be difficult to bike ride in every day unless I leave extra early or let the bus racks hold my bike while I read a book. Suppose I can decide later what works best.

Several buildings constructed in the park are out of sight from the public areas. A few structures house year-round residents. Ranger Aby mentioned, "Next to the separate storage sheds, we built a picnic table. During warm weather, workers take breaks and lunches there." I assume the place is safe and figure on storing my bike there to keep it accessible.

The human resources paperwork I completed yesterday worked out fine. Dorothy agreed I could start this Monday. She said, "You can take your two consecutive days off Wednesday and Thursdays. You'll do two weeks on-the-job-training, but we don't know with who yet."

I said my thanks. Other congenial replies followed when Ranger Aby and I left the office cubicle before my hike.

Plan to explore the apartment complex today. Once I come back, I can unpack private belongings. The parents and Eric know I'm touchy about certain belongings. Besides, who wants a stranger rummaging through their sleepwear or underwear? Not me, for sure. I heard too many tales of men with women's panties to last lifetimes. Otherwise, the place shrieks "professional decorator was here!"

No clue what cleaning company Eric used, but they sure worked magic. This apartment sparkles. That father of mine does nothing half-assed or plain other than his own decorating.

Major relief to have everything done for you. I can understand how the rich become addicted to the high-end goodies and domestic services. But I live in a different tax bracket than the one percent crowd. Nobody pampers me. I'll settle on appreciating a onetime cleaning and move-in-ready apartment though.

Eric holds my best interests at heart. I realize that, but gut instinct tugs my subconscious. It tells me something is wrong. This move sailed too smoothly. Cannot figure out how he managed. Bio-dad makes me scream in frustration. Where is Carl Jung when you need him?

I dress and later tackle the dishes; best not leave them in the sink to attract bugs. The pans and stuff can air dry.

Before I leave, I reach for a water bottle and an energy bar. Both should hold me until suppertime.

The weather bureau forecasted eighty-five degrees with a slight overcast for most of the day. When I swing open the door, I conclude whomever made today's weather report should change jobs.

Sky's so dark nobody can consider it any shade of gray. Air quality borders on a slight breeze to a non-existent one. The wall of heat hitting me is not eighty-five degrees either, though it may be without the humidity. I'll let the weatherman have that one, but I bet it was luck. Muggy days can put people in the hospital if they overexert themselves.

A sudden, brief breeze passes. It offers no relief but causes an envelope taped to the door to flap.

I remove the attached envelope. Envelope reads, "Tenant." The return mailing address shows the letter originated from the apartment office. I didn't warrant an official letter. But cannot be too sure though.

The letter reads, "Dear new tenant... our pleasure to welcome you. We hope you find... this letter provides important information. On behalf of our staff, we... please call. Joan Wilson, professional leasing manager." The back of the letter includes a list of local utility companies and contact numbers with web addresses. Could come in handy, I guess. A sticky note tossed in from a "Jody." She mentions, "Please stop by the office for your second set of keys and tour."

If I collect the second set of apartment keys, I don't need the ones Ranger Aby handed me yesterday. I toss them in a kitchen cabinet drawer under the coffee pot. The keys clank in the empty drawer. The sound chimes, "I am officially moved in." I created a junk drawer.

The delivered letter I fold into a back pocket. I rotate the lock mechanism, cross the threshold and lock myself out. A blush of stupidity washes over me, but I brush it aside. I run down the stairs and into the backwoods.

A well-worn maintenance path leads to the other side of the apartment complex. Running today can wait until the weather clears or I hit the treadmills in air conditioning.

Within minutes of wandering, I scowl at the grassy wooden path as it forks. Both bend and offer impeded sight. Which way leads to the office? Standing here reminds me of a required poem an English teacher assigned the class to memorize.

Robert Frost's *The Road Not Taken* is one of America's most familiar, if not beloved poems. Readers often misinterpreted its hidden meaning. I take the road to my left. The other, I presume, also ends up somewhere near the office.

The apartment complex overshadows what I first imaged. Made an earlier false assumption because my building is segregated from the rest of the complex. The path leads through a parking lot. A dozen or more other buildings encircle the office. Doubtful anyone can confuse this building with any of the other structures. What else can this building be? I size up a large, two-story building with a chain-link fence surrounding a sunken pool. The place strikes my interest. I could picture myself hanging out here.

The letter in my pocket listed the senders: Joan Wilson and Jody. Intuition hints that it's doubtful I'll meet any professional leasing manager who sends formal template letters. My bet is on meeting the lets-throw-in-an-informal-scrap-of-paper-with-my-name-on-it girl.

I cross the lot and reach the sidewalk. The concrete trail, I hope, leads to the front doors and restrooms.

Emerging through the double doors, I scan the relaxed office environment. Nobody inside resembles a Jody or a Ms. Wilson. The open ceiling lobby increases the ambiance. Stone fireplace built into one corner on my left. Two offices next to it. Comfy-looking, dark-green, leather sofas face the fireplace hearth. Coffee machine and a variety of coffee pods rest on a countertop on my right. Designers tucked a mini refrigerator stocked with water and colored energy drinks underneath the counter. Four bar stools stand nearby.

An office desk is smack dab in the open area between the sitting room and the drink counter. Unless Jody maintains a well-trimmed beard and mustache, she isn't the one who works behind the desk on the phone. I'm confident the young man isn't Ms. Wilson either.

We make eye contact. I whisper, "Where's the restroom?"

The man points to my right, taps his right shoulder and sticks up two fingers. I confirm my thanks and dash through the hallway to the second door on the right. Thank the gods he understood me. Pee-pee dancing in the lobby creates a poor first impression.

By the time, I return to the lobby, *mister handsome* waves me to one of the back offices.

"Hello, I'm Balin. How can I help you?" It doesn't matter whom I talk to, all I want is a quick tour and the keys. Balin serves my purpose as much as anyone would. I hand him the letter and post-it note. "Moved in last night. Found these taped to my door."

"If you join me in the office, we'll finish the paperwork. Please take a seat." Balin removes a file laying on top of the file cabinet and seats himself behind the desk. "I hope you found your apartment satisfactory? Ms. Wilson supervised every aspect with your home contacts herself."

Your people talked to my people. What am I, royalty? I made a wrong assumption. Ranger Aby dealt with Ms. Wilson, not Eric. "Yea, everything's fine."

"Glad to hear it." He opens the file and hands me forms. "Your copies of the agreements and contracts. Basic formalities but I'm required to give them to you. Although, I need you to sign this form." Balin points to the form. He says, "Please initial here, here, and sign there. The letter's an acknowledgment form stating you received a set of keys for your apartment, gym room, and a mailbox."

Mailbox? I forgot about that. No more strolling downtown to pick up mail and bother Mister Bell. Wonder if he misses me. I could call from my apartment landline and reverse the charges. Hearing my name from the operator could send shivers up Bell's spine. I smirk at the idea and sign my name on the form.

"Great. Questions so far?" Balin asked.

"Nope. Nothing yet."

"OK then. We'll take the quarter tour. Welcome to

Salerosa Hill Apartments," Balin said while filing the paper-work. We exit his office and walk through the lobby.

Balin says, "We offer free Wi-Fi. Gas logs lit in the fire-place during October through March. The drink bar opens during business hours. The gym is across from the bath-rooms. You know where those are now. Use your key for external and internal doors to enter the gym room."

We exit the back French doors. "Our swimming pool. Pool stays open May to October." He points to a separate building opposite the pool. "Laundry building, always available. Use your PIN to unlock the door. The vending machines disperse laundry detergent and snacks. Change machine for quarters until we shift over to a prepaid card system."

I note the types and the number of chairs poolside. Should be easy to find a vacant spot when I visit. Plenty of white, plastic lawn chairs with cushions surrounding the pool. "Is that a Tiki bar?" I asked.

My tour guide gives me a once over. "Yes. We use the Tiki bar on summer weekends and other special occasions. State law mandates you must be at least twenty-one for alcoholic drinks. But we do serve non-alcoholic drinks."

Balin swipes his arm in a semi-circle. "Plenty of barbeque grills around the pool, scattered throughout the apartment complex."

Nobody enjoys the pool today. Balin and I have the patio to ourselves. I turn around a few times to soak up the atmosphere. "Any grills near my building or any other amenities?" After a second, another question pops into my head. During my walk, something strange struck me. "Why is my building separate from the other apartments?" I asked.

"Three grills located opposite of your building across the parking lot. Inconvenient but they're away from the wooded landscape." His voice trails. "No other amenities associated with your building. Cannot answer the last question. Before my time. You must talk to one of the older guys around here."

"Why is that? What's the big deal?"

"The building was part of an older complex. Destroyed years ago. A private construction company reconstructed, landscaped and saved the Kent building from demolishment. No further inside renovations or new amenities are allowed by the apartment management. Management maintains the grounds, collects and keeps the leases. Unless you have further questions, I'll let you return to your unpacking."

Guess my quarter's worth expired.

"No, I'm fine. Thanks for the keys and tour." I follow him back to the office lobby.

I pause and wait a minute for the final closing. "If you think of any questions, please ask."

"Thanks, and bye." I know I instigated Balin's dialogue but too much talking before lunch. Next apartment, I ask for the nickel tour.

Yuck. What is that rancid odor? Impossible to miss the stench. The whiff hit me as soon as I left the lobby. It originates from the golf cart parked in front. Hope the odor comes from the dishwasher thrown in back and not from the driver.

I fold the contract papers into my left front pocket along with keys. Must jog away before the stench permeates my clothing.

"Hey! You the new tenant?" I look beyond the sidewalk. The cart driver scrutinizes me. "Don't believe I have seen your face around here." Before I wish he drove away, he departs from the odor mobile and waves me closer.

"Name's Carmelo Christos. Folks around here call me, ol' Gabe."

He neither looks old nor like a Gabe. "I'm Salomé. And yes, moved in last night. I'm still unpacking." I inch around backward, offering an offhanded salute. I have no wish to meet the maintenance worker.

"Boys! This tenant lives in the Kent building. Calls herself, Salomé." He directs his wave to two males shadowing behind me. "These are my sons, Colson and Cyril."

Darn, trapped.

Gabe's sons must lift weights. Colson and Cyril's bodies are solid muscle. Their broad shoulders block my sidewalk exit. Both tower over six feet. Guess a year's growth between them. The boys watch as I stare at their physique. They don't seem to mind.

No one can miss the boy's striking resemblance. "Hi. Nice to meet you. Sorry. I cannot stay and chat."

"Cyril! Drive this stinking jumble and hose it down before lunch." Gabe strolls toward the office. "Cannot have our new tenant dying on us from the fumes." He says, "Colson, take your pick."

"I'll ride with Cyril, father. Salomé, enjoy your apartment. Glad to run into you." He races to join his brother and both drive off to who knows where. The stench trails behind them.

"Join me inside. I figure you got questions that need answering. No point putting them off. I'm the one everyone asks." Gabe wastes no time as he disappears through the doorway. By the time I re-enter the lobby, Gabe relaxes on one of the oversized leather chairs near the fireplace. Two ceramic mugs sit next to a full pot of brewed coffee on the table next to him. "Your coffee's poured. Just the way you prefer."

I move the other leather chair closer to him and situate

myself in it. The white ceramic cups on the drink counter bear the complex's logo. This ceramic mug resembles the ones in my apartment. One sip of the java informs me Gabe made the coffee "the way I prefer." I'm not asking how he knew. Not asking why the fireplace flames in the middle of June either. Gabe has an influence here.

"You mentioned outside you have answers?" I balance on the edge of the chair with a coffee mug between both hands. I wait for Gabe's reply.

Gabe picks up the pot of coffee on the table and pours himself a full mug. He overfills it without spilling a drop. Gabe drinks his coffee black. He bends at waist stretching to reach the mug's rim with his lips. Both hands rest on his lap. Gabe makes rude slurping noises. He leans back empty-handed. *Ahhh.* He checks the time on his wrist-watch. "When you are with me girl, you relax."

I stare at Gabe with wide eyes. I'm unsure what he expects.

The heck with it, I make myself at home. I half peel my sneakers off and kick the Reeboks under the table. I seat myself back with both feet on the cushion, bent legs, and place elbows on knees. The coffee mug I grasp and peer over its rim. I'm as comfortable as this chair allows. "Listening," I said, sipping the coffee before it cools.

"Good, you learn fast. I admire that." Gabe reaches for his mug and reclines. He crosses his legs in a typical male fashion. His next few sips of coffee occur without the noises. "You live in the Kent building. Constructed in the forties, it's the last remaining structure of the old hospital complex."

"I live in an old hospital building? You're kidding." I'm surprised since the place doesn't resemble a hospital.

Gabe leans further back in the chair. "The hospital itself, no. Don't be foolish. You live in the old Kent building, the psych ward. The hospital and other immediate buildings, including the furnace chimney, exploded. Total oblivion. We figure a natural gas explosion. Strange how nobody kept natural or propane gas on the property."

The man grabbed my attention. I finish my coffee and refill it with the pot on the table. I wave the container in front of Gabe. He offers me his half-full mug. I top it off and place it back on the table. "What happened after the fire?" I asked.

"No fire. Explosion. Leveled everything. Strangest thing I ever saw."

"You saw it happen, then?"

"After the fact, yes. Folks came all around and saw it. Strangest thing we ever saw. People later swore the sky itself ignited for miles. Doubtful anyone saw the sky illuminate at two in the morning. They just figured it did." Gabe finishes the coffee non-stop then shouts over his shoulder. "Hey, Balin! Fetch a glass, will you?"

Balin lays his handset on the desk. He says, "Sure thing, Gabe." He walks over a moment afterward and hands Gabe a glass of water. "What else?"

"Salomé, you hungry? Chinese takeout OK? I'm buying. Good day for tales if you got the time to listen."

I check the office windows. The weather changed. Skies darken, and it drizzles. "Sure, whatever you want to order."

"You heard the lady. Place the order." Balin withdraws to the desk, punches two buttons on the phone and speaks in Mandarin. "Don't mind him. Minored in languages. Now, where were we?" Gabe said.

"You mentioned an explosion, then poof, nothing left standing." I place my coffee mug on the table and readjust my sitting posture; cross legs, straighten back and lean forward. These comfortable-looking, oversized chairs are misleading. The cushions need replacing.

"Nothing but your building. A private construction company arrived the next day at noontime. They brought earth-moving machines bigger than most people's houses. Might exaggerate but not by much. The crew cleared and gutted your building in nothing flat. The fenced in grounds forced the nosey bodies elsewhere. Also, a nursery firm planted the woodland you walked through today. Fifteen-years of growth buries plenty of history."

"How did it get owned by Salerosa Hill?"

"It didn't. A private entity owns your building. We manage it, along with other companies downtown. Before you ask—confidential information."

Gabe changes the topic. We chat for another forty minutes about his sons until the Chinese food arrives. Balin drops two bags on the table with paper plates, napkins, plastic forks, and two pairs of chopsticks. "Eat the rest with Colson and Cyril. I'm chatting with our new tenant."

At least the delightful Chinese food replaces that awful dishwasher smell.

I spend my daylight hours chatting with Gabe. My apartment can wait until nightfall.

I'll call Jim and Tina during an unpacking break. I should be able to unpack the remaining boxes before bedtime. That leaves me tomorrow for a soak in the sun poolside and taking care of any unfinished chores.

Balin carries his takeout in a cutoff box. He exits the lobby through a side door. Gabe winks. "Let me tell you a story, while we eat. Did you know Santa Fe is one of the most haunted towns in America? Settlers built the dang town on top of an abandoned Tanoan Indian village. Downtown hosts plenty of haunts…"

CHAPTER 6

The first months of any job are the toughest. Afterward, routine chores and work schedules become mundane and boring. The initial excitement fades into oblivion. I love working in the gift shop, but the job isn't what I expected. Enthusiastic the first week, coworkers nicknamed me "Eager Beaver." Hard to believe I socialize with two of them.

I dislike nicknames. Biological parents blessed me with a proper name. It suits me. People should use it or keep their mouths shut.

My school counselor once said, "You're a young adult and should learn to control your anger issues." I ignored her for years. But I learned a couple of things from her. Depending on the circumstances, best to humor people than to shove a shiny knife in their face. Most of the time, situations subside.

People tire easier if you stop feeding them their desired attention. Reasoned, if I answer exclusively to "Salomé," I could retrain coworkers. It worked. Within ten days, the nickname dematerialized. Apathy struck soon after.

I stock shelves, price items, and do light cleaning. Will move to cashier once supervisors deem me ready. Handling cash and charge cards is easy. Dealing with the public, that's the challenge. Anyone who works in a retail environment can tell you, "It sucks." People spoke the phrase so often I believe it is a technical term. I jest but reserve the right to change my mind.

The weather improved since last month. Then again, mid-July loves hotter weather. My new friends; Brianna, Alena, and Joni hang out here at my apartment's pool. We secured a Friday evening after work to party. A problematic chore considering our schedules.

Alena asks, "You want another cold one, girlfriend? Joni and I are heading inside for energy drinks."

Brianna replies, "Nah. I'm good. You girls enjoy. I'll stay here."

I befriended Brianna on the first workday. She and I own the same model bike, which made a good conversation starter. We hit it off right away. But we don't expect to hang out too much together. For one, I like my privacy. And, Brianna wears a friendship ring on her left index finger. Her boyfriend claims most of her spare time, but if time allows, we schedule girl-time together.

"Brianna, you can join them. I can tan solo," I said, squirting lotion on my palm.

"Rather not, Alena and I are going through *a thing* right now." Brianna rolls over on her stomach and covers her head with a towel.

"Do I want to know?" I asked rhetorically. I hope she replies, "No." I don't wish to argue with two friends.

She speaks through the lawn chair's teal-colored canvas. "My troubles aren't important. Alena likes this boy. She wants to double date with his brother to break the ice. I trust neither of them myself but—you know.

Don't worry about it though. We can talk the issue through."

I swing legs over the recliner's edge and lean down. "Do what you know best or change places with Joni. Wouldn't that prove an interesting date?"

Brianna chuckles. She jumps off the recliner and commanders a hug.

Brianna and I hold each other tight. Tears run down her reddened eyes. How did I miss her crying? "Why not jump in the pool?" I asked, figuring a swim could wash the tears and explain her red eyes.

We nod in unison and cannonball into the chlorinated water.

"The park certainly buzzes this time of year," I said. "Ranger Aby said the park visitors increase in the summer. I didn't realize how much." I stay near to the pool's edge and watch for Alena and Joni.

"Wait until you work here for years. The park is popular with the traveling and local public. Aby patrols a large amount of the park grounds. Amazing how she can find the time to drop in the gift shop to say hi to everyone."

"Yea, I appreciate her visiting. She has that way of lifting one's spirit with a simple smile." Brianna smiles, but it fades quickly.

"More laps?" Brianna asked.

"Sure, I'll be here," I said. And dunk my body below the water's surface. I pop up and finger my hair away from my face.

Brianna says, "Thanks. Several more laps could work wonders." Her butterfly swim strokes create splashes and comments from nearby waders. Brianna changes to side-strokes. The laps ease her tension.

Chatted with a few of my co-workers in the past month, and mostly, we cope. But, clicked with Brianna right away. I don't expect to befriend or socialize with all park employees. Sure as heck didn't rub shoulders with all my classmates. I have no wish to be *Miss Popular*.

"It doesn't hurt to be cordial with your coworkers." In the past, I credited my school counselor with that quote. Heaven knows how often she repeated it. Except for bio-dad also used the phrase last year. Not sure to whom I should give credit.

Funny if Eric saw my school counselor for therapy, but unless he attended my high school, or dates my counselor, never mind. Not amusing. Strange how I imagined him dating my school counselor.

Speaking of strange, observed this co-worker acting weird. I noticed him at the gift shop last week. Most times, I overlook boys his age. Hormones play havoc with boys. On occasions, adolescent boys act OK and then, for no apparent reason, they say or do freaky things.

I didn't notice this kid at all last month. I'm unsure why. He sticks out from the rest of the workers. He has well-kept, shoulder-length, blonde hair, an athletic swimmer build with broad shoulders, yet he's timid and quiet. Our eyes met once accidentally. Deepest, most meaningful sapphire blue I ever saw, ageless with limitless caring. Before I regained composure and bearings, he disappeared. Guess I daydreamed when he stepped away.

Younger co-workers, comment about him behind his back, yet, nobody knows the kid's name. Brianna once said, "The boy has worked in the park for years. I rarely see him doing anything though." I tried to pump Alena for more information. All she added was, "He helps keep the grounds maintained part-time, and the kid prefers to work alone." Their lack of details surprised me considering they both love gossip.

If I see him around, I plan to give him another chance

before judging. Adolescent boys are awkward. Guess the kid feels uncomfortable with girls around him. Given enough time, I'm sure he will outgrow it.

Brianna dives under the water and when she resurfaces, she backstrokes down the pool length. No sign of Alena or Joni yet. "They're still inside," I said when Brianna swims by me sitting on the edge of the pool. "Time for two more laps!"

I try to keep busy at work. Time flies when I stay focused on the job of assisting visitors. Out of state tourists ask the silliest questions. Information in the park's brochures answers most of their issues; all people need to do is to read it. I answer their questions the best I can, anyway. When I first came to the park, I felt confused too.

The toughest part of the job deals with answering dumb questions: "Are there any ghosts here?" or "Is this place haunted?" I wish I could refer them to ol' Gabe. He loves telling ghost stories. I smile and say, "No. I don't believe so." The job requires politeness, not honesty. Aby warned me I could run into issues with the public. But, dealing with ghost questions? Ridiculous and absurd fail to describe it. And, at a national park no less.

Alena is another of Gabe's children. The youngest daughter of a huge family. Alena had said one day, "Trust me, you'll run into a Christos when you least expect it. My family is everywhere." Alena and Gabe love to talk. If running your mouth is a family trait, I hope the family tree bears sparse fruit. But at least she comes from good stock.

Then, there is Joni. His real name is Jonah, but he wants the same treatment as, "One of the girls," his quote. Joni is okay to shop and hang with, but he's too busy dealing with his demons to focus on meaningful friendships.

"We ready? They're back with extra drinks." Alena and

Joni relax under one umbrella. "They're waving. We good?" I asked.

Brianna wipes the pool water from her face. "I'm never good." She smirks, takes my hand. "Thanks," she whispered.

"Anytime." We wade over to the stairs and join our friends.

"Hey, Salomé. You know about the wildlife carcasses; the ones near the Northwest corner? The area where the bats live?" Why dead animals excite Joni bewilders me. "Last week I overheard a conversation before the gift shop opened. A maintenance worker said the weird boy, the one I mentioned to you before, tends to the dead animals. So far, the main public walkways stay carcass-free."

Alena gags. "Please, we're drinking! Besides Joni, the only weird boy working in the park is you."

I answer, "No. Guess *the other* weird kid does the fantastic cleaning job."

Brianna and Alena chuckle.

"Ha-ha. Fine. I can take a joke. No Biggy," Joni said.

One of these days, I want to explore the back trails and cliff dwellings carved into the rock. The isolated cavates are the perfect spot to watch the sunset and catch up on writing. Cannot wait to climb inside and drift away into a different world, or between worlds. I sure could use the inspiration for journal entries. Lately, my entries suffer from a lack of enthusiasm and originality. Too busy right now for any night outings. Maybe after the summer when the trails are carcass-free.

Brianna says, "You girls ready to change and order a pizza?" Her demeanor improves if she is hungry.

"If you mean two pizzas, then heck yea," Joni said. He habitually orders garlic knots with pizza. Trust me. I wish he didn't.

Alena exclaims, "I rented a chick flick to watch." She teases Joni every chance she gets. Joni may dream he's one of the girls, but he favors martial art action movies. Alena, on the other hand, despises them.

Everyone's ready to head back to my apartment. We must keep the night short. We all work the morning shift. One of these days, I'm finding a night career. I hate sleeping through the best time of the day.

My mantra, meanwhile, is, stay focused on work and learn to relax. I managed to collect plenty of books these past months and can rent DVDs for entertainment. The new lifestyle is finally taking shape. Plenty of friends to spend time with too.

"All right, girls, back to my place for a movie and pizzas —plural. First, a toast. Here's hoping the rest of the busy summer season zooms by without incident."

A round of cheers erupts.

A restless summer drifted by without fanfare. Autumn promises cool air and the possibility of reconnecting with nature's harmony. The time of year when the heat of day wanes. An assortment of color and much-needed calm blooms. Leaves transform into their brilliance.

During these past summer months, I visited the Taos Pueblo Reservation, one of my excursions with Brianna. Well worth the long bike ride. If you find time to visit Taos, New Mexico, plan on a sunny day and pack your walking shoes. Make sure you spend time and chat with the shop-keepers.

We found this one exceptional shop clerk named Milap. His World War 2 stories kept us intrigued for hours. He mentioned how his father made a medicine pouch to protect him overseas. Milap said he traveled by railroad to reach the east coast. He couldn't open the rail car's window because of the black smoke the coal engine produced. Times sure have changed. You don't see black smoke billowing from rail engines nowadays.

The girls and I haunted other places, but poolside became our prized spot. We rambled mostly about work. Alena told stories about the local area. Tales I believe she embellished. Alena takes after her father, Gabe. Both are natural storytellers.

Brianna chatted up hour-long storms too. I'm surprised how she can run her mouth on occasions. Maybe she caught the yap bug from Alena. Most days I listened to Brianna while we people watched. She liked to check out the older boys despite wearing her friendship ring. But she deserves credit. Brianna tried hard to behave.

Every so often, a few of the girls and I rode bikes downtown for a change of scenery and exercise. We window-shopped or treated ourselves to frozen yogurt before the trip home. Joni joined us on occasions but became preoccupied with his new counselor. He did his best to show up when he could though.

The gift shop buzzed all summer. Long hours prevented me from visiting the cavates. But tonight after work, I'm remedying the oversight. The weather forecast predicted clear sky and calm winds. Once the park closes, I ride the bike to the northwest side of the cliffs to this perfect cavate.

The full moon shines bright tonight. I perfectly preplanned everything. Plenty of supplies in the backpack: a flashlight for the return trip, lantern for reading, a blanket for warmth, writing instruments, a small first aid kit, and my boot knife.

Hope this workday ends soon. Unsure if co-workers can put up with my humming and constant pacing. But I can push aside their comments and stares. I waited too long for the cool night breeze to brush against my skin. Too much time inside creates stress. And a night adventure beats a soak any day.

∼

A neat idea turned cold. I wrap the blanket tightly around me. The temperature dropped twenty degrees after work hours. Once the gift shop closed for the day, I walked into an isolated wooded area and hid. My backpack holds the needed packed items for later. Once everyone left the park, I retrieved the bike and rode trails.

My plan worked. Had a concern the weird kid may follow me from the gift shop. Thought of running into him during the summer but I always missed him. Guess he avoided me. Then suddenly, the kid shows up today. We had no direct eye contact. The kid kept busy doing chores. Although I sensed his eyes on me throughout the whole day.

Anyway, no more thoughts about work. I declare a private and gorgeous clear night. Another goal accomplished!

The daylight colors meet those of the night. I could get high on sunsets. Why did I delay? If a person enjoys simple pleasures in life, they should seize them. I swear, sometimes I place too much emphasis on the wrong stuff.

The vivid hues of reds, yellows, and purples fade into the velvet sky. I flip on my portable lantern, reach for the journal and enter my latest inspired thoughts.

Eight handwritten pages later, I take a slow, long breathe, exhale, and make a silent wish. Feeling moody, I stuff the journal into the backpack when stones pellet my shoulder. Someone discovered me. Shit.

"Hey, knock it off, you idiot!" I screamed, refusing to believe bats pitch pebbles.

My private time comes to an abrupt halt. It must be the weird kid. My first impulse is to throw the lantern at him. But I flip off the light instead. This way, when I toss it, his head gets one huge lump!

I wrap the surrounding blanket tighter and lean out of the cavate's opening. Teeth pinch lower lip, cutting off schoolyard slang. The sudden disturbance sends stomach stitches all the way to my sternum.

Major surprise. An adult waits at the bottom of the ladder. A stranger. Alone at night, inside a small cavate with nowhere to run but down. Just fantastic. Shit.

"Salomé, we need to talk."

The phrase echoes off the surrounding walls.

What the heck, the man knows me? Not only a stranger waiting below but a stalker as well?

Trapped inside this small space is unwise. Chances of retreating increase on the ground with plenty of running area. Best if I keep hands free descending the ladder. I heave my gear and backpack through the opening without sound or notice. Everything is thrown out at once. I hope the equipment whacks the stranger.

A quick glance triggers distant memories. The man seems familiar. Cannot quite place him but I recall him from somewhere. Too dark to see anyone while descending. Eyes adjusted to the bright halogen lantern in the cave. The stars shine on the cavern with a warm natural glow. Eyes need a moment to recover and refocus.

I reach ground level and prepare myself for a fast run. Instead of facing the stranger, the kid from work stands here holding all my thrown items.

"So, it was you. What the heck, kid?"

The kid says, "Please, allow me to explain." He steps back, allowing me space to clear the ladder.

His hands are full. Mine are empty. I reach for my knife.

"Explain, and fast," I said pointing a sharp blade at his midsection.

"The stranger you saw is known as Kajika, and he'll meet us later."

The kid further explains in a soft voice, "Kajika wishes to speak and perhaps offer something that could interest you."

Right. I bet *Kajika* does. One perfect, quiet night shot and I go visiting. Lucky me.

The kid's presence or pretense feels non-threatening. If someone else had asked me to walk with him into pitch darkness, the situation could be different. With him, though, I'm unsure.

I lower my blade and follow the kid down the path. What can I say? Curiosity trumps common sense. This kid's aura emulates trust, in a big brother-ish way.

We trek off the main park trails then traverse seldom-used, off-beaten footpaths. The paths back here deviate between dirt grooves and narrow animal footpaths. Low-lying bushes rub against my legs.

The kid peers over his shoulder. I'm trailing three paces behind him at a safe distance. The kid breaks the night's silence.

"The word Kajika means *He who walks without a sound.* The title bestowed numerous years ago in South America by a local tribe. Kajika asked me to toss the pebbles into the cavate. Although I waited until you finished your writing."

"Lah-de-dah. How cordial of you."

"I have served Master Kajika for years. I have no regrets."

No idea what this "Master" stuff is but coming from him, somehow, it sounds normal. I can still make a run for it. No need to memorize the path, or lack of one either, difficult to lose yourself inside a canyon.

"Where are you taking me? I cannot see a bloody thing in this darkness."

Silence follows my question. Pebbles and twigs scatter as the sounds of my footsteps *crunch* and *snap*. I take glimpses of the trail behind and around me but see only shadows. Finally, the trail comes to an abrupt end. We stop. A formless shadowy figure emerges.

"Thank you. Leslie, you may return to your duties," the stranger said. A calm request between two friends?

Sound and tone of the stranger's voice sound familiar too, yet distant. The kid places the backpack and other items on the ground off to my left. He backtracks and disappears into the shadows. I know my primary concern should be to focus on this stranger. Instead, my mind drifts to the kid that disappeared.

I worked with this kid all summer long and nobody I asked knew his name. I cannot help myself. An involuntary snicker passes my lips. "*Teehee.* Leslie." It makes my night.

Yea, I know over fifty years ago, Leslie was a popular name for boys, but it sounds funny. No wonder, "Leslie, *hehehe*," guarded his name and evaded coworkers.

"Salomé, enough. I don't tolerate arrogance from anyone, including you, Salomé."

A bad sign when adults use your name in sentences, especially more than once. The shadow stranger wins my attention. I note my surroundings, the best I can, and prepare to run. No trouble to replace belongings if I bolt and leave them. Might stumble through this bramble growing everywhere. If I keep steps high enough, I should be able to stomp and trump my way out of here. Assuming I make a hasty and quick retreat.

I brace myself for either a lecture or an attack.

The stranger faces me. He plants both feet on the earth. A lecture then. The night is young. I have time to listen before bedtime. Besides, an inexplicable hunch says pay strict attention to him.

His voice sounds monotone in the dry air, "Salomé, you have separated yourself from the night for too long. An unhealthy practice for the likes of you."

I trust this stranger as far as I can throw him. I mutter, "Oh please. Tell me more."

Kajika does. Guess he heard me.

"The larger population cherish their humdrum, mundane, run-of-the-mill lives. For them, life is dull. They must keep schedules and follow agendas. Ignorant sheep, who hope something on their personal planners will someday transfer happiness, but it seldom does."

Figured he would say more. He gambled a bunch of trouble leading me here. Before I could voice my views or yawn, the stranger disappears.

The stranger's words reverberate off the night air. "Don't act surprised, daughter of the night."

I pivot and shoot him a leer. My hand tightens around the knife handle. I raise the blade to waist level. I'm undaunted. And widen my stance, distancing myself from doubt.

"You say you love history, well, I'm part of history. My proud father, Antonio Fernando Florez III, named me Fernando Ventré Florez. I was conceived and born in the coastal city of Avila, Spain in the late twelfth century."

A weird, tensed facial expression washes over my face.

"Yes Salomé, I'm that old," the man replies.

This stranger offers nothing. One special tranquil night ruined. I shift my body to the left. Few bushes grow in that area. An escape route maybe. A sudden urge to vent builds.

Before Mount Salomé erupts profanities, which would embarrass a seasoned sailor, the explications rearrange themselves. I utter a single lame phrase. "Do I know you?"

The shadows abandon Kajika and visibility improves. I almost see him.

"Salomé, you live in a mundane world. Although the night abides in every fiber of your being. The darkness offers comfort. You subsist. Life should fulfill and provide meaning to existence."

The only abiding is my legs falling asleep. I shuffle to recirculate blood. This man bores me. I am also still pissed about the pebbles incident.

"You wish to speak?" the man asked.

I stand mere feet from Fernando. Pulse throbs and rubbery legs wobble. I'm unsure how much longer they will hold me upright. Despite all common sense, I hand him the attitude.

"Well, heck yes. What makes you think you know me?" Shifting stances, I offer no easement. "I'm working hard on a career, darn it. Why me? Why now?"

An expected chill runs up my arms. Spine straightens in response to changing energy. Neck hairs stand on edge. My voice lowers. "I somewhat remember. I sensed your presence. The strange missing sensation on the bus trip. The restlessness and music that first night. That was you, wasn't it?" I listen to myself ramble. "Why do I love the night so much?"

"The Moon sings a song to her children. A song you hear and feel in your heart. The warm impression you cherish illustrates her love for you. You worship it, do you not? Part of my vampiric nature recognizes the Enchantress's children and those who revere her.

"Yes, I visited your dreams. More times than you can

comprehend. You sensed my presence. To enable you the choice tonight, *Dream weaving* was necessary."

Invisible tremors course through my body. My face reddens as my hands tighten into fists. The heck with running away. I want to ram into this man and knock him on his butt.

"I don't appreciate people, or vampires, visiting my dreams, thanks. Dreams should be private! Darn it. You had no right." I change my stance and raise the blade. Aiming two inches below his ribcage. "You skipped my question. Why me and why now?"

This Fernando Ventré Florez character tilts his head to study the night sky. I cannot blame him for staring at the stars. A bright, glowing, full moon hangs high with a planet or two close by. Stars twinkle. I didn't study astronomy, so no clue what constellation he scrutinizes. Does he plan to read my palms next?

"There'll be time to answer your myriad questions." Kajika lowers his gaze. "Except for—why. You'll find that answer on your own," he said, in a monotone voice.

Do you ever wish you could kick someone in the shins and hear their screams travel for miles? I'm pissed, or rather, was.

A gambit of rage, relief, hope, and embarrassment alternate their inner battles. My mind dreams. My body fights to stay awake.

Lightheadedness transforms into clarity. I re-experience partial scenes of past dreams. This Kajika appears in them, somewhat. The figureless shapes and colors of recent visions become more apparent. I face this master vampire and squarely meet his eyes.

Kajika continues his speech. "The night calls your name, *Salomé. Daughter of the night.* Fate chose me, to proffer an alternative. One choice that lets your Soul soar to new heights. For people, such as us, the night provides unlimited freedom. Life holds no accidents. Every single action or thought leads a person to his or her destiny."

My shadowy stranger retreats to the darkness. Mists rise from the damp ground. The area develops an eerie ambiance that earmarks a classic London mystery movie. Thick heavy mist claims the tallest bushes. The once starry sky vanishes in fog.

I take no fear. I shout, "Kajika?"

The encompassing mists speak. Kajika's voice originates out there somewhere. His voice resonates everywhere. He whispers close to my ear. I swear I wear him on my skin.

"Destiny sent you for a reason, to choose. I can draw you closer to her. But your love must be complete. No room for another. This journey is challenging, and not for a weak Soul. Your destiny and the night calls to you, Salomé, do you wish to answer them? Or do you wish to walk away and live in emptiness?"

The overwhelming tale drains my energy. Here I stand, someone from a small town, holding a knife, facing a master vampire who asks if I want to be immortal.

Kajika's words strike deep. Repressed passion quivers along my skin. Arm hairs dance and lips part. My palms moisten. Flashbacks continue. Bits and pieces of faded dreams materialize.

To relive dreams is an adrenaline rush. My pulse quickens. Anger and resentment dissipate. He may have lacked consent to enter my thoughts, but the smallest inkling of understanding emerges. Kajika and I connect. No matter which choice I pick tonight, we stay linked.

I cannot hate him. Hate no longer dwells within my body.

Kajika's vampiric aura strengthens. The Moon

Enchantress sings. My heart aches at her nightsong. Throat swallows a giggle. Substantial dark waves pound a distant shore. I ascend high into the sky and plunge headfirst into comforting waters.

Stagger steps through gray mists lead to the man who calls himself Fernando Ventré Florez. Thoughts meander on future life changes. Tomorrow exists in a different world. I welcome the extraordinary venture.

Theodore said he would drop by someday. He's in for a surprise when he visits. Will miss seeing Jim and Tina but I can call. And, I cannot forget Eric. Bet me joining the undead ruins his day. Man, Eric will be royally pissed.

A master vampire's embrace is indescribable. The night and I merge. Shadows fold and wrap around us. The vampire's embrace tightens. My spirit succumbs to the ethers. My old life drifts into the darkness. A faint cry passes my lips.

Kajika places me on the damp ground. My body twitches in its last effort to survive. Scents of juniper and a hint of moss assault my senses. Darkness encloses. I drift off to sleep. There is neither fear nor regret. I know the night watches.

The night takes care of her children.

CHAPTER 8

Scented, solid earth transfigures to a plush mattress in a darkened room. Clean bare skin slides on high thread count sheets. Body squirms. Legs and arms stretched wide. A pillow hug, or two, and a swear tumbles from lips. Nothing against nudity but why sleep naked? Someone invented sleepwear for a darn good reason. If that weird kid touched me, fingertips probe gums in search of—yes—he could be my first victim.

My vision adjusts to the dim lighting. The silhouette of someone stands at the foot of the bed. I wrap the sheet around me and sit upright. Vision clears within moments. The tall, dark, and handsome man shows himself. Kajika. Mixed emotions run amok on the other night for this man, but feelings change. On rare occasions, they change abruptly without explanation.

"Salomé, thank you for the compliment. You're awake?"

Shit. I forgot vampires read minds. "Yes, I'm awake. Where are we?"

"You're safe in my cottage. Sheltered in the park. The

second cluster of buildings to the far right. The smaller cottage in the group, do you remember the place?"

"I believe so. But I didn't explore the buildings."

"Few people visit. The posted 'Private' sign discourages intruders and no direct path leads to this cottage. Leslie keeps a vigilant eye on us, one of the reasons we are safe here. Other safeguards exist too. As for reading minds, I read your projected thoughts. The technique is different. If you are up to it, are you ready to discover what your new life holds for you?"

An open-ended question and rhetorical. Kajika knows I want to know about my new life and everything about it. Who would not? I have sparse choices, right? Before I can answer his question, Kajika exits. He waits outside the doorway. Considerate and a master vampire? How impressive.

I rise and dress in the clothes I find folded on the mahogany hope chest at the foot of the bed. As he waits, Kajika explains the events that transpired on that fateful night when we first embraced.

"Not too long after your body dies, a true vampirism impulse begins, and the fledgling digs into the earth to cover itself. During this stage, I carried you to this cottage, and its protective covering, shielded from the elements. If I had left you, the elements of day and hungry carnivores could have destroyed your body. A newborn fledgling cannot take care of itself. I then buried you in the cellar's earthen floor below the room where you now stand. You laid in the earth's care for the past month."

"What! You kidding?" I stare at the door concealing Master Kajika, my jaw slacks. "You dumped and left me in the dirt for a whole month?" Cannot imagine what crawled in private orifices during that time. Heck, I was not asleep. I laid in a freaking coma.

I dress and pass the doorway. "Is this crud on my lashes or is it a dead bug?" Flat palms rub sleepy eyelids. Fingers ruffle hair and scalp to shake off any lingering sleep. A white glaze prevents clear sight. My unease doesn't stop Kajika concluding his story.

"Vulnerability plays an equal part in the strengths of a vampire's life. You cannot have one without the other." Kajika walks the hall leaving the crud or bug poll unquestioned.

We enter the living room. Four chairs surround an oblong table in the middle of the room, a brown fabric sofa rests against one wall, and scattered accessory pieces are here and there. All used furniture. Guess someone found it curbside somewhere. The frugal decorating does well for this room.

The cabin has three windows. One window in the room where I awoke and two windows in the living room. Drawn white shades cover all windows along with green, tweed, patterned drapes. Basic and unimpressive but I suspect the curtains serve their purpose.

Kajika smiles. The man heard my projecting thoughts from the past hour. He opens the cellar door. Must learn to block, or watch, my thoughts in the future. Knowing me, figure the latter.

Kajika and I descend the flight of stairs. A single, dim light bulb hangs from the ceiling. The cellar looks unimpressive.

A severe dizzy spell attacks and a mild case of heartburn joins the fun. My arms reach out for balance. My hand misses the railing. I find the opposite wall for back support. Lightheadedness causes my feet to sidestep the final two stair treads. If someone sneezes, I could fly into a wall.

When our feet reach the dirt floor, my tall, dark and

handsome friend loses his stature. The ceiling height barely clears six feet, and Kajika still has a hands' width to hit his head. Guess Spaniards in the 12th century rarely hit the six-foot mark, but I bet he can play a nasty game of hoops.

I wait for Kajika to speak. Instead, his hand motions to the far side of the cellar. Three small rooms line the full length of the far wall.

Kajika points towards one room. "Middle room is yours. The other two are off limits."

I enter my room and picture the barren monks' cells Theodore once mentioned. He read every book in the school's library about seminary life. The cells mentioned in the books do not compare to the real deal. Hard to imagine in a million years that someday I would live in one.

This cell, as the monks call them, is eight foot by eight-foot square with bare unpainted concrete walls. On the outside of the doorway a heavy open padlock hangs on the door, a thick steel deadbolt secures inside the room. The scant furniture comprises a dresser cabinet without the mirror and a storage chest like the one upstairs.

A single futon lays on the dirt floor. I double check for the infamous coffin associated with vampires. Thank the heavens the coffin is absent. Sorry, but coffins define creepy. Besides, I sleep on my side, and you cannot do that in a coffin. The futon will suffice.

I glide through the doorway to explore the rest of the basement. My excitement lightly carries me into the shadows. My thoughts grasp and wrestle my new reality. Imagine. I'm now a creature of the night! Man, I hope I never lose this feeling of euphoria.

The single bulb at the bottom of the stairs provides the solitary light for the whole cellar. No windows down here, so no need for coffins. This entire cellar is a coffin.

"Your current vampiric nature grants you a sleepless night. And any of your basic needs can be met."

"So, tossing and turning out. Toothbrush and toilet paper in. Got it."

Kajika leans into the cell's threshold. "The room's dirt floor is necessary. I'll explain more at a later time," he said, with his voice trailing.

Leslie descends the stairs. His footsteps echo off the cellar's concrete foundation walls. I complete my last survey and am satisfied with my new digs. Kajika and good ol' Leslie boy wait on opposite sides of a small table with a single pottery bowl on it.

Stomachache has grown into a case of the shakes. I cramp and grow apprehensive. Hunger massacred my ecstasy. Body demands food. That bowl had better hold something editable or drinkable or I'm raiding the kitchen cabinets.

My conclusion and hopes are confirmed when I lumber up to the table. A bowl is full of blood. I know it's blood. I can smell it.

Leslie disappeared. Palms rub both eyes in alternate directions. I squint and double-check the cellar. Nothing. Darn ache and pains distracted sight and hearing. I wildly tap my head with fingertips and refocus on Kajika, the table between us.

Few people can project their aura and command attention. Fernando Ventré Florez is such a person. I'm uncertain if his strong presence is an archetype or a Master Vampire ability.

The cosmos bestowed a *give attitude* archetype upon me at birth. But I stand on the bottom rung of this night world. My future depends on Kajika's teachings. Although I do wish to learn, it seems I may have no choice in the matter anyway. Our master vampire-fledging connection, blood exchange, or some other reason I may never know, makes my whole body yearn to listen to my Sire.

"You'll make a good disciple, Salomé. The mother of all knows her children well. Blood fills the bowl before you. Take it and fill your thirst. You hungered far too long since your second birthing. The rebirthing necessitates you experience the thirst before you learn how to hunt for your nourishment. Expect your body to experience transformations. Nothing to fear, but change is inevitable. Even in death."

I grasp the bowl of blood with both hands. I disregard my body's tiny tremors. Half of the contents I guzzle. The remaining blood I sip. No lie, it tastes good. And no, I never drank blood until tonight. It must be a required taste for the undead.

The empty bowl I return to the table. I take a moment or two to collect my thoughts. The pains subside. Blood satisfies but leaves hunger. A whole bowl full of blood and my stomach craves more. A queasiness immobilizes my body. A weird sensation occupies my thoughts.

I look at Kajika. He offers a faint smile.

"My birth name is Fernando Ventré Florez, born in the town of Avila Spain on 12 August 1137. I believe a Thursday. The exact time doesn't matter. You may know this already. Now, allow me the pleasure of telling my tale."

I stand mesmerized. Fernando wears a tailored, Italian three-piece suit. His dark hair hangs loosely on both shoulders. Master Kajika possess an irresistible aura. A unique sire—fledgling relationship intervenes. I lack the words to explain the phenomenon.

No chairs down here, so I stand. Wouldn't dare settle in a chair, anyway. The position resembles upper management, seven levels above your pay grade, speaking to you. If they stand and omit a sitting request, you stand. Period.

"My birth parents died long before I sailed to this majestic land back in the sixteenth century. Life was hard. The thought of traveling over the ocean hinted at a fabulous adventure. The trip excited me at first but that soon changed. Several vicious storms battered our ship throughout the voyage. Unlucky for the crew, and me, the *Potencia Rosa* was aged from previous adventures. She yielded to the beating of the enormous waves that crashed upon her hull. My seaward adventure was the ship's last. The *Potencia Rosa* sank off the coast of the Yucatan Peninsula in 1562. Less than a dozen men, including me, survived the shipwreck.

"The reason for our voyage? To search for gold and other trade items to export back to Spain. Gold does strange things to men. Once gold roots itself in the heart, it rots. We, the surviving members, all headed into the jungles of lower Mexico where the stories sounded too good to believe. Every man onboard heard the tales of mountains of gold hidden in this strange land. We agreed to return to Spain with the gold. With or without a ship. As I mentioned, gold blinds all men."

Despite what commanders say, just because you are at attention, one's brain continues to function. I listen to every word, but the story sounds inconsistent. The numbers don't add up correctly.

"Why the surprised expression? My life is more adventurous than you can imagine. Yes, I was over four hundred years old, when the ship first sailed. In my reckless youth, I traveled far from motherland Spain. I entered the forbidden Pireses Mountains to seek treasure and mischief.

"It was April when an unexpected snowstorm hit the mountainous region. At twelve years old and unprepared for extreme weather, my demise appeared imminent. I laid for the better part of a day on the snowy ground. The natural elements, which I love and revere, pounded my frail young body with their full wrath. But fate favored me. My cards read good fortune that day. A local shaman found and carried my body into his cave that same evening.

"With local herbs and powders, the stranger concocted an elixir. The drink saved my life and severely slowed my metabolism. We spent fruitful years together. Avalanches decimate small villages. The shaman's family died before naming him so; I took that honor. I would come to call him Bernard.

"When I sailed the wide ocean; I was older than the entire crew put together yet an adolescent in their eyes."

Wow. I'm shocked. Talk about an eventful life. I know he wouldn't lie.

"No, Salomé, I wouldn't lie to you."

"I didn't say… sorry, forgot. Less daydreaming, more listening." I take a deep breath. "Please Master Kajika, finish your story." He gestures with a reassuring nod. I take another moment to quiet inner thoughts.

"The jungle we entered held many mysteries. But the wilderness revealed none of them, including the gold. We found no treasure.

"Within months, the surviving crew perished one by one from the wilderness's diseases and dreadful jungle exposure. It took a tremendous toll on us. I was no exception. None of us prepared for such a hostile environment. The men attempted Christian burials but found the graves later dug up during the night. Bodies carried away by either predators or demons. We didn't know which. The few remaining survivors, too concerned for their safety, halted proper burials. If you dropped, we left you where you fell. It was callous and straightforward.

"Maybe the elixir ran its course, or maybe it was the

stress of loneliness in this godforsaken environment but I aged. Granted it was not overnight, but I feared my immortality was ending. Death, the ultimate seeker, now searched for me. I felt its cold stare penetrating the dense jungle. I was about to die. A realization I wasn't fond of accepting."

Master Kajika suffered deeply. His eyes hint of past remorse, and I hear a negligible quaver in his voice. Kajika's jungle experience sounds awful. Imagine witnessing your shipmates suffer and die without being able to help them. His story makes my unpleasant condition minuscule in comparison.

My muscles nag for a good stretch after lying in bed for a month. I shuffle my feet and do shoulder rolls before Master Kajika continues his tale.

"I wasn't a vampire at the time, as you theorized, but I fancied the idea of immortality. Bernard told me, 'You're destined for long life.' I wished to prove him correct."

"You ended up alone? The sole survivor with no return to Spain?" I take a moment and do a stealthily petite deadlift.

"Bernard's gift, as you surmise, left me the sole survivor. I was unsure if I should curse him or thank him. I stumbled through the jungle growing older and weaker with fatigue. Abandoned temples, long forgotten, revealed themselves but not a single soul. I believed myself cursed. And the natives were driven away for their own safety. However, fate once again felt pity. I discovered a cave. My spirit rejoiced for this simple shelter.

"With the sparse survival training Bernard taught me, I miraculously managed to stay alive for another ten years. I was in poor shape and decided not to live in the jungle's rainy season one day longer. Ironic I suppose. My immunity abandoned me years earlier. Now in adulthood, not much younger than I appear today, I gambled everything and re-entered the deep jungle to find an escape.

"Alas, my new adulthood didn't last long. Fatigue finally won its battle. With my desire for life gone, I collapsed finding and escaping nothing.

"Exhausted, I laid on the damp, cold, miserable jungle floor. Not for rest but as an offering to my maker. I was ready to die. The jungle canopy concealed the blue sky. Sunlight hadn't penetrated this canopy in who knows when. As fate would deem it, I wouldn't see the brightness of the sun or feel its warmth on my skin ever again."

I can relate to never seeing the sun again. A vampire misses what people take for granted. I chose a vampiric lifestyle; Kajika did not. The jungle robbed him of his mortal life. My eyes water and I wipe them with the back of my hands. Man, hard to imagine what he felt.

"I couldn't call the creature that attacked me human in any sense of the word. It struck my exposed neck. Strength to fight this creature left me. I fell limp on damp soil. The dense jungle swallowed my screams whole. The beast vanished when the echoes died.

"Delirium later showed its ugly face. In the years of existing in that jungle, I didn't meet a living soul. When I had regained enough strength to open my eyes, I saw what I assumed was a native. He dressed in a red and gold flowing long robe, with a black and gold ceremonial mask covering his face. My apparition held a tall walking stick. The vision, real or not, vanished as quickly as it appeared.

"Eyes grew heavy. My last breaths grew shallow. What-ever had permitted light to enter this hell was no longer interested in doing so. Darkness engulfed me. I took my last breath. Too weak to curse the ground. Dying as my crewmates did. To rot away on foreign soil, missing my homeland. I didn't plan for this future. It sickened me to dwell upon it. The sounds of the jungle permeated my mind. I drifted away into darkness."

"The moment you died. Was the guy in the mask the same creature that attacked you?" I fail to see how since the demons' descriptions sound so different. And nobody did earlier dream-work on Kajika or did they?

Kajika shrugs. "When I gained full consciousness, I didn't lay on a soft mattress as you did, but with my back chained to a dirty, damp stone wall under a long-ago forgotten temple. When my vision adjusted, the native appeared. He stood two inches from my face. I screamed and struggled with my chains. The air smelled of burning bark. I cried again. It was useless.

"I realized my fate was sealed. Hysterics did nothing to change the expression hidden behind the fiend's mask. With no hint of emotion, his gaze entered my body. I could feel his essence in every fiber of my being. A sharp pain shot up my spine. My back arched and I blacked out. A distant voice joined the pain, but darkness claimed both.

"Chained and abandoned to a wall for days is hard to accept. The chains stopped me from collapsing to the floor face first. I was alive, or so I thought. My body ached in places I did not know could ache. The ruins stood empty. I saw and heard nothing. Even my heartbeat abandoned me."

The creature forced the dream-work on him by the sound of it. Maybe started years earlier without his knowledge.

"Dead already or maybe my irrational mind imagined the whole thing. To be honest, I could not make the distinction. I tried to clear my head as my body swayed. As I hung there, I thanked the Holy Father that I endured. Thankful I did not lay abandoned and dead on that godforsaken jungle floor.

"Hanging and chained on the wall, my soul prepared itself to meet its maker. My ego wanted nothing more than to escape this prison. I fought with myself. Once I gained a certain clarity of thought, I gripped hands around the links and took the slack out of the chain. I yanked. Not too hard at first because I wanted to test the metal, but with minimum effort, the first try proved successful. The anchored chains gave away. My exhausted body stumbled forward. I landed on the stone floor. The cuffs encircling my wrists fell off with the same ease. I won my freedom."

"Kajika, did you know you were a vampire then and who was this guy that sired you?" I asked.

Kajika remains standing. We both do. I moved and jittered a bit, but Kajika stayed motionless the whole time. The story was told as if it happened moments ago. My few questions didn't faze him in the slightest.

"No Salomé, I didn't know then. I learned years later after journeying to the west coast, through the dense jungle, before the details emerged. The creature that made me left me on my own. I never saw him again. Rumors abound, but in the jungle, rumors always exist. Nothing came from them. I later called him Natanael. It means *a gift from God*. I named him for peace of mind. If not for him, I would have rotted away.

"I traveled west to Peru and discovered a massive underground cave system. It became my home for two centuries. Created rumors and myths myself. The natives kept to themselves. I felt blessed to see real people once again. So, I kept to myself too. Years later, I used the tunnels to move here. Perhaps someday you can visit them yourself, but enough of my history. You should taste the night air before dawn. Please test your new vampire powers. You'll be pleased with what you can do so soon.

Within time, more abilities may manifest. Leslie serves as your safeguard in my absence."

I want to make a long reply but a simple, "Thank you, Kajika" passes my lips.

He replies with a formal and dignified nod.

Master Kajika veers toward the door. *Poof.* He disappears before I can blink. Either he's quick, or my brain has bogged down trying to decipher his fantastic story. Wow, what a tale.

After a moment of silence, Leslie reappears and hands me a letter delivered to the gift shop earlier. I didn't realize he was present. Wonder how many times Leslie heard Kajika's story? I hold and glance at the letter. The letter is from Theodore. I excuse myself, trod up the stairs, and grab a cloak by the door before heading out of the cabin.

Leslie trails from a short distance.

I wanted to walk the night before daybreak. Fresh air does a body good, even for the undead. Taking a great chance, I leap straight upward after approaching a cavern wall. I land crouched on the ledge. First night as a vampire, it feels right. I belong here.

The kid's heart beats strong. He guards below and waits.

No unique sight yet but I have developed acute hearing. The moon hides behind the clouds. I hear her song. Her voice haunts but also comforts. Nocturnal creatures scramble to their burrows before sunrise. Too soon for the birds to sing but other animals make their presence known. Their songs echo throughout the canyon.

An hour passes, and Leslie watches.

Sweet, warm forest air fills my senses with intoxicating visions. The night embraces me. I shut my eyes and reach outward. A shout fills the night.

"Salomé!"

Body jerks and I instantly become aware of my surroundings again. I find myself upright with both arms reaching for dead air. I curse silently and take a long breath. Between Kajika's tale and recent rebirth, I'm guessing conceivable overload. I bet I'll feel better after a day's rest.

Early morning rays of the sun will appear, doubt they will harm me. My crossing-over is incomplete, but a vampire's life belongs to the dark of night. I leap off my perch and join the kid. Now's not the time to test my immortality.

One more glance around the cavern and Leslie and I quietly withdraw to the cabin. I hold Theodore's letter in my hand. Before I left the cabin, I tucked the envelope into my pocket. Somehow, I reached for the letter and forgot I held it.

This kid takes his protection responsibility personally. Was it his outburst or did I imagine the warning? Must talk to him. But it too must wait until another night.

Leslie follows me into the cabin and down to the basement. The light bulb stays off. We welcome the darkness. I bet he traveled this path a thousand times. And my enhanced sight improves. The cellar now has a particular brightness and clarity.

I head straight to my cell and bolt the door. Leslie closes the padlocks. The sound of the bolt and lock clanks. No longer will I hear the songs of birds welcoming the dawn.

No time for regret or to recite prose. Lightheadedness strikes.

Sleepwear lays neatly folded at the bottom of my futon. I'm guessing another responsibility of the kid. But I hate boys touching or handling my clothes, especially my sleepwear. Another issue to discuss later when I remember.

Placing Theodore's letter on the top of the dresser, I toss tonight's clothes into the trunk. I kneel next to the futon and say prayers. And yes, I continue to pray. I have my reasons. From the kneeling position, I crawl under the covers and claim sleep.

Sleep comes fast for a vampire. If you ever wondered if the undead dream, we don't. One reason to pray, I guess. Plenty of other reasons but they're private.

Kajika mentioned even the dead experience changes. I dislike changes. If stuff happens, make it quick. I figure why wait? Nothing I cannot deal with, anyway. Then again, no clue what these changes mean. I learn from books and movies. You know how truthful they are. Cannot imagine the percentage of truth in fictional stories. Hope Master Kajika is patient as he is handsome.

Maybe wisdom dictates patience. Hard practice when this uneasy and unexplained feeling persists. But I'll figure it out, eventually.

Kajika's voice resonates in my mind. "Tomorrow, Salomé, you learn that we're hunters and not killers. For now, sleep well and don't let the bedbugs bite. That's my job."

Vampire humor? Not very original. Nonetheless. A small chuckle surrenders to the darkness.

CHAPTER 9

At one time, I held a deep affection for dreams. They felt addictive. I remember the vivid shapes, and at times, the strange, vibrant lands I visited. Listening to Kajika that first night, I now know how he controlled and guided those dreams. Perhaps he presided over them. I imagine he had to from what he said. Did my love of dreaming apply to the visions themselves or him? Maybe both? I need time to adjust to this new reality.

Master Kajika's words penetrate through the cell's walls. "Salomé, we hunt tonight. Dress accordingly." Guess he knows I'm awake.

I withdraw fresh clothes from the trunk and dress for the night. Tonight calls for practical and functional. Clothing lacks fashion, but it suffices.

The letter lies atop the bureau from last night. I reach for the envelope and rip it open. I begin to read the message. Within seconds, the padlock outside the door unlocks. I lounge on the futon and skim the sentences. When I finish, I place the letter in the top drawer and unbolt the door.

I reel back. Leslie holds a bowl of blood. My body yearns for substance. I take the blood and hope it eases my pain. Scary sight to watch a vampire drink. We are ungraceful in that aspect, like watching the average human in the morning before their first cup of coffee. *Ah*, may miss drinking coffee.

Leslie scrutinizes my attire. He announces, "He's not here."

I don't remember asking him if he was. I hand Leslie the empty bowl, step around him, and ascend the stairs. Grabbing my cloak off the nail, I enter the night air where I now belong.

Yeah, I am a wee pissy. That kid rubs me the wrong way. Not bad, but not sure. Maybe creepy, but not *creepy*. Heck, forget it. All I wanted was to meet Kajika when my door opened.

For humans, the park trails are quiet. Vamps, on the other hand, can hear sounds that, well, you cannot. I can also soar through the air, another vampire fringe benefit.

I land on the same ledge I occupied last night. Leaping this high is easy. The extra jumping strength felt very natural. I lean against a small rock grouping. Legs dangle over the edge. What other powers might manifest tonight?

This rock ledge overlooks the vast canyon. The area already teams with all kinds of extraordinary wildlife. I'm surprised at how my vampiric sight improved while I slept. Glad too, the new powers feel so natural to use already.

Vampires perceive the physical world differently than humans. No surprise there. Humans cannot comprehend what happens in the dark of night. Sorry, but no words can describe it, but fabulous is pretty darn close. Nocturnal animals do more than hunt and kill their prey. They feed, mate, build and rebuild their burrows and homes. They live their whole lives at night as I now do.

I'm feeling uneasy. I felt the same way last night. Reminds me of staring into my parents' refrigerator gazing forever and leaving empty-handed. Maybe I'm more upset than I realize. I don't know. Life moves fast. Imagine spending a complete moon cycle, plus a day, in a coma. Yeesh. Definitely, the wrong way to spend time in bed. I dislike knowing family and friends will soon abandon me too. The reality strikes hard. It doesn't matter how tough you believe you are. Nobody can handle everything all at once.

Theodore's letter waits in the dresser drawer. I could have taken the time to fully read it, but once I do, I'll reminisce. What would he say about my new lifestyle? Couldn't mention I'm a member of the undead.

Would Theodore recognize me after the change? I'm uncertain of my appearance. No mirrors in the cabin anywhere to check my facial features. Believe I changed little from what I can see. My fangs partially retract, so I should pass for human unless sighted in a well-lit room. Which, I doubt will happen anytime soon.

Speaking of appearances, what is life without clothes? Are you convinced intellect separates one from the animal kingdom? No. It's clothes.

Tonight, I wear high, black leather, lace boots to protect my jeans. A dark, sapphire-blue blouse and light-weight, woolen cloak finish the outfit. Simple basic clothing I found in the trunk. I'll wear something original given enough time. Don't count on me saying what though. I liked being anonymous, blending into the crowds and surrounding area. Even more so now.

I hold no interest in describing myself. Your attempts to recognize me would backfire. I can walk right past you and ask for a light, not that I smoke. I could be short or tall. Built average or thin as a rail. My hair and eye color remain a mystery. You can propose any genealogical features on me to suit your fancy. I don't care.

My favorite color's cobalt blue. A girl loves her preferences. If a person drops out of the darkness wearing black leather trousers, a cobalt blue blouse and a strange hunger in her eyes, I'll save you the wonder; it's someone else.

You should see Kajika's outfits. He wears mean and sharp fashionable duds. Cannot figure where or when he ordered the custom-tailored clothing.

I began tonight on a bad start. Cannot believe how disoriented I am. Here I sit, fantasying about clothing and fashion statements. What's wrong with me? Thought I had my act together in high school.

Judgment and emotions run amok. If confusion originates from the changes Kajika spoke of, maybe I can create a grounding for myself. Perhaps focusing on the park or other topics can help.

And speaking of, where is Kajika?

I reposition myself on the ledge and sit cross-legged, both fists clenched. My head bowed; my eyes stay tightly closed. I focus on the park, gift shop, and trails. The faint stink of rotting flesh assaults my senses. I hesitate and refocus. The unwanted image redirects my thoughts. Again, my mind wanders.

What's the deal with the dead animals on the park's back trails? No official account released to the park employees. The mystery weighs on my mind. Did I drink animal blood the last couple of nights? I have no experience to notice or compare the differences. How would I know?

I must drink blood, so I do. Vampires aren't delicate creatures. Forget any previous notions. We must drink blood to survive. Don't mean to sound cruel. Just honest.

If I listen to myself, it sounds condescending. Suspect

my self-grounding technique requires practice. Thoughts run rampant. Cannot focus or control them much. How in all honesty can anyone believe I drank animal blood from the carcasses laying on the dirt paths. I'm sure I sipped human blood and nothing belonging to furry creatures. My head reels in euphoria. Cognitive thoughts intertwine and drift into weirdo-land. What happened to my rationale?

This overwhelming curiosity of the carcasses mystery surprises me. Excessive worry about dead flesh is usually not on my priority list. I cannot explain the sudden interest. Brain lingers on autopilot.

I cannot blame Master Kajika for the mystery. Cannot picture him killing animals and telling his favorite personal assistant, butler or whatever the kid's title, to pick up the carcasses afterward. It makes no sense.

Cannot blame the kid. After all, he's the one with the *pick-up the dead animals on the trails duty*. Leslie-boy cannot kill animals, suck them dry and toss them over his shoulder to land on the ground, only to pick them up the next day. If I pictured that scene, I'd picture nightmares. No. Downright confident the kid didn't kill them.

What is the greater mystery? Who or what kills the animals? Or why the possessing? How will tonight end?

Tonight is calm and peaceful in the cavern. Don't know if I can handle physical turmoil with the uneasiness in my head. This mental disarray sucks.

"Am I to assume that's my queue to enter?"

"Kajika?"

My response is rhetorical. I jump up and try my fullest to concentrate. Leaning over the ledge, Master Kajika waits on the dirt path. I don't wait for my invitation. I vault off the ridge. On my way down, I perform a front somersault with a half twist. Yep, a perfect Barani flip. I land next to Master Kajika, who by the way is unimpressed by my acrobatics.

"Salomé, we need to talk."

I remember those words. Master Kajika spoke the exact phrase when I first met him. Life has changed since that moment. He gains my full attention without asking for it. I'm confident; once again, his words will be more than just heard.

"You're a fledgling. Inexperienced is an understatement."

I was correct. Kajika's voice echoes in every fiber of my body. If bone marrow could shake in fear, it would.

"Conflicts between your old human life and your new vampire life causes thoughts and ramblings to surface. You're not required to forget your past but embrace the night's pull and hold on you. Before your turning, I did enter and manipulate your dreams. Unbeknownst to you, I have done so for several years."

"Master Kajika, why then—"

"No, Salomé. Quiet your questions and let me continue. The ancient technique of Dream weaving works, but it does cause drawbacks, which you experience. Wild thoughts of power, false inner wisdom, and superiority. Does any of what I'm saying sound familiar?

"All I can say is ignore them. The traces of my past presence in your dreams will unfold. Dream weaving causes an addiction to both parties. When you surrender to the night with your full embrace, without reserve, the obsession and my impression will diminish.

"We'll hunt tonight. Before we do, understand the feeding of human blood is necessary and prevents the incompleteness you feel. Blood provides the connection between Life and total Death.

"Salomé. Being or becoming a vampire doesn't make

you superior or grant you wisdom. Universal secrets will always be that, secret. We learn to do the best we can at any given moment. Being of the undead doesn't make you perfect. You are what you are. Nothing more, nothing less. As for your statement the other night about 'doubting the sun's rays would harm you,' if I hear anymore careless and irresponsible talk from you again, I'll chain you to a wall with bonds you cannot break. Do you understand me?"

"Yes."

"Yes what, Salomé?"

"Yes, Master Kajika."

"Better."

So much for an uneventful night.

Silver mists surround us. We both ascend from the path and into the night air where warm, dry breezes brush my face.

We descend on a mountaintop overlooking a research compound. The air calms and mists retreat. Master Kajika chewed me out. Hard to distinguish how much of his reprimand was aimed at my actions or meant to criticize. I bit my lower lip hard the whole time. I swear I taste copper.

My mind tries to reorganize and map my new reality. Feel sorry for my brain. Usually, the heart gets broken. The aftereffects of Kajika's talk caused my thoughts to do pirouettes. I figured I could handle all the new changes. Man, am I wrong. The rebirth sure is unlike what the movies depict. If you wish to understand my mental rollercoaster ride, take the word "emotional," and check the word in a thesaurus. Do you see all those words? I pray tomorrow night starts better than this one did.

The night flight helped a wee bit. However, I'm unsure

if I'm ready for what awaits. Although it's imperative, I get myself organized.

Kajika scrutinizes a nearby precipice. Preoccupied with his thoughts, Kajika doesn't bother to face me when he speaks. "The reason we're here lies below us. The two men at the far end of the parking lot are yours if you choose. Security in this area is high, but that doesn't concern us. No one will find or miss their bodies."

"To take a life is no easy undertaking. The conflict between your old life and your present one lingers until you make this kill. Salomé, remember we're hunters, not killers," Kajika said, in a distant voice.

"My pleasure." I had enough of people consoling me. I'm no child. No misunderstandings exist of what I must do tonight.

I breathe in the encompassing air to clear my head. Diminutive particulars of all life within the immediate area fill my lungs. Acute senses familiarize themselves with surroundings. Only vampires take this advantage over their prey. Nothing catches me unaware or surprises me tonight.

The two men below could be researchers or guards. Hard to tell, both men wear plain unmarked white jump-suits. It makes little difference who or what they are. Both serve as prey.

Similar to a cat when it attacks, my physical body tenses. Senses stay alert. I'm deadlier than any feline. I place trust in Master Kajika's earlier words. The decision and surrender to the darkness are easy to make. I reconcile my inner conflict, embrace the night and welcome her absolute love and protection toward her children. I allow no separation between us.

A silent oath. A promise and commitment sworn between the night and me. It takes mere seconds. The duality between two entities, one physical and the other metaphysical, cease to exist. I converge with destiny. Completeness and sensuality eluded me my whole life. They now enter the night breeze to replenish and refurnish my body with new vigor.

I target the researcher with the coffee. He holds a cup of hot java in his left hand and an oversized flashlight in the other. Does he regard the light for his shortcomings? I push the question out of my mind and leap off the mountaintop.

When attacking someone, make it quick and unexpected. These employees expected an uneventful night. I know I began tonight believing that way. The difference between them and me? These two men miss their chance to learn otherwise.

The men split up and decide to walk in opposite directions. My prey with the coffee reaches an outside corner of the building. He makes his turn. I fall out of the night sky. I position myself on his right side and come down on him hard. His exposed neck takes the full brunt of my attack.

My right hand braces his upper forehead. My left wraps the side of his neck. Grip tightens. I bite. Incisors draw blood. The man panics. His mind shuts down. The researcher makes no sound. I take him to the ground fast, sucking blood while his body falls. I hold my prey until I drain him. A few moments at most. The coffee he held falls to the dirt ground without a sound. The precious fluid loaded with caffeine spills. The earth swallows it wholly.

I snatch the departed with both hands and take flight. Fifty feet over the precipice, fingernails rip into neck muscles. A lifeless body falls and hits the rocky ground with a *thud*. An empty coffee cup gyrates without its owner.

My next prey, fifteen years younger than the first man, meanders on the other side of the building. A chain-linked fence runs the total length. No doors or windows need checking on this side. The distance separating the building to the fence cannot be over three feet. If he searches for a spot to relieve himself, he is in for a shock.

The first attack was quick. This one will be no different. Although, I must adjust my strategy. I cannot attack from the man's side without giving him a warning. I maneuvered my flight path. A vampire's surprise entrance is the best trick in their repertoire.

Again, I drop from the night sky, hard and fast. This time landing directly in front of my prey. Breasts brush against his face a fraction of a second before a spiked heel smashes into his right foot.

My cupped hand stifles his cry. Left arm wraps around the back of his neck. A simple tilt of his head and fangs find their mark. Incisors once again draw blood. The man's back arches backward. It takes no effort to subdue him despite the cramped quarters. I hasten to drain his blood. Clean-up duty awaits.

We take to the air. I treat the second victim as the other and rip bite marks from his neck. I drop him over the precipice. Two lifeless bodies overlap each other.

Master Kajika stands ten yards away. He tilts his head to the right, silently signaling me to back away. I obey without questioning.

Instantly, a rockslide begins and covers the bodies. Local carnivores can take care of any exposed body parts. No evidence of either body is destined for discovery.

Kajika hesitates. His expression serene. Eyes stare into mine. He's content with my hunt and acknowledges with a nod. For the second time tonight, the warm night breeze blows past my cheeks. We take flight and fly back to the park.

The flight back takes minutes. Kajika and I both land on the same dirt path in the park. Master Kajika lands on the same spot before we left for Los Almos. He did so purposely. No words shared but I know he wants me to remember what he said on this exact spot earlier tonight.

And yes, I remember. I say, "I understand."

"Salomé, tonight consisted of complex events. I recommend you rest. Perhaps finish your letter. Your past lingers. You should cherish friendships and family. Leslie will see you to your room and safety. You hunted, and now I must."

Leslie appears on my left. I didn't see him from the air before we landed and I didn't see him when I spoke with Kajika. The kid showed up out of nowhere. My head must be fuzzy, been a long night. I hike it back on foot. No more flying, no more attitude, at least for tonight. Temporarily blocking out everything that happened tonight. I want a clear head to sleep. Maybe Theodore's letter can help.

My escort and I enter the cabin and descend the stairs together. "The door stays open," I said, before entering my room. Leslie withdraws without a reply. I'll slide the bolt from inside myself. He can padlock it later.

I swipe the letter from the drawer and flop myself down on the futon. Once comfortable, I rescan the message:

Dear Salomé,

Saw your parents last week. They asked me to say hello and to send their love. Tina said the house seems empty without you and Jim tries to stay busy. They both know you can handle yourself and stay safe, but you know how your parents are.

Nobody knows where Eric ran off to this month. He disappeared again. I thought about taking care of the lawn. You know, make the extra pocket money for school. Eric would pay me, but then I remember the last time he disappeared. Nine months, I believe, and not a single word from him when he returned. Eric sure acts strange, well, you know. However, I thought better of it.

While you moved, my acceptance letter arrived from the seminary school. I leave soon. Parents have mixed feelings about me going. However, I swear I celebrate in my dreams. Cannot wait to discover what this career leads to in life. You know how I feel about being a Priest. You're perhaps sick and tired of hearing it.

Four months from now, I'll attend the *Sacred Heart of Theology*, in Rhinebeck, New York.

Life will be busy but straightforward. I room in one of those small cells. Can you image sleeping and studying in a tiny place? Sure is a different lifestyle but well worth the trouble. A life's dream come true, not everyone gets that to happen!

I reminisce about our times together. Know better to put any of them in print but hope to experience more someday. I'll write again when I get the chance. Hope your park ranger apprenticeship job works out for you.

Write back when you can and keep in touch. Here's hoping your dream comes true too.

Sincerely, Theodore Rumswood

Good ol' Theodore.

Better dress for bed before becoming comatose. I have no plans to sleep in these stained hunting clothes.

Closing and bolting the door, I ready myself for bed. Within minutes, I give the letter another read.

Padlock latches. The sound of cold metal screeches.

Involuntary eyelids close tight.

The letter falls from my open hand.

CHAPTER 10

I learned a lot since Kajika's first embrace six months ago.

For example, vampires need not drain their victims of blood. Imagine all the dead bodies everywhere if we did. No. Vampires can drink and lurk with no one the wiser. I have done so on several past occasions. Methods that are more natural exist, but I like choices.

Learned of other ways to get nourishment too. All without physically drinking any blood. Not offering any details, but the Night takes care of her children. Besides, I don't fancy going on a killing spree every single night, sucking the blood and life from every Tom, Dick, or Harry I see in an alley.

My vampiric lifestyle suits me. I enjoy private time with the night. In retrospect, hard to imagine living any other way. So far, life is fantastic. Yea, I know I'm a teenager and eternity awaits but one lesson Kajika taught is to live in the present.

That all said, I remember and dwell on my first kill. I recall the two researchers and the nonchalant way I disposed of their bodies as if it happened moments ago. All the other people that died, or the lucky ones I chose not to kill, I dwell not so much.

I vividly remember their faces, their feeble efforts to escape and hearing their screams. Once I decide the attack fatal, none had any chance of survival at all. None. I came, took and left. Sounds callous maybe, I don't know. Not for me to feel sentimental. If compassion was a past attribute, it vanished when I surrendered to the night at Los Almos.

Strange I didn't return to that original spot near the research center. I travel to other areas and hunting grounds. No particular reason. Much like how I end up here on my favorite perch after every kill.

Master Kajika teaches vampire survival training. He specializes in an awareness of one's surroundings. His techniques seldom resemble subjects taught in high school. Then again, why would they be?

Master Kajika commits himself to my schooling and "homework assignments." My quotes. Teach made it clear I should pay particular attention to habits. Kajika's gaze emphasized *all patterns*.

I understood the meaning. Lord knows Kajika left enough hints. My temperament will fade, eventually. Everyone grows and changes. But to be honest, I hate to lose my, combative nature.

Kajika picks our classrooms, time, and location. He insists on mandatory weekly lessons. On several occasions, Kajika said, "Without this training, you wouldn't last long living within *the night world*." He's no college professor, but he knows vampires.

Other beasties belong to the night besides vampires. More shocking to hear, other creatures live on the top of the food chain. Hard for a vampire to realize. I know that reality check hit me hard. Master Kajika left out the details but taught the basics to put me in my place, as the rebellious, impetuous fledgling. I know. Me impetuous, go figure.

Should mention Kajika closed down my apartment. He said, "The furniture can stay along with any non-perishable food items for later use. Your personal belongings are repacked and stored in a local storage unit. You can access it anytime."

Hated breaking up with the girls too. If we stayed together, we could have started one heck of a diversified group. As much as I enjoyed their company, a vampire's life is one of solitude.

I called Alena and Brianna to explain my position. Told the girls, "My parents were selling their house, and they asked if I could help with the packing." Yea, I lied. What were my other options? I kept my story short and to the point. It was best for everyone.

Alena understood my predicament at once, which took me off guard. I was unprepared for her blunt dismissal of our friendship so quickly, but I didn't complain. Alena volunteered to inform Joni. He's in rehab recuperating from, "a stupid stunt." She didn't elaborate but said she'll explain when I call again. Which left me with one phone call to make.

Called Brianna next. I dialed her number right afterward on my apartment's landline. She answered on the second ring. Brianna drilled me with questions. Watery eyes made an uneasy call worse. I was in no mood for any long girl talk, but Brianna insisted. "Sure. We'll keep in touch," I said while bowing my head. After our call, I blindly ran to the bathroom for tissues. A half-hour later, I headed straight out of the apartment and locked the place tight.

Master Kajika accepted the key. I muttered, "Made the

phone calls, everything's fine." He nodded and mentioned he talked to Parker about my park position. I'm no longer working. Human Resources categorized me as a seasonal employee.

Kajika passed on Parker's comment. "It was a pleasure working with you. I pray for your safe journeys." Somehow, my supervisor's remark sounds condescending. He and I didn't connect, but that is old history.

The night's breeze changes. It had added a crisp bite in the air. The feeling had provided an edge and focus. Tonight's my version of the perfect autumn evening.

Nostalgic winds carried long lost memories earlier. Based on the uneventful past week and tonight's perfect clear starry sky, I figured tonight perfect for reminiscing. I had put off Theodore's letter. He sounded happy enough when I read it. Even teased me with my "park ranger apprenticeship job." He knows darn well I worked as a simple store clerk. The Jerk.

Fleeting memories soar past. The winds change course. An outside force compels my body unnaturally to the scent in the breeze. Altering tonight's plans if I want to or not.

A peculiar potent stench permeates the air. A stink I'm more than familiar with, namely a mixture of male testosterone, and sweat. The smell originates from the outskirts of the park.

My prey situates themselves due east. Their scent is distinct and undeniable. I take to the air. Tonight, two unscrupulous, wannabe hunters earn a surprise visit from the undead. And that sounds poetic to my ears.

Mischievous youths inhabit every town and by definition, more times than not, are older teenagers sowing their oats.

While society waits for these youths to mature and grow up; we girls deal with their immature, domineering behaviors and sometimes their atrocious assaults.

Society can be patient and overlook things. Me? Not so much. Especially, when the main event unfolds before my eyes.

My plans changed when I picked up a particular scent in the air. That scent drove me straight here to one of the town's make-out points.

The scenic area overlooks a panoramic view of the town below, especially at dusk. When the hectic work traffic stops, the town appears tranquil from this height. Adults drive here after work hours to relax and picnic. The townsfolk enjoy the tables and freestanding barbeque grills.

The local younger folks use the area for a different reason. Instead of unwinding after a hard day's work, they use it for voyaging and exploration.

Two separate paths in this section lead to the park's perimeter. Wisdom dictates the well visible "No Trespassing" signs posted along the trail mean "Keep Out!" Instead, people hike, oblivious to the fact the upper trail washed away during the last two rainstorms. Flash floods produced mudslides and clobbered this side of the mountain. The trails are unsafe.

Maybe I could hunt here instead of traveling to other towns. Within months, people would think a crazed serial killer or a Sasquatch lives in the area. I jest. Local legends abound already. One reason to hunt elsewhere.

This outcrop oversees a closed trail. A perfect spot to eavesdrop on two overly anxious boys and the two girls inside a parked silver van.

After their movie date, the boys drove here "for the view." I know. Corny, right? The lines which followed makes me gag. I hear comments, "Come on, Babe, it'll be fun" and "It'll be our secret" and the reliable, "Trust me."

You would imagine people use better lines than that. Don't get it wrong, they tried. If I hear any more lame attempts, I swear I'll dry heave. Most of their parking ritual consisted of their hands doing the talking. Why do girls tolerate this behavior? Their dates think of one thing and their chances tonight are nil to none. The dark energy hovering over this vehicle sickens me.

As sick as I am witnessing their deviant adolescent behavior, I lack a real cause to kill them. Girls should be able to, or learn to, handle their dates. When a familiar voice speaks, I understand why Fate drew me to this particular spot.

"Why don't we call it a night, it's late." I know that voice. This the double date Brianna spoke of six months ago? She mentioned the last time we talked Alena changed her mind about double dating. Brianna repeated Alena's words exactly, "I would rather eat a pizza alone than date someone I don't care about." And if Brianna felt uncomfortable, she and Alena could watch a movie or something. Somehow, the boys convinced the girls otherwise.

"Let's all get out and breathe fresh air," Brianna's date said, with frustration trailing in his voice.

The boys cross the road and head toward the forbidden trail, forcing the girls to follow or stay in the van. Unconscious survival techniques say to keep in groups, so people herd for safety. The girls reluctantly leave their ride.

Cannot blame the girls. I imagine they felt vulnerable, but some things you don't do. Like strolling into dark woods alone with adolescent boys on a date.

Learning life from the school of hard knocks can be painful. What unfolds before me is part of life, who to trust, whom you should avoid. I can witness a parking date digress. I'm not someone's mother. I don't wish to intervene, and it's beneficial for all parties involved if I don't. Except the boys are leading their two dates into a trap!

Fate forces my hand to save friends from predatory creatures. After all my preventive plans on distancing myself from the girls, Fate now demands I protect Brianna and Alena from harm.

From this height, I see two suspicious older adults hiding out in the bushes up ahead, a short way off the trail. It would appear Alena and Brianna are about to be ambushed. Explains why the boys rushed out of the van. Figured on partying no matter what. Take it from me boys, plans change.

I survey my prey.

One of the gents, and I use the term loosely, is a stumpy, short fellow. He hides directly behind a massive juniper bush. Unbeknownst to him, he's about to become stumpier.

The leap off the ledge leads straight toward tonight's target. The full momentum exit provides enough energy to wrap the night tightly around my body. A sudden release of focused dark energy produces an expected *splat*. I crouch afterward and stay low. One knee on the firm ground. The rest of me lies on one messy low-life. You can pour his cadaver into a coffee mug.

Nothing recognizable remains. Bones, muscles, organs, you name it, is now slime. The metaphysical feat is difficult to explain and was hard to accomplish. The attack requires me to feed before the night ends.

My unexpected splash alarms the second low-life. The man whirls checking the area. His facial features tell the whole story. The idiot tries to sniff the air. Something unique and unpleasant awaits him.

"We got you now, ladies!"

The phrase booms throughout the field and maybe parts of the woods. You would figure someone used a bull-horn set to high volume but no, only an obnoxious teenager with, I'm guessing, blue-balls. I don't know the boy's name, but it was Alena's date speaking.

I wanted to wring the kid's neck, but once again, I tempered my emotions. I cursed silently into the night.

"Shawn, freaking shut up," came the reply. "Don't be so crude, bro!" This time, Brianna's date spoke. The older of the two.

"Francis, no talking back to your brother. There'll be no sibling rivalry here." This time the second dirt-bag closer to me shouted.

I'm correct on my suspicions. They're brothers on a double date. How sweet.

Shawn ignores his brother. He cannot hold his excitement. Safe bet silence and patience isn't his strong suit. If he possesses any good qualities, he artfully hides them.

Shawn screeches into the night air. "Douglas, we got the girls. Let's party." Lucky for the dead, he muted his shout. "Where's that cousin of yours?"

My guess? His bodily fluids seep into the earth. The rest of the ooze splattered on my boots.

I hide in low bushes, maybe a good fifty paces and slightly behind Douglas. Until I gain confirmation on this cousin fellow, I'm staying put. I would hate to discover someone else hiding in this field.

Douglass outstretches his arms. A broken propeller in the wind and whirls himself around in small circles. He makes me dizzy watching him. This the idiot's version of radar, maybe? After fruitless attempts, he haphazardly stares in my direction and shouts. "Yea, Chucky! Are you taking a leak somewhere? Come on and hurry. The girls are here."

"Chucky?" The name suited him. Yep, positive ID. I'm wearing Chucky, presently, *Mister Squishy*. Hi Chucky, I'm Salomé. Glad you're dead. Cleanup, aisle two. Your cousin joins you soon. Stay put.

One of the boys yells. "Now what?" The frustrated words catch in his throat.

No clue who shouted. I welcome the outburst and distraction though. Eventually, someone will expose me hiding here. But I would prefer nobody saw me, especially Brianna.

A Jeep approaches around the corner. The humans cannot see it yet. I can use this to my advantage and better yet, Alena and Brianna can ride home safely. The girls stayed silent so far. Maybe they hope a midnight angel will rescue them. Don't know. Don't care. But I will stop this madness.

One of the popular myths on vampires is we rarely yell. The belief is true. And realistically, who could we yell at, our lover, our dog or maybe our children? Tonight, one infuriated vampire makes an exception to that view. I lower my voice and add vibrato. Sounds don't frequently echo off soft woodlands. Tonight is atypical. One word instantly resonates. The word seemly originates from nowhere and radiates everywhere. A simple command with predictable results.

"Run!"

CHAPTER 11

*B*rianna and Alena scream. They dash, with arms waving, straight toward the oncoming Jeep. The three males sprint wildly and blindly into the woods. It was perfect.

The Jeep stops and picks up the girls. The ranger can make a report and take Brianna and Alena to the hospital or police station. The girls are okay and can ride home tonight in one piece.

The adults; one was melted, and the other is doomed. The two boys who helped set the girls up for a horror fest are about to earn an unexpected ride to the hospital. Turnabout's fair play. And I'm all about being fair.

Easy enough to fly low over the woods and find this Douglas fellow. A flashlight beam leads the two boys up the washed-out trail. No time to waste, the night draws to an end. Time for the shock and more shock treatment.

I descend in front of the second cousin. The two boys nearby barely sense my descent. Without warning and minimum sound, I twist and snap off the older man's head from his shoulders. Unseen in the darkness, blood gushes from the body and head. I feast on both parts.

I plant both feet shoulder-width apart on solid earth, hold Douglas' head in hand, and wait for my grand entrance. The boys couldn't see what happened in this darkness. Heck, their brains couldn't handle or determine what transpired if it were daylight. Both kids stop running when the flashlight hits the ground. My setup awaits.

Anytime now, and as if on cue, Douglas falls face forward, albeit without a head, and bites the dirt. "Hello, boys. Did you know vampires exist, and you're both alone in the woods with one now?"

I carry out the classic vampire move and wipe the back of my right hand, covered with blood, against my lips. More for my sake than for theirs. It felt the right thing to do. Living in the moment, I love it.

Left arm stretches outward holding the head of one dead Douglas. I pick up the flashlight from the ground and shine the light on the gruesome, grotesque face.

"Boo!"

They run.

I'm unconcerned if the boys believe me a real vampire or not. I don't intend to use fangs on them tonight. The boys have a lesson to learn. And they stay alive to learn it. I reach for my boot knife. The cold metal feels comforting. I chase the tall boy first.

Let's be honest, boys panicking, trampling through the woods in total darkness offers little chase. They have no clue where to run, who they run from or better yet, no clue what they can run into out here. If the boys continue, they'll knock each other unconscious. As amusing as that sounds, I don't want to waste time.

"Hello, Shawn."

Shawn tries to scream, but a mouse-ish squeak parts his lips.

I slice and dice Shawn's jacket and rib cage twice then throw him hard into a large tree. The sounding *thud* means I hit my target. Air evacuates out of Shawn's lungs. It'll not expiate for his actions but for now, he's out for the count.

Next target is Francis, Brianna's date.

Must say I'm surprised by the ground Francis traversed in those mere minutes while I dealt with his brother. He does his best to escape me by staying quiet. Francis crouches and keeps his knees flexible. The boy moves quickly and silently. Francis hopes I forget about him. He hopes wrong.

Francis doesn't realize running from a vampire is futile. I effortlessly catch up with him. Blade in hand, I introduce a long facial laceration. I hope the future scar matures him. Grasping his throat on both sides, I hold Francis up off the ground at arm's length. Before tossing him, a twinkle manifests in my eye. I stare at Francis. I cannot stop myself. Words form without thought.

"Say goodnight, Gracie."

And with that, his body somersaults through the air and slams into the base of a tree. A second *thud* verifies another bullseye. He lands head down; rear end sticks up in the air. I suspect he'll break his neck if he stays that way. I hurry over and give him a gentle kick. He falls on his side, mostly, to conclude the night's chase.

Neglected to realize how chasing boys in the woods could affect my outfit. The cloak tangles in every bush, hood catches in the low hanging branches. My boots are beyond repair. Does anyone believe I enjoy running in these woods? Trust me. I'm pissed. My journal cannot hold all of tonight's frustrations.

Glad tonight ends. This evening is my worse hunt ever.

On the positive side: I hunted, drank and saved two friends from an ugly fate. On the negative side: two dead bodies to dispose of, one super squishy and another with a separated head. Two shaken girls with parents who might investigate what happened tonight, one ranger who will check the area, and an official incident report. Last, a guaranteed police report. Tonight leans too much on the negative.

After I slice the boys, I want to shower and hit my futon for several days. I keep fingers crossed hoping Leslie knows how to sew and remove blood from leather boots. Oh well, no reason to put it off, better clean up this mess.

A nearby empty animal burrow hides the severed head. I twist and rip apart the remaining arms and legs and toss them in, uniting them with the head. A long thick tree branch helps me push all parts down the hole. The torso I stomp. Figure no big deal since I already wear Mister Squishy and soaked blood on my boots.

This pile, I bury in a second burrow located near the first one. I roll a giant boulder over both holes. Within a day or two, a hard rain should wash out all tracks and blood.

Now, to teach the boys' final lesson.

I stride toward one tree where Shawn rests. I bend down to lift his wallet and check his name. Its affirmative, name's Shawn Murphy.

Yep, the Murphy brothers. I grin and wonder if they had a law named after them. It could explain so much tonight. I remove the knife from my boot for the second time tonight. No sooner than I did, an unexpected sharp pain hits me in the left lower back. If human, the blow could have knocked the breath out of me, maybe broken a rib or two but I'm far from human.

On a typical night, I could determine what hit me so hard. Except whatever it was created enough momentum to break my balance. I head face first down the same precipice I meant to dump the boys' bodies. The service road at the bottom of this cliff could have served me well. Good odds a ranger or police would discover my victims tomorrow.

Strange how events happen. Maybe I'll have a hearty laugh when I leap back up and scare the bejesus out of their sorry asses and whomever hit me. Wished I knew magick. I wouldn't hesitate to rip their skin off their bodies right now. A simple wave of my hand, a few words said, and poof. They deserve worst.

I may yet filet the cowards and leave the pieces for the crows. Two things I don't tolerant and people who molest women rank number one. Brianna and Alena should be okay after a restful sleep. Hope they pick better dates next time or at least meet in public places. As for these two, they'll bother no one for a long time.

Feeling extra revengeful. I cannot regain footing and stop myself tumbling all the way to the bottom of this cliff. I missed the intruder approaching earlier. Losing one sense is unacceptable. Missing more can mean sure trouble.

I inhaled the night air before attacking. I should have sensed everything in the surrounding area, but somehow, I goofed. Something or someone evaded my senses. A colossal mistake for any nightkind.

Body slams into the rock bottom and slides sideways between two large rocks. A sharp rock stabs into an already sore rib. New scraps and abrasions appear on arms. It might take days to heal and return to my old charming self.

Tonight has created one exhausted vampire. Sheltering face with one elbow and clutching my stomach with another doesn't lessen the pain. The world spins. I hurt, maybe more if I try to stand. Significant payback forecasted in someone's future once I figure out what happened.

I sense the boys above bleeding. They're unconscious. Figure it fair to leave them in the same condition they planned to abandon the girls when they tired of them. I had better ascend and finish business before my surprise guest shows up again.

And I would have risen, but another problem showed itself.

Rounding the second boulder looms a shadowed figure. As tonight's luck works, the shadow belongs to a park ranger. Add yet another item to deal with tonight. The list grows while the night shortens.

Sensed another person in the woods earlier, but I had hoped they would leave and go elsewhere. Rarely make it a habit of attacking everyone in the night. But, I cannot chance anyone recognizing me. Guess tonight calls for another unscheduled exception.

This ranger advances too close. I lost track of time while enjoying the trip down the freaking cliff. That or my mind drifted. After all, this is the first time some unknown being shoved me off a cliff.

Either way, thank the moon my intruder is not Ranger Aby. I like her. Would hate to make her my exception. It wouldn't change the outcome, but I would have felt dishonest.

"Hello. Is anyone there? Are you hurt?"

The park ranger is uncertain if a person landed here. He assumes a simple landslide. The darkness protects me from recognition. Before he uses his handy flashlight, I prepare to attack.

I lean on a large boulder to keep weight off my legs. I stand, which is a difficult task. My earlier assumption "I might hurt more if I stand" no longer remains a theory.

Pain travels everywhere throughout my body. Dull pains don't faze me. Spent years at the gym working through hurt. I refocus my pain by staring at the rocky ground. The action also prevents recognition. The ranger cannot glimpse my face.

A vampire cannot be too careful. Once again, I breathe and absorb night energy. I experienced enough surprises tonight.

I calm and re-center myself. Every living creature in the woods shares my existence and I with them. The trees and the air itself whisper. The sensation simultaneously balances and exhilarates, resembling earth grounding and spreading auric Vampiric wings. Once more, I'm the predator.

Must conclude my business and check on the girls. Hope they are OK. Girls need to stick together.

Glad I grabbed the extra moment for a rebreather. I feel better, but not healed by any stretch of the imagination.

A hesitant voice suggests the ranger remains unsure of my presence. "Hello? I am Park Ranger Juan Martin. Is anyone there?" I don't know him.

Light flashes and shines upon the rock wall. The unwelcomed beam of light casts non-descriptive shadows. Shadows I use to my advantage. I lean back against a boulder and prepare to grapple the ranger.

The ranger rounds the boulder.

It would have been a simple task to catch and pull him closer for the kill. And, it would have been over before he knew what happened. But you guessed it—it didn't happen that way.

My unwanted guest showed up out of nowhere. I missed him approaching again. Before I blinked, he jumped between the park ranger and me.

You would figure a bad move on his part. Right? Usually to stand between a vampire and their victim is unsafe. Common sense to most people.

But, three more things happened afterward. My *pest guest* attacked the ranger and knocked him unconscious with minimal effort. Within the same breath and even less energy, he outstretched one of his arms, contacting my lower ribcage, and sent me hurdling backward twelve feet into rocks that were larger than the ones I landed in earlier. And then, he showed me his face.

Rarely does someone knock a vampire out for the count, myself included. I don't know how long I laid unconscious. Stars floated before the darkness closed. When I awoke, Leslie leaned in face-to-face. His hand clasped around my cloak and parts of my shirt.

He effortlessly lifted me off the rocky ground with one hand. Dazed from his blow, I didn't realize or comprehend the situation. When vision cleared, I stood on my tippy-toes, with our bodies too close for comfort. I expect he had a darn good reason to enter my intimate zone.

Leslie continued lifting me until both of my feet dangled off the ground. I was unenthusiastic about my new position. Our eyes locked in what seemed a death match. Felt as if I was losing the battle. In fact, I had no chance in heck to survive this mismatch. Much less, win it.

"Let me go!" I screamed.

Without hesitation, he did.

I dropped on the stony ground and stared unbelievingly. The darn rocks and stones poking my back hurt. The pain grew when he squatted and planted a foot on my sternum pinning me to the ground. I was pissed. How dare he? How could he? I tried to toss him off but couldn't move him.

A vampire could overturn a freaking car if they wished.

I seldom use the ability but I can. Leslie held me in place effortlessly. He stayed calm while I put up a fight. I kicked and twisted. A useless struggle. Trapped and pinned to the ground by the kid! I wondered what else could happen tonight and instantly regretted asking the question.

Leslie leaned forward and peered deep into my eyes. I swear I felt his eyelashes brushing on my face. His foot rested on my chest the whole time. Leslie bent down staring. His eyes snared my mind and sucked me into the deep blue. Nothing else in the world seemed to matter. I had little choice. The thought to resist didn't occur. Somehow, we metaphysically intertwined, the moment surreal.

Before I could comprehend, something weirder happened. The night stopped. Nothing moved or breathed. The time-space continuum froze and faded into nothingness. I lost control and was merely along for the ride. My body laid outside of existence.

Instinctually I knew—I was in Limbo.

Leslie was absent. I saw nobody. The pressure of his foot crushed upon my chest. My back no longer experienced sharp pricks of rocks, but a horizontal force acted against my body preventing me from tumbling forever into a white abyss. A plunge into nothing.

"You'll desist your resistance," said Leslie.

The kid affected me differently than Master Kajika. With Kajika's words, long story short, I hear and sense them. Words and commands forced on me, but I have a choice in following them.

Leslie's words belong in a different category. Whatever he did with those spoken words caused my whole body to enter panic mode. The cells in my body knew if they forego Leslie's command, any command, they would cease to exist.

This kid could abandon me here in Limbo if he chose

or send me to oblivion without a second thought or hesitation. I was way out of my league. Don't know how or why Leslie hid it but he's no ordinary kid.

Tonight unbelievingly worsens. First, me being so harsh, reckless, and incompetent. And then, discovering the hard way, this presumably dorky kid is a freaking god!

"Done."

Thought best to keep my reply short and quick. The way tonight had progressed, I had said and done enough damage. Once the word left my lips, we returned to where we started.

Leslie stood upright watching a trapped vampire squirm beneath his planted foot on its upper abdomen.

"You'll pull yourself together and fly to the cottage. Master Kajika awaits your arrival. Furthermore, you'll practice silence. Otherwise, I speak a word or two," Leslie said.

My body flinched at the threat. I didn't cower, but cringe comes darn close. I clamped my mouth shut. No other word passed my lips. Besides, my body wouldn't have let me spoke if I wanted to. Something is unnaturally threatening about Leslie's commands.

"I'll clean up this disorder. Go," Leslie said.

It was the basic "Leave now."

I rolled over on all fours and rose to my feet aided by a boulder. I bowed and unceremoniously ascended into the night air. Against all the odds, I made it to the cottage.

Saddened about what transpired tonight. Reflecting on past wrongs will not help either. Hoped to pull the pieces together somehow but plans fell apart. I almost made a sizable problem astronomical. Pure luck saved the night.

The girls' welfare depends on others. I cannot check on them tonight.

Presently, I stand in front of Kajika.

I forsake the much-needed shower or the change of clothing. You can imagine my appearance. If not, picture this. I slid down a mountainside, destroying most of my clothes; ran through woods, which ruined my outfit; and ripped a man's head clear off causing blood to gush everywhere. Oh, let's not forget transforming a man into a pile of goo and laying in it for a solid hour. Also, that doesn't count my episode with Leslie, which I'm trying to forget.

Did it help? I'll mention one more thing to complete my night.

Kajika isn't in a good mood.

"Salomé, we need to talk."

CHAPTER 12

$\mathcal{I}$s anyone interested in knowing what happens when someone angers a master vampire? I should first clarify. Master Kajika was beyond mad last night. He was pissed. Really pissed. As in seriously, really, really pissed.

I'm sure you're dying to discover the outcome, who wouldn't. A bunch of stuff blew up last night. What happened afterward, you ask? Unbelievably, I cannot answer those questions.

Last night establishes itself as the most traumatic and chaotic event of my whole life. Yes, my total of eighteen years' worth. Probability says I can experience a worse night. However, I pray continuously to the goddess above and below, that I don't.

Kajika's reprimand from last night vibrates throughout my body. Master Kajika spoke more than words. Last night was empowerment and warning all mixed.

When Master Kajika speaks, I listen. Imagine a master drill sergeant verses enlisted recruit. And yes, late last night, my master drill sergeant disciplined my butt about half an inch from my face. I'm sure you can picture it. It was ugly.

The main difference between the two metaphors? Kajika keeps his voice calm. The man need not yell. I feel his words when he speaks. The feeling worsens when he is upset. Go figure, right? I cannot express or put into words how that translates but can say; I wished he yelled.

After the lecture, which seemed to take forever and a night, he handed me a letter. He then said, "Good night."

I was dumbfounded. For a slight moment, I thought nothing happened. I shook my head to clear it of mind fog. One moment, I get my butt handed to me. The next moment—poof—he releases his hold.

Uncertainty is why I cannot answer questions about what happened last night. The outcome has yet to manifest. That's the scary part. I'm reserving a few choice words for later. Figure I'll use them before the night ends.

Kajika's instructions said to wait for his command. If you didn't guess already, he grounded me tonight. My orders are to "stay in the park until you hear from me. Don't feed. Don't fly. No trip to your perch."

Until Master Kajika summons my sorry butt, I meander the public park paths. The night stroll provides plenty of time to chew my lower lip and dread what might transpire.

Theodore's latest letter, which Kajika handed me last night, hides in my back pocket. Figured the letter gives me something to read, so I left it there. OK. Scratch that. To be honest, I pocketed it deliberately.

I lost my usual familiar items because of last night's fiasco. Last night did a number on my clothes. The disaster ruined everything I wore. Plenty of clothes lay in the trunk, but I own only the one pair of boots. If someone spotted me tonight, I could pass as a teen dressed in grunge.

The style is similar to what I wore on the long bus drive. Same outfit minus the boots and knife. A pair of running Nikes replaces the missing boots. Master Kajika demanded the knife.

Before walking back to my cell last night, Kajika offered me a choice. "Either you place the knife on the side table or…" You don't want to know. And come to think about it, I had little choice.

I surrendered and laid the bloody knife on the table near the stairs. Walked down to my cell and bolted the door. The sound of the padlock followed afterward. No clue who locked it. Undoubtedly Kajika or Leslie but it doesn't matter. I fell backward unto the futon without my shower. I slept without changing, wearing my destroyed outfit complete with boots, stained and soaked with blood.

When I awoke tonight, Master Kajika met me outside my doorway.

"Salomé, shower and whistle a tune, then dress." It was a partial joke, but neither of us laughed. Kajika's mood was serious. I understood why. "When you're together, see me upstairs," he said, vanishing. Didn't expect to see him again until I was cleaned and dressed.

I knew Master Kajika's underlying meaning of "together." My time in the hot and steamy shower included retrospection. No whistling or singing tonight, while I washed dry, crusty blood off my skin and hair.

Within fifteen minutes of awakening, I faced Master Kajika.

He said, "Sit."

I plopped down on one of the dining room chairs on the far end of the oblong table, facing Kajika. The air thickened. Silence lingered, searching the room for an escape route. I waited for the worst to happen.

No word from Leslie since last night. Expected a

torturous evening from him, but he's nowhere in sight. Best consider myself lucky to be alive. All right, undead, but you know what I mean. Count my blessings, move on, and hope for the best. Somehow, past blessings aside, fortune eludes me tonight.

Anyway, thirty minutes passed. My doom hangs high overhead. Master Kajika finally gave me his commands tonight. I couldn't tell what he thought but I sure was displeased with his orders. Not that I need to like them. A fledgling vampire obeys their master's commands when he gives them.

I mentioned I have a choice to obey Kajika's words. But, let us be honest. What is the chance of ignoring them? For all practical purposes, to listen and follow whatever a master vampire says is the same bloody thing. There's no difference. None.

Therefore, I walk the main loop trails here within the park, waiting to learn the outcome from last night. Calm night to stretch the legs. I once walked the park trails all the time after a day's work. I became lax. Flying is exciting and necessary for hunting but not habit forming. Flight is no replacement for walking.

Everyone requires exercise, even vampires. I just forgot about the trails, occupied with other matters. Imagine a vampire who misses their workout. Stiff joints creak. They could end up in an old horror movie, as a sound effect for creaky floorboards.

Besides, walking provides time for contemplation. I should walk more often. Spending private time might settle my thoughts.

A quiet evening so far. I didn't expect otherwise. Soon, Kajika will summon. Incidentally, intuition says, Leslie no longer lurks in any shadow. He's with Master Kajika at the cottage.

I best hurry and read Theodore's letter tonight before the calm disappears. Increasing my pace, I head toward the ruins.

The Kiva, an underground structure used in the Ancestral Pueblo culture, stands on my left. The dirt floor and inner stones offer grounding if only for a short time. After a short leap in, I open the envelope and read the letter with an equal quickness not knowing how long before Kajika's orders arrive.

I hope Theodore continues to write. Would hate to lose complete contact with past friendships. The letter says he's doing fine in New York. Good.

A re-read confirms my earlier skimming.

Dear Salomé,

I didn't receive a reply from my last letter. Hope all is well with you and yours. I'm sure New Mexico is heart-stopping, but it doesn't hurt to keep in touch. Please write back when you can.

Everything's well here in New York but let me review my day.

A big deal here about attending Mass. "The Heart of our seminary program," the priests tell us. Everyone participates in services every single day without exception.

We have mandatory prayers in the morning, evenings and throughout the whole afternoon, and quiet time in meditation before morning prayers. Then, fifteen minutes of reading and reflecting on scripture after breakfast before the morning services.

Too much expectation and that's all before breakfast. The food is excellent though. Sometimes we fast, but nobody starves. Good thing too, you know how I love food.

A crammed schedule offers little time to hang out. We must also honor the Midnight curfew. Like the priests expect a monster of the night to attack us. Man, I miss watching horror movies. I wouldn't bore you with the details. I'm pretty beat at the end of the day. Mostly, I sleep soundly. But it took a while to relax with no locks on the dorm doors.

I get along with most of the priests and other seminarians. I'm a little nervous about a future meeting with Monsignor Smith, whom I have not met yet. But I'm sure it's nothing important to lose sleep over. Like I mentioned before, all good here.

One strange thing happened since you left. Do you remember those misfits with the baseball bat smashing mailboxes?

Well, the owner of the car left his house one day and discovered his car upside! It happened during a nasty thunder and lightning storm. People say a strong wind or a tornado touched down in the area. Weird how the wind left everything else undamaged.

The town's newspaper printed the story and picture on their front page. Websites spread the news worldwide. Everyone from miles around retells the story. I figure the tale will continue for years.

My parents visit in several months. Wish you could visit too, but we're on different life paths, if not in different worlds. I think of you from time-to-time. Stay well. p.s. God bless.

Sincerely,

Theodore Rumswood.

After reading Theodore's letter, I stand and place it back into its envelope. Folding the envelope neatly in thirds, I slip it into a back pocket. Dirt from my clothing brushes off easily. I take an energetic breath of the fresh night air and exhale. I focus on immediate surroundings and regain composure. My leap out of the kiva lands me back onto the trail.

"Ready."

For the last minute, Master Kajika waited by the edge of the kiva. He forbears verbal commands. His mere presence informs me of his demands.

If it sounded like drills before leaping up, it was because they were. Simple, clear, concise and deliberate movements showed I prepared myself for whatever Master Kajika desires of me. The "ready" comment was a submission rather than a statement.

Master Kajika says, "We head west."

Our desires carry and lift us several hundred feet from the ground. Once both of us rise high enough for long-distance flight, we head westward.

For those who wish to understand how a vampire flies, I'll explain.

The vampire's embrace emulates from every cell in their bodies and attaches to dark energy in the night air. This bond allows us the ability to fly through that same dark energy. The best metaphor is to visualize a single electron traveling through an electrical wire. Electricity is the means of travel. The electron itself doesn't cause itself to move. If the metaphor doesn't help or you disagree with it then, we use magick. Magick works for me.

The other fantastic part about using dark energy? It wraps around the person using it. Do you remember Mister Squishy? When I packed the night or dark energy around my body, I increased my mass. The unwrapping and release of dark energy made, well, an issue. Not recommended for killing someone, removing dirtbags or trouble dates but it does the trick.

I discovered, after the fact, this immediate use and release of dark energy summoned Leslie to check out the source of the disturbance. Kajika said, "The massive dark energy ripple you caused was like signaling a five-alarm emergency at two in the morning, on everyone's day off!"

Heck, who knew? Not me, obviously.

Anyway, our nine-hundred-plus-mile trip takes us three hours to complete. Even better, the flight gives the impression of a ten-minute journey thanks to *no time*.

I cannot try to explain that term to you. I had trouble understanding the concept the first time too. Kajika and I both descend.

We land on a spotted grass and pebble lawn. A drought hit the area at some time. Saltwater in the breeze. The ocean lingers nearby.

Chanting originates from a large temple building across the lawn, one of several buildings on the property. Small single cottages positioned off to my right, a few, lit by candlelight. An ashram or yoga camp. I don't own baggy clothes for contemplating mindscapes. Not my style. Kajika's not assigning yoga as punishment, is he?

"Kajika?" I asked, with a hint of dread in my voice.

"Salomé, your expression is priceless."

I corkscrew in semi-circles checking the grounds. I never traveled this far west before and I never saw the ocean. The air bears unique properties. It smells wholesome. The sensation teases my senses.

"We landed in a yoga retreat center. And no, you're not here to become a member. Other plans await you tonight unless you *wish* to join this ashram. I can arrange it if you choose."

"No way! Not a chance in Hades. You kidding me?"

"Your choice of vocabulary is colorful and bombastic for this peaceful establishment. But you may wish at a later date you joined."

Biting my lower lip, I try to center myself. I note Kajika's hint or warning. "Master Kajika, what do you want me to do?"

Master Kajika faces the west. Kajika's voice sounds distant. "You must first feed. We traveled far and the night for you is young. Meditation practitioners isolate themselves throughout the area. Feed quickly."

I take flight. Famished from last night's fiasco. Kajika paces westward. He ponders, but that is no concern of mine. I breathe the night air and prepare myself for what lays ahead.

Sucking blood and life out of people donning yoga gear while they repeat, "OM" borders on cruel and callous. No cause to kill for this feeding. I'll drink less than a pint each. When the people wake up, they'll reason they fell asleep outside meditating.

People fall asleep all the time practicing meditation. If you have ever taken a Hatha Yoga or similar class, you know what I mean. Someone usually snores, dead to the world. At least with me, they wouldn't be so dead. Pun intended.

I keep my bite light. Marks fade with time. Practitioners can blame insects for their marks or push the memory away and forget the whole incident. Yoga practitioners rarely blame events on the supernatural. Did anyone ever hear of a yoga student who screamed "vampire?"

I make my rounds throughout the complex without issue. My vampiric kiss contacts three unsuspecting people. I feed quickly and join Kajika in the shadows of an Oak tree.

"Now, follow me," Kajika said.

We take to the air. Master Kajika pauses then descends. The descent is the slowest I ever saw. I follow. We land on a cliff overseeing the ocean. Yes, I said the ocean. I'm looking at the Pacific Ocean!

"Salomé, welcome to Santa Barbara, California."

"Oh, my gosh."

Kajika lowers himself to the ground and sits crossed legged. Guess Kajika plans to stay here awhile. He takes slow breaths, grounds himself and gazes at the far horizon.

Words too low for human hearing escape Kajika's lips. "And the Sea arose with a great wind that blew."

"Uh?" Something about the sea, was the phrase meant for me? I stand behind Kajika and gaze the horizon. I'm in amazement. Didn't expect to see this treatment tonight. No way. No how.

Kajika motions to join him. "Salomé, please."

For the second time tonight, I situate myself on the

ground. Instead of the dirt floor of the kiva, I camp on damp grass.

The ocean. Brimming with more life than anyone can imagine. More alive than any single creature on this planet. I can scan the whole alphabet describing my excitement.

Instead, I stick with "A" for amazing.

I stare wide-eyed at the serene vastness. A panoramic overload to the senses of any newcomer, myself included. If trying to describe what I saw last year in the canyon for the first time was difficult, it is near impossible to convey the entire vastness of the mother of all creation.

Vampire senses are acute.

Did you ever try not to imagine a pink elephant after someone told you not to? Try this. Do not picture the unnumbered aquatic life forms below the surface of the ocean. Do not hear or feel the powerful energy pulsating through your cells caused by the pounding and crashing of the waves. Try not to imagine the awe of it all.

I don't dare jump in for a swim. First, I never learned to swim. Second, the chaos created could be astronomical for the underwater creatures. If ocean life scatters for sharks, imagine what would happen if I swim around?

No. Wisdom dictates refraining from my desires. I position myself next to Kajika. A serene and tranquil aura shields him. To an onlooker, he appears to gaze into a bygone era, perhaps reminiscing about his adventures or sea voyages. Master Kajika depicts a yogi master meditating. I bet he practiced for years, maybe on this exact spot. None of that matters. I'm just glad I made it to the beach.

"Glad both of you enjoy your time. The view is spectacular."

Leslie? I twist to face him. Tried standing but Kajika places a hand on my shoulder. He expected my movements and outstretched his arm. It would appear I'm to stay seated for this meeting.

Leslie strolls to Kajika's right. "Back again?" He glances at the horizon. "No trouble finding you both. Although, if I foresaw visiting the beach, I would have dressed for the occasion." A small smirk appears on Leslie's face. His comment a joke?

"You know my fondness for this area and my history here. Plus, it works well for the other activity planned for later." Master Kajika rises to his feet. He picks a twig holding to his trouser leg and tosses the annoyance to the ground.

"I do. And yes, it does," Leslie said scanning the ocean's horizon.

Are these people talking in code? Master Kajika was here before, figured that. What do Kajika and Leslie plan for later?

"Salomé, enjoy your private time. Leslie and I wish to review our schedules."

"Yes, Master Kajika," I said, adding a respectful nod toward Leslie to be on the safe side. Leslie offers no acknowledgment. But I figured it couldn't hurt.

He and Kajika walk off and out of my direct sight. They find an enclosure with a view of the ocean. I'm a vampire. So yes, I can hear them. However, to eavesdrop on these two would be unwise. With pinched lips, I regain composure and focus on the amazing sight.

After another hour on the grass, I need to stretch my legs and walk the shoreline. I kick off sneakers and lace the strings together. Hanging the sneakers around my neck, I leap off the cliff. Wet sand gushes underneath bare feet.

I walk the shoreline leaving footprints. The incoming tide erases my steps. Evidence of their existence forever brushed away. Ocean water rushes in and covers my feet. The sensation feels calming, restorative on an inner level.

This moment is one unforgettable evening. A calm night with white crescent waves pounding the shore. Ocean sounds drown thoughts of past and future. I understand why people enjoy the beach so much. Time well spent. I must do this again sometime.

Kajika and Leslie project the impression they completed their chat. They walk the beach. Neither of them walks barefooted. I remove the footwear from my neck and slip on the sneakers. Balance and footing wobbles. With a few hops and arm waves, I conquer the uncooperative sandy beach.

"Hi, Kajika. Hi, Leslie."

The salutations flow out of my mouth without thought. The words cause an intense lip biting. Am I nuts? Could blame salutations on ocean air or intoxication, assuming nobody tosses me into the ocean.

"Hi, Salomé," a unison reply without repercussions. Incidentally, that isn't the bizarre part.

When Leslie first appeared, he wore his regular style work clothes. The same attire everyone wears at the park: different shades of khaki trousers, a park-issued, embroidered shirt, and comfortable walking or hiking shoes. Rarely do I see anyone dressed as he is now.

The closest description of Leslie is a comparison to the Indiana Jones' character. Instead of the whip, Leslie carries two mining hardhats complete with the lights, and my backpack slung over his shoulder. Kajika's attire is puzzling too, same as earlier but brighter, cleaner somehow.

My curiosity and worries focus on Leslie since he holds the extra headgear. Premonitions aren't my forte, but I wonder if it's too late to join that ashram.

Leslie hands me a backpack. While I unzip it, Kajika lays out the law.

"I finalized your park connections. Your apartment will be sub-leased until I decide otherwise. Your belongings from the apartment, I moved elsewhere. This includes the items stored in your trunk and cabin. You're exiled from the park and dissociated from me."

Impromptu numbness drains my life energy. Yea, I know I just invented the term. After all, whoever plans to be numb? Toes dig deep searching for support.

Kajika continues, "You'll train for several months, maybe more."

"What?" I find myself lightheaded, confused. The exclamation refers not solely to what Kajika says, but also what I discover in my backpack.

"Kajika?" I said, removing a pair of blue pinstripe mechanic's overalls from my pack. "You're kidding me. Prison stripes?" I stare at Kajika.

"Put on the clothing. The work boots too, they're steel-toed. Wolverines. My favorite."

I envision a smirk on Kajika's face. When I check, he's dead stone serious.

You are freaking kidding me. No chance in Heck.

Don't know what happened. Leslie threw me far, fast and hard. But I woke up in the exact spot on the sandy beach. Didn't ask what happened or how. Undoubtedly, a result of a Leslie thing. I remember slamming backward and sensations of tumbling forever out of control. Then blackness.

When I came to, the backpack laid to my side. The overalls were neatly folded on top. My boots, with the laces, tucked inside, waiting for me on the sand.

I clutch my backpack, including the new outfit, and trot off the beach to change.

Kajika and Leslie avoid me and walk in the opposite direction. I figure they prepare more pain for me. That or they want to reminisce again. Male stuff maybe. Who knows?

Kajika says, "Enjoy the rest of your night. For tomorrow night, you train with Leslie."

So, I win the grand prize and train with Leslie, for several months, maybe more. A fantastic opportunity of a lifetime, or not.

A strange numbness permeates the air and crawls on my skin. The sensation feels yucky. Intuition hints "Attitude change part of this forthcoming training." Can I trust this insight?

"Yep." The comment was short and to the point.

Peeking over my shoulder, Master Kajika and Leslie both display wide grins. Another thing I didn't think or dream of ever seeing. I sulk and walk off the beach to disrobe.

Dreadful costume. Imagine a female teenage vampire in overalls. Sheesh. Mixed surprises abound tonight. I smell more than saltwater in the air. Changes roll in from the distant shore.

I insert my earlier reserved choice words—here—you may guess my choices.

Can someone tell me what happened tonight?

I trod my sorry butt up to the cliff where I once lingered. Feet shuffle and drag the whole way. I disrobe underneath a canopy of maple trees. Using a tree branch, I suspend the backpack and strip down to bare minimum. Clothes form a privacy curtain on nearby branches.

The navy-blue, pinstriped overalls I hold at arm's length. Eyes squeeze tight. If you ever imagined a vampire moving in super slow motion or wondered why a vamp would do so, this would be the time and the reason.

My head pokes through the dark, forest-green, turtleneck blouse. Two thrusts per arm, four tugs straighten the shirt, and one item finished. I pull the overalls off the branch and easily slip into the pant legs. Never wore overalls before but nobody can call it rocket science. Easy matter to figure out how to snap the straps together.

Reaching into the backpack, I pull out the thick, extra-padded, white cotton socks and plant myself on the ground. The beach balancing act needs no instant reply. I double knot the bootlace and stand, brushing off any dirt.

I roll my old clothes into the backpack. All of my clothing fits inside, with room to spare. Someone packed extra items and necessities too. Someone thought in advance, doubtfully the same person who picked this outfit. Humility must also be a part of this lesson.

The backpack I loop over my left shoulder and step into the clearing. Kajika and Leslie, both pace on firm sand. I expect to see the pair rolling on the floor with laughter. Expectations fall short when Leslie tosses me the miner's hat. "To complete the ensemble," he said.

You can be darn sure I refrain from thoughts and any facial expressions. Kajika and Leslie attentively watch as I place the helmet on my head.

Leslie puts on his helmet. He checks the fit and rechecks it. With a ceremonial salute to the ethers, taps the top of his helmet twice in rapid succession. He then performs a pirouette.

I reply with a tight-lipped smile. Leslie's reaction doesn't show, but I bet a proud grin hides under his façade.

Meanwhile, Kajika faces the ocean. Paused in silent prayer. His gaze fixates on the far horizon. Kajika announces his next command. "We head south to the Santa Ynez Mountains."

Kajika and I ascend into the sweet oceanic air. I duplicate Kajika's flight path and speed. I stay to his left at arm's length.

Leslie repeats his disappearing act. Doubtful he returned to the park. Master Kajika mentioned training for several months with Leslie.

Ousted from one national park and thrown into another. The Santa Ynez Mountain range is within the Los Padres National Forest and consolidates old forests and reserves dating to the early Spanish 18th century. From what transpires tonight, reasonably sure Kajika has a history in this area. Uncertain about the cross-legged meditation and yoga. Undoubtedly, it was or is an interest of his.

Within a few moments, Kajika and I land high in the mountain range. Unexpectedly, Leslie awaits us.

While I dressed under the canopy of the maple trees, I adopted a new strategy. For the rest of tonight, as part of my adopted plan, I'll trudge through the motions. Theoretically, I'll eventually sleep and recuperate. Created a new mantra to help too. "If I buy time, I should be fine." Besides, doubtful much more can startle me tonight.

We hike a well-worn trail downward in silence. Thousands of people in the past traveled this distinct and established path. Unfortunately, the small boulders on both sides of us offer minimal protection. We're vulnerable to any prying eyes.

Kajika leads while I succeed a pace or two behind him. He knows our destination. I would love to ask questions, but instincts tell me to stay quiet. I choose wisely; trusting my insight and not follow my bliss.

As we hike the trail, Master Kajika channels energy. His aura amasses a ton of potential energy. The power builds and tingles. If I was prone to hallucinations, which I'm not, I would swear faint buzzing noises emanates from his body. Maintaining distance from Kajika might be a wise decision too. I back up two paces.

Leslie hikes to the rear. He drifts a dozen paces behind us. I get the distinct impression he enjoys this outing in the middle of the night. If anyone spots Leslie, all they'll see is a young solo hiker who steadies his hands on the rocks keeping balance.

What is he doing? Heck, maybe gods behave this way. How would I know?

This enigmatic evening deadens my thoughts. My poor jumbled brain consists of enthusiasm and embarrassment.

Legs are exhausted. Another case of light-headedness hits an already shaky head. Wish I could crumple to the ground but I don't dare show any weakness.

The two-hour hike abruptly ends. Kajika and I face a group of rocks. Ferns and moss flourish with scattered gray and dirty rocks. Some large stones, others not so large. Trust me. Nothing special. Isolated junipers grow here and there. This destination lacks character. A resting spot maybe?

Kajika and I admire the moss alone. Leslie fell behind somewhere. Hope he doesn't pick wildflowers for his date.

Master Kajika fixates himself, scrutinizing the rock grouping. He expands his auric energy. Leslie's shadow appears around a boulder.

I expect his return, but he joins us forty minutes later. What delayed him?

This whole adventure borders on freaky. Not much of it makes sense, and none of it feels right. What happens next stretches the imagination. I swear it comes directly out of a sci-fi movie.

Walking behind Kajika, Leslie claps both his hands on Kajika's shoulders. He whispers, "Do it."

The humming I swore I imagined earlier now amplifies. The air generates electricity. Lightning flashes trigger several explosive thunderclaps. Their thunderous *booms* scare the bejesus out of me. The borderline black night sky morphs into a stunning electric navy blue. Metaphysical energy permeates my exposed skin.

My body tingles in places I wouldn't name in public. I prepare myself to witness my epidermis peel away. Instead, I stand immobilized, beyond astonished. Whatever Master Kajika did, or is doing, eclipses all reason.

If you ever tried to follow instructions on how to build a put-it-together, do-it-yourself furniture project, you'll know what *an exploded-view drawing* is. If not, I'll instruct you in the basics.

An exploded view drawing is a diagram or picture of an object that shows the relationship or order of assembly of its parts. It shows the parts separated or suspended in space as if an explosion originated in the middle of the object.

I once skimmed through a copy of Leonardo da Vinci's notebook back in the tenth grade and studied the style. The artist inspired me. An undisputed fifteen century genius for sure but what I experience now makes da Vinci's work seem minuscule in comparison.

Those rocks and plants now float all around in the air. And I mean, all around. Rocks, plants, ferns, and moss, which behaved as they did for millennia, now hover above the ground.

Somehow, Kajika placed his willpower within the grouping of rocks and exploded it outward, while simultaneously retaining the group of rocks and plants from soaring in all directions. He controls every object of that grouping, forcing them where he wills. Suspended in mid-air!

I tiptoe through the miracle. Revolving in semi-circles as I stray from one viewing point to another. The objects radiate from their original spot. An accurate exploded view of what I sighted earlier.

This man, Fernando Ventré Florez, appears more mysterious than what meets the eye, even to a vampire's eye. As my luck runs, I stand in the presence of two gods.

"That's amazing!" I said.

My eyes shift downward. A cave opening appears in the space the rock grouping once occupied. Not that amazing compared to what Kajika does, but it explains why we're here. I can assume we're to enter the cave.

Anyone could figure our next step. Clue: Leslie and I both wear mining outfits.

Kajika turns and peers deep into my soul. "You have much to learn Salomé. And you will."

Leslie treks into the cave. He asks, "Coming?"

I take the question as rhetorical and bolt inside behind him.

The cavern exhibits the usual dark, cramped, and damp qualities. No sooner than entering, I slam my head into a rock ledge. Preoccupied with other circumstances, I lose my footing on wet moss and fall down a shaft, smashing my right ribs on a jagged rock wall. I land on my back staring straight up at the ceiling. The entrance to the cavern measures forty feet above me.

Thunder ceases. Air quiets. The opening closes. I imagine the rock grouping returned to its original state. For anyone passing on the trail, nothing exceptional happened tonight.

OK. I was wrong when I mentioned earlier that nothing tonight could further surprise me. I give. Not to mention one side of my overalls now wears a thick layer of mud.

One last thunderclap echoes, *boom.*

The sound reverberates in the shaft before the cave fills with complete blackness. I know the single lightning strike and later thunder is Master Kajika's way of saying good-bye.

But, deep down, I wonder.

Does he say, "Don't disappoint me" as well?

CHAPTER 15

My body lays sprawled out on the cavern floor, recuperating. Leslie stands adjacent to my right and leans over. He asks, "This predicament familiar to you?"

I stare into his eyes. Know darn well what he refers to. And he knows I know. His eyes betray him. I land on my backside a lot, so what. Do I answer back? Yes, it might have been the stupidest thing I could imagine doing.

"No. It isn't!" I lied.

Against all better judgment, I stand my ground. My official act requires tremendous effort. Parts of my body tremble. I ignore them. I utilize my best sales technique. But Leslie doesn't fall for the hard sell.

After a long pause, he says, "Good."

Not the reaction or reply I expect but I'm alive and in one piece.

"Salomé, from this point on, your familiarities and assumptions about the mundane world can destroy you. Down here in these caves, caverns, tunnels, volcanic tubes, and passageways, you'll live, eat and sleep. You could experience a brave and unknown world, providing you survive the first part of your training. Afterward, depending on your performance, I'll decide what ensues next.

"For the next several months, your training surpasses human comprehension. You will learn concepts beyond your imagination; topics hard to grasp and impossible to convey in any existing or known language. I suggest you change your disposition. If your brains hurt now, just wait."

A heavy, foreboding sensation of doom encompasses me. My present circumstance overshadows any realm of normalcy. If hope persisted for a traditional life, I'm sure I can kiss it goodbye.

Leslie edges around a boulder and pioneers further into the cave system. He steps on rocks and stays dry. Me? Muddy right pant leg from hip to ankle soaked through to the skin. Trust me when I say not all my past adventures ended up ruining outfits.

My new teacher shouts, "Those overalls not drying anytime soon, not in this humid air. Better to walk." Leslie continues traversing the tunnel.

I surmise that's my cue to rise to the occasion and challenge this undertaking. Be it far from me to refuse or turn down a challenge. I grab my gear and shake off my earlier misfortunate tumble. With soaked overalls, I dash straightforward to catch up to Leslie.

Leslie and I travel the darkness with our lit mining helmets. We progress through grueling passageways. Tunnels formed by ancient rivers, earthquakes, and volcanic activity. A mass labyrinth of underground tunnels precarious and treacherous to humans.

Miles and miles of undiscovered hidden cave systems run in all directions. Pathways leading to what, hidden treasure, an alien base or maybe my death? Conspiracy theorists could pop their blood vessels thinking of tales.

This underground adventure sucks. Much of our traveling is on hands and knees or climbing down sheer rock cliffs. The average passageway either confines or restricts our movements. I consider myself lucky when I reach a spot when I'm *only* cramped.

Cannot stop wondering why I didn't get my butt kicked by either Kajika or Leslie instead of visiting the beach. As Master Vampires and gods go, either one can prove their point better than this. Heck, both treat me better than I could expect. Figure the real punishment shows its ugly head when we arrive at our final destination.

If you wondered, the overalls dried out after that first fall. But fate visited and they ended up soaked on other occasions. Gave up on the idea of wearing dry clothes. No chance of staying dry dealing with underground rivers, climbing waterfalls, wet rocks scattered about, and low rocky ceilings that drip. Subterranean cave systems aren't water-free environments.

I swear moss grows on these overalls.

This journey has lasted ten days and nights so far. We traveled four straight days with three sleep periods and then repeated the pattern. We'll finish the third repetition after two more days and nights.

Leslie sleeps for one hour each rest period. An astonishing feat if you can envision it. He does another fantastic stunt. Leslie levitates. He'll take an hour nap while he hovers twelve inches off the rocky ground. My rest period consists of four hours of rock bedding, comatose to the world. When I wake up, my back aches all over. Wish I could master the kid's levitation trick. Times like these when I miss my futon.

When Leslie rests, I eat. Cannot use night energy down here, so I ingest insects, worms, and other small cave creatures. Survival mode is a humbling experience. Figure Leslie hunts while I sleep. Cannot picture Leslie eating creepy crawlies, although he must nourish himself somehow. When he wakes, we at once hit the passageways.

Leslie pushes me beyond all my earlier self-limitations. I suspect Master Kajika and Leslie attended the same boot camp. After my rebirth, Master Kajika constructed a strict schedule for me. It was similar to high school, except the hours. But Leslie wears me down and pushes me forward. I wonder if an early grave awaits if I keep this pace.

No night or moon energy down here. Earth energy infiltrates everywhere. I walk, climb, swim and crawl in a different world. Leslie allows me limited rest and the smallest food intake. If you lower your calorie intake, change your diet, rise and shine at three in the morning, you may experience a little of what I feel. Oh, and add the company of this demi-god to the mix.

We make camp in a large cavern. An underground cathedral. Stalactites and stalagmites form massive cascades. I squat on an ancient formation in a corner and munch on a centipede whose legs I pluck off one by one. No malicious conduct, solely boredom. Eating insects is an acquired taste. I've failed to obtain it yet. Bats love to hang out in caves, saw plenty. And no, I'll not eat a bat. Not even fried.

Leslie sleeps on the other side of the cavern. For the last hour, I pondered on Leslie's surname, assuming he has one. Heck, a half year passed before I learned his first name. Puzzling. Who and what is he? I know he owes me no explanations but how does he accomplish all these impressive feats? I don't believe in gods. But what other term can define him? Leslie's a real puzzle for sure.

Leslie descends to the rock ledge. "Finished?"

"Yep. Ready," I said, and toss the bug meat over my shoulder.

Backpack strapped and fastened. I leap to my feet in anticipation for more tedious trekking, climbing, crawling, and wading. Leslie uprights himself, the kid motions me to join him. I comply.

"I bear the obligation to liberate you from several troublesome queries before we continue. You'll not interrupt. Do you understand?" Leslie said.

I nod my approval.

"We're close to our destination. You and I continue at our present pace. Once there, you can change clothes if you wish. No further demands to continue wearing your present attire. You can also soak in the hot springs. Please do because you're becoming ripe. As far as my name, you call me 'Leslie' until I say otherwise. Know I'm no god, but I demand respect. Any other questions can wait."

The setting might appear to an outsider as though I love having my head handed to me. What can I say? Still a teenager.

Thank the gods this transitory adventure ends soon. Guaranteed clean clothing after a long hot soak. What more can a girl hope for in life? Leslie mentioned no more miner outfit. I'll admit the hardhat and boots came in handy with the low hanging rocks and rough terrain, but I'm jumping at the chance to clean up and wear new duds. I'm absolutely changing after two weeks straight of traveling. Why not? A bath cannot kill me. And what attire can be worse than what I already wear?

~

For another four days, we pursue our earlier rituals.

Leslie naps enjoying his shut-eye. After a siesta, I caught a beige-colored snake before it disappeared into a narrow crevice. Plenty of sharp-edged rocks in this cavern. It was easy finding a cutting tool. Hope to finish the skinning before Leslie wakes. Does snake taste of chicken? Don't know, but safe bet serpent meat tastes better than bug meat.

Time's up. Leslie passes me a sideways glance and rechecks his bootlaces. I seize a quick bite, and before taste buds can answer my riddle, shove my skinless friend into an overall front pocket.

The kid points to a spot thirty feet above us. The first order for today, climbing. At least we start dry. Countless times, we wiggled through openings or rappelled into the abyss. Plenty of opportunities await to get drenched later. Notwithstanding the promised subterranean hot bath.

We climb miles of rock and crawl more miles through crevices.

Leslie stands upright sixty feet ahead through a narrow opening. Another large cavity? Love to stretch my legs a moment. Most of my day's movements paralleled a reptile slithering through tunnels hours on end. How do cave critters manage? I snagged more cuts and abrasions than I cared for, and a dozen coats of dirt layer the overalls. Body healed amid the rest periods, but I look forward to a full day's slumber.

Anxiousness combines with my impatience. I scurry on all fours and propel myself through the aperture. My plan to tumble and raise in triumphant glory falls apart. I misjudge the depth of the cave floor and end up splattered on my back. History repeats itself. The cave ceiling dominates my vision once again.

From this angle, I see secluded stairs cut into the granite leading upwards into the darkness. The ground floor slopes upward where Leslie stands to my right. I estimate the exit portal thirty feet off the rock bottom. Leslie stares at his feet shaking his head. He can wonder all he wants. My goof was an honest mistake. Anyone could have miscalculated the perception of height.

I arise in a not so glorious fashion, gazing toward the latest chamber. Its orifice measures approximately twelve feet by twelve feet square. Hand chiseled by the tool marks.

I approach the entrance with hesitant care. Taking baby steps, allowing the living spirits to rest. Luminous golden light bounces and dances off the interior cavern's walls, spilling through the opening. A golden glow rarely heard of in legends radiate everywhere. The brilliance and radiance defy imagination. If I thought the ocean amazing, I'm lost for words on this marvel.

"Oh. My. Gosh," I said wandering through the entrance.

Leslie waves me onward. "We're here. Welcome to my humble abode."

CHAPTER 16

For two weeks, Leslie and I traveled through underground passageways. We crawled, squirmed, climbed, rappelled, swam, and with me falling on occasion. Didn't dream the outcome could lead to ultimate awe. An underlying sneaking suspicion says I may later sum up this whole experience to a stronger expression: *pissed*.

Digressing further into this vault, I discover treasure. Piles, no—mountains, stacked to the ceiling in several areas. A stockpile of gold, silver, emeralds, pearls, and turquoise. Along with gold and silver coins stored in wooden chests. Furniture, no wait—thrones with gold inlay, embedded with precious gems. Sheesh. And, I made an earlier sarcastic remark about finding hidden treasure?

Rays of light enter the cavern from hidden fissures. I was correct earlier to tread lightly upon entering. The revealing light and intruding me shouldn't be here. We both trespass. Spirits from the past reside here. I perceive them living and breathing within this cavern.

I meander and stumble through a labyrinth of pathways. Stacks and piles of treasure border the path on both sides of me. Momentary amazement halts my steps several times during my wandering. No way can I transverse this cavern in any straight line. The glistening hoard serpentines forever. Heaps of gold abound everywhere, including the cave's depressions and antechambers. The place defines humongous. How can I trust my eyes, this cannot be real, can it?

A spectacular undertaking to transport this motherlode. Hundreds of years and thousands of men hauling pound after pound of gold and silver. The more laborious task was to shield the precious metals from all prying eyes for future generations. How many other people have seen this cavern? And how many lived to see another day? This my punishment? Will Leslie kill and force me to guard the treasure as a ghost, never to see Kajika or anyone else again?

"Hardly. Although, your intuition is correct," Leslie said, sitting on the far side of the cavern.

Leslie occupies one of the ancient thrones. He squarely planted his feet wide apart on the stone floor, with forearms resting on armrests. His body and persona perfectly fit the throne. Did a designer custom build it for him? From his perspective, he has an awe-inspiring view of the encompassing treasure. The dais has enough treasure-free floor space to hold court if Leslie wishes.

"Hope you're not expecting me to kneel, Your Majesty," I said jesting.

"Your *sarcasm* is a welcome delight."

My comment hits a nerve. Leslie stares, bends forward, leans heavily on both his arms and legs bent, ready to spring forward. He says, "What I want you to do is soak in the springs. I take no pleasure in telling you this. You reek. You'll find a stone tub and necessary accessories in an antechamber off one path on my left. Once finished, you'll find several bathrobes. Help yourself to one on your way out and report back here. Girl, wash thoroughly."

I fight internal turmoil in my want to know. One heck of a treasure tale is forthcoming. Bet on it. For me to listen and be alive to hear it, I must survive Leslie's wrath. I calm my eagerness and respond. "Yes, sir."

Easy to find hot springs among the underground labyrinth, follow the sound of bubbling water. Escaping mineral springs' aroma and moisture content helped too. Without acute hearing, I suppose a norm could miss the tunnel. Unlike the main compartments, the light here is absent.

Famous archeologists discover and unearth tons of Roman bathhouses throughout Europe. The experts would be shocked to find one here. "Wow." How can Leslie call this chamber a tub? Complete understatement.

No denying it, this a bathhouse minus the marble columns and Roman statues. One substantial round hot tub rests in the center. It appears gigantic. Cannot be less than fifty feet in diameter. Massive, natural, flat limestones, four feet long, edge the circumference. Stone stairs between two distant capstones lead into the murky, greenish waters.

Bath accessories await on a shelf built into an edging stone. Folded, thick, piled washcloths and towels await on a marble bench. No bathrobes. Maybe Leslie meant they're in another alcove. A wooden scrub brush with natural bristles rests within a wooden bucket at the foot of the bench.

It takes seconds to strip down to bum naked. A wiggle here and a jiggle there and Olé! Free to breathe. Had to wiggle on the stone floor to peel off clothes. A couple of items stuck. Leslie underestimated twice. I don't reek. I'm rancid. Hard to fathom a person stinking this bad. The government could use my armpits as weapons of mass destruction. Exaggeration? Maybe, but only a little.

Except for a marble bench, décor and furniture is absent. I toss the stinking mining outfit in a far corner. If I had a lighter, the pile of clothes would burn on the spot. Slim to zero chance of finding a flamethrower among Leslie's treasure, but a girl can hope.

Descending the stairs into the waters, I bypass the bath items. Wading in the hot water wins over soap and scrub brush. I tread my way to the middle of the circular pool. Most of the bath's depth is waist deep, give or take. The bath floor is uneven. Feet slide on slippery substances. To trust my toes, I would say tile lines the bottom under the murky mineral water. Wouldn't act surprised if a secret mosaic hides beneath the aqueous surface.

This environment fosters muscle relaxation. Past tunnel exploration tension releases without effort. A good dunk erases every uncomfortable cold stream I crawled through in the past weeks.

At first, I thought the water temperature could boil a toad. I figured wrong. Gases released from the earth below form scattered bubbles. The rising bubbles mislead me. No inviting old friends down here for any pool parties though. The scalding water could burn any human. Glowing beet-red skin awaits when I exit.

Imagine executing a breaststroke in hot sweltering springs under a mountain of rock. Gliding the misty surface of the waters. The ambiance of this place haunts one's soul, accompanied by overwhelming *Ahhhs*.

"Can certainly acquire a liking to this. Maybe candles or Enya," I said.

The words die faster than General Custer did. Scrap the Enya or any music. The acoustics suck. Keep the candles though. "*Ahhh*, this bath feels heavenly."

Surrendering mind and body, I slide down the steps into the hot waters for another half hour. My body floats mere inches below the surface in a dream state. Continue this any longer and skin will prune over. Time for soap and scrub brush.

Two sidestrokes glide me to the edge. I vault out of the water and land near the bench. Carrying the cleaning items and a filled bucket from the hot spring, I walk to a nearby cave wall. The wall serves as a leaning post while I practice my balancing act.

The soft bristles loosen weeks of packed on grime helped by a beauty bar. Scrubbing changes into a pleasant experience. Five trips to refill the bucket finishes the scrubbing. Runoff from the washing drains away from the pool. One final dunk, a lap around the circumference and the new and improved Salomé debuts.

One cannonball in the middle of the hot springs sprays water everywhere. Hate to leave, but Leslie awaits in his throne room. Yearning to hear the story of the treasure. Hope it involves pirates and not ancient aliens.

I wade through the water until reaching the stairs. No hurry to leave. I take careful steps. One last quick survey for memories and I head straight to the marble bench.

"What the heck?" No. He *didn't*. "Leslie!"

I snatch one of the several robes from the bench and storm back to Leslie. Wrapping and fastening the purple terrycloth bathrobe around my wet skin, I charge barefoot into the main chamber maneuvering the labyrinth.

Uninterested in slowing down any, already committed myself. I plan to slam Leslie into the far wall. No holds barred. This kid, or whatever he is, will learn not to intrude on a female enjoying a private bath. Wanted to speak to him about touching my clothing for months. Time flew, missing earlier chances. Chats weren't high on my priority list. I had other priorities. But plans change and Leslie is about to get an earful.

Leslie roams the grand hall. Devil be damned. "How dare you!" I screamed.

Doubtful the element of surprise favors me after the outburst. Leslie stands in his would-be court. He stares wide-eyed. A deer blinded by headlights. I charge headlong and cover the short distance within a nanosecond; the kid's plastered body envisioned on the far cavern wall. Learn his lesson, he will.

"Thought it best to leave you in the position you landed. Wouldn't want me touching or disturbing your stuff, now would you?" Leslie said, from across the cavern.

Leslie's superior smug makes me want to snap and rip him apart. Whatever the illusion was, it faked me out good. I don't succumb to his taunt. "How long was I unconscious this time?" I asked.

"Funny. Not long. You're stronger since your earlier episodes. Your body heals faster. We have time if you wish to ram into the wall again, or another one if you wish."

A rhetorical question if ever I heard one.

"You don't just waltz in when I'm naked and leave robes on a bench." I gather myself off the floor and read-just my robe. "How long were you watching me in there, anyway?"

"To answer your last question first, I wasn't. As for your first question, I didn't."

"Don't *dare* lie! Nobody else is here! It *had to* be you," I said, standing my ground.

"I assure you, I entertain no wish or need to intrude on someone's bath. Your other past misunderstandings, or assumptions, are also not of my making. Master Kajika undressed and washed you that first night before *the night's dark sleep.*

"My interests focus on your present and future training. You can solve your mysterious maid issue on your own time, not mine."

Face down, flat on my stomach, and each appendage pointing to a different corner of the compass isn't one of my preferred positions. A body lands that way when running into and bouncing off a rock wall. If anyone wishes to try it sometime, I saved you the trouble. Despite the frequent occurrence of waking from unconsciousness with my derriere handed to me by others, I dislike the experience.

Facing Leslie after my foolish outburst is a difficult feat. "Was that you I ran through earlier?" I asked, forcing the question.

The kid sits on his throne. "A simple projection of myself. Placed in your mind. If you had checked your surroundings before you charged head first without regard, you would have noticed my presence here."

I should have kept watch over the whole cavern when attacking. Came in wearing blinders, tunnel vision. Beginner's mistake. Basic stuff too. Once again, I blew it.

"Salomé, perhaps it would be proper if you dress. Your trunk with fresh clothing rests in another antechamber on my right along with your bedding. Both carried down earlier from the cabin and readied for you. I believe you know of our location and what lies above us?"

Frustration builds. Lower lip trembles and both hands form tight fists. Earlier suspicions were correct. Wasted two whole weeks traveling underground with Leslie. If he wanted to show me treasure, why didn't we take the stairs?

The bloody things most likely start in another cell in the basement next to mine.

Before I offer an answer, Leslie continues his statement. "I suggest you keep your reply short."

"Go to Heck" is what I wanted to say, but I stick to, "Yes Sir. I'll make it quick."

I scramble through a different set of passageways and locate my trunk.

A light grey sweatsuit with pink striping grabs my attention. Warm, soft, and dry, just what I hoped for tonight. A plastic hair comb straightens my wet hair and removes any tangles. I plop the trunk lid shut and race barefooted back to Leslie.

CHAPTER 17

"Pull up a throne and listen. The Aztec warriors and civilians fled their cities in the 16th century. They took with them their gold, silver, turquoise and quetzal feathers. Everything the Aztec empire considered precious and didn't wish the Spaniard Cortes and his invading army to confiscate, they extracted from their temples. Legends say the Aztecs transported the treasure and dumped it down a ravine, threw it in a lake, or carried and buried it to the north."

Holy lost treasure! Real Aztec gold. I grab a golden Roman backless throne with curbed fancy armrests. Once seated, I discover the Romans didn't design benches for comfort. I slouch and relieve the stress on my lower back.

"The priests knew me well, and I befriended the majority of warriors. Although, well known didn't mean well liked. Truthfully, my presence terrified the priests, or more accurately, my past exploits. You must understand. I first reached the lands of South America in the mid-12th century. The Toltec empire ruled. I lived and trained among their Shamans for years. I dare say a fair number of my adventures outlived their priest."

"Leslie, how old are you?"

"Ballpark figure? Over seventeen hundred years so far."

"Wow. So, basically, you're an immortal."

"Basically? So are you. Depends on who places the title on you and why. I can assure you; I have held the title of 'Demon' more than once too."

He has a point. Imagine, though, living for thousands of years. I thought I understood a vampire's immortality, but the concept didn't hit home.

"How can you—"

"Be immortal? A family gift. Perhaps another story, for another time. But if you wish me to continue..." I reposition the chair, bench, or whatever this uncomfortable thing is closer to Leslie. He continues his tale.

"The Aztecs' tradition respected the old Toltec beliefs and revered the ancient masters. Priests disliked me, but they despised the Spanish more. Known as *White-devils* they murdered and stole as they conquered every city they entered.

"A priest named Taloca, his heart filled with mistrust, invited me to talk to the other priests along with a large group of warriors. After long days and nights of debate between the temple priests, the council decided I should become the custodian of the Aztec culture. No minor feat, I can assure you. Every item of worth or treasured by the Aztec empire transferred to my safekeeping."

"This is everything they treasured?"

"Everything found that wasn't already taken by Spanish ships. Yes. We used a local obsidian mine opening near Pachuca. Our group later traversed volcanic tunnels and enlarged passageways as we advanced. We transported the entire Aztec Nation's worth, a tiresome and vigorous labor, to here. Warriors, tradespeople, and peasants accomplishing the impossible.

"The priests blessed the effort by offering human sacrifices in the temples. One last ritual before disappearing in time. Several unfortunate events occurred along the way, which I couldn't prevent. To save their cultural history for future generations, even the old and sick carried what they could. I saw hundreds of gallant, brave souls perish along the way. You may see their graves when we travel the same passages later.

"Once we finished the major undertaking, I said my goodbyes and offered well wishes to each worker and warrior. They disappeared up those stairs leading into the now established national park. In this aspect, I suppose the tales are true. The Aztecs did travel north with their gold and bury it."

Explains the gold and the thousands of hands it took to assemble the piles. I bet the golden city of El Dorado hides here, but other stashes throughout the cavern are not Aztec. I see Old World, Hebrew temple items and this Roman chair for example. Poured and stamped gold bars, silver coins with crosses on them lay in chests. "And the remaining treasure?" I asked.

"Templars."

"Naturally." First legend, now conspiracy theory. "I'm listening."

"Hundreds of years I lived among the Toltec. I learned shaman sorcery. Occult practices, which I'll later teach you. When the Toltec community died out, I left the continent to return to my mother's birthplace in the Holy Land. I met the Knights Templar while roaming Jerusalem.

"A year later, I journeyed as one of their acolytes. The work allowed plenty of time to explore the land and its history. Unfortunately, my work prematurely ended. Political conflict between Church and State sealed the Templar's fate. You may know part of the story."

Everyone knows of the Templar Knights. Their legacy adventures continue to inspire authors and treasure hunters alike. "Yea. Pope and King fought for power. Knights lost."

"In short. The Knights received an early warning. It proved a facade. King Philip IV wanted the Templar treasure, his primary goal. The political control with Pope Clement V was the king's secondary concern. The Knights and their mission squeezed between the two. False confessions later ensued, and hundreds of brave, good men suffered and died.

"Before the Knights disbanded in 1310, four ships set sail from southern France. The smaller ship of the fleet, a galleon, sailed north to Spain. Then, three vessels that were more massive set sail for America. East coast of Florida to be exact. Two months later, a larger fleet of eighteen galley ships left the French docks. The ships' destination? Northern Spain, where the ships' contents were disembarked into the four winds. The galleys carried no Templar treasure but Warrior Knights who banded together and formed new orders.

"In earlier explorations of the Americas, I inspected a cave system in central Kentucky. I knew of the Mammoth Caves and its vast number of passageways. Two direct tunnels once lead from the Mammoth Caves to these caverns and would now prove useful in this Holy mission.

"A hundred and twenty-four men, two entire ship's crews, assisted with the treasure's relocation from the three galleons in Florida. The Templars, skilled in bartering, made deals, arranged fees and befriended the native tribes-people. Our trek from Florida to Kentucky proved uneventful. Once all the treasure laid at the mouth of Mammoth Cave, a skeleton crew returned to the ships in Florida. The crewmembers would restock the vessels and prepare to sail northward. The rest of the team helped with the treasure hauling.

"We orchestrated one-way traffic patterns within the cave. The more massive direct tunnel, we used to carry and deliver the treasure. The smaller second tunnel worked well for our return trip. Since the Templar's treasure comprised of different sizes and weights, the two tunnels allowed everyone to travel at their own pace without hindering others. After we finished our mission, I collapsed both passageways along with seven others branching off the central system for good measure. Those tunnels no longer exist.

"I bargained with the Cherokee Nation for the crew's safe passage eastward. The arrangements satisfied both parties. The ship's crew acquired guides and shelter for the three months travel to Charleston, South Carolina. I consider myself blessed nobody died or fell sick during the entire adventure. The men erected a temporary camp on shore until the three ships arrived for boarding.

"The Templar Knights excelled in the art of barter and trade. The Knights surpassed what I could hope to do myself. I allowed them free range of all deals in peace-keeping with Florida's native Ays tribe. Perhaps I should have placed limits on what to offer in exchanges, but I didn't.

"I understood the Ays's need to limit the number of crew settling on their village's coastal waters. The issue to support a limited crew for three galleons didn't trouble me. The ships would stay safe unless a hurricane approached. It didn't bother me either knowing the men helped build cabins inland for the natives for port fees. Hard work hurts no one.

"The Ays granted free fishing rights to all crewmen alike, as long as they camped onboard and didn't enter the villages unescorted. The treaty, constructed on short notice, worked well for everyone. What bothered me so much, you ask?"

The story sounds remarkable. But why does Leslie pause? Should a fledgling vampire ignore him? Especially the one on double-secret probation?

"OK. I'll bite. Leslie, what bothered you with a pact that worked?"

"Glad you asked," he said, with a gleeful tone.

"A handful of the knights resented my abilities and thought it amusing to include me in their deals. As part of the treaty, I would oversee and accept full responsibility for misgivings among all ship crews. And making matters worse, my contract mandated my presence at all council meetings during our temporary inhabitance.

"All Knights and workmen knew full well the distance separating our two parties and how important our mission was, but a handful of Knights insisted on amusement. I understand banter among friends, but I dislike attitude from strangers. It irritates me."

Does that mean me too? I'm not a total stranger, am I? Leslie glares his intent. His silent narrative answers my question.

"After the pact was sealed and agreed upon, I had to fulfill my duties. For months, I traveled back and forth through auric curtains to cover the distance separating our parties within the time allowed. I was displeased. Remind me sometime to explain how these trouble Knights fared afterward in their jest."

I know better than to ask that question. I nod my reply.

"One of the Ays chiefs, a man named Tsiyi impressed me with his knowledge. He asked one day if I could mentor him in metaphysical teachings. I saw no reason to refuse and agreed to return. For eight years, I responded. Tsiyi's thirst for knowledge was endless. Our relationship remained mentor and teacher. The chieftain commented on how my appearance stayed the same throughout those years. He later joked about it to others.

"I'm uncertain if the chieftain felt uncomfortable with my changeless appearance or felt satisfied with his new understanding of the world, but one day he said his thanks and we departed. In a span of two hundred years, stories sprouted in Florida about a legendary person living forever youthful.

"You're the origin of the Fountain of Youth? I cannot believe that tale."

"I'm not done. The crew restocked the ships with fruits, small animals, water and smoked meats. Ships sailed the Gulf Stream currents northward. All three arrived safely in Nova Scotia. Two of the three ships proved fit enough to travel the open seas back to Europe. The Knights and crewmembers cannibalized the third ship for its lumber and covered the rest of the ship's frame with a fabricated swamp.

"The Knights Templar buried a predetermined King's ransom in a separate location should the need for it ever arise. Europe's political atmosphere was uncertain. A reserved treasure was a wise precaution. Each ship included a handful of Templar Knights for guidance and protection. Most of the crew were not Templars, but they had the ability in tunneling and stealth. Crewmembers set in motion a devious plan. Instructions and warning etched in stone and placed predominately for any future diggers.

Upon completion and with both ships restocked, Knights and crew abandon the island for the journey to Scotland.

No way. "You're kidding. Oak Island too?" I said, shaking my head in disbelief.

"I added treasure since then; a pile here, a heap there. And, if you can create a better story to explain this treasure horde, please let me know. In the meantime, you must rest. Your sleepwear is in your trunk. Sleep peacefully. Your new quarters require no padlocks or bolts. Roam when you arise."

After hearing Leslie's fairy tales, I head to bed for a much-needed full night's sleep.

CHAPTER 18

*L*eslie said I could roam, so I'm wandering the paths dressed in brown, loose trousers and a tee-shirt. The place is amazing. I can understand how people get gold fever. All this history and gold can warp one's mind. Wonder what Master Kajika muses about when he descends the stairs to gaze upon his once hunted piles of gold.

"He doesn't."

I spin around to discover Leslie wearing formal attire. Similar to what Kajika wears: tailored three-piece Italian suit, charcoal black, woolen blend and shoes so highly polished they would make the gold jealous of their brilliance. He stands with arms clasped behind his lower back. His hair is combed tight to his scalp. Leslie appears sharp and regal. I'm impressed.

"Leslie? I was only—"

"Fernando visits none of these chambers. He deprives himself of its treasure. You surmised correctly; the gold alters the mind. Are you handling yourself OK?"

"Had no wish for jewelry or gold. Don't believe that desire changed. The treasure is cool though."

"Yes, the gold is." Leslie holds out his hands. "Take this bowl of blood and drink. We shall talk afterward."

I gracefully accept the bowl from Leslie. Human blood. No mistake about it. After gulping down the contents, I carry the empty container back to the grand room. Leslie lounges on his throne sipping, coffee?

"Want a cup? Been awhile, has it not?" Leslie asked, displaying a coffee mug with an outstretched arm.

"Now, you know darn well I cannot drink coffee anymore."

Leslie bellows with laughter.

"Salomé, enjoy a cup of fresh coffee. Vampires drink other fluids besides blood. You ate other substances. For example, the skinned snake shoved in your front pocket."

"Yea, in small bites but Master Kajika didn't mention I could drink any other fluid."

"Master Kajika's teaching methods differ from mine. He teaches what the student requires at that particular time. When a student proves ready, questions climb to the student's mind where the master offers an answer. Master Kajika's students learn within their own perceived worlds. To you, vampires drank blood. Apparently, you didn't ask if they could do otherwise.

"Vampires do exist who drink *and eat* their victim's organs. And if vampires choose, they can eat limited human food. After, of course, they learn to relax their naturally tightened stomachs. You remember your first dark-night, and your abdominal pains, no doubt. Perhaps, I'll teach you the relaxation technique, if you wish."

Darn. Caffeine free without trying.

I trade the empty bowl for the coffee. A hot ceramic mug full of java sandwiched between hands triggers plenty of memories. Sensations of comfort, the aroma of fresh coffee beans, and the thrill of the first sip, nothing in life can compare. I steal another sip, in case it's a rare dream, and move the bench next to Leslie.

"What do you want to talk about?" I asked, in an unusually cheerful tone. Morning coffee can sure perk up any mood.

"Within the week, you'll train for one year and a day in the Peruvian Rainforest. Your training will test your survival skills to their limits. You'll learn Toltec sorcery and occult subjects from local Shamans. Fernando and I decided you'd make an ideal candidate for telepathy and perhaps dream weaving. If I deem you ready, I'll teach these techniques to you. Other parts of your training will focus on teamwork.

"I'm aware vampires hunt alone, but I foresee your future adventures requiring aid from others. The possibility exist that I'm mistaken, but you best train for all possibilities. I'll not lie to you, if you pass this training, you'll be a formidable foe to your enemies. If not, you'll be dead. As in defunct."

I caress the mug and take another sip, or two before replying. "I take it; you offer no choice?" A cloud of doom sent by the Grimm Reaper hovers. The hooded specter tests me.

"One always has a choice. You can pass and live or fail and die. A choice not to train? No. Two choices. Pick one. You'll have a year to choose."

Leslie leans forward and passes me another fresh mug of coffee. I'm fascinated where this second cup of coffee originated. This mug deviates from the earlier one I held. Its round ceramic bottom fits comfortably within my palms. The mug's weight and warmth offer an unusual inner calmness. In the offering, Leslie's hand brushes against mine. The contact transfers his earnestness.

He whispers, "Warriors always train."

The words deliver no comfort. Instead, I develop brain fog. Was the phrase a trigger? A white linen toga adorns Leslie. He wears his hair much shorter and curlier in this time period. He stands on stone steps addressing Greek scholars who absorb his every word. I shake the vision off and sip familiar reality. Words leave my lips with little conscious effort.

"Who are you?" I asked in a daze.

Leslie reclines in his throne. An audible exhale escapes his lips. He stares. The thousand plus old kid glances off into the distance. I hesitate to rephrase the question.

I drank enough caffeine for one night. I place the coffee mug on the stone floor next to the other mug. Two empty ceramic mugs lay next to the golden cache of the ages. Which treasure is out of place?

This Roman bench or I could use more padding. I reposition myself once again and prepare for an answer.

"My given birth name is Athanasius, an honorable name given to me by my family in ancient Roman. It's a name I now seldom use. I gained several given titles throughout my centuries of travel: Elder, Centurion, Arahant, Abbot, Lord, El Rey Dorado, god, demon, to the latest, 'the kid' and like you, I don't favor nicknames."

"Um, sorry." But what did he expect? Nobody at the gift shop knew the kid's name. I mean, Leslie's name.

"In the summer of 1857, on one of my New York trips, I sighted a young European immigrant. My doppelgänger. His name was Leslie. I renamed myself and have used his name ever since that moment."

"If you don't mind me asking, what about all that magick, mind reading and weird stuff you do?" Training with Leslie for a whole year. Figure it cannot hurt knowing a little of his history. Assuming he doesn't mind answering questions and send me into oblivion instead.

Leslie finishes his coffee. His impression softens and offers hope. I'm optimistic and liberated when I hear his response.

"A mixture of family gifts and hundreds of years of training with generations of knowledgeable and enlightened souls. The latter taught techniques to increase one's vibrational molecular structure. My physical body, within time, transformed into a metaphysical being. I'm a true breatharian. Already possessing immortality, I furthered my studies in Forbidden Knowledge. And yes, long story short, I became godlike."

Leslie's tale explains most of what I wondered about him. He's just a 1700-year-old supernatural kid who trained years in ancient, forbidden, occult magic. Why didn't I figure this out earlier? His history was so obvious I should have known the first time I saw Leslie's blue eyes. Silly sarcastic me.

"Did Master Kajika learn from shamans too? That feat he did at the Santa Ynez Mountains was amazing. I never saw anything like it before," I asked.

Leslie leans back in his throne and crosses a leg. He says, "Fifty years before I met Kajika on the western coast of Oregon, a Taoist hermit in the early eighteen hundreds sailed from China and taught Kajika the mysteries of Qigong. These precious Qigong secrets awoke Kajika's inner spiritual nature and magnified his connection to the fabric of reality. The feat you witnessed was merely his communication with those mystical energies."

Wow. Imagine what I can learn with Leslie's personalized training in the Peruvian jungles. Wonder what marvels Kajika might teach me afterward when I return to the park. Assuming my wiseass remarks don't send me to Limbo first.

"Why the royal look?" I asked, changing the subject to the present.

A wide grin shows Leslie's devilish side. He rises to his feet and announces, "Salomé, daughter of the night, kneel and be knighted into *The Order*."

"What. Are you nuts? I kneel for one reason and you're not it." Don't know what his problem is. "Give me one reason why I should."

"Limbo. Down on one knee will suffice."

He commands me to genuflect? Shoot, maybe this quiet kid isn't so humble after all. Skeptical of this order he speaks of but I'll pass on revisiting Limbo. I add a sarcastic flourishing bow to my humiliation before kneeling.

"The Luciferian Initiation rite is brief and painless. The secret doctrines of *The Order of Awesomeness Dragons* await you. Do you accept our teachings and swear allegiance?"

Brain searches for any pass references on dragons. A few movies and books come to mind but nothing worth asking. Cannot hurt humoring him, can it? Leslie waits for a reply.

I blurt out, "Sure, why not?" What am I getting myself into now?

"Then arise. Let the four winds fear your name, Dragonessa."

"Dragonessa? I take a new name?"

Leslie throws his arms up in my direction. "Use it anytime; it's yours." He turns and takes a few steps. "You also inherit these," he said.

His Kingship steps behind the throne. He produces a book and a package wrapped in cloth. Not a candle, I hope. If Leslie wants me to read by candlelight, it might ruin my vampiric eyesight. Imagine, a vampire wearing glasses.

"This is a copy of Sun Tzu's *The Art of War*. Please read it completely. Study it. Your survival depends on your comprehension."

Doubtful Leslie joked. I take the book and skim through the pages. "Know your enemy and know yourself and you can fight a hundred battles without disaster." Fancy that. Could have used that advice earlier.

"This gift is yours to keep. It too will prove useful."

I take the bulky, wrapped item. No candle weighs this heavy. I unwrap it, squishing the wrapping into a ball. "A dagger. Wow!"

"Master Kajika supervised its construction. Fourteenth-century design using the latest modern materials with special qualities embedded in the artistry. All completed by a dear friend of his."

"Thank you. This dagger is well balanced, exceptional artistry too."

Leslie presents a letter. "The gift comes with a message," he said.

My name written with a calligraphy style text dries on the front in blue ink. I use the dagger to open the envelope.

A message from Kajika?

Greetings, I received a second letter addressed to you from your friend Theodore. The third letter he wrote since your arrival. You should respond and keep in touch. Real friends are hard and few to find. And much harder to maintain. It wasn't too long ago you thought your past dead. I can assure you, you aren't ready to forget your past life. I can also ensure you, Salomé, you'll not always have an attitude. You're sadly mistaken on both accounts.

The supplies you need for your correspondence lie inside the trunk. Please respond in kind before you and Leslie leave for your training.

You were correct in your assessment when you first fell into the Santa Ynez Mountain's cave. I wish for you to continue to trust your instincts. Be vigilant to survive the lessons Leslie teaches you.

Enjoy your gifts, and your new dagger.

Be well.

Plain, straightforward, and unsigned.

Leslie hands me the second letter.

I grasp the letter mentioned in Kajika's letter. "Thanks," I said.

Leslie slurs. I miss his comment. My thoughts drift between Master Kajika, Theodore, and the coming year's regimen.

Imagine surviving three hundred and thirty-six nights in caves and jungles. I didn't expect or discuss this career move with any school counsel. And then become a subject of The Order of Awesomeness Dragons no less. Hey, that stands for, TOAD!

I wheeled around to face Leslie. He has vanished. I march through the entranceway to the base of the staircase. Leslie stations himself on an upper landing. I raise my voice to guarantee my delivery.

"You made up the whole rite and Order. I cannot believe I let you humiliate me."

Leslie leans on the black iron railing. He chuckles. "And, if I did?"

The kid's question hints of a dare. Now that I confront

him, my tongue ties in a giant knot. I take a deep breath through my nose and wait.

"Girl, one letter waits your reading and one to write. Time abandons you. I suggest you complete both before we leave tomorrow." And with that said, Leslie climbs the stairs disappearing from view.

My feet drag on the way back to the antechamber. Glumness trails close behind. I change into sleepwear with a heavy weight resting on my shoulders. My body experienced one heck of a beating these last two weeks. The proverbial witch doctor prescribes a long sleep.

I flop backward unto the futon and skim the newly delivered letter. Theodore's letter sounds suspicious. Master Kajika and Leslie are correct. This letter does merit a response.

Supplies lump themselves together in the trunk. Found them before when dressing. Hard to miss pens, paper, envelopes, stamps, ink bottles, and fountain pens among clothing. The plain fact of stacking the writing supplies neatly in one corner helped. Master Kajika made certain the subtle hint wouldn't be so subtle.

I choose pen and heavyweight paper. Better explain a few things in anticipation of my death. My composed letter approximates a short memoir. I crease the paper tightly and tuck it into the envelope. I melt the wax and seal the flap. Weigh the letter with my hand and add a couple of extra stamps.

Theodore's return address should suffice as a delivery address. I copy the info on to the envelope. Now for my return. No apartment or work address anymore. Jim and Tina's place is out of the question, and I'm confident the postal service doesn't deliver to the Jungle of Peru or the Rainforest. I'm guessing my mail will be on hold for the next year too.

After a moment's reflection, I settle on an unobtrusive, plain "S" in the left corner of the envelope. Theodore will know who sent it.

I restock the writing supplies back into the trunk and toss the letter on top of the chest. I'm sure someone can deliver my message. Kajika doesn't come down here. That leaves either Leslie or my mysterious house cleaner. Hope a ghost or Bigfoot is not behind the maid service. I fancy a tangible object to punch should the wish arise. And, no, I don't believe in Sasquatch.

A daunting adventure approaches. Cannot wait to prove myself to Kajika and Leslie in the months ahead. Pleased Master Kajika included new notebooks in the trunk. Bet I fill them before the year expires.

Once in sleepwear, I toss myself on soft goodness. Overjoyed to lay on the futon one last time. Certainly beats jagged rocks jabbing my back. Heaven knows what I'll sleep on in the jungle or Peruvian caverns. But enough of what ifs. I'd better reread Theodore's letter before sleep.

Dear Salomé,

I hope my earlier letters reached you and found you well. I pray when you find the time you'll respond in kind. Let me know how you have been. I bet you have plenty of stories to tell.

My parents came up to visit. I showed them around town, including the village of Rhinebeck. They loved the quaint shops downtown and spent a week's pay on gifts for their neighbors and friends back home.

Both parents mentioned how proud they were of me. The praise made me feel better and happier than I have felt in weeks. Not sure if they liked the seminary. They said they enjoyed their time. I know I was a wee bit bored when I first toured the campus.

Not saying I feel bad at all but remember my last letter when I mentioned Monsignor Smith wanting to speak to me? Turns out my essay on "Fighting the Holy War Within" more than intrigued him.

Besides the assessments, interviews, letters from the local pastor and teachers, test scores, physicals, Baptismal and Confirmation Certificates, I needed to write an essay. Well, at the time last year when I wrote it, I was scared of finally reaching and accepting my dream of the priesthood. After all, the priesthood is a lofty career. I wrote how people could fight their demons and overcome through faith, resilience, and diligence.

The usually submitted articles explain why the person seeks priesthood or what their plans are afterward. The priest said, "Your article stood out above the others." But, that's not the weird part. Monsignor Smith and I talked about my article, thoughts about fear, and life choices dealing with the priesthood. The meeting lasted thirty minutes but felt longer.

When I arose to leave, the Monsignor asked if I thought Demons existed. The question surprised me. I plunked myself onto a chair. He was serious!

He wanted me to answer him if I thought live, physical, breathing demons, presumably from Hell, dwelled in the real world. Monsignor Smith's question shocked me. Didn't know how to answer. I chewed my lower lip before answering. It amuses me how we both share the same habit.

Anyway, I answered, "No way." Imagine, real demons existing.

He slowly nodded and dismissed me. I walked out of the office in a total mind-fog. But that was not the weird part.

Do you recall how we both couldn't sleep some

nights? And we would sneak out and stretch our legs? I happened to walk the same night after the meeting. I broke the curfew and patrolled the perimeter of the seminary building.

The walk usually takes less than an hour and most nights here are quiet. Thirty minutes past the curfew, two men met on one of the benches near the access street. The two people faced each other talking. I saw Monsignor Smith. Nobody can confuse him with any other one here. The second person looked familiar, but I couldn't see him. I hid within the building's shadows and waited before leaving hoping to discover the other's identity.

I waited ten minutes until the second man stood and caught a glimpse of him. The two men shook hands, and the stranger strolled to his pickup. He drove away minutes later.

Salomé, I'm not a hundred percent positive, but I'm sure your dad, Eric, is in Rhinebeck! Once I learn more, I'll write.

God Bless. Sincerely,
Theodore Rumswood

Master Vampires brood occasionally. One doesn't ask why. They can rip your throat out, drink you dry and resume brooding without hesitation.

Kajika loiters each night at the dining room table gazing at two cups of hot green tea, including two pieces of sliced lemons in each cup, complete with saucers. Understand nobody in this cabin honors formal teatime. Not me, not Leslie and certainly not Fernando.

Tonight, we repeat our greetings as we did with previous nights this month.

"Hello, Fernando."

"Hello, Salomé."

I snatch a pair of brown, leatherwork gloves hanging on a hook, grab a fiberglass, pointed shovel leaning in a corner and toss my cloak over one shoulder. With a *pfft*, I vacate the cabin and roam the lonely path leading to the northern cavern walls.

Tonight's evening breeze carries the familiar stench. I despise the humid nights of July. They suck. Wish the rains could come and clean the air. Air so dense the smell drapes the entire park. The stink of rotten carcasses permeates my clothing. Needless to mention, nasty dead animals continue to appear on the dirt trails.

I had hoped the carcass problem solved by now. This cleanup duty makes me yearn to return to the jungles of Peru. *Phew*, and what an experience that was. If I didn't mention it, I survived last year's trials! I'm still shaken up from the experience. And I have no interests in talking about any of it, at least not for now. Maybe in a few months' time if I find a relaxing atmosphere. But I will mention Leslie broke me and built me back up from the inside out.

We both won battles. Leslie won the war. Cannot say I want a retrial. However, I favor the new and improved version. Learned a bunch of new tricks and excelled in subjects I never knew existed. Already miss my four-legged friends, especially Kitty.

However, that's another story for another time.

After my return trip back to the park, Master Kajika asked if I could help with clearing the park's trails. He assured me that the request was voluntary, and I wasn't obligated.

I said, "Sure, no problem." I'm not thrilled about scouting for dead animals. Less crazy about burying their sorry butts. But I don't hesitate to share chores.

Two animals and a partial wild critter buried tonight: a possum, common gopher and parts of what suggests a rock squirrel. It appears unknown creatures attack, chomp into and drain the park animals' blood.

Discarded bodies decay in the open air. The whole scene depicts disgust. Must remember to clean the gardening equipment before returning it back to its corner.

I continue my custodial task for another two hours and zigzag the back trails until I survey the whole area.

After my trek, I officially declare the dirt paths carcass clear. Deeming the chore done. Time to return, wash the dirt off and quench my thirst. I tramp through the underbrush reminiscing.

To date, earlier attempts to locate the exact spot where Kajika and I embraced failed miserably. I thoroughly inspected the area on different occasions and estimated it near the ridge somewhere. Relocating my death spot is a hobby of mine when boredom strikes. I'm curious for sentimental reasons. The separation from the park made me reevaluate and appreciate particular things.

"Report to the cabin," Kajika telepathically commanded.

Uh-huh. Tonight's meandering ends.

Shovel in hand, cloak draping loosely around my neck, I ascend and take flight. Unfortunately, air up here smells as horrible as it does at ground level.

I return the shovel to its corner once inside the cabin. The work gloves I toss on top of one of the wooden pegs. Cloak rehangs on a single hook designed exclusively for the garment.

Specially ordered the hook from a design catalog and shipped it to the gift shop. Tired of seeing the bottom of the cloak dangle on the floor, plus the old nail left marks on the cloth. I scuffle and scrape the boots on the runner while walking to the living room.

"Master Kajika?"

Kajika motions me to join him at the table. The tea set I saw earlier no longer sits on the table. I suppose the famous and expensive tea set is boxed somewhere out of view on a top kitchen shelf.

"Salomé, please sit. I obtained information that might interest you. Your task of caretaker has come to a closed."

I take a seat. "Fernando, I don't mind helping with the chores, honest."

"Leslie and I both appreciate your enthusiasm. You demonstrated maturity these past years. Incidentally, congratulations on passing your warrior training. We haven't spoken much about your adventures. All in good time I suppose. I surmise the necklace around your neck is a gift from Leslie?"

"Yes, he presented it to me after the *Fire Ceremony*."

I attended and participated in several rituals while I resided in the jungle. The Fire Ceremony was one of them.

"Leslie said, 'Necklace is an old family heirloom, passed down through generations, from warrior to warrior.' Unsure what he meant, but I love the necklace," I said, with a hint of pride in my voice.

A silver triangle amulet hangs around my neck, believed to give the wearer protection against disease. With this particular amulet, I'm capable of summoning familiars.

The word "ABRACADABRA" inscribed on top of the necklace skips the last letter on each line as it progresses down until the last line reads, "A." Few of the letters are partially faded away from past wearers gripping and caressing the amulet, a habit I imitate.

"You found someone else to clean the paths?" Cannot imagine who else could do the chore. "What's the story behind these dead animals?" Strange how I didn't officially ask about these critters. I jumped right into voluntary cleanup duty. Go figure.

Master Kajika stalls. Does he not want to explain?

Fernando rises. His sports jacket hangs folded in thirds with the exposed inner liner on the chair's back. He withdraws an envelope from a jacket pocket and holds it close. He refolds and replaces the jacket on the chair's back.

Kajika seats himself. The manila envelope lies on the tabletop under his folded hands.

"Remnants resemble a starved kangaroo but one-sixth its size. Complete with a thick tail and protruding fangs, they can and do attack any species they wish. To date, for an unknown reason, remnants have yet to attack humans. I speculate they don't relish human blood. They use an underground tunnel system to travel anywhere in the North and South Continent of America."

Nobody sees these creatures, including me, because they burrow! I assumed a more massive beast leaving the carcasses.

"If not kept to a small population, remnants can cause total annihilation of animals, mammals, and reptiles in the Western Hemisphere. These critters crave more blood than any creature you'll encounter."

Pessimistic about intruders hunting in my park, my home. I could use a new hobby and cannot wait to start. I ask, "How many of these critters hunt in the park? What's the best way to kill and hunt them?"

"If you wish to know more, I suggest you speak to one of the *Wodemannes*, as they call themselves. These hunters are the creatures' sole predator since no known other exists. Although, I speculate a couple flourished a millennium or two ago."

I'm attentive to Kajika's story. The mystery intrigues me. Glad I finally heard the explanation. Heck, in retrospect, I should have figured part of the solution myself. I ask, "Kajika, do you know of these Wodemannes and where may I find them?" Not sure why I want to know. Doesn't matter to me but sometimes questions pop up on their own and I need to ask.

"I know three Wodemannes and heard rumors of several more. They stay to themselves and rarely settle in one locale for any amount of time. I'm sure you understand. In fact, a Wodemanne resided in your apartment until re-assigned and summoned elsewhere.

"I admired his professional hunting skills and his dedicated commitment. We quickly became friends. I must say his departing saddened me. The latest information on this particular Wodemanne's location is the East Coast, New England area I believe."

Memories flash back to the time I first moved into my apartment. I expected the place freshly cleaned and vacuumed. Jim and Tina would have insisted on it. Heck, the tub that Aby said to soak and relax in also sparkled clean. I remember commenting it shone as if Eric himself cleaned it.

I can envisage Eric creating the shopping list and someone stocking shelves before my arrival. A cabinet full of teabags, my infamous father the tea lover. Granted, I approved of the grocery supplies but… no wonder Eric was insistent on a third-floor apartment. He already had one.

"Oh, my gosh!" I blurted out, realizing the truth.

A heavy weight lifts from Fernando's shoulders. He stretches with hands laced behind his neck. Stress flows from muscles. His facial features soften. He crosses one leg over a knee.

"Yes Salomé, your father Eric is a Wodemanne," Kajika said in a warm, caring tone. "I obtained notice weeks ago informing me about the location of the past hunter but also to expect another within the year to take care of the single lone remnant who hunts our park. This letter from the Vatican can explain your questions."

I glance at the letter Kajika offers. It looks like official letterhead from the Vatican. They even signed and sealed the bottom. The message starts with a standard greeting, a basic intro, and meaningless political statement. "Expect the arrival of Wodemanne Andrea Abelli," I said reading aloud. The last line reads, "Special instruction: Hand-deliver to Wodemanne Fredrick…"

Cannot count the bottlenecking thoughts. Years of questions, comments, concerns about Eric. Not genuinely knowing a bloody thing about him. One would assume a father could at least offer a tiny clue about what he did for a living to his daughter, but nooo. This Vatican letter explains much.

"How. When. Why didn't you tell me?"

Kajika flinches. It dawns on me. I shouted my question. If no one already knew, avoid emotional outbursts directed toward Fernando Ventré Florez.

Master Kajika shoves his chair from the table and rises to his feet. "Everything has an appointed season and a time for every matter under the heaven," he retorts quoting a biblical verse. Kajika leans forward. Both hands slap the tabletop. I jerk back. The double slap produces a *thud*.

I flinch. A slight cool wave of energy races up my spine. Back muscles stiffen. My body begins to sway; my eyes study prey. I at once recognize the fight-flight response from warrior training and take a deep breath. Now's no time to pounce.

"Sorry," I said.

Kajika calms and reverts to his usual dignified manner. His persona surprises me. I swear Master Kajika demonstrates more patience than a saint. He straightens himself and folds both arms in front of his chest. Fernando's eyes meet mine. His presence dominates the room.

"Salomé, what are we to do with you?"

Since my return from the jungles of Peru, two significant changes happened. Master Kajika now allows me to address him by his Christian name. I can assure you, the practice felt awkward at first. Similar to calling your parents by their given names once you reach adulthood. And more interesting, my vamp body no longer reacts to his commands. I obtained a third-degree certificate in vampirism, as it were.

Maybe I can ask Leslie to print a certificate and frame it for me. I'm kidding. I made my peace with Leslie earlier last year. He and I rumbled more than I care to repeat throughout the entire year and a day. Afterward, we separated and ventured different paths. Leslie said it was essential he relocate to Europe. Naturally, I flew back to the park. I respect Leslie, wherever he lives. Yes, it took a while.

I respect Master Kajika too. Everyone should understand that without me saying it. The connection between me and Kajika is unbreakable.

"Um, use me as a paperweight?" I offer Kajika my brightest smile. "What do you expect? Eighteen years of cluelessness and now you hand me this news. The man hunts for the Vatican of all places!"

Kajika paces behind his chair, arms clasped behind his back. He calculates his next move no doubt. Hope I didn't push his patience too far.

Master Kajika crooks his head. He abruptly announces, "You knew the man cared about you. Some children don't ever get to know their fathers."

"Yea, but—"

"No, Salomé. You forget I hold great respect for your father. You and he ought to work through your issues together." A long pause follows. Content with his reasoning, Kajika reseats himself. He says, "As a favor, I'll grant a chance to do just that.

"By the end of next week, you'll live in New York. Your belongings shipped by private carrier. A safe house provided for you in advance. I'll make the arrangements personally." Kajika rises from the chair and snatches his suit jacket. Wrapping the jacket around his shoulders, he adds one last comment. "Before I forget, do tell Eric—I wish him well."

Master Kajika evacuates the cottage. I linger here, embedded on the chair.

"Huh." What just happened?

After two nights of rest, I accept my predicament. Yes, I forgot about the past between Eric and Fernando. Suspect I hit a nerve at some time amid my comments but why the relocation? Excommunication from the park cannot be a punishment. Maybe something to do with Theodore's letter? But Theodore wrote that letter over a year ago. Things change, people too. Heck, I'm living proof of that.

This spot overlooking the canyon served me well. It took only days to become my favorite perch. In the past, I grew fond of viewing the wonder, beauty and all the fantastic life living here. I'll continue to appreciate the canyon's allurement, but the connection is inharmonious. Tonight, I watch the canyon wearing gray filters. Everything appears duller. I sense the park discharges me. Both of us predestined to drift into different worlds.

The Bandelier National Monument incorporates its new Wodemanne, and I move to another state. The move terminates all my close personal quasi-friendships. Once again, abolished from one park to emerge in another.

Master Kajika finalizes my itinerary later this week. I'll broaden my horizons and ship off to the East Coast. In a week, I hang out with Theodore. Wonder what mischief a vampire and priest can manifest in New England? The mere thought makes me chuckle.

This plan includes meeting with Eric. Plenty of words reserved and planned for dear ol' Dad. Hope his abilities succeed beyond hunting down burrowing critters because I plan to drop one heck of a mind-dump on him.

Meanwhile, limited nights left to enjoy my perch and park.

CHAPTER 20

The clang of the padlock indicates eight-thirty, sunset. Master Kajika awaits on the other side. He promised last night he would see me off. I know no reason to delay the inevitable longer than necessary. In anticipation, I dressed and slid my latch forty-five minutes ago. As much as it pains me, I'm all set to leave.

This park means everything to me. I first arrived after high school graduation and grew into a person I barely could have foreseen. In all that time, living in this park made me compliant. Time to expand this girl's horizons.

"Please Fernando, enter." The door swings open as if a ten-year-old pushes the massive door's weight aside.

Master Kajika says, "I don't mean to rush you." Kajika stands at the doorway dressed in a simple two-piece suit. Casual attire for him. He wears this outfit when he lounges on the couch, his jacket folded over a nearby chair back. Fernando dislikes wearing sweat suits in the house or anywhere else.

"Thought you might enjoy a cup of coffee before your departure."

Kajika hands me a tall paper cup, with a lid, full of hot brew from a local coffee shop. The same coffee brand handed to me by Ranger Aby at the bus station. "This from you or Eric?" I asked, sarcastically.

"One of these nights Salomé, your remarks return to haunt you." Kajika smiles. "But not this one," he said, entering the room. Kajika hands me a letter. "The coffee I ordered specially. I hope you find it to your liking."

I take a sip before accepting the letter.

"Yea. French roast coffee. What's the letter about?" I turn the envelope over three times, no markings on it. "Who's it from, you?" I asked, placing the paper cup on the dresser. Before opening the hefty envelope, I glance at Kajika.

"Acquired the letter yesterday from the park's new Wodemanne before he moved into his apartment. The envelope and contents within are from your father. You'd best read them. Your itinerary for tonight's journey is enclosed."

"I can handle myself without Eric interfering. How hard is it to fly to New York?" I debate on either drinking coffee to calm nerves or shred the letter. A few seconds pass. I glance up to recognize Kajika's expression and slide my right index finger across the inside of the flap.

"What, is Eric nuts?" I exclaimed, after reading the pages.

I hold eight handwritten pages, front and back, of bio-dad's rhetoric. The ninth page is typed, complete with bullet points. Father of mine is crazy. Eric used PowerPoint to design my itinerary!

"Thought you were making my arrangements?" I scan the handwritten pages. "This means Eric knows I'm a vampire. He writes; follow the thirty-seventh Parallel east to meet a truck driver in Virginia later tonight. Make sure to feed before…" I blurt, "Fernando, does my birthfather know about me? The rebirth, I mean."

Master Kajika stands motionless. His arms folded across his chest. Kajika studies my composure. He replies, "Indubitably. Eric is your father. When you and I embraced, you were underage. Far younger when I first entered your dreams. I insisted on parental permission before any intrusion on my part."

"What aren't you telling me? What else is happening?" I toss Eric's pages on top of my dresser and grab the coffee. The exchange is uneven, but it works in my favor.

"Why the questions? Something else is always happening. Your earlier lessons and training should have taught you that."

My middle finger flips the cup's lid off. The plastic cover tumbles through the air. I take another sip.

"Your father and I spent hours on the phone providing you safe transport to New York. This relocation differs from your jungle stay.

"Rumors abound of the national government already sheltering at least one alien lifeform in underground labs below Washington DC. They don't need a vampire too. Unless you wish to haul your own trunk, fly over the Capital, and end up on a laboratory slab with scientists examining you. I suggest you adhere to your father's meticulous schedule."

Fernando didn't need to trail off his sentence. Nobody pokes me with a stick and lives to tell the tale.

"OK. You made your point! No hovering over the Capital." I gulp down the rest of the lukewarm coffee and retrieve the lid. After shoving the plastic lid inside the cup, I place it beside Eric's letter. "These letters mention a truck driver. I should trust this man?" I mirror Kajika's position and fold my arms. "A human I know nothing about?"

"You should trust your father. Both of us labored long hours on these decisions. If Eric trusts this driver with his and your life, then I'm sure you'll stay safe." Master Kajika relaxes his arms and smirks. "If danger befalls you while in his care; I'll retaliate and rip his throat, bleed him quicker than he can blink and shred his body into tiny pieces. And that's smaller pieces of what you thought of doing with your father's letter."

Oops. Guess I thought too loud again. "Thanks, but no. I can take care of myself."

"Of that, I also have no doubt." Fernando scans my room. "I'm pleased you packed your belongings but you'll want your sleepwear and a change of clothes. Best to carry them in your backpack. I'll see the rest of your belongings reach your new establishment by tomorrow night."

"Don't mean to change the subject, but Eric knew I would become a vampire since my grade school years?" What am I, a pawn in my father's chess game? I bury my temper. I'll unleash it later at the perfect opportunity. "Does Theodore know about my rebirth too?"

"Your parents prepared your opportunity to embrace the night. I cannot discuss this any further; it's not my story to tell. As for your friend, no. Not that I'm aware of."

Master Kajika strolls out of my cell. Kajika says, "If you pack your stuff quickly, we can spend an hour together upstairs. A couple of tales await if you wish to listen."

Stories from Kajika tonight? "Sure. Love to hear a tale or two! I'll be ready by the time you reach the top of the stairs." I'm lucky my backpack lays reachable on the side of the trunk. I jump into super vampire speed, open the chest, grab what I want, and slide belongings into the backpack. I race through the basement.

Kajika vanished out of sight.

Good thing I don't gamble.

~

Eric's itinerary says to fly the thirty-seventh parallel east and join up with a truck driver on I-95. The starlight blurs the bullet point. I reread the directions. They now read, "Stay under two hundred feet altitude and head straight to Virginia Beach. Hunt. Watch the Atlantic Ocean—then—ride in a stinky truck to New York."

Heard of a strange phenomenon occurring on this route. The thirty-seventh parallel is home to all kinds of unidentified flying objects. Conspiracy theorists believe it's a UFO highway. Why educated people conjure outer space aliens staying in their space-lane when visiting earth beats me. Common sense would dictate the phenomenon is unknown weather patterns or unknown government aircraft.

Eric designed this route in my favor. If any airport controller spots me flying fast on their radar, they'll list me as an unknown bleep. Unless an underpaid federal employee wants to fill out a bunch of paperwork, nothing more will happen.

My driver meetup is at four-thirty am. Figure thirty minutes of scout time and improvisation once I arrive. That leaves me with plenty of beach time and enough left over for recon. Eric may trust this driver with his life, but bio-dad doesn't sleep helpless, dead-to-the-world. No way in heck am I blindly trusting a stranger.

Eric's letter states to trust his experience. Like to know what training or skills he has. Why should I believe his expertise? Heck, it was only a week ago I learned Eric possessed any hunting skills. Love to see him wrestle jaguars, communicate with ocelots and command famil-iars. My jungle education tops any of his adventures. Although, I have seen Eric's organization skills. He makes an ingenious project manager. Maybe I can follow his list and back it up with what I know, always a good idea to play it safe.

"Salomé, you ready?"

Fernando changed attire since our chat. He struts a checked, dark-blue, tailored, two-piece suit, black silk shirt, and black tasseled loafers. Hair product keeps his hair tight. "Gorgeous suit. You're still escorting me, I hope." I lower my backpack to the lobby floor.

"A change of plans, but yes. A casual business meeting which I cannot postpone needs my immediate attention. We travel together until we reach Costilla near the border. You fly solo at that point."

I tuck Eric's papers in an outside backpack pocket. We exit the cabin, and I fasten the backpack tightly behind me. The dull night air shows no mercy for my departure. This part of the story ends. The proceeding nights were a prologue, which nobody read or cared about.

An indigo cloak with black piping and double fasteners complete tonight's outfit and covers my backpack. All set to travel. Fernando and I ascend into the air.

"Master Kajika? Could we circle the park once before leaving?" I asked, with an inward gaze.

Kajika's eyes soften. He spreads his hands wide with open palms. "We can, and will," Kajika replied.

We fly counterclockwise once around the Bandier National Monument Park. A place I called home. Our flight path leads us to higher altitudes. The cold, bitter wind stings and kills any tears forming.

The town of Costilla approaches us. I whisper, "Thank you, Fernando, for everything."

"Be safe, daughter. Good travels." Fernando's unspoken words echo in my mind.

I alter my flight pattern to due east. Fernando said to

locate a few landmarks along the way for guidance. If I reach the shore by three am, my alternate plans will work.

This long flight sucks though. Unlike flying comic book superheroes, I cannot spend time altering body position in midflight. This flight is strictly full speed, straight ahead, or miss my deadline. The upside-down flying, fancy acrobatics and watching the night sky must wait for another flight.

Man, hard to imagine how much life drastically changed. I made friends, lost friends, joined the undead, survived jungle training, experienced the Pacific Ocean through vampire senses, remade new friends, and lost them too. And let's not forget, meeting and training with an Immortal.

Yep. Teenage life certainly has an unusual way of changing a person.

CHAPTER 21

The coastline falls within sight after an approximate five-hour trip. The Norfolk Naval Base lies a good hundred miles west. I adjust flight pattern to treetop height. Parts of my cloak dusts the tree crowns.

I descend on the Virginia Beach boardwalk. A dark-green painted, double-railing, metal fence separates the boardwalk from the beach sand. Lighted lampposts border each side of the walkway. I fly lower and gleefully grab onto one of the boardwalk's lampposts and spiral down it. My "ta-da" moment goes unnoticed. I'm alone.

The beach's gentle roar calls my attention. I stroll over to the boardwalk's edge. The top rail of the barrier serves as a convenient resting place for ocean gazing.

A gibbous moon shines the best she can in the eastern-clouded night sky. The reflected moonlight glistens on wet sand. Ocean waves slap and smother the sandy beach. Pieces of driftwood dance with long ago abandoned shells. A seagull glides over white crest waves. The bird snatches a fish beneath the water's surface.

"Admiring the beach? Got a super deal you cannot

refuse. These timeshares are just what you need. I'll even throw in a free dinner."

"Uh? What?" I said and whip a one-eighty.

The intruder stands over six feet and rail thin. His white linen blend shirt with light-blue vertical strips heightens his appearance. He reeks of cologne. A sales rep!

"You snuck up on me!" I gasped.

"A technique I have worked on for years. If you want to survive, you must master the tricks. The Hushpuppies help. Sorry to say, they fell out of fashion. A real shame."

I step back and glance downward. The intruder wears solid, navy-blue trousers made of breeze cloth, and yep—gunsmoke pigskin leathers with soft, spongey soles. The fashion police should make him swallow the hideous footwear before I shove them up somewhere.

"Name's Penderwaller." He offers me his handshake.

Ignoring the annoyance, I resume my plutonic relationship with the guardrail. The ocean waves crash upon the beach. Good chance a storm approaches. The seagull left the vicinity. No doubt, he enjoys the fruit from his hunt, something I best work on before I go. Mister Penderwaller changes his offered handshake for a timeshare brochure. Why does this man insist on unusual business hours?

The ocean's horizon fixates my attention. Fingers drum on a metal railing. The melody taps the night's song. Words tumble from impatience and hunger. They hook the prey.

"You mentioned a free meal earlier?"

"Actually, a fifty-dollar credit for two in any four of our Virginia Beach restaurants. You can dine at any one of them—your choice. I only need you to read our brochure and complete a simple form." Penderwaller passes me a binder. "The form is on the inside left pocket, right there in front," he said, in rapid sales lingo.

"You want me to read all this? Boardwalk's somewhat

dim." The streetlamps offer plenty of light, although an optometrist would not recommend the lighting. I throw the cloak's left flap over my shoulder. "You don't expect I keep a pen in this outfit, do you?" The man doesn't hear me. I lost his attention.

"Hello?" I said.

Penderwaller fixates on my boots. Either he attempts to discover the hidden zipper, or the pervert x-rays my boots. The idea disturbs me either way. I could read his thoughts and determine his motives, but my brain will thank me if I refrain.

I plea, "Mister Salesman?"

Penderwaller staggers. He blurts out, "Umm?" He regains his composure. When he finally refocuses on my face. He says, "Call me JP, everyone does."

No thanks and I find that doubtful.

"I have a pen, any troubling questions, please ask." Penderwaller reaches into an inside jacket pocket and produces a plastic, two-tone-colored orange and white pen. The line works. "You can keep the pen," he said.

I take the writing instrument. Penderwaller's name, along with his business address and phone number, is imprinted in white lettering. "JP" sandwiched between his first and last name, not that I care. The pen I clip to the brochure's top edge.

"You already know my name. What's yours by chance?" Penderwaller re-offers his handshake.

My hand grabs his hand tightly. "Everyone calls me Dragonessa." The statement is a lie, but Leslie said I could use the name anytime I want. "I have no interest in your timeshares. Penderwaller, look at me." I stare deeply into his eyes and pierce his mind. Now for the sinker.

"I'm about to jab your pen into your jugular and suck three pints of your blood. You may live to see another day or you may not. When—or if—you wake up, you'll recall nothing of our meeting tonight. Do you understand?" The man's eyes glass over. He is mine for the taking.

I remove Penderwaller's jacket and fold it neatly in thirds. The pen pierces his artery. A jagged writing instrument cut masks vampire fang marks exceptionally well. I indulge my appetite and drink deep from Penderwaller. His cologne tastes as bad as it smells. Serves me right for allowing a human to sneak up from behind me. One humongous mistake on my part. My ocean visit doesn't excuse negligence.

Upon removing Penderwaller's jacket, I discover a pocketbook entitled *The Largest List of Sarcastic Remarks & Comebacks*, along with a travel size bottle of whiskey. I empty the entire contents of the container on Penderwaller. If I wish to unwind on the pier tonight before leaving, I better hurry and finish this cleanup.

My newfound book, I tuck into my back waistline and confiscate Penderwaller's wristwatch. I drag his body to a boardwalk bench. Blood oozing from his neck wound should instigate a call for emergency services. With any luck, a stray tourist may find him. If not, he'll expire comfortably resting on his jacket.

I leap over the boardwalk's fence onto the beach. Firm sand supports my feet while strolling towards my next goal. No wet sand surrounds my toes this trip. Instead, damp sand clings to the bottom of my boots. I'm unconcerned. I can knock off any sand residue once it dries. My black, laced up the front, high combat boots with inside zippers makes removal easy, unlike my older pair.

Treasure hunters dug exploratory discovery holes in the sand but no visual litter. Thought that maybe I would find disowned scattered items. The beach cleaning crew worked wonders maintaining this famous tourist attraction. I stroll to the pier and examine moss-covered posts. I'm unsure of the cause. The high-water content in the air might have caused the greenery. Or it's the high tide. One of these days, I'm picking up a tablet. I hate it when I don't know the answers.

The opposite north side of the pier provides cover. I leap onto odoriferous planks. They creak under my weight as I stride to the pier's end. Except for the smell of lingering fish bait, sweaty anglers, and spilled beer, the pier is barren. The angler's shop and security gate trail behind. I continue to the pier's end musing about another vampire perk—no entrance fees. I smirk at the thought and lower myself on dry, cracked wooden boards. My back rests upon a corner post. My feet dangle off the edge. Mind drifts to another realm.

In the far distance, a buoy sways in the ocean's gentle rhythm. The ocean's inhalations and exhalations lull. The white-crescent surf banishes yesterday's footprints. A shrouded voice summons. I listen.

Mother Earth's heart beats. Tender waves slap the pier's supporting structure. Chlorophyll-brined mists blow off the ocean's surface and tickle my nose. My untamed mane blows wild. Hair strains attack clandestine enemies circling from behind. This general wishes solitude before the major assault. The troops can handle this sortie. A hairbrush stands ready. Its attentive bristles specially trained for the post-battle debriefing. Trusty hairbands stay on call if in need of added support.

This second ocean trip differs significantly from my earlier one. The time Kajika, Leslie and I spent at Santa Barbara felt structured. Doom and punishment from Master Kajika or Leslie hovered over me too. Cannot forget the Pacific Ocean's first impact. I buried the awfulness of the past trip deep in my memories. However, I assure you, the ocean on the east coast also offers her stunning beauty. This time, I relax in solitude. I feel content and centered. An inner fulfillment calms my being, despite my lack of words.

An awful shame this one night cannot last forever.

Red lights flicker. The bright intrusion quickly joins blue strobe lights. They both interrupt a peaceful evening. The commotion on the boardwalk draws a crowd. Someone spotted the body and called for help. My earlier intruder may live another day. I didn't hear any screams originating from the boardwalk. Guess an employee called from the hotel. If Penderwaller's watch is correct, time for me to leave.

I toss the watch into a passing wave and leap back onto the boardwalk. I walk innocently to a side street leading to the other side of The Best Western. A side service ledge from one of the vendors serves as a table for my backpack. The long flight and salt breeze destroyed my hair. I better revive it and make myself presentable before my next bullet point.

Standing taxis line the sidewalk around the corner. I scurry and profile each driver. If I'm to reach my destination on time, I need a specific chauffeur. I jump into the back seat of the third taxi in line.

"Where to, lady?" As I expected, the driver is all business.

I unzip a side pocket of my backpack and withdraw the money Eric sent with his letter. A particular singular bill interests me right now. I flip through the stack and pass the driver a bill through the service window. "Destination is written on it. Two more Benjamins for you if we arrive within sixty minutes without any issues."

The driver examines the hundred-dollar bill. He checks the destination and then the bill itself with a currency marker. The driver checks his rearview mirror. He asks, "Conversation or music?"

I ignore his reflection and reply directly to his physical body. "Nope, neither." The driver's slight unconscious tremors and movements interest me far more than courteously. Tonight doesn't allow time for two victims. "Quiet works for me."

"OK then. Straight to Wakefield, No problem."

My taxi pulls away from the curb. The first taxi driver on line wakes up long enough to realize he missed a fare. Other waiting taxi drivers wave their arms in disgust. Guess they expect the public to use the first available taxi no matter what.

Cab drivers should read Sherlock Holmes in their spare time. Holmes instructed Watson a couple of times. "In such times of danger, one should take neither the first nor second cab to present itself." Besides, my driver is Bob Coffey. You can trust a person named Bob. I picked the right driver. So far—so good.

Penderwaller's blood cured the hunger. But my long flight here caused jet lag. I twist and wiggle the cloak from under me and fold it neatly on my lap. I pull the stolen book from the small of my back and relax. The backside title, *The Largest Lists of Made-up words, terms & phrases*, does not interest me. A double-sided book filled with useless information. The book complements my next reading material. I memorized my itinerary before leaving New Mexico but skimmed over Eric's handwritten pages. Figured, now's a good time to read what he wrote. But I don't expect worthy information from his letter.

Fifty-four minutes later, the taxi rolls into the parking lot of a 7-Eleven convenience store. "Pull over there on the side, please," I said, leaning up to the inside partition. The outside store cameras record the front doors and street side. "Drop me off here. Thanks." I hand the driver two hundred-dollar bills for the $180 fare. "I'll wait until you check them." He hesitates in insulting me, but business is business. The gold strip appears on both bills. I blurt, "Have a good night."

Grabbing my backpack and cloak, I run into shadows before Bob realizes I bypassed the store's front door. I leap in the air and cover a mile's distance quicker than the taxi can change gears.

nother low flight path west takes me to exit thirty-seven on I-95. I follow the interstate north four miles to meet my next driver at the Davis Travel Center. Eric wrote, "Find *Carolyn's Freight & Removal*. You'll know the truck when you see it." I'm unsure what he meant by his last statement. Fortunately, my father included where the driver will park the truck and a brief description. A quick flyby of the immediate area informs me my ride arrived. I land on the roof of a nearby motel chain to scout the parking lot and reaffirm my suspicions.

One dark blue Mac sleeper cab semi-tractor idles in the back corner of the lot next to a lamppost. Accurately described in Eric's letter. Fourteenth bullet point if anyone is interested. "You'll know it when you see it" refers to the invisible luminescent lettering on top of the sleeper cab. The writing is for vampiric eyes unless you're one of the limited humans who can see ultraviolet light. The heat from idling engines prevents seeing inside the truck. Heat rises, if I want to learn more, I need to approach the truck at ground level.

I calculate my next landing base at two feet behind the truck's flatbed bumper. Cannot chance running through the field separating the motel and parking lot. Also, want to avoid catching dried seeds on my boots or trousers. One good planned leap should do the trick. I'll add enough jump height to prevent any forward momentum. Falling into a greasy truck's bumper isn't the right way to start my road trip. I hope to land in proximity to the truck's blind spot.

Bird craws a mating call on the next building roof. Time to make my move. The interruption causes no concern, but I envision the sound of a starting gun. I'm off and leaping. I figured my vectors correctly and land on my mark.

I'm close enough to join the night's shadows. Doubtful the driver noticed my landing but the welcome mat I stand on hints he knew my methods and planned my route.

A year ago, I would have screamed bloody murder, and ripped the darn mat in quarters. Send each piece into the four winds, then wipe my feet on someone's face. But I learned to tamper emotional outbursts. I also learned not to become bait. Just because the mat lays under my feet, doesn't mean I should announce my arrival.

I at once squat and scan the area once more. Vampiric sight surveys everything. Infrared works better closer to the ground. The welcome mat shows a slight heat signature. Nobody touched it since daylight. Nothing buried underground near the truck and no tripwire anywhere. The ultraviolet spectrum shows people inside the travel center. A blue light glows on this truck's passenger door. I take another precaution before sneaking around the side.

I breathe in the night.

Hate to take an extreme measure this late into the night unless I'm hunting. It's too much dark energy coursing through my body this close to bedtime. Eric scheduled my departure at five am. Sunrise is six-twenty today. Over an hour to meet and greet a total stranger before succumbing to a dead sleep. The thought sends shivers up my spine.

This driver had better know what he's doing. One hour to run from all this and find a hole to burrow into before the sun shines is too short. Darn it, my life in high school was so simple compared to today.

I prepare myself and slink around to the passenger's door. A luminescent message reconfirms I found the correct Mack truck. Invisible to most humans' eyes, three distinct lines written in dark blue are there: knock once—open door—in that order."

I comply with the instructions.

An overly large man with a buzz haircut waits in the driver seat. White t-shirt shows off his biceps. Bet this man deadlifts Sumatran tigers in his spare time. Black cargo trousers cover his tree trunk legs to his combat boots. "Good to see you again. Been well?" the man said, grinning wide afterward. "Hop in and toss your gear in the back. We need to drive on the scale before we leave."

I climb aboard and seat myself on an air-cushioned chair. The door stays open with my backpack in my right hand. Am I supposed to remember this man?

"Who are you?" I asked.

This driver dresses in casual combat gear, and presumably, he kicks major butt. But, what's his specialty? If he drives a commercial truck for a living, then I'm a goldfish.

"Don't recall your old school bus driver? Two years of driving you back and forth from Jim and Tina's front door. Your high school, ninth and tenth grades if memory serves."

What? My school bus driver?

"Wore a beard and body was much leaner. Packed extra muscle since then, what do you think?" he said, flexing an arm. "Shaved the whiskers off too, cannot blame you for forgetting. Everyone forgets their bus drivers unless the driver's drunk or stoned."

"And you work for Eric?" I asked in disbelief.

"Yep, several years now. We team up on occasions. Wodemannes prefer solitude, but we also work together." He glances at the passenger's door. "Your father thought the lettering on the roof would offer us an introduction. The acronym, ACE stands for Andrea, Cadmael, and Eric." I wait for further clarity. "Eric, your father. Andrea Abelli, the new park's Wodemanne, and me—Cadmael Christos."

Mister Christos offers his handshake.

"Christos?" It cannot be. "You related to Gabe?"

My driver laughs.

"Father grew a liking to you. He's glad to have shared his stories with someone else for a change. He says to stop by any night. And yes, he knows." Mister Christos chuckles. "I'm ol' Gabe's number one son. Call me Chad. Salomé, it's delightful to reminisce, but we need to roll."

I slam the door shut, toss my backpack on the back bunk, and settle in the chair.

Cadmael says, "Time's half-past four on the button. Eric designed this trip to the minute. We head to the CAT scale next and then hit the road. Your father gave us less than ten minutes to shop from the travel center. We have time to chat, once we're on the road."

"Why the scale?"

"Tractor-trailers are required by law to weigh their loads. That includes our fuel, the load we carry, items in the cab and our bodies. I keep all paperwork legal, no second set of books. I'm fussy in my details. We drive within the posted speed limits too. Nobody stops or detains this Mack, but better safe than sorry."

Cadmael creeps the rig on the scale and sets the air brakes. He speaks into an intercom. A moment passes, he drives off and parks the rig pointing to the exit. "Weight slip's inside the store. If you want something, now's the time."

"Pick me up a small coffee, milk—no cream or sugar—and a water bottle?" Cannot go in because of the cameras. Eric mandates clandestineness. Eight handwritten pages illuminated my father's demands. For me to waltz in a brightly light truck stop, wearing this outfit and exposing myself to recording cameras could undermine this whole trip. As fun as that sounds, I'll wait it out and see what Eric's up to instead.

"Sure, my pleasure. Girl, consider this truck a Bond car but deadlier. Don't snoop or touch any of the buttons." Cadmael scowls. "I'm serious—it ain't stock."

Fantastic. I ride and sleep in a bomb ready to explode if I turn up the radio. Might as well change outfits and prepare for sleep while we're not hitting potholes at sixty miles per hour.

The truck blurts a short beep. Cadmael returned.

I shout, "Give me a minute!"

Before the driver door opens, I ready myself and plop in the passenger's seat. I dressed in sleepwear and am eager for coffee. A caffeine fix before bed is another vampire benefit.

"Wasn't dressed, thanks for waiting," I said, taking the hot cup and chilled water before Cadmael enters the cab. I plop the bottle in a center console pocket. The coffee cup lid rests against my lips. "What's next?" I take two sips and study my driver. "My bullet points continue from New York."

"The bullet points your father created for me cover eighteen pages. Shortlist considering what could happen." Cadmael places his red, white and blue sixty-four-ounce refillable mug on the floor next to him. "Root beer but half of it is crushed ice." He smirks. "Non-caffeinated, you wouldn't like it. You ready?"

"Yep," I replied, and rest my socked feet on the edge of the dashboard. "Why the extreme safety guards? It's far more than any vampire requires."

"If it hasn't dawned on you yet, you're not 'any vampire.' Your father secretly protected and had you trained for a particular task. Don't bother me with details. Eric inherited that joyful chore." Cadmael glances over and notices my feet on his dash. "You can borrow my pink bunny slippers in the back if you wish."

My feet recoil to the seat's edge. I inhale hot coffee back into my nostrils. "Hey. I'm drinking coffee!" I grab a napkin, clear my nose, and tuck the wad back in the console. His comment was so disturbing, in so many ways. "Since you cannot devolve explicit details, can you explain your truck's tricks?"

"Once we're northbound on the highway, I'll answer your questions before you hit the bunk. 'Bring Salomé up to date' is a bullet point on my list. But if you change your mind about the bunnies, they hide in the side pocket along with my black teddy and I don't mean—bear."

I reel back and cover my head. Cadmael wearing pink bunny slippers and teddies isn't a picture I want to envision. He chuckles at my response. "I'm positive Gabe told you his favorite phrase. 'Keep your thoughts straight and your spirits light.' A long adventure awaits you. Allow nothing—or anyone—to get the best of you." Except for Cadmael's cocky attitude, he mirrors his father. They both sneak words of wisdom into the simplest of phrases.

Cadmael concludes his pre-trip inspection and fastens his seat belt. I brace myself holding on to the side handle-bars. The cab jounces, bouncing back and forth out of the parking lot. The Mack's engines haul us onto the street. Air cushion seats absorb most the impact of the road.

Once we enter the ramp leading to the interstate, I reminisce on the last time I rode shotgun. It was the last week of school. I was in Theodore's car. His Mini-Cooper handles the road better than this truck does. Then again, the poor Coop would poop if it had to haul the flatbed trailing behind us. Did Theodore keep his car when he moved to New York? Maybe I'll ask when I see him tomorrow night. The fate of the Cooper makes a perfect opening question.

Fifteen minutes pass before irritation attacks. I blame the earlier long flight for my present jetlag. After all the flying time I have accomplished, this pavement-bound environment sucks. Hard to believable I ride shotgun in a Mack truck. We move at a snail's pace. I refocus thoughts and scan my immediate surroundings.

Between the overhead and side cabinets, this cab includes plenty of nooks and crannies for storage space. Bet I could store everything I ever owned in here. Heck, a tiny kitchenette hides behind the driver's seat. The water bottle Cadmael bought rests in a cubbyhole on my left. I reach for the bottle and guzzle a third of the cooling liquid. Another sip follows to swish teeth of any coffee residue. I drop the bottle in the side door pocket and lead the Q & A.

"Chad, your company sign painted on your doors advertise you're a freight company. Why haul the portable lawn?"

"Glad you asked, but we'll return to it later. First, our itinerary." Cadmael reaches for his root beer and takes a sip. "*Ahhh*, mouth's dry." Three sips later, he returns the jug to the floor. "We're heading straight to Newburgh, New York, nonstop. I'll park this baby in a Pilot Travel Center like the place we left. You'll be dead to the world by the time we arrive, but I'm maintaining a watch. You couldn't be safer."

"Ever babysit vampire girls? We can be a handful." The question sounds in jest, but I'm concerned. How can I trust strangers? They may mean well but one mishap and goodbye Salomé. "Do you know what's involved, does my father?"

"Business first. You'll have privacy when you awake. I'll park the truck in the back corner of the lot. Head to the woods when you rise. You can shower before leaving. Afterward, you head east to your next bullet point." He checks his wristwatch and double checks the time to the dashboard's timepiece. "Time for your questions."

"I'm good with what you said. I'll stick with the questions I already asked."

"The company name's a front. It doesn't exist. A friend of a friend from a friend of the Vatican filed the papers. The filing includes all government clearances. I haul any equipment we need anywhere. If a rookie cop ever should stop this truck, an immediate call blares on the police radio to release it at once.

"As for the pallets of sod, they're charmed." Cadmael checks his side mirrors and scans the CB channels. Once content, he continues. "Fernando and Eric's miracle. Your Master insisted on elemental protection for you. He didn't want you traveling in a steel container without representing the element earth. Your father did one better and enchanted two of the sod pallets."

"Don't tell me the grass talks."

"If you quiet your mind and listen intently, I'm sure it

does." Cadmael chuckles at his joke. His tone changes. "No. it doesn't." His right thumb points to the back cab. "Notice the custom rods in each corner of the sleeper? Pressurized explosives built-in to each one. If this truck runs into trouble with you in it, the top half of the sleeper blows open, exposing plenty of room for five thousand pounds of moist unwrapped sod rolls to spiral in and rewrap around you. Secondary explosives lock the roof down a moment later. You'll be wrapped tighter than a drum. Doubtful a chainsaw could cut through all the dirt and roots. The privacy curtain comprises a bulletproof material and a charmed handle, which only a vampire can unlock from within the bunk. One complete package of master spellcraft."

"Eric knows magic?" I asked, raising an eyebrow or two.

"Eric and magic? Nope. I credit him because he footed the bill. Your father is a schematic intellect. His specialty is planning, prioritizing and allocating projects. Fernando asked a sorcerer for a favor. She worked her spellcraft for a whole day. An extraordinary job if I say so myself. 'Course the truck has its own defenses; cab bulletproofing, self-sealing tires, four-point deadlocking doors with individual tear gas injectors and total electronic monitoring. You couldn't be safer."

"Unbelievable if you ask me. How long did all this take?"

"Well, I customized the cab two years ago. Extra precautions for your travels took about a week to finish. Could have been done earlier, but I wanted the external paint to match. Don't worry about the invisible lumines-cent paint, it's acrylic and washes off—nontoxic too. When you deal with professionals, and an unlimited budget, things happen quickly."

Wow. Professionals can move mountains. Kajika gave me ten nights notice to pack possessions. Eric did his specialty while I readied myself. I'm aware of my father's organizational skills. So, nothing new about that subject.

"I assume you hid explosives under the bunk?"

Cadmael chuckles. My driver reminds me of ol 'Gabe but with a more robust tenor voice. "Heck no. Nobody in their right mind travels with live explosives on the interstate. Today's drivers cause too many accidents and drive unsafe. Besides, police and Homeland Security use bomb-sniffing dogs. If discovered by the authorities, hidden explosives could cause us unnecessary delays. Rest assured. No TNT or C4 under your bunk." He recharges himself with another sip of his root beer.

"So, your truck doesn't explode? Good, because blasted to kingdom come isn't in my near future." I estimate a long life and want to stay in one piece.

"Didn't suggest that. This baby is primed inside and out with special undercoating. A powered alchemic chemical mixture bonds to everything metal. Our teammate Andrea invented the formula. The guy is a genius when it involves eccentric improvised ammunition. One massive *Kaboom* awaits anyone who activates the receivers buried deep in the dashboard. As long we stay the course, nobody steals the truck, run into trouble I cannot handle, or if your father decides he doesn't like you anymore, we'll survive this trip."

Swallowing hard, I glance at Cadmael's mug. "Why mention Eric and explosives in the same sentence?"

"We send the electronic surveillance and monitoring signals to our satellites. Eric supervises all systems. Your father has his hands on the button, so to speak."

I gawk at my driver.

"You control your own satellites?" I asked while lightheadedness introduces itself. No more questions tonight. I unbuckle my belt and swing the captain's chair toward the center console. Cadmael rechecks all side mirrors, dash instruments, and timepieces. He flips open four red switch covers and slaps a teal colored button on the dash. I'm guessing a signal. Eric's notification perhaps.

"We'll chat tomorrow night. You'll be fine. Shut the partition before collapsing and remember you're the sole person who can open them. Good night."

I mumble a reply, but my mind wanders. If Cadmael has the correct time, and I'm sure he does, I stayed past sunrise by twelve minutes. My body slowly grows stronger. It might sound lame, but it adds up after a hundred years.

Closing the protective curtain, a slight tinge of mystic energy excites my arm hairs. The charmed door handle's sensation is familiar. I felt a similar physic enhancement when Leslie handed me the dagger in the cave. At least I derived confirmation on the magical lock. Cadmael better not hit any large potholes. I don't wish to become a Salomé sod-roll.

I kneel at the side of the lower bunk for prayers. Once finished, I force an extra wakeful two seconds into my prayers.

"Heavenly Father, don't let Eric touch any buttons labeled: *Blow up truck*."

CHAPTER 23

Rain drizzles and puddles outside the window. Elongated crystalline droplets stretch forever before striking the wet surface. Ripples cascade outwards. A troupe of ballerinas swirl. Distant, unfamiliar music plays. Ballerinas spin faster and faster. The stage changes. Several circles appear. A massive stronger ripple impedes the growth of the unprepared. Weaker ripples perish without fanfare. Rings form and stretch into infinity only to collapse.

My imagination drifts. I repose gazing at the cab's padded platinum-colored quilted ceiling. Rainy lazy nights belong to vampires too. I'm thankful I appreciate Mother Nature. Her prevalent wonders, as small as pure rain, I shall always adore. Having my father pause on the "blow up my daughter button" before his morning tea is also a blessing.

Since I'm not defunct, my survival leaves me with one busy night. Cadmael said to grab my gear and step outside for further directions.

Tonight's June air holds both chilly winds and drizzling

rain. I expected neither this time of year. My first night in New York, and it rains. Glad last night's clothing borderlines on the wearable. But I intend on changing later anyway. My pajamas wait inside my backpack. Not that I distrust Cadmael. But why not step out in my sleepwear? Simple, if trouble shows, I'm ready to snap off its head.

I creep out of the truck using the driver's door. Nobody should witness my exit. The rig is parked in the back corner of the lot. Just like Cadmael said he would. A red dot from a laser pointer shines on the ground near my feet. The flash lasts a mere millisecond. I pinpoint the source.

Inching along the length of the flatbed, my back rubs against the trailer's cold metal edge. The smell of fresh cut musty earth arouses my senses. I approach the flatbed's back bumper. My arms tingle. Cadmael forgot to mention at least one detail about his truck's load. What else did he forget to mention?

My chauffeur hides in the southwest woods. I leap straightforward in his direction and balance on a tree branch opposite him. Leaves surrender their rainwater. If Cadmael stayed dry, he's soaked now.

I cross my arms. "Did you forget to explain a detail or two last night?"

"Told you what you needed to know. Nothing more—nothing less." Irritation shows on his face. He shakes off the unexpected shower. "What are you referring to, anyway?" he said, wiping down his arms.

"For one, more than the front pallet's charmed." I hold my ground with arms crossed.

"It's called need to know. And you need not know." He emphasizes each word. "*Professionals* keep backup plans in place." The last emphasis delivers his point.

"So, what's this platform, your tree fort?"

"Hardly. I bought this contraption on Cabela's website.

Handy hammock tree tent with extra support ropes for stability and the netting collapses if I use it for a platform. It's a dream." Cadmael wears an ear-to-ear grin. "Speaking of which, how'd you sleep?" I'm sure he knows vampires don't dream. Death is a more exact term, which again, I'm sure he knows.

I return his grin and bounce once on the tree branch. A gentle rain joins us. I answer, "Slept well. Thanks for asking."

"So, you're pissed. Sue me." I stare him down until he gives up what I want. It takes a full minute. "Fine, act childish. Back four pallets are enchanted, same as the front two. I carry special holy silver, iron, and dragon breathe ammo, not counting my usual stash. And if it makes you happier, your father isn't the sole person with his hand on the button." He reciprocates my stare. "Knowing all this beforehand, would you have slept better or felt safer? Does it matter whatsoever? Girl, you best trust the professionals. We work as a team. We depend on each other."

Teamwork, the one lesson Leslie drilled into me. I understand the concept, but I'm solitaire by nature and species. Old habits are hard to break. It could help if I knew all the team members. Forgot Cadmael was a member of ACE and working with others, including shadowy ones. Although the acronym is singular, I should play along until I talk with Eric.

"Fair enough, what's next?" Cadmael holds on to a support rope and steps forward. We overlook the down-pour. We both know the lousy weather shields us from prying eyes and ears.

"Bullet points have you taking Pilots' backdoor for a shower and change. The truck's jammers block the Wi-Fi cameras. I reserved shower number eight for you. Take this key. Since you travel faster than sight, knock off the red marker flag on the roof of the building before you leave. Unless you want me standing here with a loaded rifle when the sun rises."

"The temptation's great, but no, it's no trouble. Hope you're taking a hot shower too. Dude, you're soaked." Amazes me how professionals go the extra mile no matter what the consequences. "I follow my bullet points from here?"

"Directly after the knockdown, yep. As for the shower, I plan on soaking in a hot tub with my rubber ducky and finish my double shift with a large mug of hot cocoa." He lowers himself on the hammock tent and lays flat on his stomach. His facial expression hides but I bet he's grinning.

Like father—like son, I guess. "One more item, it's not a bullet point, though. My teensy sis, Alena, mentioned you saved her and a girlfriend back in New Mexico. She left out the details, but I want to thank you personally. If you ever need a favor, you got it. No questions asked." He targets the backdoor with his scope. "Safe. Go."

"Chad, good to see you again. And thanks."

"Ditto. Right back at you. And, you're welcome."

Neither of us postpones our duties further. I'm hesitant about long goodbyes. Cadmael is too. I plunge feet first, sliding close to the tree trunk and ricochet off any intrusive branches. From the tree base, I sprint to the back door of the building and test the handle. Unlocked, no surprise. I give a thumbs up and enter. Cadmael allows me ten minutes for a shower and a change of clothes before he raids the place. Plenty of time if I hurry.

Wish the rain stops before my meetup with Theodore. Hate to have him see me looking uncivilized, or worse, a demon from hell. Plan to arrive at the diner early and eat to get a wee bit of color before Theodore arrives. My shabby appearance, I'll blame on the long truck ride, not that he'll notice much. With food, Theodore has a one-track mind.

I unlock shower room eight on my left. Two rolled dry white towels and toilette supplies lay on a wooden teak stool. I toss my backpack into a corner and strip. The countdown starts.

After a warm shower, a quick change of outfits, limited minutes of mirror work, thirty seconds remain of my allotted time limit. I crack open the back door. The rain stopped. I take to the air. One loop around the building's roof and I tilt the red marker.

I take my sweet time flying above the highway east for eleven miles and arrive fifteen minutes early. The I-84 Diner and my destination lies below me. Scratch another bullet point off my list.

Fishkill is rain free. I hope Theodore hurries. Hate to change clothes again tonight. Fantastic luck if the rest of tonight stays rain free, but that's doubtful. A low-pressure wind blows the storm this way.

Peruvian jungle training taught me the hard way, to dispense with non-necessities. A Jaguar attacked me once while I was preoccupied. The fourth change of outfits in one night cost me dearly. All because I wanted to stay in dry clothes. What can I say? The humidity in the rainforest sucks.

I made a new outfit policy that states, "One clothing change per night unless dripping blood creates a safety hazard or if fabric tears show more flesh than I'm comfortable exhibiting." I reserve the right to tweak the policy.

Meanwhile, several parked SUVs shelter me in a southeast-darkened corner. For my next task, I must blend into a small group of humans and stroll up to the front doors like I own the place. A white Escapade enters the lot and solves my dilemma. It carries a party of six. Once they disembark from their tank, I join the back of the pack when the last person enters the diner.

Timed my approach into the diner perfectly. Nobody spots or holds the door open for me. My craftiness continues. I worm around the small crowd, inching my way to the front of the line. I quicken the distance between me and the cameras eyeing the cash register. A scan of the place says wait for an available booth. I turn down counter seating for apparent reasons.

Everyone arrived paired or is dining with friends. Even the counter patrons are eating with other people. I'm the sole single person except maybe the hired help. However, I blame no one for enjoying the food and atmosphere. The gods created weekends to enjoy with others.

My luck holds. Romeo and Juliet stand up and toss their tip on the table. This couple practiced lip locking since I entered. It's incredible they could eat with their mouths glued to each other. They must be newlyweds by their actions. Good guess they'll return to their hotel for dessert. Luckier for me, this couple cozied up in a back booth out of the way. The exact position I hoped to claim. I can also watch the front door from there, a strategic advantage in any restaurant.

I grab the nearest server's attention. "Booth over there is available. OK if I grab it? Thanks," I said before the woman can take a breath.

The server blurts out, "Sure, but it's not cleaned yet." She talks to a kitchen helper. I pay them no mind. I got what I want.

I hurry over to the back corner and plop myself into the booth. Two sets of empty plates lay on the table, along with a ten-dollar bill. The last couple leaves a bountiful tip, almost fifty percent of the tab.

Half tilting a soda glass, two small ice cubes slide out onto the table. I pop both in my mouth without hesitation to cool a dry mouth. Vampires don't worry about catching germs from saliva spittle. I snuggle myself into the corner and blend into the upholstery.

A kitchen helper stops and clears the table. He wipes the surface and goes on his way. I reach for a handful of paper napkins from the table dispensary and dry the table.

A server says, "What can I get you, dear?" Her nametag reads "Shirley."

Cannot lounge in a busy restaurant at an empty table and hide in stealth. I say, "I'm waiting for a friend. In the meantime, I'll have a coffee and the cheeseburger platter."

If any employee should question my eating habits tonight, I tell the server a lie. "Feeling a little sick tonight. This corner seems dark and quiet." A force smile precedes my request. "Can I have a little privacy and have the check now?"

Shirley double nods. She says, "I'll fetch your coffee and your receipt if you're finished ordering. I'll make a separate bill for your friend when they arrive." She scoots off to place the order.

I say, "Thanks Shirley," and hold in a snicker. Why did the old television shows always have a waitress named "Shirley" in them? If I see a waitress named "Alice," I'm losing it.

Another server, her name tag says "Ann" comes around with the coffee. Ann swiftly arranges a hot mug, spoon, and three creamers. The server then walks off completing her rounds. I recall a couple of TV waitresses named "Ann" too, and hope this one is no vampire slayer. However, typecasting amuses me.

Three fingers pinch both my lips tightly shut. Roaring laughter wouldn't serve my incognito visit. But sometimes, you have to laugh. I reach out with a free hand and hold a white ceramic mug. Hot Columbian coffee releases a much-needed aromatic distraction.

Coffee smells good. I take a sip. Fantastic! A fresh pot. My luck tonight continues. It'll be another ten minutes before Theodore arrives, plenty of time to relax and ponder.

With popular Hollywood horror movies, scores of vampire and werewolf books filling bookshelves, I stand a chance of anonymity. Nobody expects a real-life monster to patronize a family restaurant.

Kajika and Leslie said all kinds of mystical creatures roam the planet. The public lives in delusion. And, I hope it stays that way. A vampire can hide from governments without worry. But if the total population forms hunting parties, that can complicate things. Then again, knowing kids nowadays, they may ask for an autograph. Maybe getting a wooden stake through my heart isn't such a bad an idea after all.

And speaking of steaks, an order of prime rib awaits a hungry teenager. She sits two tables away from the register and is about two years my junior. Almost impossible for her to finish her slice of a cow in one seating. Her server should have known better than to let the girl order it. A good four inches of the meat hangs over the edges; even the plate cannot hold the steak. Meat's extra thick and on the rare side. Strange how I didn't notice the girl when I passed her booth. I lower my gaze before she catches me staring.

My order arrives and I lie to Shirley once again. "Everything's great." She includes the check with the platter. "Thanks again," I said with a fake smile.

Food could be appealing under different circumstances. The long truck ride bothered my nerves. Glad no bright overhead lamp exposes my facial expressions.

My earlier fib fails as an excuse to return food un-eaten and untouched. Although the coffee I can sip while chatting with Theodore, I cannot perform stomach-relaxing exercises here. Meat and potatoes might cause me *refeeding syndrome*. And vomiting in a diner creates one heck of a disturbance.

The burger I break into pieces and spread the fries. A massive squirt of catsup breaks up the white space. A lame coverup but it serves my purpose. The technique doesn't fool parents, but a server is uninterested in your eating habits or health.

I twist and turn in the booth to check the diner's windows. No sign of any incoming traffic that I can see. I better review my plan before Theodore arrives.

I figure the server will remove my plate when Theodore enters. Theodore will deduce I finished my meal. I then order a java refill. He orders half the menu while I caress my coffee mug. We chat and have a pleasant time. The plan should work out fine. But I need to *finish* my plate here first.

After ripping the steak fries in half, I scan for the abnormal. Would hate it if lousy luck ruins my night. People come and go. The coffee mug pushes on pursed lips.

The girl with the humongous steak stares in my direction. She displays her empty plate. Every scrap, including fat and grizzle, eaten. A single streak of prime rib juice lingers. All strange enough, right? Her index finger wipes the rest of the sauce. She licks her finger in an un-ladylike fashion. A hint of exposed fang shows through plump lips. She winks.

Somehow, I blew my cover. By the time I reach into my pocket to leave a ten-dollar bill on the table, she disappears.

The hunt is on.

Vampires can fly. We also move so fast to the human eye we can almost be invisible. Trust me; both are hard to do in a busy diner loaded with patrons.

I bolt through the diner keeping my feet on the tile floor.

Two things stopped me from catching the junior vamp. The girl was much faster than I first expected, and I ran into Theodore when he rounded the corner. Good ol' Theodore. He's right on time.

Leslie would kill me for this mishap. I forgot to focus and prepare myself before tramping out of the diner. I offer no defense. My response was stupid and a beginner's mistake.

Calming my temper, I help Theodore to his feet.

"What the heck!" Theodore pushes my efforts away. He says, "Never mind. I'm all right." Acute vampiric hearing notices a disturbance in his voice. His comment isn't entirely accurate.

"Sorry, I'm experiencing an upset stomach." I reassure my best friend, "Had to run before vomiting." Add another lie to the growing list.

Theodore wears a simple black polo shirt with black dress slacks, black loafers, and a black overcoat. The latter dampened by the wet sidewalk. A light drizzle hit the area. Guess I missed its arrival.

"Well, good to see you. You have changed little since graduation. Except for the blue, hooded cloak, you haven't changed at all. You been well?" Theodore said, rising to his feet.

"No complaints. You appear well, wet clothing aside. You OK?"

"We'll catch up on the ride back. I phoned in our order before I left. It should be ready. Do you want to add to the order? Your father's treat." Theodore pauses for my response, his back toward me. He expects a quick, "No."

I study Theodore's posture and test his patience. "Sure. Order me two coffees, chocolate milkshake, a large order of cheese fries, fried onion rings and liver with anchovies. Thanks."

Theodore plants his shoes on the wet pavement. Both his fists and legs tense. He tilts his head. "You don't eat anchovies. You hate the stuff!"

"Yea, but if Eric's buying," I said, with words trailing. "All I want is coffee." I offer Theodore my best grin. "I'm dumping the rest."

He refuses the bait. Theodore lowers his head. He says, "I'll add a coffee to the order. You can drink it in the truck. In the past years, you haven't lost your attitude, have you?"

I boast, "Nope. Same old, same old. Nothing's changed much."

Theodore buries both arms deep into his coat pockets. He talks stiff, matching his stance. He asks, "You drive or come by taxi?"

Is this an interrogation?

"No car. Eric's list said to meet you here. I'm here." Heck, now I think of it, I have no driver's license, credit cards, or photo identification. Add another item to my discussion with Eric. Maybe he can create a special package. He works for the Vatican. He could obtain a Swiss Passbook or better yet, diplomatic immunity. Now, that would rule. "You know me, free-spirit. I go where the wind blows."

Hope I sound normal. I'm pissed about the vampire

imp. Curious to know why she was eating in the diner. Master Kajika mentioned no creatures to fret over in this area. Vampires roam everywhere, including the Hudson Valley. I shouldn't act surprised to spot a fellow *Nighter*, but her wink showed a tease, not a greeting. I best keep both eyes open for any more unwelcome visitors.

"Meet you by the truck. I parked it under the light. The order shouldn't take long." Theodore sulks towards the diner and enters. He removes his overcoat when the door closes behind him.

Guessing a five-minute wait at least. Theodore said to wait under the bright light. Slim chance that'll happen anytime soon. I'll tell Theodore I wanted to stretch my legs before the ride. It's a good excuse as any.

I dash behind the diner.

Fragrant hints of expensive perfume linger in the mists. The imp's scent. The girl has money to afford this stuff, or she prefers to vampire-shop at private perfume booths. Whatever the case, I need to discover if she returned to haunt. And, I need to do it before Theodore returns. Having a strange vampire attack could be catastrophic. Theodore's one of the last remnants of my past human life. It would tear me apart if he found out the truth.

The night sky welcomes my presence. Dense mists and fog veil me against any intruder on the ground. Although no rightminded person ever looks up in bad weather, I should hurry.

A counter-clockwise spiral survey pattern may cause dizziness but better safe than sorry. Using full vampiric sight and the limited minutes allotted, I scan the diner and the surrounding area. I recheck my findings and assume nothing.

The imp cannot be a pure vampire. She traveled at a

fantastic speed, leaving no trace of herself except the scent of her perfume.

Three minutes of airtime later, I cover a ten-mile radius and believe the airspace on both sides of the interstate clear. I descend back to my original landing spot. No one arrived or left the lot since my absence.

My distraught friend will make his appearance within the minute. The cashier takes his money. Parts of his overcoat show through the glass doors. Best to return toward the truck before Theodore asks questions.

When Theodore arrives, I say, "Guess you couldn't drive the coop all the way to New York. Does this F250 Super Duty pickup belong to you? Doesn't exactly say—priestly." Don't mean to insult him but this monster isn't Theodore.

The sound of double beeps. Theodore unlocked the doors. I wait outside until he places the bags in two empty milk crates on the floor behind the driver's seat. "Door's open. Hop in," he said.

Theodore stares out his window adjusting the side mirror. He subconsciously taps the steering wheel with his fingers. The tumble pissed him off royally. But in all fairness, I did apologized and said I was sorry.

Bet he wanted a comfortable, and dry, dinner date with a table full of food. I, at least, looked forward to our meeting. Well, the dry part anyway.

Strikes me strange why Theodore ordered take out before he arrived. He knew we were meeting for dinner. Guess plans changed. "Look, about earlier," I said.

"Forget it. All set?" Theodore directs his reply toward the dashboard. He fumbles clicking the seatbelt.

"No. What's going on tonight?" I pivot in the passenger seat and face Theodore. "I want answers." The position reminds me of last night's meeting with Cadmael. Are males ever upfront?

Theodore twists. The steering wheel digs in his side. He grimaces. His moody appearance transfigures into pure disgust. "You distrust me of all people? Did you believe you could deceive me? I know——" He reaches and flips two switches above the center console. Bright LED dome lights beam down filling the cabin with a light blue hue. "You're a vampire!"

Theodore's emotional outburst heightens my reflexes. I at once reach for the door handle and manage an exit before the doors lock. Four automatic clicks follow a slam of the passenger door. I'm out of Theodore's immediate reach. But now what? He knows about me!

Damn it.

Theodore knows.

CHAPTER 24

In a single heartbeat, a loyal friendship dies. Daggers, made from a trusting relationship, stab internal organs. A colossal wave of sorrow crushes my ribs. My broken heart tears apart into little pieces. Once healthy muscle pumping blood throughout my body now transforms into blacken ash. Ashes carried away by the four winds. If anyone ever mentioned the undead don't feel pain, these people would be wrong.

I retreat out of the lamplight and withdraw into familiar darkness. The night offers no comfort. Vision diminishes. Tears rob me of sight. Legs buckle and desert me. Fearing the taste of sadness on my lips, I collapse on the pavement. Insides constrict into a protected ball.

My luck runs out. Tonight's previous rainstorm arrives. Droplets fall. Distant thunderclaps howl my name. The night grieves for my heartbreak.

A familiar phrase interrupts my solitude and desolation.

"Salomé? We need to talk."

I flinch. Kajika? The words help to refocus on the

present. I pull myself together and rise to my feet. My back slouched. Left hand rests on my knee for support.

Rain soaks my clothing. Drenched hair dangles loose and covers my face. I wipe the hair and water away. Exposed fangs scrape against the heel of my palm. A few drops of blood ooze from the slight cut. I lick the precious life fluid. Theodore watches from under a lamppost. I lift my head and glance up in the drizzle.

Theodore's shoes scrape the blacktop. The light rain doesn't deter me from sensing his indecision. Maybe he's allowing me a private moment or maybe he hopes the light offers safety, but either way, Theodore is uncertain if he should advance. My mind played a trick. I imagined Fernando's voice.

I cast off despair and stand erect with both fists clenched. Unfocused words are grumbled aloud. "Who told you what I am?" Arms swing wide relieving tension. My chest cavity fills with air. I bellow, "Who told you I'm a vampire!"

Any bystanders, witnesses and past friends overhearing my outburst are now fair game for a kill. I march up to Theodore.

Six feet separates our physical bodies but it's years that separate our friendship. "You caught me unprepared, but I had my downtime. Explain. Who told you?"

Theodore's life hinges on his answer. Cannot allow him to continue knowing my vampiric nature if he proves untrustworthy. I have too much at stake.

"Eric, Monsignor Smith, and I met a month after I wrote you my third letter. We discussed what's been transpiring for the past year." Theodore's voice tremors as much as the tree branches around us. The rainfall turned misty. However, the wind picked up speed. Theodore pauses his excuse. The back of his left hand wets his lips.

"Events have been happening. You don't understand." The response falls short of supplying the info I want. And I cannot take all night to drill him.

"Theodore, things are always happening. You wanted to talk. Come here…"

I allow him to approach at his own pace. When he reaches arm's length, I grab his coat collar with both hands and toss him eight feet into the shadows. Protected by darkness and hidden away from any prying eyes, Theodore lies flat on his back on the ground.

I straddle him at his waist and lower myself down onto him. My knees touch and rest on the wet earth beside his chest. I let Theodore feel my weight on him before I pull his collar and lift his head off the ground. I snarled in his face with exposed sharp pointed fangs.

Theodore stutters, "Don't. I didn't." His brain experiences spatial confusion. His present uncertainty benefits my plan. I tilt Theodore's head downwards. The awkward position forces his eyes to strain. The added eyestrain will hinder him if he manages any internal resistance.

"You're safe here. Rest and look at me. Deeper, breathe and relax. Allow yourself to drift and go to your safe place. And breathe." A vampire's rapid induction takes less than a moment. If I wanted to read Theodore's mind, I would use another technique. For now, I'd rather hear the story in his own words.

After long minutes of questioning Theodore, I'm satisfied with his continual loyalty. My concern now lies with my friend's safety. "When I release my grip, take a deep breath and keep your voice low." I step backward. "What did Eric ask of you?"

Theodore falters on the grass. He's unbalanced and disoriented. I allow him a moment. "Keep *my voice* low? You already woke everyone up for miles around with your yelling!" He massages his neck. Theodore's lucky I kept his questioning short. His mind should clear in a moment.

"Bugger girl. What did you do?" After a moment, Theodore returns to his old self.

I offer him my hand. "Need help?"

"No. I can stand on my own. Thanks." Theodore stands and removes his jacket. He inspects his clothing. "Twice in one night? Dirt, mud, a slight tear, and grass stains?"

"Yeah, well, sorry about that. I'll buy you a new one." Heck. I ruined all of his clothes tonight. "You want me to take care of the dry cleaning bill too?" I asked, half-jokingly.

"With what! You don't work—do you?" Another outburst? "Forget it. I'm not mad about the clothes." Theodore stomps right pass me and heads towards the pickup. He whips around.

"No matter what the size or importance, we all hide secrets from each other," he said, in an assuring voice. "Do you remember the freshman in school who you insisted ate his peanut butter and jelly sandwich with the jelly side upwards? You swore he checked and rechecked his sandwich before every single bite. You commented on how he kept the jelly side up the whole time while chewing. You remember the dude?"

I stand dead to the world with wide eyes. This condescending lecture had better lead somewhere.

"Well, he may have been a stranger to you, but he's my cousin. I was unhappy with you teasing him. I said nothing. He and I weren't close, but it goes to show I have kept secrets from you too." Theodore breathes deep and uprights himself. He adds, "I'm upset because you tried to hide from me. Me—of all people! After everything we did together. Vampirism is no big deal unless you make it one."

Father Theodore trying to offer priestly comfort? My, has he changed. But I have too. "Vampirism *is* a big deal. Movies don't portray the whole story, but I'll drop this for friendship's sake, for now." Tonight isn't the time to teach him Vampirism 101.

Patrons exit the diner. They head in the opposite direction from where we stand. Luck held while Theodore and I had our private discussion, but luck doesn't last forever. I repeat my earlier unanswered question.

"What did Eric get you into?"

Theodore replies, "Fair enough. I'll drop this too, but we'll talk in the truck. Food's getting cold and people wait for us back at the lodge." He walks around to the driver's side and hops inside the pickup. I straighten my soaked clothing and trail behind him.

I get in on the front passenger side and adjust the seat. Theodore hands me my coffee. I say, "Thanks" and remove the plastic lid. The coffee cooled. I offer him a blank stare. He lowers my window. "Where're we heading?" I asked, tossing the cold brew out.

The seatbelt clicks and I check out the truck's interior. Beige leather covers seats and dash. The new truck smell mixes with strong hints of testosterone. I smell Miss Fang's perfume in the cabin too. Strange how her fragrance lingers. Theodore had better dry-clean her scent off his coat.

We leave the parking lot and drive onto a secondary road. Theodore quickly turns onto I-84.

"We're heading to Rhinebeck, be there in about fifty minutes. You can see the Kingston-Rhinecliff Bridge from the lodge. The building has no formal name, but I nicknamed it, *The MT B&B*. The place feels empty."

Theodore waits for a reply. I pay him no mind. His lame joke fades as fast as his tight grin. He says, "I take casual strolls in Ferncliff Forest nearby, so please hunt south or cross the river." Theodore flips a dashboard switch and bright yellow fog lights beam down the highway.

"Thanks for the info," I said, twisting around and checking the interior of the truck. If I thought lingering perfume was strange, this is stranger. Video cameras hide in secret places: in the far back corner speakers, in the dome light above the second-row bench seats, and microphones in the top ceiling trim disguised as plastic fasteners. Spyware matches the equipment I discovered up front with us. I eye one of the hidden cameras near Theodore. "This truck belongs to Eric, doesn't it?"

Theodore blurts out, "Why the concern over the ownership?" He squints and waves a hand in the air. "Fine. I give. Eric told me to drive it tonight. Said it would be safer for you. First time I'm driving this monster, so give me a break." Stress tightens his voice. "Bugger this night. I miss my Mini-Cooper."

"Nothing, just wondering." I relax in my seat and focus on the microphone buried in the dash air vent. "You abandon the coop back home with your parents?"

Theodore turns off the interstate and onto a secondary road. "Had too, school policy, no student cars."

"I'm sure it's fine. You're doing fine with the driving." I beam my vision down the foggy two-lane roadway. "Although, you may wish to give the dude on the scooter some extra room."

The truck swerves a bit. "What scooter? I can barely see the edge of the front hood in this weather." He corrects steering and slows. Theodore's steering grip widens. Knuckles whiten.

"Relax. The man drives five miles down the road around a bend. I'll shout when you get close."

Theodore shoots me a look. "You pierce through the fog, and around bends?"

"Vampires can see, hear and sense all kinds of stuff. Speaking of which," I said leaning toward the dashboard.

I speak into the nearest concealed microphone. "Dear Santa, we both need showers and clean, dry clothes. Buy Theodore a new jacket. I want coffee. You know how I like it." I stretch back and ponder. Is there something I missed? Eric's bullet points didn't list Theodore's revelation, running into another vampire, and jeopardizing a friendship. Items I can deal with later. Nope, I'm good. I lean forward and add, "Oh yeah. Dear Santa, I want a pony."

"What was that gibberish? You're acting weird. You OK?" Theodore hunches over the steering wheel. A jacket button rubs against the leather-wrapped steering wheel. He tries to spot the scooter that drove onto another street. Human vision cannot penetrate this thick fog. But he still tries. Tonight's stressful driving takes a toll on him. I can save my antics for another night.

"Nothing. Just clearing my head with levity, after a long trip." What is one more lie to my growing list? "From what you said, we have ten minutes before we arrive. What did I miss? The scooter turned into a driveway. You got a clear road ahead."

Theodore leans back and relaxes his grip. He does weird squirmy movements with his shoulders and derriere. "With these road conditions, I figure a good fifteen, but OK. Where do you want me to start?" he said, after settling into his seat.

Good question. "The last strange letter you wrote said Eric was in Rhinebeck. That was over a year ago. Hit me with the high points. You can fill in the gaps afterward."

Theodore's eyes glance upwards. His teeth pinch his lower lip. He frowns. Wrinkles manifest on his forehead.

How complicated can this story be?

"OK. I got it, remember it as if it was yesterday. It's not every day I get called to the principal's office you know."

I sit back and prepare myself for a long story.

Theodore turns right off the secondary road. Red and white "No trespassing" signs border each driveway corner. White fencing borders the driveway. It continues a thousand feet all the way to a large building. Fencing is in the surrounding fields too. In its heyday, this place must have been a horse farm.

We stop at a black decorative high steel gate. Two security cameras, both in full view, one on each side of the driveway let the house occupants be aware of visitors. Theodore disregards the outside intercom protruding from one gatepost. He waits, a moment later, the gates automatically open.

We continue down the driveway until Theodore stops. He parks the pickup right by the front doors. I estimate the size of the lodge at least four thousand square feet, not counting the garages, two barns, a guesthouse, and woodshed. It would need a flyover to discover what hides behind the main house. Remember, I wear cloaks, not capes. I don't possess x-ray vision.

"We're here. This is the MT B&B. What do you think?"

"Little foggy. I'll let you know after the grand tour."

"Love to show it to you, but later. People wait for us, not to mention dinner."

Theodore carries the takeout order while I open one of the lodge's dark green front doors. I let go of the solid brass hardware and pass through the threshold. Energy tinges on my arms. An enchantment spell protects the entranceway. Cannot say I'm surprised. Eric meets Theodore in the front lobby.

Eric tells Theodore, "I'll take care of these. You change."

Theodore replies, "Sorry. Weather delayed us. Reheat the food." He smiles and twinkles his eyes before walking away. Theodore telling a half-truth? What can I say? I'm a terrible influence on people.

I stand in the lobby staring at my biological father.

Our stare down lasts forever. Each of us studying the other until one gives way. Eric's freshly shaven face yields first. His chin points towards the stairway.

The fourth step holds a navy-blue travel mug. I abandon Eric in the lobby, pick up the coffee, and continue up the stairs. A simple twist of the top opens the spout. The aroma emulating from the lid shows Santa granted my wish. I take a sip and make a mental note to add Santa in my early morning prayers.

Oversized houses mean long staircases and this lodge is no exception. I trod sixteen steps, including the landing, up the L-shape staircase. Medium oak stained wood paneling floor to ceiling cover the hallway. Wall lighting fixtures line one side of the hall between three doorways. A half round oak table with white crochet doilies holds brass bowls of lavender-scented potpourri.

The opposite side hangs different types and sizes of framed oil paintings. The ten-foot ceiling complements the hallway's five-foot width. Recessed ceiling lights stay off, allowing the wall lamps with Tiffany red glass to cast an eerie calm. Of the eight hallway doors, only one door stays open.

I enter the bathroom and flick the wall switch. Shades

of brown and white ceramic tiles cover walls with an accent tile border adding green to the décor. Double white porcelain sinks contrast with their polished brass fixtures. Several thick, fluffy, dark-green towels and matching wash-cloths complement the room's color scheme. Two rolled towels rest on the sink counter. A corner Jacuzzi tub by the double windows awaits a willing soul to relax in its comforting warm waters. With a touch of a button, yes—touch adjustments—one can soak their stressful day away.

My dry clothes hang on hooks near the ceramic-tiled shower stall. A pair of polished, black, ankle boots from my truck lay in the corner. Before I clean up and meet guests, I better strip and take care of personal business.

Damp clothes and backpack I dump in the corner. Dual rain showerheads quicken my shower. They beckon my return. As much as I liked to answer, I dress and parade downstairs. Eric already awaits in the front lobby by the time I reach the bottom step.

"Ask Santa for a refill," I said, holding the travel mug at arm's length. My dear father takes the cup. I blurt out, "The Vatican! Seriously?"

Eric speaks through cringed teeth. "We'll talk afterward, alone. I need to introduce you to someone."

We leave the front lobby and walk through a standard plain living room: standard eight-foot ceilings, walls painted with plain beige, and gloss white trim. I examine the furniture set. Someone shopped at a warehouse furniture store. They said, "Give me a six-piece living room set. Whatever you think best," and marched out.

Why did they bother? The cushions appear unused. They're old. Dust and pollen coat the fabric. Why not add a game room or billiard table? Those I could use.

Eric leads the way. We pass the kitchen, a half-bathroom, and two closed doors. In the far northeastern corner of the lodge, we pause in front of a set of glass French doors. Eric says, "Believe it or not, this meeting is important. Stow your emotions and try to act civil."

"Have I ever behaved otherwise?" I grin wide and lower my stare to the mug in Eric's hand.

Bio-dad's patience grows thin. He replies, "I'll get your coffee in a moment. You should drink tea instead of this mud. It's better for you."

"Promise someday I will—when I'm old and gray," I said, prancing towards the glass doors. Which means, not anytime in this century or the next.

Eric pleads, "Would it kill you to… oh hell, never mind. I'll take my chances." I stifle a laugh. He swings open both doors. We take two steps down and I get a clear glimpse of pure wonder. Add another thousand square feet to my earlier estimate.

Jim and Tina's whole house can occupy this room. A billiard table is at the far end of the room. Coin-operated game systems line the wall on my right. Doubtful the game machines accept real currency, but I'm only guessing. A lanai, in the middle of the left wall, serves as an entrance to a covered, screened outdoor pool.

The paneled grand room's walls soar twelve feet high. Above the eight-foot wooden paneling hangs framed theater posters from Hollywood movies. A large popcorn machine on wheels stands next to the large sitting area on my immediate left. The latter is where everyone waits. This place is one heck of a customized downtime room.

I absorb my new surroundings. Eric ushers me to the sitting area where an elderly silver-haired man roots himself in a brown leather chair. Reading glasses hang on a golden chain around his neck.

"Reverend Monsignor Terence Smith, please allow me

the honor to introduce my daughter, Salomé." Eric bows when he makes the introduction.

"It's an honor to meet you," the monsignor praised. "Eric and Theodore both have spoken well of you." I glance at Eric and ponder. Have they?

The upper back of a leather sofa supports my hands. I hesitate in answering the priest and scan the large room a second time. Theodore and Cadmael both enter through the doorway and seat themselves on the sofa. Cadmael's head partially blocks my view of Monsignor Smith. He did it purposely. The move forces me to circumvent the couch and meet the elderly priest.

I ask, "Monsignor. I'm not a practicing Catholic. My father's introduction sounded formal. Am I supposed to kiss your ring?"

"Monsignors don't offer rings, only their hand. But tonight's meeting is informal. Why don't we forgo the formalities?" Monsignor Smith signals to Theodore who reciprocates with a thumbs up. Theodore jumps to his feet and scrambles out of the room. The monsignor gives me his full attention. "This meeting is also unofficial." He lowers his voice. "We have much to talk about tonight."

Cadmael lifts a leather-bound tome laying on the center cushion and places the large book on monsignor's lap. Cadmael lowers himself back unto the sofa and waits with both hands on his lap.

Eric watches from the opposite side of the sofa. A leather loveseat is next to him, but he remains standing.

I stay motionless next to the sofa's armrest during the uncomfortable silence.

Monsignor Smith interjects through the silence. "Daughter, please be seated. My neck strains to see you from this angle."

Eric's eyes dart to the leather chair next to the monsignor. Brief defiance flies through my thoughts, but I recline in the chair. Theodore enters the room with tea and my refill. The monsignor's chair and mine sit catty-cornered together. Our adjacent armrests spaced by mere inches.

Theodore hands Monsignor Smith his tea. A blend of green tea with honey from the smell. Theodore hands me the travel mug and gestures with his other hand. I say, "Thanks." And offer him a silent, "What?"

A deep inhale of java improves my mood.

"All right monsignor, I'll humor you, but please make it short. I want to chat with my dear father. We haven't seen each other in years, and I traveled a long distance to see him."

Cadmael says, "Show respect. You'll have your talk but listen to the good Monsignor." Cadmael takes a long breath and assures the priest. "Please monsignor, continue." Last night's chauffeur seems touchy tonight or overworked. I savor my coffee. Eric settles himself in the middle of the loveseat. His eyes examine every move I make.

"I understand Salomé's impatience, Chad. When one reaches my age, one learns to develop a thick skin. I'm also well aware of her history and her present nature. Not to worry." He opens the cover of the tome. He asks, "Daughter, what do you know about exorcism squads?"

A shower of java spurts out of my mouth and across the sitting area. I get lucky and only fifty percent of the hot coffee lands on Cadmael's boots, but as my luck runs, the other fifty percent ends up on his pant legs.

Nobody should ask a vampire with a mouthful of hot coffee in her mouth questions about exorcism squads.

I gasp, "What did you say?"

CHAPTER 25

"Your reaction was captivating. Hard to decide which of you two jumped more." Monsignor Smith smirks. He then drinks his tea. His stretched-out arm offers the empty cup to Theodore. The priest observes each person occupying the sofa. "Chad. Theodore. Please offer us privacy?"

Cadmael sculls.

Theodore takes the monsignor's teacup and picks up the saucer.

Cadmael and Theodore leave together heading, I assume, straight to the kitchen. Eric stays quiet on the loveseat. He displays calm, but his patience drains. Monsignor Smith comforts himself. "My apologies, Salomé, if any coffee spilled on your clothing, obviously I was too forward in my questioning. Perhaps we should begin anew. Do you like history?"

I disregard my father's impatience and face the priest. "History was my favorite subject in school, Monsignor Smith, and no, no coffee on clothes." As soon as the words leave my mouth, I recheck my clothes. I ask, "Hope Chad's not mad over the spill."

Monsignor chuckles. "Don't worry about Chad. I can attest to the fact. He has worn far worse stains than coffee. He'll be fine."

"What history are you interested in discussing tonight: political, social or my latest favorite, military?" I asked.

"Tonight, we're discussing my favorite, religion—pre-flood—to be exact."

What did I expect from a Catholic priest? I feel myself sinking deep into the chair already.

"The Sumerian Empire thrived before the recorded biblical flood. Sumer was perhaps the most significant and most influential civilization ever to have existed. Archeologists credit humankind's major advances developing during the Sumerian Empire. Its rediscovered clay tablets recorded the civilization's history of celestial visitors twelve thousand years ago.

"According to Sumerian mythology, *the Anunnaki* taught enlightening divine wisdom in Sumer. The Sumerians believed these ultra-knowledgeable beings descended from the Heavenly skies. Several groups credit the Sumerians for creating the original secret society.

"If you know Genesis in the Old Testament, you'll recall Abraham. He carried the Sumerians' ancient myths with him when he traveled to Canaan. The Church doesn't officially recognize this, but several Old Testament stories are revitalized versions of ancient Sumerian's myths. The Canaanites renamed the Anunnaki, Fallen Angels. You might have heard of the Watchers, *the bene ha Elohim* or the Sons of God?"

This fad of Biblical history is all too familiar. "Umm, Monsignor? I don't mean to interrupt, but I do hope you skip tales about Ancient Aliens. When I see that garbage on TV, I get an impulse to toss the set out the window. Extraterrestrials don't belong in the same sentence with history." I glance over at Eric. "I have other things planned tonight."

"I find the Ancient alien topic enlightening myself, but I understand your motive and your impatience. To understand the importance and depth of the current events; I thought best to start from the beginning. I meant to simplify a complicated bit of history. My apologies for any misunderstandings. Your generation resists the past norms."

"Don't take it personally. My generation hears that comment often. Can you fast forward to the end? What's happening?"

"Well, my daughter, it saddens me to say but you have a 7,000-year-old Extermination Order on you. An adjurstine rogue Priest, authorized by an ancient branch of the Ecclesiastical Court, seeks your demise."

I straighten my posture and focus. "I'm being hunted by a priest? Nothing cliché about that scenario." But the mental picture gets my attention. Imagine a Van Helsing family member stabbing me with a wooden stake while I'm sleeping! "Perhaps Monsignor Smith, if you don't mind, maybe you could rewind?"

"Have you heard of the Ecclesiastical Court?"

"Yes. I have heard of stories of the Ecclesiastical Court once or twice." Heck, I heard several tales from Leslie when he and I were in Peru. Leslie has this thing against the group. His body cringes when he hears the group's name. I believe the word he favored was—despised. "Is the term adjurstine a title?"

"An adjurist is a strict follower of religious teachings where an urgent demand is made upon them. The particular demand creates a solemn and irresistible sacred oath in the name of God. An adjurstine follower is a formable foe. If you study this block print, maybe you would better understand."

I take the tome from Monsignor Smith and study the image.

"The intermarriage between the fallen angels and human women produced giants called, the *Nephilim*. This interbreeding leads to the Nephilim's extinction. The block print unveils the horrors that transpired. Your eyes see the truth, the Nephilim were no simple giants."

"These Nephilim were vampires?" I asked.

"The term and their description have changed over the millenniums, but yes. You're looking at the oldest original block printing of Nephilim offspring known to exist. No wonder the Christian ancestors hunted and slaughtered them throughout ancient and medieval times. A secretive branch of the Ecclesiastical Court has continued to seek the ruthless and bloodthirsty creatures. It matters not if vampires, such as yourself, are not Nephilim. In their eyes, you are, and they must destroy all demonic beings."

"Well, that's mighty righteous of them. Guess I cannot blame them too much though. If they're basing their motives on this picture—"

"Yes. If that print matched the period's reality, an extermination order could justify the massive slaughter. But the Nephilim no longer exist in today's world, and neither does any of their offspring. Unfortunately, now and then, a rogue priest takes the law upon himself and continues the outdated practice.

"We don't have an exact number of these priests, but we know they work in clandestine, secretive tribunals. We also are certain; they have deep connections within the Vatican itself. Their communication network is too vast. Your father is doing his utmost best to narrow our leads.

Not to fret, daughter, we'll track these self-righteous pompous pricks. Forgive my language."

Holy shit! Cannot believe what I just heard. My fondness for this old priest just rose a point. I tighten my smile, but I would rather offer him a high-five. "I know Eric will find them," I said, glancing in Eric's direction. Will I lay defunct in a grave by the time Eric learns the answers? "Monsignor, in the meantime, what's being done to find this guy who hunts me?"

"Everything we can," the monsignor said, plain and drily.

Eric strolls over and takes the tome. I hand him the oversized book and my travel mug. He withdraws from the room.

Bio-dad returns with two bottles of water. He tosses a bottle in my direction and hands the other to Monsignor Smith. Eric reseats himself on the loveseat.

Heard a bunch of stories tonight, and little of it concerns me other than being a target. The air in this room thickens. Monsignor Smith holds back the real deal. "Like what?" I asked, twisting the bottle cap off.

Now that the tome no longer lays on my lap, I stand and reposition the chair. Once reseated, I wash down the room temperature water. Sitting directly in front of the priest eases the awkward neck strain. Eric ignores my redecorating.

Monsignor Smith sips twice from his water bottle, recaps it and tosses the bottle to Eric who catches the bottle with his left hand. "I started my study group *The Conmilitium Ineteriorem*, years ago. Its role allows studies and debates on metaphysical sciences, ideas, and promote comradery within the Seminary. With bright, inquisitive young minds in the group, the study group often has sidebar discussions on spiritual and occult topics. Typical for young males to explore other philosophies. Although, I recently suspect members of my group practice secretive occult rituals against my orders.

"One of our senior priests named Father Moretti created his inner group, COATROSA two years ago. The group's acronym stands for Celestial Order Against the Rise of Satan's Army."

Sure sounds better than TOAD. One of these days, I'm joining a better secretive club.

"Father Moretti based his group on the exorcism squads endorsed by the Vatican earlier this century to tackle the rise of Satanism. This inner group might be, and I emphasize *might be*, connected to the threat to your life. We're getting information from an inside source. You need to trust us."

"Trust you? I know the 'inside source' is Theodore! How do you expect me to trust you? Theodore is a close friend of mine. He has no business spying on dangerous lunatics."

"I don't know how you know this, but yes, I asked Theodore to infiltrate Father's Moretti's group a year ago. He does so voluntarily. Theodore has strict orders to leave at the slightest hint of danger. I trust his judgment, as should you."

"Is that why I'm here? The Vatican wants me to take care of the big, bad, and evil priest. I would think they should be able to handle their own people."

"No. That's not why we had Fernando send you. We can—and will—deal with Father Moretti on our own, once we positively know what he plans and with whom. For now, his agenda eludes us. We have learned he fancies himself a master Astrologist. He draws and studies astrological maps of the heavens. Nobody can pinpoint why. With Theodore's persistence, we have also learned Father

Moretti waits for 'brothers.' We checked his known contacts but found little worthwhile. Possibilities exist that Father Moretti and his group have nothing to do with you. Theodore may be our only hope in learning otherwise.

"The night shortens. I'm sure you have much to talk about with your father. Eric, please send Theodore around for the car? Time for us to head back. Salomé, I understand your hesitation and concern for your friend, but this isn't my first mission where lives are at stake. Eric will inform you of my address should you wish to continue any further discussions. My door stays open for you."

Monsignor leans over and clasps both my hands. "May the Lord always watch and protect you. Please, don't be too hard on your father. He worries and dwells on other important matters."

We all stand and stroll to the front lobby.

Eric exits with Monsignor Smith. A black Suburban waits outside the entrance. The pickup truck I rode in earlier is nowhere in sight. I assume Cadmael parked it somewhere while we chatted. Theodore waits in the SUV's driver seat. Stuck driving another large vehicle tonight. Poor Theodore.

The living room includes a few unusual items. Unlike the grand room, little catches my eye. Moments later, Eric bursts through the lobby doors. He exclaims, "We need to talk. Follow me."

"Sure. Whatever," I said, making a satisfied smirk.

Eric struts past me. I trail behind him. We turn right before the grand room. A digital clock on the wall reads 11:05. After listening to the Monsignor's long talk, the time feels later. Eric leads us down a hallway and through two doorways. We stop in an office room. Eric says, "Shut the door behind you."

Bio-dad faces a mahogany wall unit and picks up two

sets of playing cards on a shelf. I ask, "We going to talk over a game of cards?"

"Don't be rambunctious. Place the black deck here. Then, place the white deck over here. In that exact order, in these exact spots. Got it?" I nod. "Afterwards, remove this book." Eric pulls out a hardcover volume of Britannica volume number twenty-five labeled, Number/Prague. Once the book clears the shelf, the top half of the wall unit raises into the ceiling. The bottom half lowers into the floor. "Take the volume with you. The doors will seal behind you."

"You're kidding me! You got a secret elevator in your office?"

"It'll take you down to the safe room. If you cannot handle a situation on your own, you go down. Don't play hero."

Eric lifts and restacks the two playing decks. Both halves of the wall unit silently closes once Eric replaces the book. Nobody could guess an elevator hides behind the wall unit.

"Next stop inside the closet," Eric said, leading the way.

Where else would I go?

I closed the door once we both enter. The office closet is six feet by eight feet and cedar lined. Clothes hang on two closet rods. Simple pine shelving above each rod. Eric says, "Turn the right wall switch on, not the left, nearest to you. Push in the trim panel above the shelf in this corner. The hinges hang here on my right. Push the opposite side. Mechanisms reset once you shut the door from inside."

Eric swings the bare wall open and red interior LED lighting highlights edges of the stairway.

"We walk down two flights." I hesitate after his statement. Intuition warns dear bio-dad would love to deliver a kick, sending me flying down headfirst. Eric bows and waves me forward. "I'll reset the door behind us. Please, after you—Daughter."

My eyes bulge and give Eric a quizzical expression. Bet bio-dad cannot wait for our chat. I tippy-toe around him. Once on the stairs, I prance down the twenty-eight steps.

When we reach the carpeted bottom floor, Eric volunteers a cordial tour of the place. "This is the sub-basement. My official workspace when dealing with ACE. The regular basement entrance is off the living room stairs. We use it for storage and supplies."

My father's office is huge. Although, a conference table takes up most of the space. I count twenty hidden revolving monitors built into the tabletop. Eric reclines in one of twenty office chairs circling the table. Ten monitors hang on the right wall. International world clocks display different time zones over each monitor. Twelve smaller size monitors hang on the wall to my left.

All monitors have nameplates fastened under them listing their owner's codenames. Four of the twenty-two monitors glow blue indicator lights. In the corner of the room on my right, a small wet bar with a single-cup coffee machine waits for any thirsty ACE agent.

I mosey over and examine a blue mug. They're the same type in my old apartment. "You get a special deal on the case?" I replace the mug and stare at Eric. "Before we begin, this room bugged?"

Eric swings his chair in my direction. Both forearms rest on the desk's edge. He deepens his voice. "This is a *live-room*. The room is not *bugged*. If you mean if other people are listening then—yes—they are." Eric reclines and waves me to a chair. "Help yourself to a seat."

I stroll to Eric and purposely flop down opposite of

him. Crossing a leg over a thigh, I rotate my chair with the one foot on the floor. The room spins.

"So, how're things? What's new in your life? Your family and health OK?" I abruptly stop and stare deep into Eric's eyes.

"Rest… you want, you must…answer." Our minds link. Let's see what dear daddy hides.

I search deep into Eric's present thoughts. An immediate vision appears. A large group of people dressed in white t-shirts and blue denim overalls. Painters? No, builders. People are building a house or structure. The people pause. They see me watching. They all appear similar. I concentrate and get a more unobstructed view. They are the same! All the builders have chubby round faces with exaggerated handlebar mustaches. The men resume building. Their masterful handiwork indicates remarkable skill.

My perception changes and I float upwards. A wall of bright red brickwork with white vine piping grout grows. Men work faster, more diligent. The wall reaches an incredible height. The meaning dawns on me. They're blocking me out!

Common red bricks transform into ultra bleach white bricks. The vine piping shimmers. Pulsating energy flows, circling each brick. They spin counterclockwise. The wall whitens until the vision irradiates brilliant white. The scene blends into a memory. A flash, and the connection breaks. I tumble back into the chair dismayed.

"Drat, darn it."

Words pound in my head. "When you return to Earth, please let me know." I refocus, shaking the vision from memory. Eric reclines. His arms crossed.

"Glad you're comfortable using your new abilities," Eric said. "Liked the spinning distraction you did with the chair. Professionals use whatever they can find in their environment. That showed initiative and innovation. Hold both tight. You'll need them. But you lack a strong grounding. Too much in your thoughts. Stop thinking so much."

"You seem mighty comfortable with mindreading and having someone in your head, not to mention your favorite daughter becoming a creature of the night." OK. I'm his only daughter, but it helps to make my point. "What loving father would allow his child to join the undead or hide a double life from her?"

"My work dictates the hows and whys. You didn't lack a single thing. I made certain of that. My history is unimportant. Besides, you didn't ask or show an interest in my work. As for 'my favorite daughter,' I don't play favorites. Trust me. It's harder than you think." Eric smiles wide. He enjoys his private joke.

"OK. Fine, be that way. You say girls are difficult to raise. My fault then, I didn't drill my father. Trust me. Girls are far worse when we have fangs. What is happening? A menacing exorcism squad isn't why I'm a vampire. Why order Fernando Ventré Florez to dream-weave and offer the vampiric gift? Why get me involved?"

"Short answer? An ancient, powerful supernatural deity desires your life-force for a pick-me-up. He already knows of your existence and will hunt you down sooner than later. Simply put, a Djinn wants to suck you dry and spit you out."

"A what?" Did I miss something?

Eric explains in his dry and flat tone. "The Supreme Being, in His infinite wisdom, created Angels, Humans, and Djinn. You may know the latter as Genies. Their origins vary down through the ages. Although inherently neither good nor evil, the demon after you is a monster."

Oh, fantastic. Unauthorized killer squads and magical

genies want to either obliterate or kiss me to death. I tell you, a vampire's life holds no dull moments. Darn, on rare occasions, I miss my old school life.

Eric adds, "Your mother and I thought you might want to defend yourself someday. Were we wrong?"

A hushed whisper, "Mom" passes my lips. I straighten my posture and give Eric my full attention. He notices my cue and continues.

"Keziah and I meet in Seattle, Washington on a Sunday afternoon. I had recently graduated from college. During the daylight hours, I scavenged the city for an accountant's position. Long story short, I failed finding a job worthwhile. But, on one clear blue-sky day, fortune shined.

"A local lumber company had won a substantial contract. One of their hiring agents caught sight of me one night in a dive called, *Beer & Tap* eating pretzels and caressing a beer. The place was so shoddy it couldn't afford a real name. I swear the sawdust on the floor came from bugs and termites. This man, think his name was Greg or Gregory, figured I drove trucks and offered a job. The lumber company needed drivers. I needed an income. So, I took the job driving their rigs.

"Met your mother two years later at a family-run truck stop. She rushed in at the same moment I was leaving. We ran into each other. Keziah said she was driving non-stop south. We talked. She decided to stop over for the day. That day turned into months. I gave the lumber company my two weeks noticed. Keziah and I both traveled south together. She never mentioned what she saw in that young strapping gawky kid, and he never asked. Your mother and I fell deeply in love, married and eventually bought the house where you spent your early years."

Haven't heard my mother's name spoken in years.

Seems awkward hearing it now but comforting at the same time. "What's this Wodemanne chore you do?"

"That'll take all night."

"All I got is the night. Spill it."

"I'll give you the highlights. You already know the basics. If you want the whole story, talk to Andrea. He tells it better than I do."

"Am I meeting this Andrea too?"

"He's solitary much like yourself. You two should get along fine. He arrives sometime early tomorrow night if plans hold."

I drift to the wet bar, grab a water bottle. "You want anything, while I'm here?" I asked, after chugging down the contents. Eric shakes his head. I crush the small bottle and screw the cap back on before it reshapes itself. The irritating noise disrupts the stillness in the room. The transparent creature of art stands on top of the serving tray. One of the world clocks labeled "Local" shows the night diminishing. Eric's brief version allows hunting time if we hurry.

I sit myself in the closest chair and cross my arms. "You hunt down critters?"

"*The Wodemanne Society* exists for hunting remnants. Every government on every major continent enlists the services of the Wodemannes. A Vatican Bank funnels and pays our fees. Another entity called *Old World Bank* operates and supervises the clandestine missions. Guaranteed bet, *Old World Bank* operates under another organization.

"The Christos family worked with Wodemannes since the twelfth century. Hunting these creatures runs in their bloodline. I met and befriended Cadmael Christos in Saint Petersburg, Florida at a trade show. Chad ran a complete background and clearance on me without my knowledge. Once I acquired the clearances, he introduced me to the fine art of remnant hunting. We worked together for years until the Vatican received information on a man blowing up remnants without preauthorization. Chad's superiors sent us to Santa Fe, New Mexico to confirm the reports.

"When we arrived, Andrea Abelli was decimating remnants with explosives. He made a specific chemical compound of his design. The mixture drew the creatures straight to their deaths. Andrea would locate a burrow; bury a specialized *Kaboom-stick*, his trade name for it, and *boom*! No more critter.

"Chad and I reported back with our findings and waited until further notice. The notice arrived when an abandon hospital complex disappeared one night in an instant. The Vatican's black-ops launched into overdrive to cover the incident and bury the damage. No small feat. Well, you heard ol' Gabe's tales.

"Andrea Abelli already knew of remnants and was no stranger to hunting them, so the team recruited him. Andrea is a born genius with improvised engineering. ACE couldn't exist without him. But eccentric falls short of describing him when he was younger. Heck, we were all young back then."

"What about Master Kajika? How'd you meet him?"

"Didn't. Fernando met me when I was hunting in *His* canyon." Eric pouts. "Let's say; I didn't make a great impression and drop the subject."

"Getting pissy aren't you?"

"It's been a long day."

Long night too, and I'm hungry. "We'll get back to this later. Before we leave, what was the deal with the intro you did earlier?"

"I formally introduced you because not only do I respect the Monsignor's office, but he's also my boss. Although we belong to a larger worldwide organization,

ACE is under Monsignor Smith's direct control. Based on Fernando's praise and recommendations, I thought you might want a new career. Unless you enjoy perching on a rock cropping all night."

"Oh. Sorry. You're offering a job reference and not beheading me because?"

"Orders from the monsignor. He wanted me to back off a while and give you slack. He thinks I gave you enough strife as a teenager. I'm thinking *a while* counts as two weeks. So, prepare yourself for more strife."

"Sure. OK. I can take everything you could hit me with, and more."

"Be careful what you ask. Experience will trump youth every time."

"Speaking of youth, Theodore doesn't get it. No one prepared him for the dangers ahead. If he gets hurt—"

"I assigned him back up. Theo will be fine and safe. Let me worry about him. You focus on your plate. I'll schedule you more training. In the meantime, if you're content with our chat, you up for the tour?"

"Later. I'm heading outside to walk this evening off." And hunt for blood.

"Fine. Be that way," Eric said. "But before you sulk, I'll show you to your new quarters."

We trod back up the two flights of stairs and through the walk-in closet. Retrace our steps down the hall and head to the back lobby.

"If you fancy secret elevators, you'll love this. I stole the idea from an old television show back in the sixties. Fernando assisted. You'll know why in a moment."

Eric and I stand in a windowless mudroom off the back lobby. White painted walls and trim reminds me of the walk-in closet without the rods and cedar paneling. A wooden bench rest against one wall with coat hooks above it. A full-length mirror hangs on the opposite side with wall lamps bordering each side. Gray slate tiles cover the mudroom and back lobby floor. A closed door is off to our left.

"That's the laundry room and a double garage. Use the laundry anytime. Motorcycles inside are off limits. Don't even think about touching them." Eric points to the mirror. "This is what you want."

"A mirror? I'm not vain. And if you didn't already know, I have seen my reflection. My Soul is intact. Thanks."

"You're not looking. You're putting your back to it."

"What am I supposed to see, dancing coat hooks?" My mouth prepares to say a bunch of one-syllable words, but I clamp it shut. Why bother? "OK. I'll humor you, but my stomach growls. And that's unhealthy. Trust me."

I walk over, turn around and face the wall. "Now what?"

"Reach up and pull the lamps." Eric's grin and eyes grow wide. He reminds me of a dog going for a walk. "Pull down the lamps with both hands and use your full strength. Don't worry about the lamps. The brackets are made of a titanium alloy." I hesitate, but if I postpone any longer, Eric will burst in anticipation.

I lean back against the mirror and tug the lamps. The mirrored panel and a small part of the floor give away. My grip tightens. Panel swings and reveals a concealed space. "Wow! That's cool." I release the lamps. The panel rotates and re-shuts, sending me back into the mudroom. "That's the cellar?"

"Hardly. The spiral staircase leads down to your quarters. One of my better-designed safe houses. Tell no one. You, Fernando and I, are the only ones who know of its existence. No human can open that door. One reason

Fernando assisted in its making. Theo has strict orders not to ask questions about your sleeping quarters, and members of the team already know better than to ask."

"When was Master Kajika last here? When is he coming back?"

"Fernando visited a while ago. I couldn't say. You know how fickle master vampires are, but he said he left gifts for you downstairs. I'm unable to enter your lair. I cannot answer questions." Eric sticks his hand into a pant pocket and pulls out a key. "The key to the back door. Keep it with you. We'll talk more tomorrow."

I drop the key into a pocket and head toward the door.

"Yea. We will," I said, over my shoulder, heading into the night air.

CHAPTER 26

I slept in late tonight. Usually, I wake up about a half hour before sunset. But last night wiped me out. Between Theodore's revelations, the priest delivering my death notice, and bio-dad's tale, I felt exhausted. My scant feeding afterward helped, but barely. Need a better hunt tonight, right after this game.

"You got better, been practicing? But don't think you can beat my reflexes," I said, boasting.

"This controller rules. Nice piece of tech, especially with the preprogrammed moves. But you could give me a modest handicap, you know."

I laugh. "What fun would that be?" Theodore frowns when I beat him. "What's that, four wins now?" Playing video games on the floor for three hours put my butt asleep. "You up for a movie?"

"Sure." His controller soars and lands on the sofa. "My male pride could use a break. What do you have in mind? We stock plenty of DVDs."

We both jump up when the front door buzzer rings. "You expecting someone?" I asked.

Theodore offers a blank stare. Eric shouts from the kitchen. "Got it!"

"Make the movie scary with lots of screams. I'm checking out our visitor. Be right back." Theodore places a finger to his lip. A second later, his evil grin could make a vampire proud.

I round the corner just in time to see Eric opening the front door. A well-tanned deliveryman wearing a green tartan flat cap carries several pizza boxes stacked head high. The man's matching short-sleeve shirt and cargo shorts accessorize well with his desert boots. My father invites the burly man into the lobby.

The deliveryman and I glimpse each other.

"What! What are *you* doing here?" I exclaimed.

"Pleased to see you too. Hope I didn't miss much. Pizza for everyone." The man swallows deep. "While I had the time, I picked up the mail," he said. "You fix that mailbox yet?"

The deliveryman's grin reveals shining bright white teeth. He must have stopped at his dentist too.

"Salomé, meet Andrea Abelli. The third member of ACE."

"But you're Mister Bell from the Postal Service. I cannot believe it! You're Andrea Abelli, a Wodemanne?"

"Yep. It seems my fame precedes me." He chuckles. "Been watching over you for years. Heard word the jungle beat your butt a time or two. Glad you're still alive and in one piece."

No clue how he heard of my Peruvian episodes. However, I did have a few narrow escapes. Eric closes the door and latches the deadbolt.

"Pizzas are getting cold. Someone else I'm supposed to meet tonight, right?" Andrea asked.

Eric says, "One more." Bio-dad and Mister Bell, I

mean Andrea Abelli, head toward the grand room. Eric comments before we pass the double French doors. "The kid shows promise."

Andrea grows an inch of satisfaction in hearing the words. However, concern washes an inch from my statue when Theodore raises to greet our guest.

Andrea stacks the pies on the round table in the corner.

Eric introduces Theodore to Mister Abelli. "Theo, meet Andrea Abelli."

Theodore drops a movie on a wall shelf. He runs around the couch stopping short of colliding into the pizzas. "Good to meet you, Mister Abelli. Heard much about you," Theodore said, shaking hands.

Andrea pulls Theodore close with a double grip. Andrea says, "You got a good firm handshake, Theo." Mister Abelli checks Eric and nods. "Heard much about you too. Keep up the great work." After the introductions, four heads turn and stare at the pizza tower. "Before we dig in, you two call me, Andy."

"Help yourselves and get acquitted," Eric said. "I'll fetch the plates and drinks from the kitchen."

The three of us attack the pizzas. Who needs plates?

When my father returns, he finds us on separate chairs and sofas. We each have our pizza box on our laps, although, we varied our slices. Eric grabs a slice.

I ask no one in particular. "Chad hiding somewhere?"

Andrea replies, "He drove the van. You don't think I placed a stack of pizza goodness on the passenger's seat and drove, did you?" Andrea munches on a piece of crust. He mumbles, "Chad has his pizza. He's fine."

Eric dumps an assortment of slices into a pizza box. "I got another meeting tonight." He folds the box in half under an arm. "See everyone in a couple of days."

I slide my pizza box onto the cushion and stride across

the sitting area to confront Eric. "You disappearing again? What about our talk? We're not finished, you know."

"It's important. You can take care of yourself. Questions, talk to Andy. You two should catch up." Eric and Andrea share a telepathy stare.

Andrea nods in agreement.

Yes, I noticed their thoughts, but nothing significant. "If you want a tour, Theo will give it. We'll talk later," Eric said, before leaving the room.

My head bounces off the air in disgust. "Too difficult to talk with your daughter?" The question, again, meant for no one in particular. I return to the sofa and my pizza.

Eric exits the lodge, and a vehicle drives away. I'm alone with two grown males. What mischief can I make? Scare the bejesus out of them, naturally.

"Theodore, did you pick the movie? We're ready when you are." I study Andrea. "Hope you're not a scary cat."

"If I am, keep in mind my full stomach. And I know how to projectile vomit," Andrea said, with dimples dotting his grin. "I heard Eric has a theater room in this lodge. Let's relocate our upchuck contest?"

I flash a look at Theodore. "A theater room?" This place grows by the minute. "I want the grand tour after the movie. No excuses." I grab the rest of the pizza boxes. Andrea and Theodore split the chore of carrying the drinks. I outstretch an arm. "Theodore, lead the way."

We head toward the video machines and down the side hall. The hallway is about ten feet long and lined with a padded black décor wall covering. The bathroom, with its painted black door, is on my left. Theodore passes the door and stops at the end of the hall.

Theodore says, "This panel is the door. It doesn't lock, push it open." The wall lighting casts dim shadows. The theater room is multi-leveled and designed with a black and gray color theme. Three rows of five recliner chairs fill most of the room. A humongous screen hangs on the far wall. "We'll set the food and drinks on the back table, near the bar. I'll set up the movie and lower the accent lighting. Save the middle seat." Theodore walks behind the bar and disappears.

Andrea and I unload the snacks and lower ourselves in comfortable movie seats. We each take different end seats. That leaves an empty place between all of us. Plenty of elbow room and space for our food and drinks.

The lights dim and I twist around in the seat. Theodore closes a set of black velvet curtains across the door. If any stray light wants to join us, it'll be disappointed.

Theodore plops down and gets a double thumbs up from Andrea. I ask, "So, what's playing?"

Does Andrea show any hidden fears? After him spying on me for untold years, I would love to add a little concern of my own. But plans fall short when Theodore holds out on me. "No spoilers. Relax, put your feet up and watch."

Sheesh. Third wheels suck. I walk back to the bar and grab a drink. The opening credits roll. I stroll back to my seat, with cola and pizza in hand. The movie score doesn't ring any familiar bells. I recline in my chair and soon fall deep into the movie.

All right Theodore. Good choice.

Theodore's movie pick lasted three hours. As a bonus, he added two mini-movies. We had plenty of time to finish the pizzas. Our tour added another hour. Andrea and I both agreed this lodge is a mansion.

Mister Abelli hasn't visited this place before. He lives

somewhere in Colorado. During the tour, Andrea said, "There's plenty of room to blow equipment up and work on experiments. My industrial complex beats living in a box anytime."

If he considers this lodge a box, I want to be a shoe.

Andrea and Theodore assigned themselves clean up duty. I excused myself and changed into my night gear. My limit of food, movie, tours, and chitchat reached its limit for one night. I swing the kitchen door open. "Sorry guys, but time to leave. Theodore, I had a grand time, catch you later. Andy. Thanks for the pizza." I toss the cloak around my shoulders. "Vampire stuff. Don't wait up for me."

Andrea washes dishes at a triple basin sink. If I forgot to mention it earlier, this lodge has a commercial sized kitchen. Andrea places a plate in the middle basin. He replies, "Use your key. We'll be upstairs sleeping late. I'll tell you tales about your father if you choose, tomorrow night."

"Fantastic, but I'm pizza'd out. Make it over coffee," I said.

Andrea winks. I head outdoors.

CHAPTER 27

*L*ove to patrol the property's perimeter, or check on Theodore's park, but I need blood. The lodge borders on the Hudson River. Plenty of hunting grounds on the other side of the river. I'll check the parks out. I ascend the Rhinebeck night air and at once regret it.

Thick summer humid air suffocates my lungs. The updraft from the river must have kept the humidity away at ground level. I'll need to head deep into woods for any comfort from the muggy weather. An open wooded mountain range lies due west. Mountain terrain limits hunting, but I can make do.

Circling the mountains, I pick the least favorite peak and descend onto a hiking trail.

I hike the trail until I run into an unexpected victim. Animal blood curbs my hunger along the way. The hike up to the top serves two purposes; I burn pizza calories, and the moss-scented air calms my thoughts. Last night's mind dump still unsettles my brain. Vampires cannot mull ideas over while we sleep or dream. So, prowling woods are ideal for contemplating.

The night's long quiet stroll helps me to reorganize my thoughts. Monsignor Smith and Eric both gave me a full plate of worry. I might need another couple of nights to digest it all.

An hour of twisting trails leads to a small plateau overlooking a lakeside campsite. The scene is picturesque from this height. Moonlight reflects the goddess's profile on the calm waters of the lake. The clearing below glistens in a brilliant silver hue. The moon outperforms herself tonight.

A nocturnal artist has set up her canvas and easel in the middle of a clearing. She paints a lake scene. Her painted moon hangs high in a starry sky. Iridescent pink clouds float in the air. Artistic license, I guess.

The night's canvas has no stars twinkling and the moon balances on treetops. I'm at a lost with the pinkish clouds. My neck muscles strain peering upwards into the night sky. I return my gaze to the artist.

The artist appears twenty-ish. A college student maybe. She wears a strap-on headlamp. A second lamp, clamped on her easel, shines downwards. She uses the fixed light for her palette and a folding table with brushes. The nocturnal painting technique, using natural outdoor lighting, piques my interests. But humans shouldn't travel the unsafe night alone.

An older male creeps along the perimeter hoping to interrupt the painter's session. The stalker hid behind bushes spying on the woman with his binoculars. I kept the man in my peripheral vision in case he retreated.

The gods might have shined on him if he returned to his camp. I would have offered him a simple love bite and left him alive. As it now stands, the sleazebag's luck ran out.

My slim chance of grabbing the man unnoticed shortens. I could let the man attack her and kill him afterward.

The lake makes a natural spot to dump two bodies, but I rather skip that choice.

The sleazebag takes his sweet time sneaking around the perimeter. His type enjoys preying on innocent women. Fate offers two minutes tops until the painter notices her stalker.

Using my necklace is out of the question. I don't dare release familiars on one kill. My dagger makes a perfect throwing weapon if nobody minds the man's death yell, body crashing on the ground, or me pulling the blade out of a corpse. Heck, I might as well jump the dude. A sling-shot would be perfect if I carried one and knew how to use it. That limits my options. I must improvise. So, what is here I can use?

I rush away from the ledge hoping for fresh ideas. Any ideas. The one-minute countdown begins. Vampiric senses jump into overdrive. My mind races for distractions and weapons: branches for spears, vines for nets, rocks for throwing. Eyes dart everywhere. Stones, pebbles and dirt roll down the ledge where I stood before rushing away. Maybe, make it look accidental. I suppose it could work.

I peek over the ledge. The downward incline looks right, and if I angle it properly, this stunt might work. I dash into the woods.

Running with a massive stone above one's head through woods isn't easy. Tree branches break and detour my path. But a minute later, I make it back to the ledge. However, I have little time to rejoice.

Peering over the ledge, I plan my attack. Cutting it close, but enough safe space separates the good from the ugly. Cannot wait any longer. I scrap my boot heel into the ground. Dirt and grass give way to form a guideline. Whipping to the back of the boulder, I aim and push the large ball. This better work. I cross my fingers for a strike.

Boulder rolls straight towards the man. My aim is true. Leaning against a tree, I rejoice. Sleazebag has written his epithet. "Wanted to attack a young woman at night, but instead, a falling boulder crushed me tight." Witnessing his demise sends shivers up my spine.

The moment of impact drags. The attacker hears a loud, *crack*. He searches for the source and spots me instead. We lock stares. A second later, we both watch in amazement. The boulder takes flight and soars high into the air!

The attacker makes a beeline run towards the artist. He cannot see the boulder clearly or calculate its trajectory. I'm uncertain what he plans. Before I jump into vamp-drive and throw him into the lake, I watch with an open jaw. The boulder's center of gravity shifts the massive weight. I'm helpless. The deadly projectile heads in the wrong direction.

"NOOO!"

I leap straight towards the artist. Maybe I can shove her aside. But the gods and physics are against me tonight. I reach the target zone at the same time the boulder lands on all three of us. I shield the woman with my back. Jagged edges tear my attire and rip flesh. My scream rises two octaves when the ground itself gives way. The boulder crashes through earth taking the three of us with it. We collapse in a forgotten mining tunnel.

The debris pins me down flat. Iron mine dust and carbon dioxide make the stale air unbreathable. Must move the woman. She's within arm's reach but she's not moving. I twist, turn, and wiggle through the rumble. This shaft reminds me of my times in the Southwest tunnel system, but less habitable. I gain clearance, flatten my back on the ground and push the boulder.

Standing upright, I grab support beams, one at a time,

and shove timbers out of the way. The lifeless man whose heart stopped when a ceiling beam crushed his chest can stay dead.

The woman has a faint heartbeat. "If you can hear me, stay with me. I'll get you out of here." I kneel by her side and check for damage. The woman sustains a broken leg, cracked ribs on both sides, and a collapsed lung. Nothing I can fix. A wooden fragment impales itself deep in her back. She's bleeding out. The piece must have hit an artery. Dammit. I cannot move her.

What happened? I stand up and scream to the skies.

"Somebody. Help!" Why must she die like this?

"I'm sorry you got hurt. I didn't mean you to. Honest. I wanted to save you," I said to the dying woman.

The stalker lays lifeless a foot away from the boulder. "Why do people like you exist? What purpose can you possibly serve?" I gaze skywards. Would I ever hear an answer? "Kajika, I'm sorry. I should have known better. Dammit! Fernando. Please."

A faint voice interrupts my plea. "Fernando? Umm, I'm Dorothy." Her voice bleeds. I bend to hear her words, my ear close to her lips. I cradle a hand behind her neck. She says, "My name is Dorothy Dene."

We stare at each other. Dorothy smiles unknowing what I did. I hold her. Dorothy's lips part. Her life slips away. Her lifeless body goes limp. A young talented soul blends into the night where I pray she finds peace.

"*AHHHH*!" The scream attacks the night air.

The outburst drains energy. My balance wavers. I steady myself on the boulder.

The boulder. Its massive size and weight created this mess. It killed an innocent woman. I grip the stone. Sheer willpower prevents me from crushing the damn thing. I bury emotions, steady my footing, and heave the damn boulder out of the way.

The dead woman lays at my feet. She deserves better than abandonment down here alone with her attacker. Her death was my fault.

Attacker's body already decays. *Mister Stinky Guy* needs to leave. I grab his collar and drag him under the tunnel's opening. I leap to the surface with the man over my shoulder.

Nobody responded to the earlier commotion. The area is free of intruders. I have to remove any evidence of us being here, but I must hurry. Sunrise cometh. Birds already chirp their early morning tunes.

I drop my dead weight and head to the artist's campsite. The tent's interior is undisturbed. Good. I stage her belongings outside the tent, pull the stakes up and fold the camping tent flat. Piling her property in the center, I wrap her belongings tightly together. The whole package I haul back into the new tunnel entrance.

A broken tree branch removes our footprints within seconds, which leaves two more chores. I check the dead man's pocket for identification. The driver's license lists Ernest as his first name. I slide the license back into the wallet and fling it far out into the lake.

"Ernie," I said. "You're going to hate this." I grab Ernie by the waistline and fly him to the lakeshore where I pulverize him into pulp. Blood oozes, pours and splatters everywhere.

Sticky blood, mine dust, and mud coats everything I wear. Not one item of clothing is salvageable. Maybe if I had used my fists to pulverize Ernie instead of two large flat rocks, I wouldn't have gotten all the splattering. O'well, unpleasant stuff happens when you don't practice foresight.

All of Ernie's fleshy pieces end up in the lake. The fish will enjoy their change of diet. The sun shines its pink and orange rays over the horizon. Dawn. My night departs.

The dark clouds drifting off to the west may carry a storm, but I need to vamoose. If the sun's golden-yellow rays shine, I'm a goner. I eye the tunnel's entrance and swan dive in for dear life.

Once I'm in the tunnel, I carry the artist and her equipment out of direct sunlight. The earthen tunnel shields me from the sun. The darkness provides me with another ten minutes. I travel farther and deeper into the mining shaft. I squeeze around the massive boulder and discover a narrow exploratory mining tunnel sloping downwards.

After taking two calming breaths, I listen for sounds originating within the tunnel and hear dirt and rocks tumbling. I transfer the artist and her equipment into the shaft. Hike back to the opening, as close as I dare, and pick up one of the fallen support beams. I dislodge all the support structures and loosen the dirt ceiling until the ceiling caves in.

A weak section gives way and sunlight busts through the tunnel. Daylight burns my face. "*ARRRGH. UGGH. Dammit.*" After a quick leap, the boulder provides instant cover.

I roll the boulder, and my protective shield, through loose dirt and jam it in place blocking any more invasive sun. If stray light seeks to harm me, it can try another time. I make a mad dash and skid around the side tunnel. The ceiling above collapses with my help.

Thicker ceiling down here means no chance of the sun invading. I tiptoe around the artist and travel thirty paces deeper into the darkness. The wooden beam assists me one more time. This last cave-in guarantees safe sleeping quarters and protection for the night.

My body slides down the loose earth. I collapse at the barrier's base.

CHAPTER 28

I sway side-to-side, both knees tucked tight to my chest. I stare into the abyss. Darkness won the last battle. At the opposite end of this black void, lies the young woman. Lifeless. Dead.

An hour passes before I pull myself together and accept the facts. I messed up, and life sucks. It makes little sense to dwell on the past. I force myself up and stroll over to check the body.

Teeth bite hard into my lower lip. The pain helps to focus. The taste of metallic copper, I ignore.

One of Dorothy's pockets conceals an envelope. I discover no other identification on her. I open the envelope and pull out the card. It reads. *You are cordially invited to the Hudson Valley Plein-Air Painting Party.*

Fantastic, a party. Which means, other artists are in the immediate area and know she is here painting. Darn it. So much for burying her myself.

Time to leave this shelter and head elsewhere. My best exit is to open the closest wall. I walk back and grab the wooden beam then return. It'll take me a while to hack through, but I can manage.

I climb up the earthen wall and pound dirt. The wooden beam is awkward to handle, although, the tar coating helps my grip. I wish for a hard hat and goggles. Rocks and roots pound my head while dust and dirt dry my eyes. If I dig with my eyes closed, I cannot see the best place to clear a path. The next time I cause a cave-in, I'm doing a more miserable job.

Thirty-minutes later, I clear a three-foot clearance and break into the central tunnel. The tight fit will have to do. Dorothy and I roll together through the opening. I wildly shake my hair. Loosened dirt falls to the ground. The back of my hands dries watery eyes, trying to stay clear of sunburned areas. I lift Dorothy over my shoulder and run.

I keep running until I find an upward tunnel. One passageway promises hope. With the woman held tight in both arms, I lean forward at speed—and crash through the sealed entrance. The mine's entrance collapses. The exit re-seals. We tumble into a mud pit staring at each other.

Remorse drags last night's memories to the surface. I bow my head low and grab the woman. We ascend into the night air. A thunderstorm passed an hour ago. Energy lingers offering a refreshing pick me up. The night air with its strong wind feels invigorating. I take deep breaths and spot a resting place for my cargo.

A hospital west of the park includes a helipad on its property. I descend and place the woman in the center of a large red painted "X," and take flight. Someone will discover her and perform a proper burial.

I fly several miles north. Below, a male prepares his fishing gear near the river. I have no way of knowing if he fishes tonight or prepares for early morning. Either way, he will nap first. I land and knock him unconscious with a backhand punch. The unconscious angler loses a pint, and I toss him on deck. He can sleep it off in his boat. I head back to the lodge and call it an early night.

The perimeter of the lodge looks somber. Two heat signatures on the property. Unable to tell who is inside, but I can see Theodore waiting outside on a bench near the back door. I'm in no mood for chitchat. Planned to head straight to my lair, however, I cannot avoid running into him. Darn it.

I descend fifty feet in front of Theodore and wait for my cue.

The lodge's yellow floodlights illuminate my stage. I'm ready to start the main act. I could bury my head elsewhere, but why put off the inevitable? Theodore needs to understand the real world of vampires before he gets physically hurt. This night provides the perfect opportunity. Hate to manipulate Theodore, but it's for his own good. If this play affects our relationship—so be it.

Theodore stands. My cue. I march forward keeping my head down. My cloak blows in the wind. Theodore says, "I worried about you. Thought you would join us last night."

I raise my head and face him. "Unless you're here to tell me someone I care about is on fire—it can wait."

Theodore gasps and stumbles. He tumbles over the bench. His hand braces on the wall catching his balance. "Oh, what happened?" He stutters, "You're hurt."

Andrea enters the scene from stage right. The second person I saw earlier walked on the opposite side of the building. He must have raced to get here.

"Salomé, stand down!" Andrea hastens to Theodore.

Andrea puts his arm around Theodore's waist and escorts him away.

Theodore pleas to Abelli. "She needs help—"

Andrea says, "No. What she needs is a long shower and

have everyone leave her alone." Andrea glances over his shoulder and scowls. He projects his rage. "What the *Hell* were you thinking? He need not see this. Not yet."

Andrea escorts Theodore after the main act. When they disappear around the corner, I use my door key and exit the stage. I enter the back lobby and gasp at my reflection. Leaning against the mirror, I pull down the lamps.

Titanium alloy handles activate hidden levers. The door swings open, revealing the secret compartment. I slink down the spiral stairway reflecting on my horrible reflection. Tonight's play sickens my stomach. Theodore saw my monster side.

Andrea was right. If any of Theodore's residual, "Vampirism is no big deal unless you make it one" lingered, tonight dissipated it. Heck, our friendship might have ended too.

I reach the inner lair's door and bolt it shut. Fernando made this place comfortable. Plenty to entertain myself with but only one thing I feel like doing.

And the tears are already falling.

CHAPTER 29

Rhinebeck's downtown shops display the quaintest items in their windows. I'm tempted to shop but could draw unwanted attention if I entered alone. Theodore and I must Christmas shop sometime. Theodore left a message on a clipboard near my lair's hidden door earlier. I had told Theodore, "I use the back lobby. Leave messages on the bench, and I'll read them." Heck, I'm surprised he still wants to associate with me after that stunt I pulled on him three weeks ago.

Andrea remains disgusted. He sends mental reprimands every time we meet. Andrea knows I hear every syllable he emphasizes. The man's routine grows thin. Guess the badgering will continue until I apologize to Theodore. Promised Theodore, I'll make it up to him. I just don't know how yet. I gave myself until the end of the year. Deadlines help if you wish to finish a schedule on time.

Speaking of deadlines, Eric scheduled mine tonight, in his unique way. He ripped a sheet of paper out of the clipboard, wrote a two-part message, and clipped it on top of Theodore's note. The extra chore took an hour but I didn't mind. Besides, what fun is it, if you cannot do surveillance for a family member?

Eric's instructions also said to circle Rhinebeck and look for a sign. The note said: "you will know it—when you see it." So far, I see nothing important.

Two buds exit a bar. They spot me, cross the street, and head my way. I pause on the sidewalk and scrutinize their every move. One man raises a phone. He says, "Yea babe, how about a pic? We'll make this moment last forever." Both men are in their thirties and wear golden wedding bands. People shouldn't stroll the streets drunk.

I grab the phone, notice the time, and toss the phone in the middle of the street. "No. Definitely not," I said.

The man shrieks and runs after his property. His buddy laughs wholeheartedly. "What's that, forth rejection tonight? You should walk home because you're not scoring any here."

"Weeknights are like that. Not my fault," the man said, inspecting his phone. He sticks it back into his pocket. Both men stare at the empty street. "Hey, where did that girl go?"

Up. Where nobody ever looks.

The fool's phone read 10:05 pm. Time for my surveillance. I fly a spiral grid pattern and survey downtown. No abnormalities below, although it would help if I knew what I search for tonight. The nation's big holiday doesn't help. Fireworks shoot pass and emergency vehicles respond to calls, but no signs jump screaming, "Over here."

My search expands. A field below displays a commotion. I pick an inconspicuous spot and descend. The flicker of familiar luminesce catches my eye. I readjust my descent and land next to a blanket with a painted luminescent "S" on it.

"Do you always travel with your blankie?" I asked Cadmael, landing an arm's width away from him.

"Woman, I wouldn't dream of traveling without it."

I comment to no one in particular. "Not the fireworks I expected."

Andrea and Eric stroll over to join us. Eric says, "The group practices Druid rituals with influences from the old Hellfire club. You look like shit. You OK?"

"Nice to see you again too. Yea. I'll live, in a matter of speaking."

Bio-dad and I keep missing each other since he walked out that night. We haven't had our chat, yet. My episode in the mine tunnel and worrying about any facial scaring prevented me thinking about the issue. Until tonight, nobody said a word about my looks. Leave it to Eric to do otherwise.

"What did you find?" Eric asked.

"Not much. Unless you want me to kick major butt." I study Eric and take a long breath. "OK then. Under the third bridge south of here, on the west side, armed soldiers dressed in dark blue camouflage accepted a delivery. Two groups of armed personal guards surrounded the delivery point. Someone anchored boats near buoys as a reserved backup. Frogmen waded in the water and one SUV parked on the bridge. Guessing the SUV provided a satellite link, am I right?" I wait once again. Cadmael and Andrea pause their activity and glance at Eric.

Andrea says, "Sounds like a large delivery—"

"Or one heck of a diversion," adds Cadmael.

I hold my stare on Eric. The man processes the info. He glances away and replies, "It's neither—and it can wait.

Back to the task at hand." I turn and face Cadmael and Andrea. They offer no responses.

The four of us take positions and watch a group of people celebrating in an open field. From what I see, they're in their late twenties. "What's happening? A guy coming out party?" I asked.

Eric tilts his night goggles up and walks over. "Father Moretti's inner circle, COATROSA. Take a moment and learn their faces, then tell me what you see."

This the infamous hunter group? I burn their faces into my memory. "A celebration? Lots of food on a portable table, a cooler of drinks. Young men dressed in mixed styles of dark clothing jump around like maniacs. No Fourth of July party I have ever seen. You said ritual?"

"Move your scan outside the group, at your ten o'clock."

I follow Eric's suggestion. At first, I see nothing special. My sight drifts. "There, further out. A Jeep Wrangler parked on the grass near a grouping of trees. A heavyset man paces, not paying any attention to the younger males in the field." I shift to infrared and do a complete scan. "Twelve acolytes, one driver," I said, before a pause. "And one, Father Moretti in the Jeep?"

"We suspect so. Theo discovered the secret meeting and called ACE. Said Father Moretti would arrive here with his group. Safe bet the priest waits inside the Jeep. Theo believes Father Moretti awaits an important delivery tonight, and I need to discover what. This priest is a pawn. We need to learn who's financing him."

"You figure the platoon has a connection with Moretti?"

"Grab a tree stump and wait. We're staying for the show."

∼

Within minutes after midnight, an SUV rolls off the road and parks itself in front of the Jeep Wrangler Rubicon. Lights turn off, and five soldiers disembark. The armed men surround the Jeep, their weapons trained on the inside occupant.

If Father Moretti is inside and makes the wrong move, this sortie ends right here. What's so important to demand all the security?

Another infrared scan shows more people inside the SUV. I hold up three fingers and point toward the vehicle. Eric nods. A man in body armor leaves the SUV and walks to the Jeep's driver. Its driver paces the whole time, and strangely, no rifle points in his direction.

The armored soldier places a grenade in the large man's left fist and pulls the safety pin.

Moretti's driver doesn't flinch. He holds out his other hand.

Driver's right hand latches onto a brown wrapped package, tied with a cord. The armored man says, "The Grand Scribe honors your second contract as promised."

The driver nods.

Armor-man strolls to the Jeep. He tosses the safety pin on the hard top. Soldiers pile back in the SUV. Headlights come on, and the SUV drives off the property.

A Jeep's occupant leaps out. He demands, "The package! Give me the package."

The driver strolls over. The Jeep's occupant swipes the package from the driver's arms.

The driver says, "Father Moretti. You hold what you seek these past years. Rejoice."

I add one more face to memory. "Father Moretti, you're targeted."

The driver reaches for the pin and reinserts it back in the grenade's handle. The man can stop pacing tonight. He tosses the weapon in the back seat and leans against the hood. Moretti shouts and dances with his acolytes for a solid thirty minutes.

"What's Moretti doing? Why wave at the moon and squash every ant in the field?" I asked.

The four of us stand. Eric announces, "We have seen enough. Mandatory squad debriefing at o-three-hundred hours, meeting room. Chad, tail the SUV."

Andrea swings his rifle over a shoulder and heads back to his car.

Cadmael gives a two-finger salute and a second ACE member disappears.

Eric stands with a hand on his hip. A stiff finger points at my chest. "You saw yourself what we're dealing with tonight. This setting will worsen before the summer ends. Unsure what happened in my absence but you better pull yourself together. You have experienced enough of life to know damn well, it sucks. I don't care a rat's ass if you gag or choke. Shallow your damn troubles. Nobody hinders or jeopardizes this team.

"We all have jobs to do, and I expect everyone to do them. That includes you. You need to recheck the drop-off area and cleanup. Professional security doesn't leave much behind them. Doubt you'll find much but if you do—take care of it." I was ready to cut in on bio-dad's speech until he continued with his story. "As for your juvenile chat you have been moaning about, consider this it."

I throw up my arms in disgust. "Fine." I give bio-dad a devilish pout and ascend far from the madness. If I stayed and argued, I increased my chance of missing my secret rendezvous.

Theodore's message said to meet him at "the witching

hour," less than an hour from now, which leaves no time to waste on Eric.

CHAPTER 30

When Theodore and I have a need-to-meet, we head to the local cemetery. Graveyards are dead at night. Pun intended. The witching hour comprises the night's darkest hours. The time humans belong in bed. Humans believe midnight the darkest hour, but that's a misnomer. In a metaphysical sense, anyway. Anyone working the late shift knows staying awake between two and three in the morning is near impossible. The human body wants to shut down during this time. It's a survival instinct. If you wander around when the beasties do—you lose.

A taxi arrives outside the entrance and parks curbside. Passenger door swings open and Theodore exits the cab. "Thanks for the lift, Joseph. No later than one hour. OK?"

Driver replies, "One hour. No later." Theodore shuts the door. The taxi drives around the corner out of sight.

Theodore whispers, "Salomé?"

"Inside. You want to leap or walk?"

"I'll walk. Thanks."

I grab the padlock on the chain and pop it open. When Theodore clears the gate, I snap the lock closed.

"Let's find a quiet spot," he said, jokily.

We stroll deeper into the cemetery and recline under a large maple tree. Mobile patrols focus on the cemetery stones and not the scenery. Although we should stay unnoticed, I can always grab Theodore and leap into the branches if the need arises.

"OK. You called the meeting," I said, leading the conversation.

"How did it go with Eric? Did Father Moretti show up? Was I right?"

"Yea. Moretti snatched his package and then danced the night away. We left afterward. Eric called a meeting later tonight. In the meantime, bio-dad is researching this nutcase. Moretti receives support from the higher-ups. Eric wants more Intel before acting. Me? I rather snap the man's neck and be done with it."

"You cannot! He's a priest."

"Trust me. I can. If you have forgotten, Moretti's the one who put the target on my back. Monsignor Smith is unsure, but I'm not. And if Moretti isn't the one, I bet he knows who did. If by some slim chance I'm wrong, I'll apologize to his corpse.

"Besides, I didn't like the vibes I experienced tonight. There was this huge secret black-ops payoff earlier. An armored bodyguard passed a package to Moretti while a mysterious man hid in a black SUV. The soldier wearing the armor suit mentioned a deal between Moretti and 'the Grand Scribe.' You ever hear of him?"

"Yes. I have heard the term mentioned. The man is a legendary Bigfoot in the metaphysical community. Stories originate back hundreds of years. Members of The Conmilitium Ineteriorem talk and occasionally joke about him. People have been searching for the Grand Scribe for ages. You should hear the stories. The man collects every item dealing with immortality. He finances his obsession by consulting with people who seek magickal items. The Grand Scribe hopes he might run into something that may interest him along the way."

"So, what's so funny about him?"

"Well, for one, he's searching for everlasting life, and the tales date back hundreds of years. Get it?" Theodore pauses and waits for my reply.

"Oh." Four firework rockets explode in rapid succession. The multi-color display distracts my thoughts. I should have known Theodore's hint but was reminiscing about Leslie's conspiracy theories. Theodore's tales don't compare. "OK. What else?"

"The man doesn't throw garbage away. Rumors label him a real eccentric hoarder. We joke about him storing junk in houses until the malarkey pours out of his chimney. The stories we share can get weird. You know how guys can get sometimes."

"The person with all the heavy protection tonight was no ghost. Be careful whom you laugh at from now on. They may be listening." I scan the cemetery and wonder if I do so out of habit or because of Theodore's story. "My time here grows short. Why the meet up?"

"As you know, I'm working my way into COATROSA. It's taking forever. Father Moretti instructed me to meditate on the seventy-two names of God. Any idea how long that took? Let me tell you, my butt felt sore for months. After that initiation, I learned their blasted secret cipher. They call it, *The Cryptic Rosary*. The code has five decades or levels. A guardian protects a key to their particular decade or level of code. Worked on the third decade this past spring. Moved up the ranks and gained enough trust to attend the group's meetings.

"Inform Eric, Father Moretti's no simpleton. People are wrong about him. He isn't crazy. He's mad. Father Moretti obsesses with ruling the planet, or in his words, 'all the kingdoms on earth.' He claims, 'my time has come to rule them all.' I figure he spent too much time reading J.R.R. Tolkien."

"Why Tolkien? *Lord of the Rings* a prerequisite for priests?" I asked.

"The epic has many undertones of Christianity, but most likely, he enjoyed reading the books. Heck, who didn't? Father Moretti is an avid reader too, or at least he was before he bonkered. Father Moretti memorized an old spellbook and mastered the spells. He later studied ancient and modern astrological charts. The man breathes the occult. Heard tales of people cutting him and watching his wounds heal by themselves, although I have seen none of the miracles myself.

"What I have witnessed is Father Moretti anointing a necklace last April. The man was freaky crazy about getting his hands on it. He acted like a child opening their presents from Santa Claus. Father Moretti wanted all his acolytes and special guests to celebrate. Let me tell you, I love rituals and incense burning, but stripping down with a bunch of fellow males under a full moon isn't my idea of fun. The things spies must do. You were right. Life isn't like the movies."

"Yea, about that—"

"I told you, forget it. You gave me a few rough nights of sleep. Chad and Andy helped me through the first couple of days. I don't hold grudges. Friends forever? I should have known better. Glad most of your scars healed though."

Theodore stands and brushes himself off. "If it bothers you that much, you can buy me a Christmas present, although I don't know with what. You get a real job?"

"Ha-ha. You becoming a priest or a clown?" I jump up and scan the area. "Unlike your story of Father Moretti, I don't heal instantly. Scary thought if the stories you said about him are true, but don't worry. Other than my facial scar, I'm fine. The night fades. I need to pass your information to Eric. You find any more info?"

A taxi arrives at the entrance gate. The cab leaves its parking lights on and waits by the curb. Theodore says, "Joseph is here. I cannot linger. The man likes helping, but he has a family waiting for him." Theodore glances at where we planted ourselves and checked his pockets. "No. That's everything, and before you say it—I'll be careful if you are."

"Deal. I'll walk you out and snap the lock for you."

"Don't bother. The stonewalled gate is only fifty feet long. I'll walk around this time. Better hurry, you know how punctual Eric is. If something else happens, I'll let you know."

Theodore enters the taxi. The cab drives off. I ascend into the night air. Eric thrives on punctuality. The main reason I take my sweet time heading back to the lodge.

If Eric failed to decode my earlier pout—shame on him.

I enter the back lobby. My summer cloak I toss on the bench. Familiar voices originate from the grand room. ACE members lounge on their chairs and sofas.

"What you're telling me is Chad tailed the scribe and lost him?" Andrea said.

Eric shakes his head in disbelief. "He *never* loses a tail."

Cadmael points his finger at Andrea. "No, I don't. The man is a phantom. I couldn't get a clear glimpse of him, so I left a tracker on his vehicle." Cadmael throws his arms up in disgust. "The darn SUV blows up fifteen minutes later. And don't tell me it was any grenade. Only high-grade explosive could leave the disorder I witnessed."

Andrea asks, "What about the people inside the vehicle, including your target?"

"No idea. Either the group blew themselves up or escaped sometime earlier, or I trailed a remote-controlled drone. I'm unsure what I feel worst about."

"The Grand Scribe got away from you?" I asked.

"Looks that way, first time for everything but don't worry none, he'll show his head again," Cadmael said, eyeing Andrea.

A humming noise resonates throughout the room. From everyone's demeanor, none of the humans can hear it. I listened to a faint hum entering, but the sound is stronger in this room. I grimace, trying to pinpoint the source.

"Salomé, we're meeting up here. I'm broadcasting jamming signals on the walls and windows. The signals blend and block any laser or satellite microphones. Whatever you're hearing, block it out," Eric said, sitting at the table. Stacks of files cover half its surface.

My palms hold my head tight. I visualize the moon singing her song. Her voice offers comfort and focus. "Can do. Why the change in plans?"

"Andy and Chad called an early day. How was cleanup?"

"As you predicted, scant leftovers. Theodore had much more."

"I take it you saw Theo? Where?"

"Where isn't important, but what is. We have a major problem with Moretti. He went Saruman on us. The priest grabbed all the cookies and joined the Dark side. Father Moretti picked up superpowers along the way too. Theodore mentioned a necklace and Moretti wanting to rule the world. I dislike carrying a target, but it's the least of our worries."

Andrea, Cadmael, and Eric tighten their circle. Three pairs of eyes squint their interests.

"COATROSA no longer serves the boys as a study group. The Father teaches the boys occult rituals. Theodore confirms it. The details are forthcoming. He also commented on our other POI (person of interest). Rumors say the Grand Scribe has roamed the planet for the last couple hundred years. Regular kleptomaniac that one," I said.

Eric spreads out folders in front of him. He says, "Makes sense. Monsignor Smith feared they might do secretive meetings and unauthorized magickal practices. I rented time from the University of Alaska and used HAARP (High-Frequency Active Auroral Research Program). The program studies the Earth's magnetic field in the Ionosphere. I pinpointed mystic anomalies by using specialized algorithms and links to our satellites. The upper portion of atmosphere picks up and holds onto different energies much like the physical effects in the human aura."

"You ran off to Alaska last month?" I asked. The night Andrea showed up, no doubt. "Don't tell me. ACE owns a jet. What about Mister Spook?"

"We charter," Eric said plainly. "It cuts down on expenses. Chad, call ol' Gabe to check on this myth. Send all folders, info, and tales your father knows about him. Andy, check with our recordkeepers. Have them search as far back as they can, to the source, if possible. I want the

Keepers to check and recheck if this scribe exists. Tell them 'highest priority,' let me know once they complete the file.

"Chad, you have your orders. Andy, after the Vatican —call Fernando. Tell him, 'Send them.' Fill him in on the latest info. The research will take weeks. In the meantime, I want everyone rested and equipment checked."

"Who do you want me to call?" I asked.

"No one. You could find a hobby to keep yourself busy, but since that's asking too much, scout Monsignor Smith's place. Watch for unusual traffic. The back of your clipboard lists his address. Keep unseen unless it's an emergency, and even then, keep incognito. I'm not revealing our hand, not that we have much."

Three sets of eyes stare at Eric.

"That's it, folks. *Meeting's over.*"

The humming stops. Bio-dad heads to the kitchen.

Andrea reclines in a leather chair. He says, "We reserved a roll of quarters for you."

"I'll pass. My journal beckons followed by a long hot shower. You guys interested in Nine Ball tomorrow night?"

"Sure, and we'll hold you to it. Just spell our names right and get out of the shower before you prune over." Cadmael forms a tight smile.

I stroll past the table, take a magazine, and throw a "later," over my shoulder.

CHAPTER 31

"Hey, listen to this. Moonlight acts as a synchronizer with water temperature, tides, and sunset timings to initiate egg and sperm cells release. The coral possesses photoreceptors that fine-tune the gamete release occurring to moon phases."

I glance up from my reading. Scattered white containers, cold drinks, an ice bucket, and paper plates cover the cocktail table. Andrea and Cadmael relax in the leather chairs. Both hold plates of food piled high. Cadmael points his fork at Andrea and talks between bites.

"Mind telling me once again, why you bought her that?"

"You know Eric said she should find a hobby. I figured that if she has her own tablet, it couldn't hurt. Who doesn't savor the entire world at their fingertips?" Andrea stands and helps himself to another drink. He examines my body with an exaggerated slow nod. "Besides, she doesn't seem the knitting type."

"Sounds like we're getting a lesson in sexual education, beginning with plankton." Cadmael gulps the rest of his drink. He rises and fills his cup with ice before adding the cola. "While I'm up, anyone want more before I finish the bottle?"

Closing the tablet's cover, I walk to the corner table. Sports, science and financial magazines are scattered on the table's surface. I display two women's fashion magazines in the air and get two headshakes for my trouble. I gather all the magazines in a single pile. Unlike the men in this house, I prefer eating at the table. Placing my tablet on top of the heap, I pat and straighten the towering stack. The idle chore doesn't improve my mood.

"You couldn't finish all that food if you had a week to do it, but I suppose I should eat before you make yourselves sick." I walk over to the coffee table and check out the choices. "I'll claim a half plate of pepper steak, and if no one minds, all the Buffalo wings."

Andrea plays the mother role. "What, no veggies?"

"My system barely tolerates human food. You don't want me to exceed my limit."

Cadmael takes two paper plates and double layers them. He plops down four Moo Shu wrappers. "So, no Moo Shu pork?" Cadmael forks Moo Shu pork on his plate. "Oh well, more for me."

"No. Cabbage would make me cramp and—"

"Stop! A rhetorical question if you didn't recognize it. Nobody needs to hear sentences with 'cramps' in it, while people are eating." Cadmael waves to the table. "Talk about plankton if you must."

Surprise why nobody else eats at the table, far more comfortable than balancing a plate of saucy food on one's lap. "Sorry, my mind was elsewhere. OK. Did you know seals are at a greater risk being eaten by a shark during the full moon since bright moonlight silhouettes them?" I nibble on a wing and then realize a Full Moon shines tonight. "Anyone interested in seal burgers?"

"She could have *learned* to knit you know?" Cadmael jokes.

I return to the drinks and fix an iced cola for myself. After a quick sip, I say, "Three weeks of scouting and we have nothing to show for our troubles. I have an itch that says a major battle brews. We heard stories of Moretti practicing and summoning nasty magick. The priest might be indestructible by now. So, where is he? What's he waiting for?"

The two men gaze off. Both focus their eyes on the Chinese takeout. Cadmael says, "Eric and Monsignor Smith learned little of value. The last time I heard, Father Moretti awaited the brothers' arrival. He vanished into the shadows last week. He told his inner group to meditate until he returned. Monsignor Smith is looking into it. Eric said, 'be ready,' so we're standing on call."

"How is eating food being ready?" I asked.

Andrea says, "We thought you would enjoy real food before we kick your butt."

Cadmael takes Andrea's plate and walks off to the kitchen. Andrea slides open a drawer under the lamp table next to him. "You recognize this?" He holds what could pass as a marble box. The unique hardwood called Tigre Caspi, fools many people. The first time I saw the orange-brown irregular wood grain was in Peru with Leslie.

"Where did you get *that* box?"

"Bracelets arrived earlier today by special courier."

Frown marks run down my forehead one at a time. "You know what's inside?" I said, hoping I can ask a rhetorical question too.

"We do know." Cadmael returns holding a second box. Identical to the first one. A smug smirk confirms his secret.

Cadmael hands over the second box to Andrea who interlocks the two tops together.

"Fernando informed us we needed to perform an offering, but neither of us knows the background. If you wish to fill your friends in, we would appreciate it." They plop themselves down on the sofa. Andrea separates the boxes and hands one to Cadmael.

"I'm not ready to tell my whole story in the Peruvian jungle, but an intro couldn't hurt. Understand this background story doesn't leave the room." I lower myself on the edge of a chair across from Cadmael and Andrea. They both lean back with a box on each lap.

"One box includes a set of Peruvian weave friendship bracelets. I imagine the second box holds similar items. I wore the bracelets in the jungle. Wearing them enhanced my schedule and removed years off my training. Trust me, the less time one lives in a jungle with certain people the better. I wore the wrist bracelets willingly. I didn't know the shaman created a second pair.

"The wristbands consist of several burrowing animal types of leather, soaked in a ritual brew, and strands of my hair woven with silver threads. A shaman asked for four strands of my hair, but I assumed he spun them into the single pair of wrist bracelets. The magick within the leather bands severely hinders my abilities and keeps me earthbound.

"Knot magick is specialized and limited. A shaman customized these bracelets for a particular vampire, me. You need strong magick to strip me of the goddess's hold. Blood magick excels all other magicks.

"Blood rituals have pleased gods and goddess alike since forever. Once you complete the ceremony, the night god presents the offering to the night goddess. We pray she grants the bracelets' magick to work. You must understand she always protects her children. She'll not allow long separation between them. If the goddess accepts the offering, bracelets will work for one night with a full moon.

"I'll experience slight withdrawal symptoms, but I'll live. Don't worry. You cannot un-vamp me. The goddess and I share a metaphysical bloodline. We cannot be completely separated."

Andrea says, "Well fancy that. We're in luck; there's a full moon tonight."

I stand and say, "Right now? I made plans to scout for Moretti. He hides under a rock somewhere. And, I intend to find him."

Cadmael jumps in on the conversation. "Father Moretti can wait. ACE figures another week until word arrives about his whereabouts. People like him cannot hide forever, and we cannot wait until another month.

"About time you get real battle training," Cadmael said, handing his box to Andrea. Cadmael stretches and fixes himself another drink. "We'll start with general tactics: night combat, reconnaissance, and smoke screening." He wanders the room, cola in hand. "This fizz tastes better when it's diluted." Cadmael twirls the ice before gulping the rest. A thunderous burp echoes.

"What are you, a child?" I said while making rocking cradling arms.

Cadmael tosses the cup in the waste. He focuses his stare on me. "Afterwards, we'll move to small unit tactics. Then, we train in hand-to-hand. Take a water bottle with you. Make sure you stay hydrated. We don't want you fainting on us."

Andrea asks, "That clothing comfortable enough?"

I say, "I'm always prepared to hunt—or fight—it's a vampire necessity."

"Good. Our training equipment awaits us in the back

pasture. Tie these things on and get moving. We got a long night ahead," Abelli said, sliding both lids open.

The wrist bracelets I recognize right away. Flash memories flood my mind. I shake them off and focus on the second box. Two bracelets inside, more intricate than the others with different leather and weave. Andrea notices my inquisitive stare and smiles. He says, "Ankle bracelets. Take off your boots."

My old boot knife hides within one boot. I'm tempted to keep the dagger hidden, but I remove the blade and lay it on the seat cushion. The boots, I unzip and kick off. I regret the quick action at once. Ever do something private and assume nobody would find out in a million years? I stare down Andrea and Cadmael who both have their mouths agape.

"Don't even think about commenting!"

The men watch each other. Their brains calculate their next move. I lift the dagger and place it on the armrest. The move should help them figure faster. Eyes bounce between the blade and me. Eyebrows dance, noses and lips twitch. In unison, they say, "What's there to comment?" Cadmael and Andrea take turns tying the wrist and ankle bracelets. They snicker but stifle it quickly.

"Now what?" I asked.

"You put your boots back on. We hike," Andrea said, surveying the leftover takeout. "The food will keep until we return. You can keep your dagger. Dagger is unnecessary, although, it may come in handy." Andrea tosses any garbage lying around the room. He seals the food containers. "OK. Looks good."

"I have the cooler and ritual supplies. We set up on the side deck. How long do we wait until the goddess accepts the offering?" Cadmael asked.

"On earlier ritual offerings, I felt the separation immediately or close to it."

Cadmael acts shocked. "Offerings? Plural? How many times did you perform this ordeal?"

"Several, and thanks for uncomfortable memories."

"Sorry, but you can take it out on us later—or try to," Cadmael said, with a trailing grin.

Andrea heads to the back door. He says, "Let us set up. You lay down in the yard. The moon shines brightly. Go do your part and we'll do ours."

I stroll out to the center of the yard and lay down on moist grass. The heavy dew eases my spirit. The moon shines in a cloud-free sky. In the years of sky-gazing, the moon persists in her beauty. For the bracelets to work, I must willingly disconnect my love of the night. If luck holds, the moon's devotion will only fade.

Fibbed earlier when I told Cadmael and Andrea I would experience, "slight withdrawal symptoms." Nothing slight about this ritual. The statement 'I'll live' is also a fib. If the night goddess believes my willingness to leave her permanent, she claims my life.

Leslie had mentioned stories about Tibetan monks willing their souls to vacate their earthly bodies. The monks could pick their moment of death. The technique is ancient and a guarded secret. Students rarely learn the practice. However, if the old gods recognize a boon, they may grant it to those they favor. I must make sure the goddess approves my request but still holds me earthbound. Andrea and Cadmael need not know my problem.

With eyes closed, I take a deep breath and center myself. I focus and hold my desire tight. Moments pass. Andrea and Cadmael ask, "Did it work?"

I answer, "Yea." I roll on my side and stand upright. Rising to my feet takes longer than it should. The guys notice it too. "It worked." Fragmented words echo in my head. The moon's hold fades but faint metaphysical odds and ends, in my head, seek a new home. All their moving around causes one major headache.

Cadmael asks, "You OK? That doesn't look slight of anything I have ever experienced."

"As long as I'm alive and my eyes don't glow red. I'll be OK."

"Your eyes turn colors?" Andrea said bending down to stare at them.

"No dummy, teasing. We training tonight or not?" My brain weighs heavy. Experience has taught me the pain will subside. I shuffle my boots on the ground trying to focus on any reality outside my head.

Cadmael points northeast. He says, "The battlefield is in the sheltered pasture. Nobody can disturb us, and no one will come to your aid. The rigorous workout starts right after a warmup jog."

Andrea jokes, "That is—if—you can run in those *Hello Kitty* socks." The two goofballs laugh at their joke. I let them have their fun and wait to see who gets the last laugh.

I cross arms over my chest and tap my foot. If you tease men, you aim for maximum effect. "Guys, you better hope the night goddess keeps her offering, because if she changes her mind," I said, holding my thoughts unfinished.

Cadmael and Andrea stare at each other. Andrea says, "Shit. Nobody said a word about refusing the offering." Before I can open my mouth, two macho men bolt toward the backfield. I laugh until the pain returns. And sprint after them.

So much for the warmup jog.

～

The northeast field differs from the other sections of the grounds. A double row of forty-foot high hedges sandwiches the white fencing. Privacy we have. Although with all the low-lying smoke Andrea dumps on us, nobody can see what we're doing anyway. Heck, my line of sight barely extends three feet in front of me.

Cadmael says, "You did well on ACE general and small unit tactics. You're accustomed to night combat. But you're having trouble with the smoke. Don't breathe deep, time your breaths."

I ask, "Why are we fighting hand-to-hand using smoke grenades, anyway? I thought you used them for D & E?"

"We do," said Cadmael, as we stray through the smoke. Its penetrating veil dissipates around us when we reach the field's outer perimeter. "Distractions, if we're coming in and extractions, for exiting. But in your case, you need to deal with the in-between. What could you do if you were already in close combat when the grenades explode? You must ready yourself for any unexpected diversions in the field."

The fresh air offers me renewed energy. Squatting low in a deep horse stance, I raise my knife to Cadmael's face. "Like this?" I asked. My empty hand tightens. A hammer strike awaits if he avoids my blade.

"Hahaha. I warned you earlier about that. Your knife will not help you any." Before Cadmael's smirk registers: he disarms me with a combination grip and nerve pinch then sweeps me off my feet and shoves my body to the ground. Within seconds, a forearm digs into my neck. "Knives scare children—not your enemies." He leans in with his forearm.

Cadmael's voice resonates seriousness. "When in close combat, you also deal with your attacker's weapon. You must commit yourself to *the violence of action*. Use all your speed and strength. Surprise the enemy, not warn them of your intent. In combat, there's no room for hesitation." Cadmael grabs my arm and twists it. His elbow digs into my neck. "The next time you pull a weapon on me or someone else—use it—or don't bother. Want to try the lesson again?"

I cough. "No. I'm good."

In truth, these two men wiped me out. I'm soaked through with sweat. My headache dispersed into nothingness hours ago, but every muscle I own aches. Years of acrobatic training toned my body for vampiric feats, but not for combat fighting. From what I experienced tonight with Andrea and Cadmael, unsure martial arts ability could have helped me either. I lay on my back and gaze upwards. I ask, "What move was that?"

He says, "Nothing I can teach you in one night. If you promise not to break bones, we can continue disarmament and takedown techniques once we store the bracelets in their boxes."

I drag myself back to my feet. Thigh muscles tremble and pulse throbs right out of my neck. I could massage my aches, but I can barely lift my arms. I half squat with hands resting on upper thighs and force deep breaths. Experiencing human fatigue sucks.

Andrea lays down his grenade launcher. He says, "Well, that was fun. Salomé, I have two percussion grenades left if you wish to learn another technique or two."

I grab a water bottle from the cooler and wave the smoke smell from my face. Who but Andrea could think of designing scented grenades? "No, thanks. Another night maybe." Andrea had better sense my sarcastic tone. One night training with ACE is enough. I quench my thirst and listen. From a distance, a ferocious whine originates from the main road. I have suspicions it'll travel in our direction.

A motorcycle slices through lingering white smoke. Eric huddles behind the handlebars. He kills the headlights. "She survived in one piece?" The remark sounds more of a statement than a question. He sits upright and removes his helmet. Eric asks, "Well, what do you think?"

"Yes. I'm breathing." I take a deep breath and stand upright. "Sweet ride. What's the deal with the smell? Drive through a rose hedge or two?"

I remember the scent. Hints of it have haunted me since my arrival. Now, the smell smothers Eric's motorcycle. Darn, another bullet point to add to my watch list. Bio-dad and I may have the same stalker.

Eric waves his hand in front of his face. "No. Picked up this Triumph Tiger Explorer XRT beast right after first light. I have been putting her through her paces. Used all five selectable riding modes and so far, this bike may make my favorite top three list. Now for the bad news, Father Moretti showed his head today."

The three of us gather around Eric.

"Someone outside COATROSA discovered our spy and reported their findings. Father Moretti was mad upon learning about our infiltration and took it personally. A brother overheard conversations not meant for his ears. Monsignor Smith is interrogating him. Theodore could recover in a week or two. Once he regains consciousness—"

"Theodore's unconscious?" I knew his assignment was dangerous. "You said Theodore would have a backup! Where were they?"

"Nobody's perfect. We couldn't protect Theo while he attended the meetings. Once inside, he was on his own. Theo knew the dangers when he agreed to the assignment.

It was no one's fault. Another brother set him up from inside the rectory. Monsignor Smith summoned medical help in time. Theo's safe in the hospital."

"You best make sure Theodore stays out of danger. And Father Moretti had better pray day and night nothing else bad happens or I'm ripping his head off his shoulders!"

Eric hunches over the gas tank. "How did that stunt work out?"

What? My father knows of that night. Guess Fernando and Eric exchanged a story or two. Hope Leslie entered none of those conversations. I can deal with existences of immortals but doubtful any human could. Immortality is too hard of a concept to grasp. Even though Leslie and I developed a cordial relationship after our time together in the jungles, his nature still scares the bejesus out of me.

Cadmael interrupts my mind wandering. "You did what? You ripped off a guy's head." Both he and Andrea turn and face me.

Now isn't the time to interrupt.

"Christos. Shut your trap before I shut it for you!" My eyes drift back and forth between Cadmael and Andrea. Neither of them retreats from my outburst.

Andrea creeps closer, inching outside of my peripheral vision. "Chill girl. Your father said Theo would be fine. Which means, he will be. Besides, ACE works with plenty of specialists. Monsignor himself watches over him."

"Abelli, don't you start!"

Christos says, "Don't know what came over you for the past months but move on. Shit happens. Calm yourself. We can handle this."

"The Heck you can," I said.

Eric puts on his helmet. "Andy, you better stay. She's about to go ballistic."

"Explosions are my specialty. I could stay and go for seconds on the Chinese takeout. Plenty leftovers."

"You cannot stop me from hunting Moretti and you know it. You'll need an army. So, unless you hide one up your sleeve, back off."

Eric says, "You're acting irrational and leave me no choice. Chad, you're with me. Andy, you get to watch them both." Bio-dad starts his Triumph.

Motorcycle whines fill the night. "Everyone else ready? Andy?"

Intuition says to run, but I lunge into a warrior's stance and ready myself for a fight. "We're not done here. What about Theodore and Moretti?" Abelli, Christos, and Eric wait. Abelli stands with his arms at his side. Christos sits behind Eric.

Abelli answers, "Ready."

Christos hops on the bike. Eric throttles his Triumph. *Barrooms* blast in the night. Abelli spreads his arms outward. A sucker punch connects. Sweaty arms and rose scent cradle me tight.

The night vanishes an hour earlier than planned.

CHAPTER 32

"Clark, you forgot your glasses."

"Don't push it, Diana. I can fly to the hospital, hang on the window ledge, and watch from the outside if you prefer."

"And have you crash through the glass when you see Theo. Not a chance. We have all seen—and heard—your temper."

Andrea's remark reminds me, I owe Cadmael an apology for being such a hothead.

Missed Leslie after his sucker punch a few days ago. I don't dare ask anyone the reason Leslie showed up or where he went. I must settle on guessing his Europe trip is over, and he misses my company.

Andrea waits in the living room. I'm using the couch to help pack a get-well box loaded with goodies. "Is Theodore that bad?" I asked, pausing my packing.

"Theo will pull through. He's tough and young, two great qualities to have in one's favor. You'll see for yourself if you hurry. Visitor's hours don't last all night you know." Andrea tosses a set of keys in his hands.

Kajika stocked two closets full of necessities when he built my new lair. Every style and combo I could imagine wearing. That includes the items for my plain Jane attire. Blue denim jeans, light blue polo shirt, and canvass shoes apparently make my new style tonight. My incognito disguise also has me with flat-combed hair, which I'll tie up later. A pair of glasses would complement this dorky Kent outfit.

The disguise allows me to blend into the background unnoticed. The hospital employees and anyone who spies on Theodore will forget my visit. I hate looking dorky, but sometimes you have to do what you have to do.

For the last couple of nights, I downloaded movies on my tablet. Theodore should enjoy watching them until he gets better and leaves the hospital. He might want to snack too, between scares. Heck, who doesn't? So, I include goodies with the horror shows.

Andrea paces. I had better hurry or miss my ride. The tablet I tightly tuck in the box. All the food packages look secure. Snacks should last several days. If they don't, I can shop for more. Headphones lay on top of the box.

"All set." I stagger to Andrea. "If you don't mind?"

Andrea exhales a long slow breath. "You realize, I know you can carry a small truck through that door if it could fit, don't you? Don't tell me you cannot shove that box under one arm and open the door with the other."

"I'm extra careful not to crush Theodore's gifts." I give him my best provocative look. "If you don't mind."

"Not at all, princess. I suppose you want me to open the truck doors for you too?" I bat my lashes. "Drop the gear on the floor. Let's go," Andrea said, locking the door.

I remove the noise-canceling headphones and place the box behind the passenger's seat. Once in the F250 Super Duty, I reach into the glovebox and pull out a red portable music player. Andrea drives this monster with a heavy foot. We hit the main road in no time.

Flashbacks of Theodore driving this truck surface. I readjust the headset's volume and cancel unwanted memories. Reclining the seat, I zone out. Andrea appreciates my solitude. He listens to AM radio.

The ride takes longer than I expect. I assumed Theodore stayed at the local hospital. I guessed wrong. Andrea backs into a parking slot. I unplug the headphones and toss the player back in hiding. The headphones I place back in the box. Before lifting it, I ask for our itinerary.

"What now?"

"We act like regular visitors. Visitation hours don't last all night. Once checked in, we stay as long as necessary. You ready?"

I remove the box from the truck and take a deep breath. "Ready as I'll ever be."

The F250 sounds its double beep. The truck locks and ACE equipment secures. We hike to the hospital entrance. Automatic doors slide open at our approach. Andrea heads to the reception's desk.

Andrea hands the receptionist a business card. Woman gives him an envelope with two passes. I tuck my pass in a back pocket. We head to the elevator and exit on the third floor. The stink at once assaults my senses. Nobody can mistake *hospital clean*. How do people adjust to this odor?

We make a left turn and pass the nursing station where we make a right. Andrea and I wear non-marking soles. We add no sounds to the already quiet workspace.

Two men guard the hallway. Men dressed in brown suit jackets stand at the ready. Unless the hospital policy allows tan combat attire and tactical boots, neither of them is a hospital employee.

Andrea says, "We have guards on the floors above and

below too." He enters room 387 without further comment. I trail behind him.

A man in his forties paces the room. Dressed in black; the white collar indicates priesthood. I assume Monsignor Smith sent him since I don't see the monsignor. Andrea asks, "Father Joseph, how is he?"

I wait by the door. I'm hesitate to intrude upon Theodore's privacy.

"He's doing well. The first night was the hardest," the father said, with a gleam of hope. "I believe the worst has passed. He'll sleep through your visit. The doctors have him sedated to ease the pain."

If the priest tries to console me, he failed.

As two men greet each other, the receptionist's envelope passes hands hidden in their handshake. Andrea steps off to one side of Theodore's bed. "I have someone I would like you to meet. Father. Salomé. Eric's daughter," he said, waving me into the room.

The priest pockets the envelope and steps closer to the door. "Monsignor Smith mentioned you would drop by tonight. You have grown into a remarkably fine woman since the last time we met. It's unfortunate to re-meet under such circumstances."

"This is the first time I have seen you. I would have remembered if we had met before now."

"Hardly. You were inattentive to Catholicism classes much less to the people who taught them to you. And unless one of your talents is a super memory, I find it doubtful you would remember the priest who baptized you."

I try to remember but come up with nothing. "Huh?"

"Ha-ha. Girl, your expression is priceless," Andrea said.

"Don't trouble yourself daughter. I understand your

dilemma. Monsignor Smith asked me to travel to New York and care for Theodore. I was Theodore's mentor when he attended school. Although untraditional, my duty continues to prepare him for the priesthood. We traveled in different circles, you and me, so I understand your forgetfulness. But you could have visited the church more often."

"I'll be honest. Childhood memories faded years ago. Besides, I rather visit the library than any church." Speaking the truth shouldn't hurt his feelings. But the comment he made earlier bothers me. I must use care to ask questions in this environment among witnesses. "Father Joseph, what did you mean when you mentioned one of my talents?"

I shift the box to a two-hand position. A box edge rests on my belt. Andrea studies my movements. Does he believe I could attack a priest in the hospital with the door open? Silly human. If you see me shut a door before speaking, then worry.

Two shadows outside the room join Andrea's concern.

Why the issue? Other than my emphasis, I kept my voice level regular, which means one thing. Someone planted a bug in the room. Eric said Theodore was safe. I should have expected this security. When will I ever learn? I tighten my grip on the box and refocus my attention on Father Joseph.

"You're aware Theodore spoke of you in private? He often mentioned how amazed he was on how you both found mischief yet maintained high grades. Theodore nicknamed the balancing act cosmic buddyship." The priest walks closer and takes the box. He says, "Scholarly achievement should be cherished. I hope you continue your higher learning?"

Father Joseph places Theodore's care package on an

empty side table. I answer, "Let's say I study technical courses at the moment and leave it like that."

The priest slides the curtains open. My closest friend lays in a hospital bed with IV tubes in his left arm. Black and blue marks cover Theodore's swollen face. A suspended sling supports his right arm cast from wrist to shoulder. White sheets cover Theodore up to his chest. Hard to tell if doctors cast or wrapped his ribs. The occasional facial grimaces show Theodore's pain.

"Oh, no. Father Moretti did that?" Andrea reaches for my arm. I evade the gesture and sidestep him.

"Four members of Father Moretti's group caused most of the damage. Father Moretti finished the job. A brother saw the attack. He said Theodore took four straight punches in the face. They took turns passing him around before he collapsed to the ground. The group then preceded to kick the young man's ribs. Father Moretti used his boot to smash Theodore's right arm. Daughter, I'm sorry it had come to this but—"

"Don't be sorry, Father. Tell Theodore I dropped off a care package. And, I'll take care of it. Andy, I'm leaving. I need to jog this off. Do yourselves a favor. Stay out of my way. I'll find my way out."

"You're not alone in this. We can help."

"Father Joseph, don't stop her. She needs fresh air. Let her leave. *She's fine.*"

Andrea's emphasis buzzes through the earpieces of two undercover guards. I lower my head and quicken my pace down the hallway. No one trails. My ride down the elevator is uneventful. I pass the receptionist's desk and ignore her plea for my visitor's pass. Doors swing open and I at once head skyward. I invade the bitter coldness and the blackened sky. Screams stab the clouds below me. The thin atmosphere delivers my frustration and hatred.

~

My disgust for Father Moretti and his thugs lingers. My earlier attempts at releasing stress helped, however, I cannot shake the inner hatred this man has caused me. It gnaws at my insides. Don't know what Moretti's problem is, but I bet greed ranks on top. If I'm right, I'll do humanity a favor and pound it out of him.

I lost track of the number of laps I have completed on these footpaths. The only reason I jog in Ferncliff Forest in the first place is that Theodore cannot. I want a pleasant memory, so I'm borrowing one of Theodore's. He said he enjoyed the tranquility of the area. Figure I would try it, but I have yet discovered any peaceful moments myself. Before gloom or doom overtakes me, I embrace night energy and take to the air.

Father Joseph explained Theodore's injuries. I would prefer collecting info from the source. Which means I visit Monsignor Smith. The impromptu trip is a pleasant diversion. I need to erase the image of Theodore lying in bed helpless with an IV in his arm. And who knows? Maybe hunt afterward. A bite does a vampire good.

Tonight's summer breeze carries a rare slight chill. I need not confirm the number of townsfolk who now sleep with open windows. People seldom get the chance to turn off the air conditioners and fans in the middle of summer but when the opportunity arises, most will.

I remember plenty of times I slept with open windows. But no person I know of leaves doors wide open. The dead of night harbors the criminal element. Although the blackest hours of the night benefit vampires, I find it doubtful Monsignor Smith baits the sinful tonight for the confessional.

Eric assigned me to watch this building for any unusual

activity. My past recon showed little importance. While I made sure nobody spotted me spying before, I take no precautionary measures now, descending on the back patio. I slink by the patio and observe inside the rectory.

The priest hangs up the wall phone. A young dark-haired male lies unconscious next to a staircase. "Salomé? I know I said anytime, but—"

"Monsignor, what the heck happened? You OK?" I invite myself in and study the young man on the floor. "Who's the kid?"

"That's Brother Aiden. He has been assisting me this past week. We had break-ins. Best you stay hidden. They may still be outside spying. Emergency personnel are on their way."

"I'll check outside and be back before the EMS services arrive. If any spies are outside lingering, they wouldn't be for long." I step outside and head to the shadows.

Infrared picks up heat signatures and tracks. Easy to detect where four people penetrated the perimeter. They gathered by the tree. Two sets of footprints left the property. Two people stayed in the tree keeping watch. Not only can I see handprints on the bark but also two large blobs in black cloaks hug the main trunk eight feet off the ground. Tonight, I hunt *fiends on a tree*. A vampire's menu is seldom dull.

My playtime with Frick and Frack must be short. Authorities arrive soon, and I want blood before speaking with Monsignor Smith. I didn't drink in two nights. ACE training exhausted me, and my concern for Theodore didn't lessen the stress.

I jog up to the base and climb the tree. The first male I meet, I knock unconscious. My love tap allows the second male plenty of time to scream. His scream sounds pleasing. If I was a psychic vampire, his terrifying scream could make a refreshing snack, but I'm not, and it doesn't. I want —and need—blood.

The yell stifles once both my hands wrap around the young male's neck. Fangs pierce human flesh. I suck out over a pint of blood, enough to make him woozy. I stare deep into his eyes. Top of our foreheads touch. "Payback for Theodore. Forget. Forget everything." I steal more blood and drop him, feet first, to the ground.

The second male I wake up and allow him to voice his fright. The kid's horror feeds my satisfaction. However, only his blood will quench my thirst. I take what I want and remove his memory. He'll not recall what transpired tonight. I drop his body and leap to the ground. Sirens blast through the night.

Both bodies hang over my shoulders. Their cloaks wrapped loosely around them. I carry the men inside the rectory. "Ambulance and police are a block away. I found these two spies. They forgot today's events. You want to take care of cleanup?"

"I believe my study will suffice. The front room on your left. Please draw the double doors closed behind you. We'll have a good *talk* later. Stay there until I open the doors. Read a book and do nothing else foolish."

I turn away and stare at the unconscious body. "Monsignor, this the dude who ratted on Theodore?"

"Brother Aiden confessed his actions. He saw what transpired and later confided what happened. I forgave him and assigned him penance. He's not your concern. You need to hide while I deal with our company."

Monsignor sweeps his open hand toward the study. Brother Aiden? The name sounds familiar. I have heard the name before somewhere.

"Looking forward to our chat, Monsignor."

I twist around Aiden's body adjusting the bodies on my

shoulders. Their legs knock the wall pictures. Luckily, no frames fall and crash on the wooden floor but I end up stepping on Aiden's hand. Bones snap under the combined weight of three people. I smirk. My foot twists and turns flesh, tendons, and muscle.

"Forgive me, Father. I have sinned."

The floor rat should consider himself lucky I didn't wear boots tonight.

Strobe lights shine through the windows. Doors open and shut. So much for my brief enjoyment and forgiveness. I hurry down the hallway and dump the bodies inside the study. Pocket doors slide shut. I search for a latch but find none. I drag the two unconscious males behind the Monsignor's desk. The already closed blinds prevent peeping Toms. I untie the curtains and pull them tight together, adding more concealment.

Floor-to-ceiling shelves line two-and-a-half walls full of books. An extensive collection, but no point starting a book if I cannot finish. A magazine sounds better to my liking. Catholic-themed magazines fill a cardboard box next to the sofa. Stacks of geographic magazines warrant their own bookcase under the window. Other reading material and catalogs are scattered on the other shelves.

I pull a random issue out and plop myself down on a high-back chair. A table light offers enough reading light and creates shadow if the need arises.

The tone of the detective's voice in the hall hints I might be here awhile.

CHAPTER 33

The ambulance drove away ten minutes after it arrived. Two detectives question the monsignor on the break-in and Aiden's injuries. Detectives linger in the hallway talking shop. The detectives' questions hide accusations. My hearing kicks in overdrive.

Other seminary residents' homes had break-ins. The detectives wonder if this crime relates to previous attacks. The monsignor said he wasn't aware of any robberies. But strangely, this news offers comfort to him.

Monsignor assures the detectives of his safety. He'll call Brother Aiden's emergency contacts and pray for his injuries. Monsignor Smith knows his psychology. He doesn't usher the detectives out. The priest waits and allows the officials all the time they need.

His plan works. The detectives lose interest and are leaving of their own accord. They know something's amiss but are unsure what.

Study doors slide open five minutes after the detectives' departure.

"Water?" Before I reply, a bottle whizzes in my direction.

It was an easy catch. I place the magazine on top of the other two I read. "Thanks. You knew of the break-ins?"

Monsignor Smith slides the doors closed behind him. He strolls to his desk and notices my two-body pileup. "Father Moretti removes all loose ends behind him."

"Was it Father Moretti who attacked you?" I open the bottle and sip. Chilled water. I take half a mouth full and swish. Thought of gargling but I finish the water instead. "You know Moretti's location?"

The monsignor settles in a chair behind his desk. He ignores my art piece. "I wasn't attacked. I met with three of his students in our library. Father Moretti instructed his study group to disband earlier today." Monsignor Smith pours water into a teacup and drinks.

"The break-ins, the rat, and Theodore are loose ends?"

"Father Moretti surrounds himself with his most loyal of acolytes. Any other past contacts of his, he treats as a threat. My reports say Father Moretti wants to purify and cleanse himself. Not only from outsiders but also for his ritual."

"Tell me where I can find him. I'll rip him apart and remove the target on my back at the same time."

"I'm not convinced Father Moretti is the one targeting you. He focuses too much on other matters. Besides, I want to question him. That means we need him alive.

"Your friend Theodore compiled information on Father Moretti." A single-note fart *pops*. The monsignor cringes and surveys the small pile off to his left. "Excuse me, while I make a call." After two rings, someone answers. "Please prepare my limousine. Thirty minutes should be fine. Thank you, Father." The monsignor replaces the receiver on the headset. "Where were we?"

"Theodore."

Monsignor Smith straightens his back. A recollection and a calming breath are revealed in his movement. His posture slackens. He leans on one armrest. "Yes. The information he gained gave us great concern. COATROSA consisted of a few members outside of this seminary. These strangers joined and replaced the members who had their family homes broken into lately. Before you say I lied to the authorities, the question they asked was if I knew about the other break-ins. Which, I didn't. But I recognized the names the police mentioned and surmised the rest."

"I can do simple math too. I cut the serpent's head off and the body dies. One-minus-one equals zero. No more threat."

"Isn't there? What about Father Moretti's sources, his superiors, the Grand Scribe?" the monsignor said clasping his hands on the desk.

I cannot believe I'm about to say this.

"Monsignor, you must know I'm no saint. I kill people and drink their blood until their body drops. Most of my victims deserve death. A rare exception didn't. She died anyway. I know death. Soon, Moretti will too. Trust me."

Within a few years, I progressed from a high school graduate to priest killer. Am I a demon?

"Salomé, daughter, I know of your academic background. You're an astute student, no doubt. I understand your nature and its necessities. I have dealt with vampires and other nightkind. When you feel stressed, you must learn to trust and gain support from others. People who love you. I cannot say what troubled you so profoundly these past weeks, but please understand you're not alone.

"I cannot condone killing. However, Father Moretti may know of your existence. He has been a dozen moves ahead of us this whole time. Although, I expect Eric will give Father Moretti plenty of strife. Trust your father in this affair. Trust your friends too. We must all make choices and later live with them. My child, whatever troubles you will gnaw at your insides until you release it."

"The night takes care of her own. Make no mistake. I'm a daughter of the night, child to no other. I know my duty."

No sense delaying, time to leave. I rise and stretch my arms. "Thanks for the chat. We must do it again sometime."

"Father Moretti is a worthy adversary. His magic is strong."

I pause at the doorway, one door slid open. "Vampires sense and use magic, Monsignor. We exist, in part, because of moon magic. Magic isn't kryptonite to vamps."

"By itself, perhaps not." A pause stills the air. "Unless—"

"Darn it." I turn around and face the priest. "Unless what?"

"Eric informed me about the amulet you wear. Nothing in detail or personal just the basic principle. Is it true you're able to call demons?"

"They're known as *familiars*. They do my bidding. I command and summon them when necessary. So?"

"So, could you summon them without your amulet?"

"Heck no. The amulet houses and provides the neces-sary—oh, shit." A nasty sour feeling burns my stomach. The bad news is coming. My body shuffles toward the priest in a zombie-like trance. "You're not telling me Father Moretti has an amulet too, are you?"

"Worse. I discovered what 'brothers,' Father Moretti

waited for these past years." The monsignor checks his wristwatch. "You better sit, it's a long story."

I lower myself on the sofa and stretch my legs on the seat cushions. An armrest and two pillows support my back. "OK. You know who the brothers are?"

"These brothers are a what, not who. Our story begins with *The War of Two Brothers*. The year was 1807. The Napoleonic campaigns in Portugal created political strife. Portugal's royal family and court fled Lisbon for Brazil taking their gold, silver, and jewels with them. John VI showed no interest in ever returning to Portugal. After much deliberation, he, with his wife and second son Dom Miguel, returned to Portugal in 1821, leaving his eldest son Dom Pedro governing Brazil.

"When John VI died, Dom Pedro inherited the Portuguese throne. However, Dom Pedro declared Brazilian independence in 1822 and became emperor. Dom Pedro planned to abdicate the throne in Portugal if his brother Dom Miguel married Dom Pedro's daughter Maria when she reached the proper age. Dom Pedro later sailed to Portugal and created a new Constitutional Charter as Peter IV of Portugal. He left Maria the throne and Dom Miguel as Regent. Dom Pedro returned to Brazil afterward.

"Politics entered the equation. One of the country's political parties were loyal to Peter IV. He was their rightful king by birthright. The other party favored Dom Miguel. They theorized Dom Pedro was Brazilian while Dom Miguel was Portuguese. Rebellions surfaced in Lisbon. Dom Miguel nullified the new Constitutional Charter shortly after its creation with his backers' aid. His supporters proclaimed Miguel II king of Portugal in 1828. Peter IV regretted the decision."

Love history but not tonight. My patience grows thin. I

point my water bottle in Smith's direction. "You said Moretti waited for brothers, a what, not people."

"Yes, I did," said the monsignor, brushing me off with a breath. "Dom Pedro abdicated his throne to his son and sailed to Britain. He funded a military fleet to defeat the rebellions and keep order in Portugal. Long story short, Dom Pedro restored the peace six years after his brother claimed Portugal's throne. Dom Miguel was exiled from Portugal forever, and this left Maria, at age fifteen, the ruler.

"This is where the story interests us. Court witnesses state the brothers wore Ruby necklaces at the Constitutional Charter's creation. A belief exists that Dom Pedro sold his necklace to raise funds for his army. I have a sketch I'll show you in a minute."

"This *Dom* thing a title?"

"Yes. It's a Portuguese title for family members of the nobility. As Legend has it, both rare twin rubies originated from an exclusive Sri Lanka mine. Nobody knows for sure where or when. The Rubies ended up in Burma, and in the 16th century, a group of Tibetan monks traveled there to work Tantric dark magick on both rubies. The twin rubies resurfaced in an Eastern Indian temple a hundred years later. When the Portuguese invaded India in the 17th century, they brought treasure back to Portugal with them. Historians believe the twin rubies were part of that treasure and later added to the Royal Court treasure."

"Good. If Father Moretti wears a ruby necklace, I'll recognize him. Makes my job much easier."

"Hardly. You should learn about the gems. Earlier alchemists treated the rubies. The gems' internal structure changed. Inclusions formed inside where none existed earlier. An impossible asterism formed; a six-pointed star miraculously appeared in each ruby. Also, both twin rubies contain trace elements of unknown origin. Indian mystics worshipped the gems. Following generations of mystics shaped the rubies into cabochons and wore them as necklaces.

"People recognize rubies the world over as powerful gems. They amplify cosmic energies." His last words trail off. A stillness intrudes. "Daughter, make no mistake, this unique pair of rubies carries dark and mysterious tales associated with them. They're known in occult circles as the Burmese Doms or—*the Brothers of Burma.*"

My lips part. I exclaim, "The brothers aren't people, but gems? No wonder Eric had trouble locating them. He'll not be relieved when he finds out though."

"Eric spent hundreds of hours researching the brothers. No. The news will not amuse him," Monsignor Smith chuckled.

The monsignor's posture slumps an inch. He strokes his chin, his mind in deep thought. He says, "Father Moretti tested the necklace last Easter summoning Shades. Spirits of long-dead ancestors to aid the living. Father Moretti was foolish enough to test the necklace farther. One night, he jumped into a pit. And his disciples dumped poisonous taipan snakes on him. The amulet protected him. As long as Father Moretti holds onto the amulet, I fear he might be indestructible."

"You said two brothers, two rubies. Where's the second necklace?" I asked.

"Historians believe traders sold the stones independently years ago. Slim chance the twin ruby shows up anywhere. Although, Father Moretti mentioned he waited for the brothers. Plural." Monsignor Smith opens a desk drawer and pulls out a file. "A sketch of the doms wearing the necklaces."

The *splat* made by the dropped file leads to a quick

glance and a long stare at the floor. After a reluctant creep to the monsignor's desk, I pace the room with the file in hand. A technician retouched the sketch with some type of image ware. What I surmised was a charcoal rendering is, in fact, a colorized version of royal jewelry.

Two rows of diamonds surround each of the cabochon-shaped rubies. Six-pointed stars gleam in each gem. The tech used too much white. Large links of gold make up the chains.

"To each his own. I don't wear tacky oversized jewelry." I drop the file back on the desk. "That's my target then. I remove Father Moretti's amulet. He loses his power."

"We don't know for sure, but you must retrieve the amulet or amulets." Monsignor returns the file to the drawer. "We have another problem."

My body cringes. I clasp my hands.

"Father Moretti appropriated a package last month. You saw the delivery."

"You refer to the crazy dude handing out hand grenades?"

"Father Moretti covets ancient knowledge. Knowledge so old and lethal, it should have been destroyed eons ago. The father hired a specialist to locate the artifact. You saw the security behind the book's delivery. Vast resources could only mean a large shadow organization. Theodore uncovered one item of Father Moretti's and your friend suffers because of it. If you interfere with their organization, prepare yourself for the worst.

"Inform your father; tell him Father Moretti has the *Tablet of Eluppu*. Travel quickly and report what I have told you. Be careful. Don't underestimate your adversary. We'll talk again." Monsignor peeks behind his desk and picks up the phone.

Guess that is my cue to leave, and I best before the driver enters.

I exit the study, trod through the hallway and freeze dead in my tracks. A full-length antique mirror hangs in the back lobby. The monsignor didn't comment on my disguise. Gads, I hope he doesn't believe this my typical attire.

Footsteps echo. Shoulders dance and hands fasten a nonexistence cloak. With fidgeting fingers, a reflected plain Jane says goodnight. I hasten my exit into the night air. Tonight's flight requires a quick return to the lodge.

Time and essentiality permit a fashion change before talking to Eric. Bio-dad could die laughing seeing me in pigtails. Monsignor Smith's latest news demands seriousness. This Tablet of Eluppu sounds evil. Eric had better discover its details quicker than he did with the brothers.

CHAPTER 34

The secret door swings and closes behind me. My clipboard lays upright on its bench. Eric left a message: "We roll tonight. Dress appropriately. My office."

"Yes!" About time. I hope Father Moretti surrounds himself with a dozen of his acolytes. I feel extra hungry tonight. Theodore's injuries deserve a thousandfold payback, and I'm the one about to deliver it. Moretti, wherever you are, you had better pray.

My blue hunting attire is inappropriate. Tonight's festivities demand special preparation. I return to my lair and head to the closet. I pass the khaki and camouflage patterns. Military clothing is too impersonal. An odd mixture of dark greens and brown leathers suit my taste. Now, to check the trunk and accessorize.

This old trunk stayed in my ownership since Master Kajika said, "You may keep it with you always." I couldn't imagine back then that the trunk would travel parks, caves, jungles, and New York safekeeping my belongings. When this mission finishes, maybe I can sand, stain and varnish the wood. The trunk's steadfast dedication deserves the extra care.

The Wolverines from my prior cave training also deserved care. I treated them with mink oil and wrapped both in an old newspaper. The boots are the one item I kept from the outfit Leslie gave me. Their steel toes and heavy protective soles top my accessory list tonight.

My gifted dagger I remove from the chest. Kajika commissioned the blade. As much as I love the piece, ritual charmed items belong in a safe place. This gift is strictly for special occasions.

A shaman asked one Peruvian night what I would wish for a reward. Already accustomed to jungle life, I couldn't picture any wants. Much like the night, the jungle also cares for her children who listen to her song. I told him, "Surprise me."

The shaman later honored me with an alpaca leather holster. It holds my charmed dagger and includes an extra covered pocket. The holster is a thoughtful gift, and handy if I don't wear high boots.

I wrapped the holster, with my dagger, around my calf. Wolverines I double tie and stick any loose lace inside the boots. My roomy sleeves I tighten with leather cords. I tuck a bandanna in a pocket and head upstairs.

Cadmael and Andrea are descending the stairs when I round the corner. Cadmael pauses on the landing. "Who do we have down there, Robin of Rhinebeck?"

Andrea slings a large duffle bag over a shoulder.

"Is this a jollying old man with his ogre helper? You two stick out wearing green camouflage against a red wall. You ruined my belief in Santa," I said.

"I don't consider myself old," said Andrea. He studies Cadmael. "Or am I the ogre?"

Cadmael and Andrea step down into the living room.

"In this light, it's hard to tell. I'll let you know after coffee," I said.

"Coffee sounds great. I'm sure Eric has a pot or two waiting for us. What say you, Robin, we continue our jest over our favorite brew?" Andrea half-heartily slaps my back.

Cadmael leads us to the secret entrance into Eric's abode. He opens the interior closet wall and we trot down the lighted stairs. "Maybe later, Andrea can find a feather in his bag for your outdoorsy outfit." I could kick Cadmael's butt, however, Andrea walks between us.

I make my reply brief. "Keep in mind guys, magical bracelets rest safely in their storage boxes." One tease deserves another.

A full twelve-cup coffee decanter awaits us in the corner. Two brown paper filters with fresh ground coffee wait off to the side. We'll use them before the meeting's end.

We take our turns preparing our drug of choice. Cadmael heads the line. Andrea dumps his gear on the table. I wait behind Cadmael.

I tell Andrea, "Ladies first."

Andrea bows low. "After you, my lady." His left arm sweeps to his side.

My knee bends high in his direction.

Andrea jerks upright.

Cadmael swings wide holding his coffee. Not a single drop falls.

I glance at the far end of the room. Teeth pinch my lower lip.

Eric scowls. He doesn't appear pleased with our pre-battle banter.

Last night, I repeated Monsignor Smith's intel upstairs in Eric's study. Eric was enraged when hearing of "the

Brothers of Burma." More so about their charmed magic. Andrea and Cadmael lounged in sleepwear sipping tea. If either of them listened, it was inadvertently.

Eric ended the meeting at three o'clock. Said research called. Andrea and Cadmael both sleepwalked to their rooms. What followed later in the day, I don't know. The lodge's daylight schedules are unknown but the early night meant I could hit a hot shower, add entries to my journal and allowed time to catch up with reading.

However, tonight has a different vibe. Files lay on the table with our names on them. Eric's idea of place markers, no doubt. As long as I kick butt tonight, I don't care where I sit. We lift our four mugs and make a silent toast. We take the first sip and slurp in unison. We open our respective folders. Eric starts the meeting.

"Another HAARP report came in from DARPA (Defense Advanced Research Projects Agency) last week. Disruptions of unexplained weather patterns showed Father Moretti's activities in South America. Moretti was practicing his sorcery or scouting for another target. It explains why we couldn't locate him. Monsignor Smith interrogated former COATROSA members and learned of Moretti's intentions in South America. Also, the monsignor discovered Father Moretti's plans for tonight."

Eric stands taking his coffee with him. "I'm refilling. Abelli, show Salomé her new hardware, while I brew another pot."

"My pleasure." Andrea unzips the duffle and displays the contents on the table. "The large heavy gear belongs to Christos. You get these three."

I stand and walk over to Andrea.

Andrea says, "This specialized flare of mine emits black smoke with a chemiluminescent indicator. I added a self-propelled directional turbofan to keep the smoke vertical. We'll spot the smoke miles away. You also inherit, at no added cost, an ACE custom red percussion canister. For extraction, use this special yellow smoke grenade. I found spare time so, I handcrafted this matching holster for your mini-grenades. The flare, stick it somewhere."

"I'd rather have a rocket launcher and blow the guy to bits," I said.

Cadmael leaves his chair and heads for a refill. He says, "Heavy equipment belongs to yours truly. If you hear a missile whizzing pass you—run."

"Don't worry. We'll extract you before someone gets trigger happy," Andrea said, pausing long enough to refill his mug. "Questions?"

"No." Best fill up on coffee myself. One long night lies ahead of me.

Cadmael says, "Well, I got one. How does she tromp through the woods without her feather? Better recheck that duffle." He roars with laughter at his joke.

One tease deserves another.

I remove a clean mug from the tray and exchange it with the one Cadmael drinks from faster than his eye can detect. To add a special effect, I don't return to the coffee machine. I empty Chad's refill with a *slurp*. His bellying laugh comes to a sudden halt when he realizes I'm no longer at the coffee marker.

"Hey, where'd she run off to?" Cadmael said scanning the room.

Cadmael spots me standing next to Eric. He picks up his coffee mug and finds it empty. "Darn it girl. Taking a man's coffee and drinking it crosses the line." He walks over to the brewer and fills the mug. "At least you saved me enough for a second cup."

"Glad you're all enjoying your pre-battle jitters. When you're all reseated and serious, we can continue our meeting. Christos, while you're standing there, make yourself useful and make another pot of coffee," Eric said.

Eric plugs a power cord into an outlet and flips toggle switches. Concealed monitors appear out of the conference table. All monitors automatically turn on displaying a broad vertical bicolor banner of gold and white. A horizontal red bar with the word, "active" appears on the bottom part of the screen. The room wall monitors mirror the same display. I focus my attention on the meeting.

My father checks his wristwatch. "This meeting is officially live." A moment later, a letter "S" superimposes on my screen. I recheck the wall monitors, and each displays a different emblem. None show a simple single letter.

"Last night I learned the owner of the *Tablet of Eluppu*. This information originated from Regent Smith and then passed to my daughter Salomé. For those who are unfamiliar with the Tablet of Eluppu, allow me to explain." My bio-dad finishes his coffee. He glances at me and side nods in my direction.

Unsure what Eric asks for, I twist and check behind the chair. Stacks of eight-ounce bottles, balance themselves in the corner. I mouth, "Water?"

Eric half-nods.

I leave my seat and break open a pack, placing a bottle in front of everyone. Saving a bottle for myself, I drop the extras with wrapper at Eric's feet. If dear dad wants seconds, he can help himself.

"Our research teams couldn't locate reliable sources referring to the tablet. And beyond 30,000 years ago, the tablet doesn't exist by name. At least any names we could find. Himalayan sages mention disruptive mantras that date the pre-flood era. The yogis confessed the mantras originated from an unreadable manuscript, which a monk translated from a much older piece. How someone accomplished that feat, nobody knows. Two Tibetan scrolls showed promise. We secured them for further study.

"Cultures throughout the world cherish their creation myths. The Aborigines of Australia speak of totemic ancestors who roamed the land at the time of creation. During this *Dreamtime*, these beings would sing the name of animals, reptiles, mammals, and elements into existence. For life to continue, as the ancients created it, the Aborigines enact the totemic songs and stories. Aboriginal ceremonies continue Dreamtime into the present world.

"We believe the Tablet of Eluppu does the exact opposite of Dreamtime. What the totemic beings created, the Tablet of Eluppu uncreates. How the tablet works, we don't know.

"The folders in front of you include files with several other possibilities for the tablet: Lilith's instructions for speaking God's true name, the ultimate poison, an alien technology, and the world's first heavy metal sheet music. A joker sent that last entry anonymously. We have an opening in our research department if anyone wants to recommend someone. You have my contact numbers."

A dozen plus files in this folder and nothing useful. I peek in Andrea's direction and across the table to Cadmael. They both skim through their records. Andrea glances up at Eric.

"We locate Father Moretti yet?" Andrea asked, closing his folder.

A PowerPoint presentation projects on monitors. I memorize the slides. Eric continues with his commentary. "Legends say the practitioner who reads the Tablet of Eluppu, must possess a particular ritual tool at the time of reading. Lucky for us, ancient forbidden sorcery demands ritual instruments that no longer exists. However, it also forces people like Father Moretti to build their own.

"We traced Father Moretti's travels from South America. I figure he searched for meteors and either couldn't find one or didn't like what he found. According to the charts we gathered from Father Moretti's old room, he summons sky-iron tonight. Directly from the asteroid belt."

"Darn, I hate want-to-be Doctor Evils," said Cadmael. "Why do these power-hungry fools insist on destroying the world they want to rule?"

Bio-dad continues, "We have a target. Doodletown. The town derived its name from the Dutch word, *Doodel*, meaning Death Valley. The place is now a Ghost town surrounded by a natural park across the river.

"I speculate Father Moretti's ritual works on the principle of like attracts like. One reason he may have picked Doodletown. Iron in the area also repels and constrains fairies, ghosts, witches and any malevolent supernatural creatures. If I'm right, Father Moretti couldn't have picked a better place for an undisturbed ritual."

Eric labeled and circled several important sites on the slides. The intel can be handy if Father Moretti's group plans their ritual in Bear Mountain Park. If not, Eric wasted hours making this presentation. I finish my water, lean forward into the table's edge, and memorize the park's layout. Bio-dad continues with his meeting.

"Major rituals need significant grounding. The old mines under Doodletown provide the father's requirements. Authorities closed the mines but watch out for old entrances. Moretti's followers might use them for exit routes.

"Five mountains surround Doodletown. Four roads lead in, not counting the other escape routes. Growth covers most entrances. It provides cover, but it also shelters Moretti's men. Make sure you keep your peripheral vision moving. We need no surprises," Eric said, warning the three of us.

"Salomé. Signal us to confirm the location. I don't want to spook him. He disappeared before on us. No telling where he'll hide next. We can arrive within thirty minutes. Stall until we do."

Andrea asks, "What's the story on our other POI?"

"Nobody within the Vatican archives concedes his existence. I used the video monitors to send my requests. I threaten to fly to Italy myself and beat the files out of one of the clerks. Screamed I didn't care which clerk. All four clerks watched when I phoned the airlines. In all my years, I cannot believe such resistance. They're shipping copies of the Grand Scribe's files overseas. The archives cover three hundred years and will take decades to read them.

"From what the stories say, he's a hired archeologist. Father Moretti already has what he wants. Unless the Grand Scribe also supplies weaponry, and the tales don't show this, I figure he's no longer our concern. We can deal with him later but for tonight, watch for any armed security.

"If no further questions?" No one replies. Eric pushes his mug away. "Meeting's over." Wall monitors switch off and display default screens. The table monitors return to their stealth positions. "Salomé. After the mission, tell Theo only what he needs. Keep it to a minimum."

Eyes blink twice for my reply. Eric's meaning is clear. Once we remove this Moretti fruitcake, we could possess three powerful ancient—and deadly—magical items. Nobody wants Theodore getting grandiose ideas.

Eric mentally sends a message, "Do what you need to do. No hesitations."

Secret orders? An involuntary eyebrow raises in

response. I gather my gear, strap on my new holster and recheck my dagger. I'm ready as I'll be.

I say, "See everyone on the other side."

"You mean the other side of the river. Right?" asked Cadmael.

"What else could I have meant?" I pause and ponder my reply. "Oh, yeah. Sorry guys." I tuck the flare in the small of my back. "Father Moretti is the one who needs to worry. Together we own this sortie. Let's go."

Eric stands. His hands rest on the table. He says, "You heard her. Move out and stay alert."

Fathers. They sure love to give orders.

<h1 style="text-align:center">CHAPTER 35</h1>

"Two bridges south and fly west," Eric said. "Begin your search at the first lake you see." I have minimal direction in locating a power-hungry madman, but I must make do. Everyone depends on me finding Moretti, detaining him, and summoning the team for cleanup. But my plan varies a degree from Eric's. My ideas generally do.

Before I travel further, I need a pit stop. Coffee before a battle has a negative downside. The park below provides plenty of logs and cover. But it also offers clean restrooms. Why rough it when a girl can get privacy?

I drop and pop the lock on a restroom door. I pull out my old friend from my boot and wedge the dagger under the door. The blade will halt any four-legged creatures intruding upon my privacy.

Once I have taken care of business, I tighten my gear and head to the mirrors. I don't accessorize, but a braided feather in my hair might improve the look. Who knew Cadmael and Andrea had fashion sense? I wash up, cover hair with the bandana, and hit the night air.

The lake Eric spoke of lies below. I head to its center and ascend straight upwards. A thousand feet above ground level, I search eastward. Then fly counterclockwise. A vampire's advantage from this height cuts scouting to mere moments. If only I can find the right sign… Bingo!

Two people stand on a mountaintop. Four bodies patrol four road entranceways. Small groups wander the paths. Guess I found Doodletown. For a ghost town, the population is high. I bet Father Moretti walks in the middle somewhere, which means I work my way into their circle.

Dropping out of the sky, I attack a mountaintop guard. His neck snaps before my feet hit the ground. "Don't you know night hunting is illegal?" I said, facing his companion. The second guard leaps forward. I strike with my hip and toss him. His neck breaks a second later.

Two dead men in gray camouflage, more in wait. I search through their gear. Both held assault rifles with scopes. My search halts when I reach the miniature ear mics. Whatever else they carry can wait.

Eric said Doodletown is surrounded by five mountains in a seven-mile radius. My vision cannot pinpoint people past a one-mile radius no matter what height I scan from, at least not yet. If these guards communicate with each other over several miles, I best hurry. Eight more guards need my attention.

Anyone carrying assault weapons on the surrounding mountaintops scores a broken neck. All eight of my latest victims hide earpieces and wear similar gray camouflage. How is it I'm not surprised? Had I run into any campers, they would have awoken miles away with a severe headache.

Detectives know the dead tell tales. And this stripped-down corpse can tell a doozy. I hope. So far, I'm disappointed. Protein bars, spare batteries, military-grade mace, and a stun gun, which shows these men are overpaid scouts. On closer inspection, the earpiece appears one-way. Receive only.

I secured the outside perimeter. Time to move inward. I'm betting the guards patrol the entrance roads with post orders not to leave, no matter what. ACE can handle them later. The inner patrols win my attention first, one at a time, and then Moretti.

Doodletown lies due south from this mountain. I leap outward, flying at treetop height. The rollercoaster flight causes me motion sickness. I ride the discomfort out. One thing matters tonight and only one thing. My mission.

Mister Lunch patrols a wooden path alone. I swoop down and tackle him. Clamping my hand over his mouth, I drain his blood without remorse. My peripheral vision reads clear. The patrols have split up. I ditch the body in a rock grouping. The cemetery located off the nearest path shows movement. Good. I could use someone to wash down Lunch.

Trees and overgrowth provide cover most of the way. Gravestones shield me in the graveyard. Although hallowed ground, vampires feed where they wish.

Mister Wash-me-down strolls pass. I stand to brush up against him. Both hands clamp on his face. I take him down. He breathes dirt. Within moments, he breathes death.

A wave of energy riffles through the cemetery. The air quiets. A bright red net crisscrosses over the area. Magick.

As much as I prefer Moretti for myself, I don't want him escaping. I remove the flare from my waistline and activate the built-in spring mechanism. Andrea spent days designing this beauty. The spring activates the flash and timer. A battery hides under the small blades to power the turbofan. Once the flare emits black smoke, I unfold the housing's built-in side stakes and stick them into the ground. Now I must wait for ACE's arrival.

And this is where we reach the part where my plan differs from Eric's proposal.

Eric wants me to nap on my rump and not do a bloody thing worthwhile. Bio-dad and I see life differently. The way I see things, the quicker I remove Moretti's acolytes, the better. Weighing both strategies thoroughly in my mind, I ease farther into the woods.

Another patrol at my two o'clock. Two armed men; one of them leans against a tree vaping. I bypass these two and ascend through the red energy netting discovering its limited range. The net only covers the graveyard.

I fly higher and find the other local cemeteries have energy netting too. Father Moretti tries to control the ghosts in Doodletown. Guess he seeks privacy. O'boy is he in for a surprise.

My next victim stands by a small lake. I descend and double fist the guard's skull. The body collapses.

I whip around. "Latin?" I said, before seeing the source.

A sharp blow hits my chest. Paralyzing pain blasts through my body. Two men hide under a rock shelter. One man aims. Two gunshots ring out. I twist, contorting my body. A dragon breathes. Fireballs—two of them—devour me whole.

My body scorched, I fall motionless on a soft corpse.

A thirtyish-year-old man dressed in traditional priest garb stands over me. His short cut dark brown hair and clean-shaven face jumps from my memory. Father Moretti! Beside him, stands an acolyte with a shotgun. The grin on the latter invites an attack. I would oblige but cannot move my limbs.

"We finally meet face to face, *vampire*." Moretti's emphasis on vampire sounds grainy. The sounds of two slugs sliding in the shotgun bother me too. A *clank* indicates a reload. "You look different. On earlier occasions, you seemed younger. Love the outfit or what remains of it. All badass and tough. Are you tough? *Vampire*."

Again, with his emphasis. My night worsens.

"What are you blabbering about, priest?" Magick immobilizes my arms and legs. The dragon breath ammo burnt the better half of my body. Few positives in my favor but at least I can stall.

"What did you do?" I asked.

The priest is carefully holding an old grimoire. Its distressed leather binds about four hundred vellum pages. Whatever book it is, it's no Table of Eluppu. The priest pats the grimoire's spine. "I crucified you. A spell I learned in my travels."

"Moretti, your ritual here is finished. Surrender."

"It matters not you know my name, demon. My ritual can wait. The heavens align within the hour. You and I shall talk afterward."

I'm positive Moretti didn't spot me last month. What does Moretti refer to when he said I look different? And what is wrong with my outfit? Moretti can answer my questions later when we're alone. One item remains on my list.

Moretti commands, "Call the rest of our brothers. We have a Holy mission to carry out." *Shotgun-man* radios the order.

Five enthusiastic unarmed young men respond within moments.

Father Moretti clutches his book close to his chest. His other hand tightens around the lower right corner of his jacket. "Brothers, beware of demons traveling the woods," he said.

The crucifixion spell spares my head and torso, but my arms and legs are inert. Each time I move, I flop like a fish out of water. Helpless.

The five latest arrivals circle my body. Father Moretti and *shotgun-man* stand to the side. The signal flare's thirty-minute limit draws near, as does my stalling time. Where are they? If Eric forgot to fill the vehicles with gas, tomorrow he ends up in the middle of the ocean!

Best to stall until I have no choice to use my backup plans. I'm guessing that maybe five minutes tops before the man with the shotgun blows my face off. Better, pump Moretti for information while I can still speak.

"You hid in wait, at the ready. You knew I was here?"

"My acolytes spotted you on seminary property several times throughout the past year. I have seen you with the spy. I was confident you would stick your nose in where it didn't belong. A simple spell cast over the cemeteries alarmed me of intruders. Where else could a demon hide if not among the already dead?"

He said he spotted me with the spy. Theodore? I wriggle in a try to break the spell. The corpse underneath gets the sole benefit.

"I recommend you halt your resistance unless you choose the taste of fire. Although Disciple Paul's marksmanship abilities are unquestionable, he lacks patience." Father Moretti waves his arms in a circular pattern. I flinch, expecting another spell. I get no relief when he commands, "Carry her to the pit!"

"*ARRRGH.* Shit! Damn you, Moretti. *UGGH.*" Ten pairs of hands grab my body. Half of them support me over burnt flesh. My brain recoils. I scream to the heavens and curse the ground. I officially declare tonight my worst night ever. However, Moretti isn't getting the best of me yet. Time for "Plan B."

"Hey, crazy priest-guy. What direction is this pit?" A telepathic message trails my question. I focus it at Moretti.

"For you, straight downward." Father Moretti slips on the loose ground. He mumbles a swearword and regains his balance. His lapse of judgment proves helpful. He outstretches his arm and points in a particular direction. Moretti says, "That way. Hurry."

I don't care a rat's tush where we march. Can deal with that issue later. My eye tracks the priest's hand. It returns to the lower right jacket corner. Father Moretti clenches something important in that pocket.

Wish my telepathic abilities were stronger tonight. Father Moretti blocks my attempts into his mind. He falters but quickly regains his balance. Guessing he uses a protection spell.

I next order the five goons to lower me on the ground and attack both Moretti and the man with the shotgun. But it too fails.

I'm too weak. Although, I invaded my carriers' minds enough to overlook my weapons and lessen their pressure on my burns.

After a beautiful sightseeing experience through the woods, we come to an abrupt halt. Best to prepare for "Plan C."

"Drop her in," the priest commands. Four disciples heave. The fifth disciple delays his release. I land like a ragdoll. My arms and legs fold at awkward angles. "You should feel honored. That pit once belonged to one of our country's esteemed inventors," the priest said, easing up to the ledge.

Wished this esteemed inventor removed all the sharp stones before he left. My back loves attracting the bloody things. One stone sticks into my right shoulder blade while another stabs my hip. Binding spell holds. Cannot move easily. If they move elsewhere, I might find time to breathe.

"No *real* priest wants to destroy the world. What the heck are you doing?" I asked.

"What I'm doing is no concern of yours, and the word is Hell. You're old enough to speak the term. Or is that *was* old enough? Hahaha."

Father Moretti opens his grimoire. He thumbs through the pages. Within a second or two, Latin spurts from the priest's mouth. Who uses a dead language? Don't understand a single word he speaks, so I focus attention elsewhere.

Peeking at the grimoire's cover, I mutter to myself. This night just fell apart at its seams. "Shit."

The night quiets. Father Moretti closes the cover with a cabochon ruby embedded on it and leans over the pit. His grin disappears. A serene expression fills his face. "Any last confessions, my daughter?"

Is this nutcase serious? "Priest, you're no father." I manage to move a finger. Moretti receives my answer. Although, I find it doubtful he noticed.

Five disciples ready themselves at the pit's ledge. Their postures are solemn but the acolytes' faces display tight-lipped smiles.

Moretti calls attention. "Brothers?"

The young men wait with their hands in prayer position. The disciples watch their master. It takes forever until Father Moretti barks his orders.

"Stone the demon. Stone her!"

CHAPTER 36

*P*lan A and B failed miserably. Implemented Plan C when we reached this pit. The plan waited because diverting pain and not losing consciousness took precedent.

I allowed myself to enter a deep meditative state before the rocks fell and crushed my body. Father Moretti's madness and evil plan, I wrapped, forced, and placed in my mind-cave. I now travel the inward passageways.

I visualize bursting flashes of colored light flowing through my chakras. Crimson red floods the bottom of my spine. Bright orange fills my stomach area, followed by a canary yellow. Emerald green with specks of pink enter my heart. I breathe the higher, vibratory colors of true blue and deep indigo. Each color, in their respective chakra, works their healing magick. When vivid violet reaches the top of my head, I take a deep, concentrated breath.

My mind exists outside of time and space. Heck, I might be dead for all I know. I hold on to the vivid violet and allow the transformation. The color diffuses into lighter shades until I'm bathing in brilliant golden-white light.

I imagine myself healed, even my clothing. I overlook the park on my ledge. A gorgeous night with glittering moon and stars. My body looks in prime shape: healthy, relaxed, stress-free, and ready to attack. I chant a mantra. Either the amulet's Gatewayer will restore my body the best he can, or this pit serves as my grave. If I'm not already dead, Moretti and his followers will soon finish their job.

Peeking with one eye, no clouds or harp players anywhere. Better yet, no fury blazes, sulfur smell, or agonizing screams. I'm alive. A sky-blue glow encompasses the pit. The Gatewayer's presence. Father Moretti practices nocturnal magick. Well, two can play that game.

Tossed into a pit could mean a dangerous situation. The *gruesome five-o* dumped my body on its side. Right arm shielded my face from their direct hits. Most of my wardroom malfunctions hide underneath or against the pit's edge. Also, my left leg bends behind off to one side. My knee is hyper-extended.

I'll limp in the future, but this position helps my predicament.

My enchanted dagger lies within grasp. One perfect stomach crunch should do it. Ready, set and, "Aww! Arrrgh."

I reel back. Dammit.

A quick mental damage inventory says I broke my right arm. Maybe in two places, one above the elbow and another near my wrist. A bone sticks out of my right thigh, clean break. I hope. Any fractured ribs I overlook. No pain —no gain. Right?

Teeth bite hard.

In the last effort, fingertips grab the handle. They flip

the dagger into the air. My left hand snatches the leather handle. I tighten my grip. Leaning forward, I cut.

I don't recommend using your scalp as a cutting board. But I only have a single choice. Father Moretti's resurrection spell holds my extremities. Need to break the hold. And I *need* a blood ritual.

Leslie once said, "Learn the basics first. Improvise later if you must." I'm uninterested in witchcraft. Spells take forever to see results, sometimes a whole month. I'm a why wait girl myself. Rituals need sacrifices. That knowledge, I can use.

I lean forward once more and snatch my offering. Blood, hair, and dagger rest on my amulet. The Gatewayer's light pulsates. A million zillion stings, dull hypodermic needles penetrate my body. The sharp pain causes me to double over and straighten both legs. If my vocal cords could vibrate, they would scream. I hug myself hard. The fact of moving my extremities shows the spell's removal. A positive sign but the pain continues.

My mind flashes back. Rocks and timber pin me. Two dead bodies lay in a tunnel. I killed one of them—no—I killed them both. One deserved his death. The other died by my negligence. A boulder, resting next to them. The size of… an asteroid!

Dammit. I cannot let Moretti destroy innocent people.

I shout, "Release me. Now!"

The temperature in the pit drops twenty degrees. The amulet's light disappears. My surroundings darken. I'm no longer in the Gatewayer's care. Whatever healing he did, will have to suffice. Lucky Moretti left my brains intact and me semi-unconscious. Must return his thoughtfulness, right after this one chore.

I have miscalculated and underestimated the priest's mission. My mistake and I take full responsibility for it. If I cannot complete this mission solo, and ACE cannot back me up, I know who can.

I hold the amulet in my dominant hand and proclaim:

> *"Hail Makari. Wise and Faithful to the Loyal*
> *Three.*
> *I seek your aid and summon Feker, Amha, and*
> *Bahmat.*
> *Their price promise in blood, paid this night*
> *two-fold.*
> *Grant my request and assist me against my foe in*
> *combat.*
> *Gatewayer, mighty sage, my desires for your*
> *aid extol.*
> *May the gods favor your name beyond the end*
> *of days."*

Sky-blue light bursts from the amulet. My eyes close shut. My body tightens. The light entombs and attaches itself to my aura. I gaze upwards. Three of the strangest supernatural beings wait at the pit's ledge, each with an inquisitive expression.

"Great to see you again. I have a chore for you. Afterward, we party."

Feker and Amha help support my weight on our way to Father Moretti. They did their best patching my wounds. Feker cut my trousers to shreds while Amha used the strips for bandages. Amha used small branches and the leather cords to splint my forearm then sling the immobilized arm to my chest. A whole pant leg worth of material wraps ribs.

Any unnecessary remaining material, Feker, and Amha used for resetting my right leg.

The four of us didn't fit in the confined pit and I wanted someone to stand guard. So, I instructed Bahmat to gather sturdy wood for my leg splint while keeping eyes open for intruders. He was all for the idea. Despite Bahmat's stout built of four feet two inches, long dangling arms, large far-width eyes, he's a sweetheart.

Feker, Amha, and Bahmat are incorporeal spirits. They shape-shift and take on a physical form depending on what their last offering supplied them. Consequently, that varies tremendously.

Technically, they are Tulpas or Thought-forms. Makari, the Gatewayer, is the Tulpamancer who created the Tulpas with the unmanifest concentrated matter in the earth's atmosphere. He lives in the amulet. I don't know why or how.

I communicate with my inarticulate, charcoal-colored, putty-like humanoid familiars via telepathy. Their survival depends on offerings. During the time my familiars inhabit the amulet, I burn incense. When they roam, I offer blood or other liquids.

We arrive at one of the local cemeteries. I halt the team and point at the gravestones. This section of the woods looks familiar. I cast a glance upwards over the consecrated ground. Father Moretti said he spelled the cemeteries. I saw the red netting myself when I descended earlier. This place is where I landed and set the flare. The cemetery's red mesh glows darker than it once did with diminishing luminescence. ACE didn't, and cannot, spot my signal!

Fate dealt me a dirty hand. Just what I need in my condition. It's time I reorganize.

"OK. We can make this mission work. Father Moretti

placed a spell on the graveyards. Stay away from them." Bahmat hastens behind us. His shorter foot strides cause our delay. I wait until I have his attention. "When we spot the disciples, you take the point," I said. "Feker, Amha, and Bahmat, you each take two apiece. The priest is mine. We clear?"

Their telepathic response is immediate.

Our mutual grins seal the pact.

My right arm wraps around Feker's neck while Amha supports me at the waist. Father Moretti and his disciples all squat circling a small campfire. The priest reads aloud from his book. He calls and summons the Watchtowers. Strange to witness a priest do ritual while sitting but Eric mentioned an important grounding in this area. To interrupt the priest in the middle of his magickal circle could be fun, and chaotic.

Bahmat catches up to us. I ask, "You ready?" He offers a handmade six-foot staff. The supportive staff lacks aesthetic beauty, but it's the thought that counts. "You made this? Always watching after me, aren't you?" Bahmat blinks twice, for yes.

I lean my weight on the staff. Feker and Amha take their places behind Bahmat. "OK, lead the way." My right hand grasps the amulet. A sky-blue light encompasses our group and creeps towards the campsite at Bahmat-neck speed.

The Gatewayer shields me against any further attack spells from Moretti. But, his presence comes with a price. The million-zillion blunt hypodermic needles once again penetrate my body. Instead of doubling over, I scream. I scream bloody loud.

My outburst serves in different ways: it helps me focus on my mission, it grabs Moretti's attention, and the yell got ACE's attention—if they're in the neighborhood.

"You mentioned earlier about a confession, priest?" Father Moretti jumps to his feet. His disciples stare, unsure what transpires. "Bless me father, I died. Descended into Hell and returned with real demons. I have sinned and will sin again."

Panic-stricken young men arise. They herd. Heads turn back and forth. An acolyte or two face me but most stare at my familiars. The men's faces droop and turn white. A putrid smell enters the air. Six acolytes beat a hastily retreat deep into the woods.

My familiars pursue them. Bahmat pauses at the campfire to pick up an abandoned rifle. My ever-thoughtful Tulpa gawks at Moretti before continuing.

Father Moretti sickens. He holds his book and jacket corner tight. Two shotgun blasts ring out. Agonizing screams succeed bursts of flames flashing bright orange.

Moretti and I stay our grounds. The priest stands motionless. He's overwhelmed seeing actual living demons and lacks the know how to compute it all. Me? I wait for the finale.

The screams stop. Silence. One can listen to the distant running stream. A distant hope arrives too, which tells me the night soon ends.

Father Moretti catches his wits. He moves in my direction. I shake my head sideways and point down the path. The Tulpas drag six dead young men back to the campsite.

My familiars stay within a tight perimeter unless I command otherwise. I granted their release to redeem offerings. They now return to eat. Well, sort of.

Each Tulpa attacks and digests their victim differently. When Tulpas eat, expect a smelly, chaotic and disgusting cleanup. A person needs ice in their veins to witness a Tulpa's eating habits.

Three familiars slouch by the fire's perimeter. Tulpas cannot digest flesh. They're energy creatures. Tulpas metabolize the blood and other bodily fluids. Any solid tissue, muscle fibers, and bone pass right through them.

Feker and Amha break the men's extremities off in pieces. Feker prefers to use a stick to pry the juicy parts away from the bone, while Amha squeezes and sucks the goodness out. When Feker and Amha work their way to the larger pieces, both smash them with rocks. Sometimes they thrash their prey on the ground.

Bahmat is different. His eating varies depending on the local atmosphere. Take tonight, for instance, Bahmat shot dragon breath ammo into his offerings. The direct shots opened the men's chest and faces. Payback and convenience at the same time. Bahmat is indeed thoughtful and witty.

Father Moretti doesn't appear to appreciate the irony. He parodies the art piece *The Scream* by Edvard Munch. Who knew I affected lunatics so much. Must be my new look. As amused as I am, my pain tolerance dwindles. I have an unaccomplished mission and an ACE helicopter approaches. Unless I want to share Moretti—and I don't— I had better hurry and finish this fight.

"Hey, Moretti! Forget the demons. You and I have a reserved dance together."

The priest whirls in my direction. He hisses, "You dare to challenge me?" He stumbles. Teeth grind in anger. "You can barely wear clothes, much less stand."

I send Feker and Amha a telepathic command. They respond in unison. The priest rattles off Latin. His facial muscle tightens; his envious green eyes narrow. Moretti projects his right hand. His index finger digs in my direction. The man winds up his arm, shouts a yell, and releases one whopper of a spell that fizzes into nothingness.

"It won't work, I'm protected." Father Moretti projects an aura of determination. He flips through his book. I cannot trust luck. This priest may find a spell that could work. I command, "Do it."

A double handful of burning coal pours down the back of Moretti's neck. He screams.

"Profanity? I'm surprised. Father." He ignores my jab and swats imaginary mosquitoes. The book falls to the ground. The good father senses someone nearby. He pauses his shuffle long enough for a second double handful of coals down his front jacket. His tune changes. He now jitterbugs.

"You cutting a rug by yourself or can anyone join?" The priest mumbles but even with my hearing, the sounds are unrecognizable. He unbuttons and drops the jacket at his feet. He checks himself for embers. By the time he rights himself, Father Moretti notices his grimoire and jacket lay by the fire. Bahmat guards the items.

"You don't want to imagine what he can do with that empty rifle Moretti, trust me."

"Vampire, you're less than what you were earlier." The words conceal his disgust. "What makes you believe a demon spawn can stop a man of the cloth? This night belongs to nobody but me. I spent years studying scrolls and manuscripts. Hours spent in thought charting the heavens. I worked too hard to quit."

Father Moretti glances at the campfire. My familiars munch on his disciples' remains. "I killed you once tonight. I can do it again. Demon spawn, prepare to return to Hades."

"You despise me, don't you? Something I said?"

The priest attacks and lunges for my throat. I drop the

cane and sidestep. When Moretti passes, I sidekick him in the butt. Hard. My wounded leg at once disapproves of the impromptu defense. Before the priest can attack me again, I grab the staff. I forward roll, hitting the ground hard, thrusting the staff upwards. Rough broken edges scrape and lacerate Moretti's face. He bleeds.

Father Moretti circles away in disbelief. I inch closer to him. I'm finished if he retreats. My broken body cannot give chase. I must keep Moretti within arm's reach.

"Don't see your cuts healing, priest. Your gods abandon you. One doesn't trifle with unknown pagan magick. Maybe you could stick to confessions," I said teasing.

Moretti stares over the rims of imaginary spectacles. Neck veins convey his hatred. He boasts, "I held the boxing title in college three years running." Moretti charges. "We fight another round."

Fisticuffs with a vampire? A partial *Art of War* quote comes to mind: "… if your opponent is of a choleric temper, seek to irritate him." I say, "You always this conceited or is the moon pulling out the lunatic in you?"

Father Moretti tucks in his chin and pummels my ribs.

I block with my elbow and forearm. Moretti's smart. He sees one of my arms in a sling tightly wrapped to my chest. And one of my legs poorly splinted. He fights on my weaker right side.

A sideways left jab breaks the priest's nose. Another jab cuts Moretti's lips. And a lucky backhand smashes his ear.

Moretti baits with matching jabs, bashing my jaw. Teeth clamp on my tongue. The force of the blows throws me off balance. Intuition screams. "Here it comes!" Didn't need to ask what. Everyone knows what takes out a superior adversary.

I squat and perform a back roll. Rolling on the ground

with a splinted leg off to one side hampers mobility and inflames my burns, but I succeed. By the time I stand up, Moretti's uppercut reaches its peak.

My body acts sluggish. I'm in lousy condition to fight. Moretti readies himself for round three. Unless my fangs sink deep and drain him, I have one reserved move left.

Difficult to maneuverer a fighting staff with one healthy arm but I manage. I swing, focusing my strikes on his arms and hands. A swift kick in his privates could help me, but my splinted leg refuses. I brace the lower end on my hip and twist, fast.

Moretti blocks my headshot. He changes his stance and karate chops the staff in half!

Shit. "Martial arts too?" I said.

"Beginner's lessons but enough to resend you to the depths."

What else does he hold up his sleeve? I can take no more chances. The mini-grenades hide under my waistband. Father Moretti and his followers overlooked my weapons. Cannot rely on my luck to continue.

If I present knives or a percussion grenade in this fight, Moretti realizes I carry weapons. He can use them against me or retry a spell. Neither choice works in my favor.

I remove the yellow grenade, stick it under my underarm, and twist the cap. Andrea designs his toys with options in mind. This beauty performs multiple duties, including a particular knockout gas formula. I toss the grenade behind Moretti. Yellow smoke bellows and rises.

"A signal?" The priest spits into the smoke. "Had plans of collecting the bounty with you alive. I could have ended your pathetic life, you know."

"You made the contract?"

"Not me, girl, but I intend to collect. One way or another."

"Yea, right after you rule the world with your tablet. Where are you hiding it away?"

"*Ha-ha*. As if, Vampire." Father Moretti advances.

The *whup-whup-whup* of the helicopter reaches the clearing. "Willie Pete" joins the dance. White-gray phosphorus smoke grenades bombard the entire area. Gas grenades land at my feet. Father Moretti, already woozy, coughs and gags.

Bet his eyes sting too. The ACE training prepared me for this environment. I can assure you it was an unpleasant experience. However, I cannot take pleasure in Moretti's discomfort.

The smoke screen provides a cover. I recall familiars to the amulet. Their joint energy drifts Father Moretti away. I shout, "Hey, Moretti!" He stumbles in my direction. "A gift from Theodore!"

I jump up and kick both feet out fast and hard. I land flat on my back. If Moretti yelled, I missed it. Pain runs through my body. Splints fall apart, bones pierce flesh, ribs collapse, and my head smacks the solid ground.

"Over here!" someone yelled.

I stare upwards. A young woman dressed in a maroon pantsuit kneels. Scents of rose and sandalwood linger. The helicopter lands. Moments later, the girl's long, chestnut hair blows wildly. Smoke dissipates. I recognize her.

"Who—"

"Don't worry, sis. I got you." People exit the helicopter. She waves. "She's hurt. Hurry."

Cadmael and Andrea bolt from their ride, armed with their rifles. If my lungs worked, I could take a breath of relief. Cadmael says, "Inform Eric and your mother, she survived." He pauses. "Have them summon the complete team plus one. We're immobilizing her."

The girl kneels. She says, "You're fine. I promise to watch over you."

I call out to Cadmael. "Moretti? Rubies. Book. Jacket. Separate them." My voice fails after each word.

Cadmael says, "Father Moretti collapsed. Heard his knees crack across the field. He lays unconscious, dead to the world. Don't fret. We came prepared. You did a commendable job."

Andrea returns with a polyethylene neon orange board. "Good to see you survived your first ACE mission. Wait until you see our future adventures." He aligns the spinal board against my side. Andrea says, "This might hurt a bit."

CHAPTER 37

"Kitty. Stay away. You could..."

"She's out of it!" Words blast in my ear. "Eric!"

I roll on my side. A hand pushes me back. "Check your surroundings first, sis. You're back at the lodge."

Dim room, no artwork, and walls painted beige with gloss white trim. "Am I in the living room?" I prop myself up on a cot. Six other cots stored in the corner, four IV poles, and people wearing white lab coats watch monitors. And, some bright soul remembered to include the hospital scent. I ask anyone listening, "You transformed the room into a hospital?"

I recognize the girl. She spotted me after the Moretti affair, although her strong rose scent is absent. "Dad. Salomé's awake," she said.

Eric enters the room from the kitchen. He says, "About time. Get her the drink." The girl runs off. Eric rests in a folding chair next to the cot. His shoulders hunch forward. "You all right?" He takes a breath straightening his posture. "How much do you remember?" he asked, peering into my eyes.

"I remember *my room* with *no siblings* and a dream. Hey! I dreamed while I was unconscious?" I asked myself.

The girl returns with a glass and pitcher. She pours a half glass. She says, "Fernando's special blend."

"Drink or these doctors stay another night," Eric said, waving around the room.

I sip the drink offered. "What is in this? Tastes weird." The second sip, I swish around my tongue. Before anyone answers my question, I guzzle the rest. My eyes ask for a refill.

The girl fills the glass. Bio-dad answers, "Mostly a blend of blood and organic mint tea mixed with fresh ginger."

I straddle the cot and savor my drink. "Must get the recipe. Now, who is the girl?"

Eric says, "Let me introduce you to our newest member of the team. She tells me you two already met. She helped to back up Theo."

Images of Theodore flash in my mind. I stare at the girl. "She could have backed him up better." Pieces of ginger spice swirl on the bottom of Kajika's blend. He added green and red minuscule flecks of herbs too. "What is this dad and sis crap?"

"The family discussion can wait until tomorrow night. I'll explain the whole matter then." Eric rises. "Doctors, I appreciate your help and valuable time. Lilliane will hand you my thank you on your way out."

A brief round of applause follows. Four people remove their white lab coats. Another four exit the game room, tossing their lab coats in the same box.

The doctors nod their salutations when they pass. When the last doctor leaves the lodge, Eric places a short call. "We'll ship your equipment overnight as agreed," he said.

The front door swings open. A team of men packs up the equipment and supplies. Eric asks, "You able to stand? They need the cot."

Lilliane says, "Promised to make a call when she woke. Sis, we can chat over window-shopping. I know this quaint shop in Madrid." She smiles with eyes sparkling and bolts out the front door. A half-moment later, she pops back in next to the cot. "And before I forget, sorry about hitting you that night. It bothered me all those nights you stayed unconscious. Hope you don't hold any grudges. Toodle-oo," she said, disappearing faster than she entered.

Eric pushes a chair in my direction. I ask him, "She always flaky?"

"Afraid so. Lilliane likes to drop in and out of places. Loves to travel too, which helps my nerves when she's gone."

Explains why Leslie didn't stay around. He wasn't here in the first place. Also unravels my housekeeper mystery. I'm assuming, but it makes sense. Night hunting is out of the picture for a while. I better prepare myself for one heck of a story. Maybe we can get that popcorn machine running.

I steady myself on the armrest and plop in the chair. "Legs felt weak. I'm OK," I said, squeezing my thighs.

Bio-dad rips away the blackout curtains, reaches behind the blinds, and hands me a metal bar. "Bend it." He folds arms across chest and studies my reaction.

"Huh?" I turn the bar over a few times. I grasp the middle of it and test the weight. One plain metal bar three feet long and an inch thick. I squint at Eric. He edges me on with his awkward impatient chin.

"OK." I grasp the ends and twist the bar into a horseshoe. I continue twisting. "Want this for your truck?" I asked.

Eric snatches the spring from my hands. "Your attitude certainly returned to normal."

"What did you expect?"

"What I and everyone expected," Eric said, emphasizing each word. "That bar isn't steel. You shouldn't have been able to bend it so easily. Good thing Fernando re-enforced your entrance to your lair."

My lair? I stare toward the back lobby. "Does she—"

"Know the location? Yes. But she holds other interests. Lilliane prefers luxury suites. Her tastes run high and expensive."

"What happened to Father Moretti and his rubies?" I straighten my posture and rub legs to improve their circulation. "Dead and safe, in that order, I hope."

"Monsignor Smith sentenced Father Moretti to 'penance and prayer.' The rubies brought out an old family bitterness toward the Catholic Church. They fostered his madness. He now works in an archdiocese filing department. Thanks to Lilliane's mind-wipe, the single memory Father Moretti remembers is the alphabet. The rubies, we locked in lead-sealed boxes. One rests at the bottom of an undiscovered Antarctica lake. The other buried in the deep depths of an Indian temple."

"What about the tablet? The priest refused to tell me where he hid it."

"The Father's Tablet of Eluppu proved a fake copy, which means the original might exist elsewhere. But that's another issue, for another time."

Eric's cell phone rings. He checks the incoming number and answers. "Yes, Monsignor? She is. Yes, we are. We await their arrival. Yes, Monsignor I will. I'm sure she'll be pleased. Thank you, Sir. Good night, Monsignor."

"Monsignor Smith said to tell my daughter, 'Brother Aiden recovers and could regain usage of his hand with therapy.' Didn't need to ask which daughter. He mentioned about expecting guests. You best change."

"Before I do. What happened? Why this?" I point at the packed portable hospital equipment.

"You received greater damage than you thought. The amulet held your injuries at bay until you dismissed your familiars. When the amulet closed, your wounds opened. You bled out."

"To make matters worse, the amulet didn't break Father Moretti's spell. The amulet diluted Moretti's spell into different metaphysical layers. It spread throughout your being in weakened states. Mind, body, emotional, and spiritual shells—all infected. The infection caused your weakness that night.

"I called in every favor owed. The group you saw was the tip of the iceberg. Armed guards protect the grounds, doctors, and you. I scheduled a physical therapist while you were out. Three shifts, round the clock, watched over you, including Lilliane. Fernando donated blood transfusions. He supplied the dream weaving too. Fernando mentioned you might experience changes. Said you would understand."

"Yea. Hey, wait." I jump out of the chair. "Physical therapy? How long was I unconscious?"

"If you wish to trick-or-treat, you better hurry and design a costume," Eric said.

"What?" I count the days, months. "Over two months?" The chair catches my collapse. "What happened?"

"I have paperwork and projects to finish. You best throw yourself together. Be careful of your new strength. Fernando said you would find everything you require, and to your liking, in your lair. He may pay you a later visit." Eric checks his cell. "Don't quote me but I'm glad you are in one piece."

Bio-dad waits by the stairs while I stand. My legs wobble a wee bit. I hold on to the armrest and push my feet downward. Muscle memory kicks in after a moment. I stand upright.

"Gee thanks. *Dad*," I said, sarcastically.

"Don't push it, girl. You should check under the floor of your lair sometime."

I gasp and scrutinize Eric. His mouth forms a wide, tight grin. He withdraws to his study.

My feet scuffle along the floor. I wobble to the rear lobby with no further handholds. My back lays flat against the mirror. I cautiously pull down the wall lamps. The secret entrance door swings. I take one step at a time down the sideways descent and pause at the inner chamber door.

"Kajika, what surprises did you leave this visit?" I asked, aloud. Hearing my voice offers comfort. How many strangers poked and inspected my unconscious body for months? The thought makes me uneasy.

I ease open the steel reinforced door.

"Oh, my. Fernando, you're the best."

An hour later, the men lounge in the game room. I walk in wearing a black heather workout suit. The bandages limited my movements, but the zip-up hoodie works fine. Black sports shoes help keep my footing. My boot knife hides inside a pocket. "Pizza and balloons. What's the occasion?" I asked.

Theodore strides up the steps. "My going away party. Monsignor Smith notified his superiors. They invited me to

Rome and a Vatican tour. Sort of a thank you and getaway vacation. Doctors want me to chill a few months. It means I miss the next semester, but I'm fine with that." Theodore checks outs my bandages. "How are you doing? You OK?"

"Back to my undead status. With a few improvements. Did I miss much?"

"You missed signing my arm cast. And you slept through the itchy part. Thanks for the movies. They helped. Your headphones are on the shelf near the DVDs."

"Thanks." Cadmael and Andrea recline on the sofas. I whisper, "Theodore? The bastard paid for his actions. I made sure."

"Yea. I heard. Kind of wish none of this had to happen. Life sure isn't like the movies."

"No. It sure as heck isn't," I said. Eric steps pass us and joins his teammates. "How long until you leave?"

"A limousine waits in the driveway. I stay with my folks and fly to Rome with Father Joseph in two weeks. Semester starts in January. Then back to normal."

"Good for you. Keep your dream alive." I escort Theodore down the steps. "Let's attack the pizza. Shall we?"

Pizza boxes spread out on the corner table. Drink bottles scatter the grand room with balloons. A large, white Igloo cooler guards the pizza. Between its red lid and sprout beams a label with an "S." Ten-ounce glass tumblers are stacked nearby. White, adhesive medical tape on the red lip reads, "Shake first."

I follow the label's instructions. Then grab one the tumblers and hold it up to inspect its cleanliness. The glass passes the test. I fill it half full.

Theodore loads his plate with pizza and garlic balls. He says in a low voice, "We celebrate your un-deadness too you know. Andy said your battle wounds were worse than the last fiasco. He thought best I stay away these past months. Seeing how you fare now, I agree with his advice. You look terrible."

"Vampires heal quickly. As for my looks, you want the other arm broken?"

Theodore scatters around the table. He says, "Pass, considering how much fun it was the first time." He inches back around and dumps red sauce next to the slices. "Father Joseph said to visit anytime. He's staying with Monsignor Smith."

Theodore marches over to the loveseat and claims both cushions. He scatters plates of food on the first cushion he reaches. He sits on the other cushion and rests his feet on the cocktail table. An iced drink of orange soda balances between his thighs.

My glass contains the same concoction Lilliane served earlier. A younger sister raised by wealthy foster parents. Some people have all the luck. I ease down the steps, balancing my drink. Fingers tremble ever so slightly. I lay the glass on the cocktail table and join Cadmael on the sofa.

"Glad you're up and moving," said Cadmael, twisting sideways facing me. "Thought you might sleep through the year and miss our Christmas party."

"Felt like taking a nap. Be ready for another adventure in a day or two." I reach for my glass and glance across at Andrea curled up in one of the single chairs.

Andrea wears a light-blue causal golf attire and a navy-blue tartan flat cap. Strange since the other men in the room wear denim trousers and short-sleeve polos. "Andy? You shaved your head. You're bald!"

Andrea removes his cap and wipes his shaven head with his left hand. "Easiest three pounds I ever lost," he chuckles and places the cap back on his head. "Met your master, Fernando Ventré Florez as the park's new Wode-manne. He and I made a friendly bet. In short, I lost."

Kajika's iced drink washes down my giggles. "Well, I'm just pleased everyone made it through Moretti's madness in one piece."

"I'm pleased the doctors left," Andrea said, standing. "I swear one of them observed my butt every time I passed the hallway. Normally I wouldn't mind, but she made a silent purring noise deep in her eyes."

Andrea walks up to the sofa. "Good to see you are scuffling along," he said strolling into the back hallway.

I finish my drink and lean back into the soft cushions. "Chad, you mentioned a Christmas party? You serious or joking?"

Eric reclines in the other single leather chair across from Cadmael. Eric puts his glass down on the side table and answers for Cadmael. "This year, we celebrate Christmas here. Gifts galore. Girl, you can count on the largest tree and at least one big surprise. Guaranteed."

A New England Christmas in a lodge. That's a surprise by itself. This life keeps on changing. But if we're in October, snow and ice can fall any minute.

I slide on the sofa next to Cadmael. My right arm, holding the glass, drops to my side. I wrap my other arm around Cadmael's shoulders and whisper in his ear.

"Chad? I'm calling in that favor."

ABOUT THE AUTHOR

William Freeman was raised in Stony Point, New York. He is retired from the TSA with twenty-six years of federal service. William now resides in Charlotte, North Carolina, where he is currently working on his next novel.

AUTHOR'S WEBSITE:

WFreeman.net

FOLLOW ON TWITTER:

William Freeman@desksquire

REVIEWS:

The author welcomes all honest rates & reviews. Feel free to add yours on your favorite retail & social websites.

ACKNOWLEDGMENTS

My deepest appreciation to the many YouTube channels (Ellen Brock, The Write Channel, Jenna Moreci, Derek Murphy, The Creative Penn, Cy Porter, and others), for their informative videos.

Special thanks goes to the following: M. Plummer, L. Dolle, and J. Reed. As humble as you all are, you deserve credit for advancing Salome's adventure. Thanks for your help!

I also thank my past English teachers and professors. Without you, this novel wouldn't have gone very far.

Past due thanks goes to my parents Marie & Bill for implementing a solid reading foundation. Those Classic Editions didn't go to waste. Thanks mom and dad.

And to Lilly, who diligently read and edited like the professional she is. A very special loving thank you.

FUTURE RELEASE:

SALOMÉ - PATH OF THE JAGUAR

Salomé catches her breathe in time to enjoy Christmas at the lodge. After gifts and a quick bite, she's ready to share her past Peruvian cave and jungle adventures with ACE and family. With a warm mug of mead in hand, Salomé's tales reveal mysteries and surprises all the way until dawn.